NO MAN'S WORLD
THE ALLEYMAN
PAT KELLEHER
D0556095
ABADDON BOOKS
WWW.ABADDONBOOKS.COM

"When ants unite, they can skin a lion."

– Iranian proverb

An Abaddon Books™ Publication
www.abaddonbooks.com
abaddon@rebellion.co.uk

First published in 2011 by Abaddon Books™, Rebellion Intellectual Property Limited, Riverside House, Osney Mead, Oxford, OX2 0ES, UK.

10 9 8 7 6 5 4 3 2 1

Editor: David Moore
Cover Art: Pye Parr
Design: Parr & Preece
Marketing and PR: Michael Molcher
Creative Director and CEO: Jason Kingsley
Chief Technical Officer: Chris Kingsley
No Man's World™ created by Pat Kelleher

UK ISBN: 978-1-78108-024-5
US ISBN: 978-1-78108-025-2

Printed in the US

ACKNOWLEDGEMENTS

I would like to thank all those people who have helped bring the true story of *'The Broughtonthwaite Mates'* to light. As ever, I am indebted to the members of the Broughtonthwaite Historical Society for their tireless efforts in collating the new information that has come to light since the publication of the first book. I would also like to thank Robert Scotton of the Media Museum North, for an insight into the work and career of the kinematographer Oliver Hepton, including his early pre-World War One erotica. I am grateful to Elizabeth Thompson of the National Archives for helping to trace the RFC service record of Lieutenant James Tulliver. I must also thank Jon, Jenni, David, Ben, Simon and Michael at Abaddon Books. Without their enthusiasm and unstinting support for this project, it wouldn't have happened. Once again, I must thank my wife, Penny, for her continuing love and support. Finally, I would like to thank all those descendents of the men of the 13th Battalion of the Pennine Fusiliers who spoke to me, still hoping that the truth about the fate of their loved ones will come to light.

13th BATTALION PENNINE FUSILIERS: COMPANY PERSONNEL

Battalion HQ.

C.O.: 2nd Lieutenant John. C. Everson
2C.O.: Sergeant Herbert Gerald Hobson
Company Quartermaster Sergeant Archibald Slacke
Pte. Henry *'Half Pint'* Nicholls (batman)

Royal Army Chaplain: Father Arthur Rand
(CF4) ('Captain')

War Office Kinematographer Oliver Hepton

Signals

Corporal Arthur Riley
Pte. Peter Buckley
Pte. Richard Tonkins

'C' Company

No 1 Platoon

C.O.: Lieutenant Morgan

No. 2 Platoon

C.O.: 2nd Lieutenant Palmer

1 Section

I.C.: Lance Corporal Thomas *'Only'* Atkins
Pte. Harold *'Gutsy'* Blood
Pte. Wilfred Joseph *'Mercy'* Evans
Pte. George *'Porgy'* Hopkiss
Pte. Leonard *'Pot-Shot'* Jellicoe
Pte. David Samuel *'Gazette'* Otterthwaite

RAMC

Regimental Aid Post

RMO: Captain Grenville Lippett

Red Cross Nurses

Sister Betty Fenton
Sister Edith Bell

Driver Nellie Abbott (First Aid Nursing Yeomanry)

Orderlies

Pte. Edgar Stanton
Pte. Edward Thompkins

Stretcher Bearer

Pte. Jenkins

Machine Gun Corps (Heavy Section) 'I' Company

I-5 HMLS *Ivanhoe*

C.O.: 2nd Lieutenant Arthur Alexander Mathers
Pte. Wally Clegg (Driver)
Pte. Alfred Perkins (Gearsman)
Pte. Norman Bainbridge (Gunner)
Pte. Jack Tanner (Gunner)
Pte. Reginald Lloyd (Loader/ Machine Gunner)
Pte. Cecil Nesbit (Loader / Machine Gunner)

D Flight 70 Squadron: Sopwith 1 ½ Strutter

Lieutenant James Robert Tulliver (pilot)
Corporal Jack Maddox (observer)

For Elliott and Miles

PREFACE

"Keep the Home Fires Burning..."

THE BRITISH OFFICIAL History of the Great War, *Military Operations: France and Belgium, 1916 Volume II (1938)* simply states that on the 1st November 1916, the nine hundred men of 13th Battalion of the Pennine Fusiliers went over the top at dawn to attack a German position in Harcourt Wood on the Somme. They advanced into a gas cloud and vanished, leaving a crater nearly half a mile wide and eighty feet deep. The official explanation was a mass explosion of German mines dug under the British positions using an experimental high explosive. This is still the official position.

And it would have remained that way, had not a chance find in a French field by a farmer, ten years later, sparked a controversy that exists to this day and led to the one of the greatest mysteries of the First World War.

Known as the Lefeuvre Find, it contained several rusted film canisters of undeveloped silver nitrate film, along with, amongst other things, journals, letters, keepsakes, notes and what purported to be the Battalion War Diary. When developed, the black and white silent film – believed to have been shot by Oliver Hepton, a War Office kinematographer who had been assigned to film the attack – showed the Pennines apparently alive and well and on an alien world.

The film was dismissed by the Government as a hoax, playing on the hopes of the relatives and loved ones of those missing. However, there were those who believed its provenance and campaigned for the truth. Some of their descendants still do.

It became clear from the items recovered in the Lefeuvre Find that there were other casualties of the Harcourt Event, and that the phenomenon even extended up into the atmosphere. The Hepton footage (HF232) shows a member of the Royal Flying Corps, who has since been identified as Lieutenant James Tulliver, who was presumed to have been shot down and killed and whose body and plane wreckage were never found.

The First World War was one of the first truly technological wars, where industrialisation changed the nature of warfare. Manned flight was barely ten years old at the outbreak of the war, and within months, it was being used to kill. The war in the air developed into an arms race, with technological advances rendering machines and engine designs obsolete within months, as the push for advantages in speed, height and manoeuvrability drove huge leaps in innovation.

To those at home, the war in the air was a romantic notion that the RFC fostered. It seemed like an echo of a previous age, of chivalrous knights duelling in single combat. The mixture of romance, adventure and technology caught the public imagination, and many adventure story magazines of the time featured tales of derring-do in the air. None more so than *Great War Science Stories,* which featured a series of highly colourful pulp tales about *Tulliver, Ace of the Alien Skies* as he battled everything from flying dinosaurs to robotic sky pirates until the magazine ceased publication in 1932.

This third volume of the *No Man's World* series continues the account of the Pennine Fusiliers' true fate. It is based on the accounts of those who were there, where possible, although some events are inferred. All major events have been drawn from primary sources, including the papers of Arthur Cooke, author of *The Harcourt Crater: Hoax or Horror,* personal letters, and entries from the Battalion War Diary, as well as from the Flight Log of Lieutenant James Tulliver. This is now in the hands of a private collector in Australia, who wishes to remain anonymous but for the truth to be known.

1st November 2016 will see the one-hundredth anniversary of the disappearance of the Pennines. Renewed interest in the fate of the Broughtonthwaite Mates is constantly bringing new evidence and facts to light and so, while their hometown of Broughtonthwaite prepares to commemorate the centenary of the Heroes of Harcourt, we may yet finally discover the true fate of the Pennine Fusiliers.

Pat Kelleher
Broughtonshaw
Easter, 2012

PROLOGUE

"They Told Me He Had Gone That Way..."

THE GREAT BATRACHIAN ironclad tumbled into the crater, its tracks gouging broad ruts as it slid down the steep slope towards the tangle of alien jungle below. Poisonous barbed vines lashed its ironbound hide as the *Ivanhoe* ploughed through them, ripping them out at the roots and dragging them along with it.

Trills, howls, roars and whoops of alarm reached a crescendo as the intruder blundered through the undergrowth.

The great steering tail broke free and tumbled through the jungle on its own lazy trajectory, spewing hydraulic fluid as it spun.

The *Ivanhoe* plunged on, every impact slowing its momentum, the ironclad only coming to a halt as it collided with the buttress root of a huge trunk with a thunderous, hollow *thud*.

Overhead, the canopy thrashed as startled creatures bolted in terror and a tense silence descended. The jungle seemed to pause.

No predatory growl rose from the intruder to challenge them.

Half hidden by the dappled shade and torn foliage, the intruder clicked and groaned. Large leafy fronds sprouted from its tracks, caught in the track wheels. Shredded leaves and broken boughs lay strewn over its hull. The drivers' visors hung shut and the ironclad's great guns lay listless and bowed.

It was just another dead thing. Nothing to fear.

The sounds of the jungle began to trickle back into the silence, timid at first, but slowly gaining in confidence. Soon, the raucous chorus resumed.

Emboldened, scavengers loped through the undergrowth towards the ditched ironclad, perhaps sensing easy prey.

Inside the belly of the tank, Alfie Perkins opened his eyes.

Although the festoon lights had died, shafts of light punched their way in through pistol ports, boring down through the smoky haze that filled the compartment, criss-crossing the dark space like searchlights seeking out a Zeppelin.

He coughed as he breathed in the smoke. It smelled of burnt grease. He dragged himself into a sitting position, so his back was against the sponson door. The spasm of coughing set off a chain reaction of other pains, which only subsided when he stopped hacking. He was slumped in the gangway. He looked up to see the starboard six-pounder gun and Hotchkiss machine gun, its spent cartridge casings rolling around him with a tinkle of brass as he moved.

To his right, filling the centre of the compartment, the huge Daimler engine ticked to itself as it cooled.

His hand was covered in blood that had collected in a sticky pool on the gangway planks. In a surge of panic, he checked his body. His forehead felt tender, swollen. He shifted his weight and sharp pain flooded his right leg. His hand groped down the leg of his coveralls. Another jangle of pain. Broken, probably. At least he'd still got his leg. For the moment. He felt something warm and sticky below his knee. It was blood, but not enough to cause the sticky pool around him.

The blood that lay thick and pooled about him on the gangway wasn't his.

He saw a crumpled shape further up the gangway.

"Lieutenant?"

There was no answer. He waited a moment for his nerves to stop screaming, and for his eyes to adjust. Lieutenant Mathers, the tank commander, was crumpled on the starboard gangway, having fallen from the commander's seat at the front, his leg twisted and caught awkwardly under the bucket seat.

"Sir?"

There was no answer. Alfie struggled to recall what had happened. It would be easier if the pain in his head would stop. The last thing he remembered was the fire extinguisher flying towards him.

Frozen pictures, like shell-flash afterimages, burst in his mind. The *Ivanhoe* toppling over the edge of the crater. Falling. Mathers. A gunshot. The pyrene fire extinguisher. Blackness.

He looked at the slumped body in the gangway. He saw the glint of the Webley revolver and the sheen on the blood as it spread from Mathers' head. Alfie remembered now. Possessed by some alien parasite, in a moment of lucidity, the Lieutenant had shot himself.

Alfie tried moving again, but couldn't find the strength. He searched around, his hand groping among the scattered ammo boxes and tools within reach. It closed around a wrench. Steeling himself for a moment, he banged on the side of the sponson with what strength he had and yelled with as much gusto as he could muster.

"Help! In here! Anybody?"

Panting, he waited for a reply. None came.

He tried again and again, each time weaker and with less conviction that there was anyone outside to hear. Eventually he lost his balance and his broken leg twisted. He screamed, and when the pain had passed, he closed his eyes.

His voice low now, almost like a prayer: "Anybody."

He woke up. Minutes later? Hours? He didn't know. The only thing he knew was that he didn't want the *Ivanhoe* to become his tomb, as Mathers had known it would become his.

Alfie breathed deeply of what faint traces of petrol fruit fumes were left to dull the pain, and then hauled himself to his feet. He waited for the nausea to pass. He pulled the handle on the sponson hatch and pushed. The hatch gave a little, but didn't open. He put his shoulder to it and shoved. It gave a little more, but recoiled back. There was something against it outside, preventing it from opening.

Feeling his strength ebb, he kept his weight on his good foot and shoved again. This time light briefly flooded the compartment, and he could see a mass of russet leaves.

Gathering his strength, he shoved the hatch again, roaring. This time it gave, swinging open. Alfie lost his balance, tripped over the lip of the hatch and fell out, screaming as he caught his broken leg.

His fall was cushioned by the tangle of shrubbery in which the tank had come to rest. He shook his head, trying to clear the fug of pain that threatened to smother him.

A deep, mucus-addled panting filled the air. Alfie felt waves of warm, foetid breath wash over him.

He twisted his body to see, barely twelve feet away, a huge mouth, lips pulled back in a snarl, long serrated incisors dripping with drool. From deep within its thick matted pelt, two dark eyes regarded him with seeming contempt as it crouched on its six legs, pondering.

A growl began building in the back of its throat.

Never taking its eyes off Alfie, the creature let out a roar and pounced.

CHAPTER ONE

"At Some Disputed Barricade..."

THE SMALL, FLIMSY flying machine puttered across bright blue space, defying possibility; the persistent putter of its tiny engine echoed through the vast vault of the alien sky, belying its small size, like a skylark rising to sing.

In the forward cockpit, Lieutenant James Tulliver wiped the speckled build-up of oil from his goggles and revelled in the cold air. Fresh and sharp, it made him feel more alive than he ever did on the ground. Beneath the scarf wrapped round the lower part of his face, a broad grin spread until it almost ached. This was why he'd joined the Royal Flying Corps. At a thousand feet, the two-seater Sopwith 1½ Strutter had the alien sky all to itself, while winged creatures wheeled and soared on unseen currents below.

Lieutenant Everson had sent him up on a recce flight out to Croatoan Crater to check on the stranded tank crew. It was a simple flight. It had to be; compasses didn't work on this Godforsaken world. He had to fly by sight, from landmark to landmark, and that meant keeping below the cloud cover as flocks of cumulus drifted along overhead. While Everson rightly valued the aeroplane, he was as a needy child with a cock linnet in a cage who never let it spread it wings. Tulliver resented that. What the hell use was a grounded pilot? Granted, the alien sky wasn't without its dangers. There were jabberwocks, mountain-dwelling wing predators, and the huge atmospheric jellyfish-like Kreothe and a dozen other vicious air raptors, any one of which could reduce his bus to kindling and rags. But then, dodging airbursts of Archie on the Western Front hadn't exactly been a joyride either.

On top of that, for the last several days, dud weather had kept him grounded. Still, he was up now. He felt a tap on his shoulder. It was Maddocks, his observer-come-gunner, seconded from Lieutenant Baxter's Machine Gun Section. It always paid to have two pairs of eyes up here, although his own were keener than most; things seemed brighter, sharper, as though he had just got spectacles after being myopic for years.

It was all thanks to the petrol fruit fuel the bus now ran on. Some hapless Tommy had distilled it in secret. The resulting alcoholic concoction proved to have undesirable side effects, and the commanders had declared it unfit for human consumption, although it did solve their dwindling petrol supply problem. It was another bone of contention between Everson and himself. Ever since they had discovered that the crew of the ironclad tank *HMLS Ivanhoe* had suffered from the psychoactive effects of its fumes, Everson had been more than a little suspicious of Tulliver, and had him up before Captain Lippett, the Medical Officer. Tulliver had explained at great length that the confinement of the crew within the tank for long periods had increased their exposure to the fuel vapours and heightened its psychotropic effects. He, meanwhile, was in the open air and travelling at almost one hundred miles an hour. Whatever vapours were expelled from the engine were whipped away by the aerial winds. The MO's examination seemed to bear out this hypothesis, and reluctantly Everson had let the matter drop.

Tulliver decided to keep his new acuity to himself. He didn't want to be grounded, and besides, what harm could it do?

Maddocks was pointing down. A couple of hundred feet below them, a pair of jabberwocks were engaged in territorial aerial combat, luckily too busy to notice the Sopwith.

Ahead, Tulliver could make out the depressed green circle of the jungle-filled Croatoan Crater. Almost a mile across and over two hundred yards deep, it was darker than the surrounding jungle, its bowl-like depression obvious and ominous. The strange strip of faded, discoloured foliage that cut across it was quite marked from this perspective. It didn't seem quite natural to Tulliver's eyes.

They came in low over the jungle surrounding the great depression. Without warning, the air came alive with cracks and bangs, like gunshots. Tulliver pulled back on the stick, gaining height.

Across the jungle canopy, huge vine-like things – whipperwills, Maddocks called them, anywhere from twenty to nearly a hundred feet long, sensitive to a combination of air movement and shadow – cracked above the trees, like whips. The fast-moving shadow of the Sopwith set them snapping ravenously behind them, like a living wake.

The treetop field of whipperwills gave way to the ruins of the Nazarrii edifice, which had belonged to a long-dead colony of chatts, the race of intelligent arthropods that dominated this planet. It now lay completely destroyed after the Fusiliers' encounter with the Dulgur that inhabited it, and which had cost them the tank. The ironclad *Ivanhoe* now lay scuppered somewhere down in the crater. The crew had refused to abandon it and the two members that had gone over with it.

Tulliver banked the plane and circled over the brush leading to the lip of the crater. With his eyesight heightened by the petrol fruit fumes, they were easy to spot. He waggled his wings. Six small people waved back. A seventh Tulliver took to be the urman guide, Napoo. He seemed to be intent on some kind of work, squatting on the ground, ignoring the plane. Tulliver turned and nodded to Maddocks, who leant over the side and dropped the tin. As it fell, he saw the tank crew run towards it and then lost sight of them as he pulled out of the bank and set a course back to camp, following the line of the Strip that fortuitously pointed back to the trenches.

"Hold onto your lunch!" he bellowed out over his shoulder.

Tulliver performed a few rolls, simply for the joy of it, and then pulled the stick back, climbing up to meet a small flock of clouds. The bus soared over the bright white fairy-tale landscape. Up here, above the clouds, Tulliver could almost believe he was back on Earth again...

Barely five months ago, on the first of November, 1916, at six twenty ack emma, he and his observer, Hodgeson, had taken off with the flight from the aerodrome at Fine Villas, along with Captain Parkhurst and Biffer, with orders to take down a German observation kite balloon behind the lines near Harcourt Wood.

Thousands of feet below, flashes of artillery fire glittered like fallen sequins as they bombarded the already pitted and pocked German positions.

As they closed in on the observation balloon, the Hun observer in the basket beneath spotted them, and his ground crew began winching the tethered sausage balloon down.

Then Tulliver saw the two Hun Albatros D2s protecting it.

Parkhurst, red flight-commander's streamers trailing from his outer wing spars, gestured that they should break and try to gain the higher ground.

Tulliver pulled back on the stick and indicated to Hodgeson to keep his eyes peeled. Hodgeson, as well as being the observer, also had a Lewis gun attached to the rear of his cockpit, mounted on a ring that allowed him freedom of fire, unlike Tulliver's forward-facing gun.

Tulliver raced after an Albatros as it tried to escape them when suddenly, from round the huge mountain of cloud high above them, swooped a third.

A burst of machine gun fire from the new machine raked across Parkhurst's Strutter. Tulliver saw smoke streak from its engine before an urgent thump on his back from Hodgeson alerted him to the fact that there was another Hun on their tail. While the 1½ Strutter outgunned the Albatros, the Hun machine was quicker and more manoeuvrable.

Tulliver banked hard to avoid a stream of tracer bullets and caught a glimpse of the Hun in his rear-view mirror. Hodgeson let out short bursts from the Lewis gun as the Albatros dived, trying to get below the Sopwith.

He felt the thud of bullets sewing themselves along the fuselage. Behind him, the rattle of Hodgeson's machine gun ceased. He risked a glance over his shoulder to see Hodgeson slumped in the rear cockpit, his head lolling back.

"Hodge!" he yelled. "Hodge, old man?" There was no answer.

Above, Biffer was trying to shake off another Hun. Tulliver went after it. He came up below the Albatros and, without pity, strafed the machine. Gone were the days of playing the game, of chivalric aerial jousts. These days it was kill or be killed.

It went down, threading a smoky trail across the sky.

There was just the glory hound to worry about now. He liked to hang high and dive. Tulliver searched up and around for it, but everything seemed wrong, even the clouds. His compass began spinning wildly. The engine sputtered, misfiring. Try as he might, he could no longer find the horizon. He found himself suspended in a featureless grey miasma that billowed sluggishly around the bus. All sense of movement, direction and speed ceased.

A deep bass rumble filled the air about him.

Turbulent currents buffeted the machine, threatening to snap off its planes.

As he fought with the spade-handled stick to regain control over the Strutter, Tulliver felt a sticky warmth in his ears and tasted the metallic tang of blood trickling from his nose and down the back of his throat. His breathing became rapid and shallow. His eyes flickered shut and lights burst against his eyelids.

The noise died and the buffeting ceased abruptly. From above, a bright, diffuse light illuminated the encompassing haze. He breathed a sigh of relief. He was in cloud, that was all. He eased the stick forward and dropped. He could get his bearing and fly back along the front line until he came to a landmark he knew.

He wasn't prepared for what he saw. Spread out below was an unfamiliar landscape: a blaze of green plain and glistening rivers with mountains in the distance. Beneath him, set in a valley that existed on no maps or aerial photographs he had ever seen, he spotted the only remnant of the world he knew: an ugly circular scab of land, pock-marked with shell holes and raked by crenellated fire trenches. A pitiful, pulverised corner of earth on a world that was not the one from which he'd taken off...

All that was in the past now, and the alien world was momentarily hidden by the undulant white landscape around them. Vast billowing mountains rose about him and he flew his bus through their wraith-like canyons and gorges; the cloudy cartography of an insubstantial world. At play in the fields of the Lord, as his old flying instructor used to say. He chased their contours until the rigging wires sang and he let out a whoop of exhilaration that the wind snatched from his lips the moment he uttered it.

He caught sight of something out of the corner of his eye. A fleeting shadow rippled across the face of the cumulus mesa above them. Was there something else up here? A predator? He turned to Maddocks and jabbed a finger in its direction. Maddocks nodded and swung the Lewis machine gun round on its Scarff ring. Tulliver pulled on the stick and banked the bus to look for its source, his head constantly moving as he held up a hand to shield his eyes from the uninterrupted glare of the alien sun.

The shadow flitted into a narrow chasm between two great cumulus tors as he raced up the vertiginous slopes after it, scanning the shifting vista as mountains roiled up and melted together.

High above, a haze of cloud moved across the sun and the shadow vanished along with whatever cast it.

Perhaps it was just as well, Tulliver thought. Nothing up here was ever friendly. The thought that there was a fast and predatory creature existing at this altitude, sliding through cloud like a shark through water, filled him with trepidation. He'd hate to give Everson cause to curtail his flights even more.

Sooner or later, he would have to find this creature and kill it. He knew that. It might be that it was a rendezvous with death, but it was one he would not fail.

He throttled back, dropped below the drifting clouds and found himself over the Fractured Plain. It was a barren expanse of uneven cracked and tilted slabs of sand-covered bedrock that looked as if someone had smashed the landscape with a giant hammer.

He pulled out of the dive and followed the great rift face along the edge of the sunken plain until he saw the gorge that pointed the way back, its mysterious metal wall flaring in the sunlight.

As they neared the valley that the marooned Tommies now called home, Tulliver felt his mood sink with every foot of altitude he lost.

LIEUTENANT EVERSON, ACTING CO of the 13th Battalion of the Pennine Fusiliers, heard the droning approach of aeroplane.

"Back in one piece. Thank God for that!" he muttered, before returning his attention to the ongoing repair work. The circular rings of defensive fire, support and reserve trenches that now protected the precious circle of Somme soil had been pulverised in recent weeks; not by a German barrage, but by an animal stampede precipitated by a storm front of Kreothe, giant aerial creatures that drifted in herds on the wind. The decomposing corpse of one of the jellyfish-like creatures lay up the valley, not half a mile beyond the trenches, like some tentacled, demonic leviathan washed up from the depths. The men had already become accustomed to its stench, having lived in a charnel field of rotting corpses on the Somme.

Hobson, a barrel-chested Platoon Sergeant whose most prominent feature was an immaculately groomed handlebar moustache, followed behind him, catching anything the Lieutenant missed, snatching words with other ranks about undone buttons and the other hundred and one petty breaches of Regulations that blighted the life of a private, even here.

Everson felt the weight of his responsibility keenly. He had gone to Oxford with the intention of escaping the weight of his father's expectations. With the outbreak of war, in the summer of 1914, he joined the patriotic throng of other young men in front of Broughtonthwaite Town Hall and signed on as one of Kitchener's volunteers. When his father found out, he was furious. Over his son's objections, he used his considerable influence to buy him a commission, as a Platoon Commander, in the local regiment. In seeking to avoid responsibility, Everson had found himself saddled with it. He hated his father for that.

The longer they remained here, the harder it was to maintain the men's morale. He felt the respect they held him in being eroded week by week. They wanted leadership, and all he could offer was survival. It wasn't enough. A slow drip of deserters sloped off to take their chances in the alien wilderness, whittling their numbers and further undermining the men's confidence in him.

Now, though, they had a solid lead on Lieutenant Jeffries. There was a deeply held belief among some of the ranks that Jeffries was responsible for their transportation to this hellish place, one Everson tentatively shared. Jeffries was a self-styled diabolist and rival of Aleister Crowley. He was also a con man and a wanted murderer. It was Jeffries' boast that they were here on this planet as the direct result of some obscene ritual he had conducted, powered by the staggering scale of human sacrifice on the Somme. Before he vanished, leaving them at war with the chatts, Jeffries declared that only he knew how to get them back.

For over three months, they had searched for him and now, at last, they had a lead – the Croatoan Crater. Not only that, they also had the chatt prisoner, Chandar, and a collection of ancient sacred scent texts unearthed at the Nazarrii edifice. They could give him leverage with the Khungarrii, the local colony, on whose territory they had materialised and under whose attacks they had suffered in recent months.

With these, Everson felt he could finally *act*, rather than react. He could galvanise the men, give them a purpose other than survival. He only hoped it wouldn't be too late. First, though, he must arrange a salvage party to recover the tank if at all possible.

Following the jinking traverses of the radial communications trench, they turned left and clockwise into the support trench ring. Soldiers saluted as they passed. Some looked him in the eye with defiance. Others averted their gaze. Everson smiled briefly and nodded to all in acknowledgement.

He noticed an awkward figure, his right leg missing below the knee, hobbling on crutches round the traverse ahead of them. It was a hard figure to mistake.

"Nicholls?" The man had been in his own platoon. Half Pint, the rest called him, on account of his constant grousing. He'd lost his right leg below the knee in a battle with the Khungarrii. Anywhere else but here it would have been a Blighty wound, poor sod. Since then, Nicholls had served as his batman, at least until his new peg leg had tried to kill him. Now he was just a Category Man, unfit for active service.

"Sir?" Nicholls attempted to turn but got one of his crutches stuck in the duckboards that ran along the bottom of the trench. "Damn thing!"

"Sergeant, give him a hand."

"It's all right. I've got it, sir," said Nicholls from between gritted teeth as he gave the crutch a vicious tug. It came free. He let out a strangled cry and lurched backward against the revetment. The crutch clattered to the ground.

Everson stooped, picked it up and handed it back to him. Nicholls took it, reluctantly, avoiding his gaze.

Everson's brow furrowed with concern. "Everything all right, Nicholls?"

"Fine, sir," said the Fusilier. "Never better. Everything's tickety-boo."

Hobson leaned forward and pinned the man to the revetment with a gimlet eye, a note of threat in his voice. "Any complaints?"

Nicholls shook his head. "No, none at all, Sarn't."

"Very glad to hear it. Hop along now."

HALF PINT ROUNDED the traverse and shot a furtive glance over his shoulder, to check if he was being followed, but he'd left Lieutenant Everson and Hobson behind.

He stood at the top of a set of the dugout steps and called hoarsely down into the gloom. "It's me, Half Pint. Someone give us a bloody hand, then!"

There were footsteps and a Tommy, his tunic undone, emerged into the light at the top of the steps. "About bloody time too," he said. "Where've you been? Bains is waiting."

Ungraciously, Half Pint allowed himself to be manoeuvred down into the gloomy dugout lit by a single hurricane lamp, where he was dropped unceremoniously onto an empty bunk. Sat and stood around him were a collection of discontented Fusiliers, brought here like himself by word of mouth. He wasn't surprised to see Hepton here, either. Officially a War Office kinematographer, he always had a nose for trouble, or a "story," as he preferred to put it. His rankless officer's uniform covered by an Army Warm, he smiled affably and nodded at Half Pint as he entered. Half Pint ignored him.

"It's not easy getting round on one leg," he said, kicking out his stump to illustrate the point. "You should try it sometime."

"If I thought it was a Blighty one, then perhaps I would," said Wilson. "But it ain't any more, is it? And that's the bleedin' point, i'n't it?"

Across the way, Rutherford groaned. "Oh, don't start, Wilson."

"Look, I signed up for the duration," Wilson retorted. "I did me duty. I volunteered to defend my country. But look around you. Is this la belle France? No, it bloody isn't. As far as I'm concerned, my war is over. And so's yours, and yours," he said, jerking his chin round the dugout at the gathered Fusiliers.

"You don't know that. The Lieutenant will get us back somehow," protested Carter, but there was little conviction in his voice.

"Look, if your officer bloke don't know the way home," said Rutherford, addressing Half Pint, "then I do think he should tell us. If there isn't one, if this is it, then fine. Let us make a new start, I say. Out there." He gestured vaguely at the dugout roof.

"Well, you would say that," said Hepton with a leer. "A little birdie tells me that you've got yourself a piece of urman skirt."

"Her name's Duuma," Rutherford insisted. "And her enclave has got this place sussed. I'd rather be out there with them than stuck in these trenches, or back in a crumbling terrace, any day. Not that I could go back anyway, not after what I've seen. I wouldn't fit in there no more."

Wilson snorted with derision. "So what do you think, Bains?" he asked the silent figure in the corner.

The shadows hid Bains' features, his face only visible in the red glow of his burning gasper whenever he took a drag. Blue smoke drifted up to the roof, snaking its way through the hanging knapsacks. Sitting on an upturned ammo box, he leaned out of the shadows, his elbows resting on his knees. He was an unremarkable man with large ears and untamed eyebrows. His cheeks were speckled with flecks of dried blood, nicks from a blunt razor. He had a chevron-shaped patch on his sleeve, slightly cleaner than the khaki serge around it, where once had been a Lance Corporal's stripe. It was faint, but it was there if you knew where to look, and everybody in the dugout did. He took a final drag on his cigarette before dropping it on the dugout floor and grinding it into the dirt.

"We've been here nigh on four month now," he growled. "I think Everson has had his chance. He doesn't know anymore than the rest of us, I reckon. Like it or not, we're here for good, I'd say, and I've had a bellyful of doing what the Army tells me. All I want is a fair chance to make summat for myself, and I'm prepared to take it if I have to."

Monroe piped up. "But blokes have been doing that; desertin', I mean. And patrols have come back saying they've found their bodies barely miles from here."

"All right," said Bains. "But how's that any different from getting blown up by a Minnie, eh?" He looked round the gloomy dugout of malcontents and grousers. "Or ripped apart by shrapnel, or dying of a gut wound in a shell hole? We're sitting ducks if we stay here."

"But this place is all that we have left of Earth," said Cox.

"And you're really going to miss all that, are you?" said Bains. "People say the world will change after the War, if it ever ends, but I doubt it. Them as has money will still have it and them as hasn't still won't. I'm going to be no worse off here. But at least I can be me own master. And so can you. Starting right here, right now."

"Why, Bains, you're beginning to sound like a Bolshevik," said Hepton with an oily grin.

"So what do we do?" asked Cox.

"It's already being done. Word has gone out. Some of our brethren will be on sentry duty. They'll let us pass. All I ask is that if you don't join us, stand aside and let us take our demands to Everson. We just want a say in how things is run from now on, and we'll man the barricades to get it if we have to."

Half Pint heard Bains' speech with despair. Grousing was one thing, but this was another kettle of fish altogether. It had started out innocently enough – they had genuine grievances, after all – but now it seemed to be gathering a momentum all its own. Bains spoke with passion, though it wasn't altruism that was forcing his hand. He was letting his ambitions get the better of him. He hadn't lost his stripe for nothing. Bains wanted power and over the past few days he had been giving the same speech to many small discontented gatherings like this. Half Pint, his glass by nature being half empty, expected the whole thing to blow up in their faces.

"And what on earth makes you think Everson's going to listen?" needled Hepton.

Bains grinned. "He won't have a choice."

AT THE APPOINTED time, gangs of men, many with their faces covered, took advantage of the chaos caused by the mutineers, and rampaged through the trenches, and across the open ground between, in a spirit of mischief, revelling in the irresponsible respite from daily military routine.

Other men had darker motives.

Padre Rand, the army chaplain, knew the men felt lost, far from home as they were, and far from the sight of God. He knew because that was how he felt himself. However, he had his faith, or at least had rediscovered it out here. And with the largesse of the shepherd he knew he must use it to protect his flock from straying.

So it was that he found himself stood on a firestep, pleading with a mob of unruly men who sought to pass by. He raised his arms in the air, appealing for calm, but his uniform wasn't helping. Although they held no army rank, chaplains wore an officer's uniform with a dog collar and black bib.

"Let us past, Padre," a voice from the masked crowd called out. "We just want to talk to Lieutenant Everson."

The Padre, middle-aged and sandy-haired, looked down at them more in sorrow than in anger. "Then why cover your faces and go armed with clubs?" he asked, attempting to look them in the eyes. "Go back to your dugouts. This isn't the way."

A large bruiser of a soldier pushed his way brusquely to the front and stood before him. "Don't be a martyr, Padre. This isn't your fight. Step down."

The Padre smiled sadly and shook his head. "I'm very much afraid, my son, that it is. You're going down the wrong path. I am, for better or worse, stood at the fork in the road. You would do well to listen to me."

"Then you can't say I didn't warn you." The man pulled back his arm, drawing a gasp from the surrounding mob crowding the fire bay.

A man surged forward, ripping the kerchief away from his face as he did so, to restrain his arm. "Wilson, have you gone mad? You'll lose your name."

Wilson turned and snarled. "Take your hands off me, Rutherford."

The Padre watched, startled, as the two men struggled. The soldiers around them tried to move back, away from the grappling pair, but in the cramped confines of the fire bay it wasn't possible. An arm flailed out and caught the Padre on the jaw; he lost his footing and slipped, cracking his head against a revetment post.

An accusing cry went up from Wilson."Rutherford, what have you done?"

Rutherford stood, looking shocked.

As the Padre went down, the mob fled in panic, and Rutherford with them.

Beyond the trenches, the first shots rang out.

The world faded and the Padre found himself sinking into darkness. There, the nightmare vision he fought to keep at bay, the one he experienced in a heathen Khungarrii ritual, waited for him...

TULLIVER TRUDGED ALONG the trenches to his dugout, lost in a moment of maudlin introspection. He still felt bitter. The RFC had fought for two years to be taken seriously by Brass who couldn't see how to use them. And now Everson was making the same mistake.

A group of rowdy Tommies filed along the kinked communication trench, singing and shouting, and jostled him from his thoughts. Some wore gas hoods, others covered their faces with scarves or kerchiefs. From all about came raucous shouts and yells. This was far from boisterous high spirits.

One man, a balaclava and scarf round his face, seized Tulliver roughly by the arm.

A mate, catching sight of his double-breasted RFC tunic, quickly dissuaded him. "Leave him, Spokey. He's Flying Corps, not even a proper soldier."

The fellow let him go with a grunt and moved on.

"What's going on?" Tulliver called after the mob.

"The proletariat are rising up!" said another jubilant Tommy, shoving past, rifle in hand. "Some of the boys are off to tell Everson what they think of him. We've got no argument against you, sir. You keep out of our way and we'll keep out of yours." He ran after his comrades.

Tulliver understood their resentment, even shared it to a degree. The camp had been on edge since the Khungarrii siege and the animal stampede. But he hadn't expected this.

From up beyond the trench, there were angry shouts and barked orders, answered by jeers as disorderly soldiers rampaged recklessly across the camp, dismissive of the NCOs' calls to order.

"Damn!" Tulliver shook his head and drew his revolver.

He raced along a comm trench, swerving round the traverses, in an attempt to get to the command post.

The points of several bayonets brought him up short.

He slipped to a stop on the wet duckboards, inches from the glinting steel as a small section of men, led by a Lance Corporal, glared at him.

"Just what the hell's going on here?" Tulliver demanded.

"Mutiny, sir."

CHAPTER TWO

"Hold Your Hand Out..."

TULLIVER POINTED HIS revolver at the Lance Corporal's head.

Lance Corporal 'Only' Atkins didn't flinch, confident in the clatter of several rifles he heard behind him as they were raised and pointed at Tulliver.

The RFC officer cleared his throat, but didn't lower the pistol. "We're not the mutineers, sir," said Atkins. He glanced over his shoulder at the men behind him. "Lower your weapons, lads."

"You sure, Only?" asked the tall, lanky one.

"Uh huh."

The men behind him lowered their Enfields, albeit reluctantly.

Warily, Tulliver lowered his gun too, but kept them pinned with a sullen stare.

"What's your name, Corporal?"

"Atkins, sir."

"Atkins? Everson's Black Hand Gang Atkins?"

"That's one way of putting it, I guess," he said with truculence. "Though we prefer 1 Section, 2 Platoon."

"Oh. Right you are," Tulliver said cheerfully.

Tulliver studied the soldiers in their worn, ill-fitting uniforms; the tall lanky one must be Pot Shot, no mistaking him. The one who never took his eyes off him, that must be

Gazette, the sniper. The other with the roguish good looks must be Porgy. He'd heard the stories that had circulated around camp about them, and the ones about Atkins in particular. He knew Everson trusted him and his section implicitly, and decided to do the same.

Tulliver raised an eyebrow. He held out a hand. "Tulliver, Royal Flying Corps." Atkins took it warily, and Tulliver gripped his hand firmly. "So you're Atkins, eh? Glad to meet you."

His eye caught the telegraph pole overhead, the cable now hanging limp in the mud.

"Damn them. They've cut the telephone wires. Signals won't be happy. You and your men come with me. We'll have to report the situation in person."

EVERSON SAT WRITING up the Pennines' recent fantastical experiences on this foreign world in the Battalion War Journal. They were totally at odds with the dry reports of troop movements, battles and trench raids of earlier pages. Sometimes he wondered if he wasn't mad, and if all this wasn't the product of a febrile shell-shocked imagination. He even thought that might be preferable.

The sound of faint jeers and gunfire leached through the gas blanket.

His forehead creased with annoyance and he looked up as Atkins and Tulliver clattered down the steps into the command post, closely followed by Sergeant Hobson. "What the devil is going on out there?"

"The men are running amok," said Tulliver in a tone of incredulity, as he paced around, gesturing wildly towards the door.

By comparison, Hobson and Atkins stood smartly to attention.

"Seems to be a bit of a riot, sir," said Hobson, delivering his assessment with wry understatement.

"Seems?" Everson turned and cocked his head, listening to the gunfire and sporadic shouts. "There doesn't seem to be any 'seems' about it, Sergeant."

Atkins chipped in. "No, sir. But the majority of the men are staying out of it. Mostly it's a few malcontents stirring up trouble, but we should nip it in the bud, sir."

Everson paused to listen to the chaotic sounds a moment longer. "Do we know what they're mutinying about?"

"You name it, they're grousing about it, sir," replied Hobson.

Everson shot a questioning glance at Atkins, who gave a near-imperceptible shake of the head. That was something, at least.

He struggled to subdue a rising feeling of guilt. If the men had known what he and Atkins knew, then they would have cause to riot. For they both knew that the Pennine Fusiliers weren't the first or only people displaced here from Earth. There had been others. Atkins and his section had found the remains of a party of American emigrants in the Nazarrii edifice. The Bleeker party had been travelling west on the California Trail in 1846 when they suddenly found themselves here, much as the Pennines had. If there was a way back, they didn't find it and they died here. They survived barely three months. Everson had ordered Corporal Atkins' Black Hand Gang to secrecy. He needed it kept secret; he believed the only thing holding the battalion together was the hope that they still *might* be able to get home.

Today, though, it looked like even that might not be enough.

He slammed a fist on his desk in frustration. Just as he was getting on top of things, he could feel them slipping away. But this was the Army and, like it or not, he needed to quell the potential mutiny and reassert his authority, if they were to survive at all.

"God damn it. I hoped it would never get to this." He looked up at Hobson, his face set, determined, his voice as hard as stone. "Sergeant, read them the Army Act. They get one chance. One."

"Leave it with me, sir," said Hobson, saluting smartly and making for the doorway.

"Thank you, Hobson."

Everson turned his attention to the flying officer, who was still pacing about in an agitated manner. "The gall of the fellows!" he said, still stung by their impudence.

"Tulliver! I'd be obliged if you'd fly over the camp; see if you can't help break up some of the larger groups."

"What? Oh, now you want me to fly," said Tulliver, archly.

Everson wasn't in the mood. "Just do it," he said wearily, "or you may find that once this lot get hold of it, you'll have no flying machine left at all!"

Tulliver stood for a moment, about to say something, then thought better of it, turned on his heel, and left.

"And me, sir?" asked Atkins, standing at ease.

"You're about the only man I can trust right now, Corporal. I want you and your men to mount a piquet outside. Are they all with you?"

"All apart from Evans and Blood, sir. They're guarding Chandar, sir."

"Oh, God, the chatt!"

"Don't worry. They'll keep it safe, sir."

"I hope so. Like it or not, Atkins, we need it."

Everson took his Webley out of his holster and, with a deep sigh of regret, began to load it.

MERCY AND GUTSY, of 1 Section, stood on guard duty either side of the gas curtain to the dugout where Everson held the chatt, for its own safety. For theirs, they tucked their gas hoods in knapsacks on their chest, for ease of access. They were supposed to wear them all the time when on guard duty with the chatt. But they were hot and foul smelling, and neither wanted to be mistaken for a rioter.

Mercy, as wiry as a terrier and an inveterate scrounger, was listening in sanguine mood to the drone of the aeroplane and wash of rioting and looting that ebbed and flowed around them.

"Thought you'd want to be out nicking a few things yourself," said Gutsy, a stocky man with large, meaty hands, a ruddy complexion and a balding pate beneath his battle bowler.

"Nah. All the bon stuff's long gone, mate."

"Really?" asked Gutsy. "Where to?"

Mercy just smirked and tapped his nose.

The wave of noise grew louder as a rabble of men approached round the traverse.

"Eh up." Mercy nodded and he and Gutsy turned to face the direction of the noise, bayonets fixed. Mercy's short, sharp bark brought them up short.

"Halt."

The leader, a scarf wrapped round his lower face, didn't seem concerned. His confidence bolstered by the men behind him, he stepped up to Mercy's bayonet point.

Mercy could see the length of rope in the man's fist. This wasn't a rabble, this was a lynch mob. "You've not really thought this through, have you?" Mercy said.

"We were passing and thought we'd pay the thing a little visit. Those things killed my mates. So are you siding with one of them murderous insects against your own kind? Have you got no shame?" he snarled.

"No," said Gutsy. "We've got orders."

At that, the men surged forward. Unwilling to use bullets or bayonet their own men, Mercy and Gutsy swung the shoulder stocks of their rifles into the first wave. Men fell to the duckboards, winded, or careened off wattle revetments before sliding down into the mud.

"Bloody 'ell!" said Mercy, ducking under the swing of a trench club to land a hard punch in a soft belly.

From behind the gas curtain came a thin skittering sound that made Mercy's skin crawl. A prolonged hiss followed.

The fight broke off as everyone's attention turned toward the rubberised cloth covering the dugout entrance.

Something tore the curtain aside. In a swift, inhuman motion, a pale, chitinous creature leapt out of the dugout and onto the trench parapet before scuttling back down the revetment behind the mob, who now found themselves trapped between the guards and the chatt.

It stood like a man, had the height of a man, but that was all the humanity one could ascribe to it. The chatt reared up on its backward-bending legs to its full height, a posture of threat. It spread its chitinous arms wide, exposing the small vestigial limbs at its abdomen. Then it splayed its mandibles and hissed again, spraying an atomised mist into the air, enveloping the men.

Within moments, the lynch mob's expressions softened, changing from fear and anger to contentment. Their unifying purpose forgotten, they began to wander off individually, in a daze.

The chatt sank back down and advanced toward Mercy and Gutsy, who turned their rifles upon it.

"This One has merely blessed them," it said. "By GarSuleth's Will they are at peace. They will not harm us now."

Mercy and Gutsy looked at each other, wide-eyed with amazement, as the chatt returned to the dugout of its own volition, the stake and rope that had kept it imprisoned still tied to its ankle.

"Well, bless me!" said Mercy rubbing the back of his head and exchanging bemused looks with Gutsy.

Gutsy watched the mob staggering off like happy inebriates. "Best not," he said, reaching into his knapsack for his gas hood. "Not on duty."

NURSE EDITH BELL looked over the beds, filled with recently blinded patients newly under her charge, all of them victims of chatt scentirrii acid spit. She still berated herself for the loss of the shell-shocked men, led to their deaths by alien parasites and flayed alive by the huge airborne grazing Kreothe. However, she had experienced the death of patients before and, as Sister Fenton reminded her, the dead weren't her purview, the living were.

Sister Fenton interrupted her thoughts now.

"No time for shilly-shallying," she said, nodding towards the end of the tented ward. "Warton needs a bed pan."

"Nurse!"

There was a desperate tinge to the voice. As the matron left, she bobbed in an almost imperceptible curtsy, her nurse's apron sitting oddly over her part-worn khaki serge trousers. "Yes, sister."

She walked along between the two rows. She reached the end bed and searched underneath for the hollowed-out gourd that now served as a bedpan.

"Can you manage?" Edith asked.

"Yes, I'm sure I can, nurse," said Warton in a strained tone. Bandages made from an old army issue shirt covered his eyes, but didn't hide the extent of the livid acid-etched flesh.

The gourd vanished beneath the blanket. Warton's features softened with relief.

Edith turned her back. She heard a fast stream splash against the inside of the gourd and subside into a rising gurgle. The trickle died. She turned round as Warton carefully manoeuvred the gourd out from under the army grey blanket and handed it back to her.

"Here you go, nurse. Sorry, nurse."

"Nonsense," she said softly.

The gourd was heavy and warm, and sloshed. She put it under the bed for collection later. The urine wasn't wasted. The experiment with gunpowder was still ongoing. That was one good thing to come out of the animal stampede. There was a surplus of dung. They added urine to the dung, in the hope of making saltpetre, apparently. With ammunition running low, even crude gunpowder would be welcome.

She became aware of a rowdy jeering outside. It wasn't unusual for the men to become boisterous and rowdy, but that was usually in the evenings.

"What's going on?" asked Warton, cocking his head toward the sound.

Edith pursed her lips. "I don't know."

Several men burst into the tent, throwing back the flaps.

Edith bustled towards them, arms out, preparing to herd them from the tent, out of concern for her patients.

The men stood in the entrance, leering as they looked about. Their tunics were undone. One wore a kerchief over his lower face; another wore his PH gas hood.

"Privates, what's the meaning of this? This is a casualty ward. Please leave," she insisted in a stage whisper.

Several other men attempted to enter behind them, and the masked men staggered forward. Gas Hood stumbled into Edith's arms and clung to her. His mates cheered him on.

"What about some fun, nurse, eh? How about a dance?" The mask muffled the voice. "If you were the only girl in the world, and I were the only boy!" he bellowed in a rough baritone. She found herself staring at her reflection in the mica eyepieces. She looked startled and afraid, and she hated herself for that. She braced her hand against the man's shoulders and pushed him back.

"Get your hands off me."

The blinded patients, confused by the noise, called out in alarm from their beds.

"What's going on?"

"Leave her alone."

His grip tightened around her waist. His head leaned in for a kiss, the gas hood's red rubber non-return valve poking out obscenely. Repulsed, she twisted her face away and took a swing with her foot. Her boot connected with his shin. The private bellowed in pain and let her go, her hair askew and tumbling down from her hair pins, her chest heaving with adrenalin.

"Ooh, quite the wild woman, eh?" The others began to circle her.

"I haven't had a woman in months," said one.

Warton groped his way out of his makeshift bed. "You men ought to be ashamed of yourselves." Rising to his feet, he thrust his hand out, feeling blindly for obstructions. He found a tunic. He gripped it and pulled the man toward him. "Who the hell are you, eh? Not a man, that's for sure. I'll have your number for this," he snarled.

A large hand planted itself in his bandaged face and shoved him to the ground, to the accompaniment of mocking laughter.

Someone shunted Edith. She lost her balance, tripped over Warton and landed on her back, on the vacated bed.

A cheer went up. Kerchief loomed over her. "Them trousers won't protect you, darlin'. I'm a dab hand with trousers," and to illustrate the point he flung off his tunic, flicked his braces off his shoulders and began to unbutton his flies. Edith, alarmed, tried to rise from the bed, but found herself pushed back down.

Her hand searched blindly down by the side of the bed for a weapon, something, anything. All she felt was hard, dry soil. Her fingers clawed at it, trying to get a handful of dirt, but it was too compacted. Her hands met something hard and warm.

He loomed over her, khaki trousers down round his knees exposing pale hairy thighs. She lashed out with a foot between his legs. His eyes bulged and he grunted into his kerchief. Edith swung her arm upwards, the hollowed gourd in her hand, and flung the contents in his face. There was no mistaking the smell of urine.

Edith scrambled from the bed and, panting, faced her attackers. Before, she had been scared; now, she was angry. That same righteous fire that once urged her to denounce Jeffries burned within her now.

A howl of derision went up, the men enjoying the turn of events even more.

A gunshot silenced the laughter.

Half Pint stood in the tent entrance, leaning on a crutch with one hand, his other crutch cast to the floor, the better to hold the revolver.

Sister Fenton arrived on his heels to see the aftermath.

"What the hell are you doing?" yelled Half Pint. "Get out! You've got no argument here! Your grouse is with the officers. The next one who makes a wrong move gets plugged. And you can bet your arse it won't be a cushy one, so just remember who's going to have to patch you up. Now move."

The rowdy mood deflated almost instantly, leaving the shame-faced men to shuffle out, their consciences pricking.

Kerchief, his eyes red rimmed, his hair plastered to his head by warm piss, struggled to pull up his trousers.

"Not you," said Sister Fenton and belted him round the head with the fallen crutch.

Edith watched, her mouth a perfect 'o' of surprise. He crumpled to the floor. Fenton handed the crutch back to a bemused Half Pint.

Hobson stood beneath the flagpole on which the battle-tattered Union Jack fluttered with little enthusiasm, as though infected by the general malaise affecting the men.

Backed up by 4 Section 3 Platoon, he confronted the disorganised mob heading towards him. They stopped, more out of amusement and curiosity than discipline. Many were wearing gas hoods or kerchiefs over their faces to hide their identities.

"Just what the bloody hell do you think you're doing?" Hobson roared. "Get back to your duties."

The mob stood around insolently, interspersing the resulting sullen silence with the occasional boos, jeers and catcalls, like a rough music-hall crowd.

Hobson was disgusted. He'd helped train these men. He'd wiped their arses, patted them on the shoulders and listened to them when they cried for their mothers.

He took a piece of paper from his tunic pocket to a rising sarcastic "Oooooh," from a crowd that grew bigger as other rioters drew closer.

Hobson unfolded it to more mock amazement.

"Hey up, lads, he's going to read us a monologue!"

Hobson's lip curled as he glared at the ill-disciplined rabble in front of him. He cleared his throat. "I have been ordered by Lieutenant Everson, Acting Commanding Officer of the 13th Battalion of the Pennine Fusiliers to read from the Army Act of Nineteen Hundred and Thirteen."

"Give us a song!"

Hobson ignored the lout and began his recitation. "Every person subject to military law who causes or conspires to cause any mutiny or sedition in any forces belonging to His Majesty; or endeavours to seduce any person in His Majesty's forces from allegiance to His Majesty, or to persuade any person in His Majesty's regular forces to join in any mutiny or sedition; or joins in, or being present, does not use his utmost endeavours to suppress any mutiny or sedition; or coming to the knowledge of any actual or intended mutiny or sedition in any forces belonging to His Majesty, does not without delay inform his commanding officer of the same, shall on conviction by court-martial be liable to suffer death."

Every word was as bitter as bile to him. He never once believed he would be reduced to reading these words. He stood and stared down the insolent glares not obscured by gorblimey cap peaks, gas masks, scarves or kerchiefs. Some, at least, looked shame-faced and cast their faces down.

"Sod this for a game of soldiers," someone yelled from the crowd. The throng began to scatter, dodging the clumsy-footed soldiers who had no heart to engage them. Some sprinted straight past Hobson, whose face flushed with rage as he bellowed. "You men! Come back here!"

Before him, the remnants of the mob, perhaps two thirds of their number, shuffled uncomfortably.

Hobson, looked at them, disappointment etched on his face. "I don't want to see your faces. Get back to your dugouts and remain there unless otherwise ordered."

The men, their mood subdued, removed their hoods and kerchiefs once their backs were turned. They began to disperse, although not quick enough for Hobson. "At the bloody double!" he yelled.

He felt the weight of his trench club in the frog at his hip. Right now, he could really do with breaking a few heads.

THE STRUTTER FLEW over the field of red poppies that had sprung from the Somme mud, before it dived low across the camp, causing men to duck, or to dash for cover.

There was a time when Tulliver loved doing this. He and Biffer had often flown down French roads buzzing staff motor cars, sending bloated red tabs scrambling for the car floor or columns of soldiers diving into ditches. All jolly good fun. Here, though, the sport palled.

He chased and harried, breaking up large mobs, herding them back from the open ground and into the trenches, watching men sprawl in the dirt as his landing wheels roared inches above their heads.

"Christ, what am I doing?" he muttered.

All the rage at being grounded, at the loss of his squadron mates, at the lack of understanding; he balled it up and screamed at the unearthly world in frustration.

The indifferent roar of the engine drowned it out.

AS THE RIOTOUS din rose and fell about them, Atkins and the rest of 1 Section stood to arms in the trench outside Battalion HQ. Thin columns of smoke rose into the air from indiscriminate arson.

"You can't blame them for rioting," said Pot Shot, remonstrating. "We've had no rest or pay for four months. We haven't suddenly found ourselves back on Earth, and it doesn't look like we're going to, either, does it?" The lanky Fusilier shot a sullen glance at Atkins. "Don't you think the rest of those poor buggers deserve to know, too?"He was talking about the Bleeker party, and Atkins knew it. They all did.

He wanted to do the right thing, and of course, he had sympathy with those rioting, all of which made his choice to stand here right now all the harder.

He shook his head. "That's not our problem. Lieutenant Everson ordered us to keep it secret, remember? And for good reason."

"Doesn't mean I have to like it," countered Pot Shot. "Even so, if there isn't a way back, then we're not exactly anybody's army anymore are we? Maybe we should all have a vote," he suggested.

"What, the women, too?" said Porgy, never usually given to deep political thought.

Gazette poked him in the shoulder. "You're only worried that if they get to vote on everything, they'll never let you walk out with them again," said the taciturn sniper.

Atkins watched the mob approach the Battalion HQ, hands bristling with trench clubs, sticks and rifles. Porgy, Gazette and Pot Shot stood beside him, blocking the way.

"Go back," he warned them.

Bains stepped to the fore, the shaft of an entrenching tool in his hand and a greasy smile on his face. "Well that's the whole point isn't it? We haven't gone back, have we? We're still here. All we want is a chance to make a new life for ourselves."

Impatient, the men behind Bains began to jostle, bracing for a fight.

Atkins raised his voice and addressed the rabble. "Is that what you all say?"

Bains took a step forward, daring Atkins to react. "They're not going to listen, Atkins," he said, "not even to you. You don't have any believers here. In fact, most of these men think you're a bit of a sham. Those campfire tales of you fighting Jeffries, magic bolts of lightning, demons, all that?" He wrinkled his nose in contempt. "Don't believe 'em. You're no better than I am. You're just a jumped-up lance jack who wants a bit of glory. Well, they don't give out medals for bullshit." He paused and shrugged. "Unless you're on the General Staff, of course."

"You ain't half pushing it, Bains," said Porgy.

"On the contrary. It's Everson that's been pushing it for far too long, and it ends here. Where's Everson?" He looked around and began singing. "If you want to find the CO, I know where he is, he's down in the deep dug–'"

A gas gong rang out. Everson stood on the trench bridge above them, the artillery shell casing hanging at the end of the bridge still swinging where he'd struck it with the butt of his Webley.

"You men! Stand down. That's an order. I've asked once. That's more than generous, given the circumstances. I won't ask again."

"We don't take orders anymore," yelled Bains. "We've done our duty, but there are no Huns left to kill, no King to tell us what to do, no country to fight for."

"It doesn't excuse mutiny," said Everson, looking down at him.

"It does if you don't recognise military law anymore."

"Your uniform says different. Now disperse and go back to your dugouts," Everson ordered.

From around the camp, indiscriminate rifle fire popped and crackled.

"You hear that?" he said. "Every bullet you and your fellow mutineers squander means one less creature we can kill, one less horror we can dispatch. So each round you waste only hastens your own deaths."

"Or yours," countered Bains with a sneer. "At 'em, lads!"

The mob rushed the Tommies in the trench.

Porgy grabbed a sandbag from the parapet and swung it round. It smacked a mutineer on the side of the head with a thick, wet thud, slamming him into the trench wall.

Atkins hooked the shoulder stock of his Enfield behind a mutineer's knee, snatching the man's leg out from under him. A shunt of his shoulder sent him over.

Striding forward, he drove the shoulder stock of his rifle into a stomach of another and brought it up, cracking the gas-masked man on the chin as he doubled over, then swung it down on the back of his head, driving him onto the duckboards.

He never thought he'd be fighting his own. But he fought with a desperation born of fear, knowing that everything he held dear depended on Everson staying in command. Every man jack of these mutineers was an obstacle to a goal that was his guilt and his disgrace. He knew that they were stuck here. He knew with more certainty than these poor bastards did. He chose not to believe it. He chose to hold on to a possibility so slim it could be said to be barely there at all. It was the one Everson had pinned his hopes on, too. Every moment he was stuck here in camp was a moment lost, a moment when he could be pursuing Jeffries, the only man who might conceivably know of a way back. Back home to Flora, his missing brother's fiancée and, to his eternal shame and joy, the mother-to-be of his own child.

Bains grabbed Atkins' rifle.

"What makes you better than me, eh? What really happened in Khungarr between you and Everson and Jeffries?" he grunted.

"Really?" snapped Atkins, snatching the rifle from his grip. "I saved a chatt's life."

A shadow crossed his face and he flinched instinctively. Bains took advantage of the distraction and melted into the mob.

Atkins glanced up at the parapet to see Sergeant Hobson leaping over the sandbags, using the firestep below as a springboard as he leapt into the fray, swinging his trench club. Atkins didn't envy the mutineers now. He'd seen Hobson in trench raids and he fought with a brutal efficiency.

Atkins' brow furrowed with mock concern. "I was worried you wouldn't get here in time, Sarn't!"

"Thanks for saving me a few, lad," said Hobson, raising his trench club, and as he waded into the skirmish, skulls cracked and punched faces flung bloody mucus into the air.

* * *

Bains, seeing the tide turn, scrambled up the side of the trench and made for the makeshift bridge that spanned it, where Everson stood. All pretence at negotiation was gone now. This was a bloody coup.

Everson caught the dull yellow shine of a brass knuckle-duster and a glimpse of a short blade. A dirty little weapon, he thought, as Bains charged him; a Hun souvenir.

He moved off the footbridge to meet Bains, blocked the first punch thrust and grabbed Bains' wrist. He stepped past and brought the handle of his revolver down on the back of Bains' head. Bains' momentum carried him across the bridge into the gas gong. It *clonged* as he slipped, lost his footing and tumbled over the edge into the trench.

His unconscious body lay awkwardly on the duckboards below, a red stain spreading over the wet wood of the duckboards and bleeding into the muddy sump below.

Standing on the footbridge, Everson combed his hair back off his forehead with one hand, establishing order and decorum in his own mind once again. He looked around for his cap, picked it up by the peak and placed it on his head, just so, with a nod of satisfaction.

"Mop this lot up, Atkins," he said.

INTERLUDE 1

Letter from Lance Corporal Thomas Atkins to Flora Mullins

29th March 1917

My Dearest Flora,

We've been back in camp for a while now. Don't worry. It was still here when we returned, despite my fears. At least we have fresh rations now, if you can call what the mongey wallahs cook up fresh.

I thought coming back to camp, I'd find some peace, but it seems there's none to be had anywhere here, least of all here. Some of the lads are unhappy with the situation and want to be somewhere else, but 'C'est la Guerre' as they say. Lieutenant Everson is trying to do his best, and believes it's for our own good, but there's always some barrack-room lawyer who thinks they know best.

I've been thinking about what happened between us. Sometimes, I think of nothing else. I don't regret it for one moment, but I feel so helpless stuck here so far from home, so far from you. I know some say that what we did was wrong, but that night I didn't believe it, I still don't, and I hope you feel the same.

It's human nature, I suppose. You'd think with everything else out there against us, that we could show some common sense. Sometimes we can be our own worst enemy.

Ever yours
Thomas.

CHAPTER THREE

"I Was Their Officer..."

EVERSON WALKED DOWN the hutment ward towards the Padre's bed. Captain Lippett, the MO, had assured him that the chaplain's injury wasn't serious, although it had resulted in a mild concussion.

Hearing of the Padre's assault had a profound effect on Everson, perhaps more so than the riot itself. How was it that the morale of the soldiers under his command had slipped so low? A chaplain, of all people. He was glad that the man who did this was under guard and would face retribution under court-martial.

The Padre looked wan and older than his years. A bandage was wrapped around his head. An odd, almost comic tuft of sandy hair stuck up from the middle of it, like a tonsure in reverse. He sat in bed reading the black-leather-covered Bible that rarely left his side. It was, as he had said many times, his only weapon. As he saw Everson approaching, he put the Bible down and smiled for him, but it was a weary smile that took effort.

A chair had been put out for him. Everson took off his cap and sat down.

"You look tired," said Everson.

The Padre waved a hand. "I haven't been sleeping well. A few... nightmares."

"Night terrors, Sister Fenton said. You wake up screaming."

The Padre shrugged off his concern. "So do many here," he said, gesturing around the small ward. "You forget, Lieutenant. There are no reserve trenches here. You can't take them out of the line. There is little relief for them, even here."

"Or you, Padre. You seem... troubled," said Everson.

The Padre ignored him and continued to press his point. "The men have a legitimate grievance," he continued gently. "They have homes and families far away, with no knowledge of if they will ever see them again. They've endured more than they ever should. They have done far more than you expected of them. But even they have their limits, John."

He was more forgiving than Everson. But then, Everson reminded himself, that was his job.

Everson bowed his head. "They're not men," he corrected. "They don't have that luxury right now. They're soldiers. They have to be. It's the only way they'll – we'll – survive. We have to maintain discipline. Unless we stay together, unless we remain as a battalion, we're going to get picked off, one by one. Each man that dies or deserts lessens our collective chances of survival."

The Padre looked into his eyes and clasped Everson's hand in both of his. "Then you have to find a way of keeping them together. You need to give them hope."

WHAT FEW OFFICERS there were, along with the NCOs and compliant soldiers, managed to re-establish order and calm within the camp quite quickly, suggesting perhaps that ill-feeling didn't run as deep as the ringleaders had hoped. It took less than a day to round them up. Everson surveyed the camp in the aftermath. In truth, the rioters had caused less damage than they might have, but that wasn't the point. They could be dealt with swiftly, but it would take much longer to deal with the consequences of their actions. In the wake of the Khungarrii attacks, the Pennines had sought to ally themselves with local nomadic urmen enclaves, offering them protection from chatt attacks. Now, thanks to the riot, and the behaviour of some of the men, those alliances were in jeopardy as some enclaves prepared to move out.

Most of the men, their immediate frustrations spent, returned reluctantly to the routines that had structured their lives these past few months. Most of the men complied because it was all they knew. Ultimately, they sought comfort in the companionship of their comrades.

Everson didn't fool himself into thinking that this was an end to his problems. For months he had held the battalion together. He had been relying on their respect for him, but that currency had diminished rapidly. He had been given a warning. How he dealt with the mutineers would send a warning back.

The courts-martial ran for two days. The court dealt with most minor charges by forfeiture of pay or field punishment. It heard the more serious charges toward the end. They were the cases that Everson dreaded.

The bell tent requisitioned for the courts–martial was humid and smelled of damp tube grass, sweat and fear. Army justice was often brutal and uncompromising.

Everson sat at the centre of the table, with Lieutenant Baxter, of the Machine Gun Section, to his left and Lieutenant Tulliver to his right, as they dealt with one case after another.

The Padre's assailant was one Everson took a particular interest in. He sat impassively as Second Lieutenant Haslam, prosecuting, read out the charge sheet. "The accused, number 9658798, Fusilier Francis Rutherford of the Pennine Fusiliers, as soldier in the regular force, is charged with striking a superior officer, being in the execution of his duty. The maximum punishment is death. How do you plead?"

The prisoner Rutherford, who stood to attention in front of his escort, looked visibly shocked. "Not guilty, sir."

Despite the plea, the case itself was straightforward. Rutherford had taken part in the riots by his own admission.

"I was trying to stop Private Wilson, sir," he protested. "There was a struggle. During the incident, I may have struck the Padre by accident."

"By accident," said Haslam, unconvinced. He waved a sheaf of papers. "There are eight witnesses – eight, including Private Wilson – who testified that you struck the Padre deliberately, in an act of malice and insubordination."

"What? But that's not true, sir," Rutherford protested. "Ask the Padre!"

"Unfortunately the Padre isn't fit to give evidence at these proceedings. And may I remind you that you have already admitted to taking part in the mutiny. Do you wish to further address the court?"

Rutherford, when faced with these facts, merely hung his head, realising the futility of any further protest. "No, sir."

To his dismay, Everson felt no satisfaction in pronouncing sentence.

Wilson got away with field punishment.

Private Nicholls' intervention on behalf of the nurses had seen him acquitted as he had done all possible to prevent the actions.

The ringleaders, though, were of a different cloth and were court-martialled jointly. They stood together surly and resolute: Bains, Swindell and Compton.

Bains stood to attention, his face swollen and bruised with a dark red hatching of scabs on his left cheek. He refused to make eye contact with anyone in court, a look of undisguised insolence on his face.

The charge against him and his fellow conspirators was mutiny.

He offered no plea, just a sullen, defiant silence.

"Bains," said Everson wearily before he passed sentence. He waved a fragile piece of paper in Bains' direction. "You drafted these demands, I believe."

Bains looked straight ahead, refusing to be drawn.

"Damn it, Bains. We're all trying to work together here. You don't think we all want to get home?"

Everson saw Hobson behind the prisoner lean forward and whisper something he didn't catch. Bains' eyes flicked to the side before staring straight ahead again.

"This is your chance, Bains. Your only chance," Everson said. He read from the scrap. "Your demands here: one, to recognise the fact that we are no longer at war and that our duty to King and Country is done. Two, to allow those that wish to do so to leave and seek their own fortune. Three, that those men who wish to stay be allowed to do so on equal footing, that a council should be elected and voted on by all.

"Laudable sentiments, Bains. But I'm afraid I can't allow it. You signed up for the duration of the war. And, if you haven't noticed, we are still at war – with this entire world. Our lives and safety depend on well-ordered military discipline. It represents our best chance of survival.

"The court sentences the accused to suffer death by being shot. However, the court recommends the accused mercy on the ground that they have been present in the line without relief for over four months and this may have gone some way to contributing to their behaviour."

Bains' Adam's apple bobbed as he swallowed. He didn't meet Everson's gaze, but he nodded.

"May God have mercy on your souls," said Everson heavily.

Everson ordered all men fit for duty on parade at dawn the next day. This was not something he wanted to do, but punishment had to be seen to be done.

The prisoners were marched out, under guard, past the Union Jack, out across the rings of defensive trenches and between the waiting ranks; the two full companies that were all that was left of the battalion, a couple of orphan platoons from the remaining two and several loyal Karno platoons. The men were escorted to the old bombed-out Poulet farmhouse, which now served as a gatehouse and watchtower to the camp.

Everson stood stiffly to attention as he addressed the condemned men, his voice hard and cold. "If I carried out the sentence as required it would, frankly, be a waste of what bullets we have left, and mercy has been recommended by the court. Privates Bains, Swindell, Compton and Rutherford, I hereby exile you from the camp. You will be sent forth with such provisions as we can spare and forbidden to return on pain of death. Is that understood?"

Company Quartermaster Sergeant Slacke handed the men two days' provisions, water and one magazine of ammunition of ten rounds for their Enfields, which he felt was more than they deserved given the circumstances.

Everson wasn't entirely sure how merciful the commuted sentence was. It was in effect still a death sentence, expecting them to survive out there for any length of time. At least they had a chance. Rutherford had a 'wife' among the nomadic urmen. Everson knew that her urmen enclave was planning to move out, unsettled by the riots. It brought him some comfort. If the men survived long enough to meet up with them, then they might improve their chances.

They walked past the poppies that spread out across the scorched cordon sanitaire and strode out into the veldt of tube grass. Only Rutherford turned to glance back. It was a look of hurt, betrayal and sorrow, and it shook Everson to the core.

Standing up on the observation platform on the remains of the ruined first floor, Everson felt duty-bound to remain long after the other ranks had been dismissed, not to make sure they actually left, but out of a sense of guilt.

"It had to be done, John," said Lieutenant Baxter, coming up and standing at his shoulder. He watched with him as the dwindling figures were finally swallowed by the veldt. Although a couple of months younger than Everson himself, Baxter, with his full moustache and easy smile, exuded the air of a favourite school master. Everson found his company comforting.

From behind, within the wireweed-bounded camp, the barks of NCOs urged work parties on, a little harder than necessary in revenge for the rioting.

He looked out across the camp. "I've lost them, Bernard."

"They'll come round, John. They need you, more than they think."

THE OFFICERS GATHERED in the Command Post. Their mood was sombre and subdued. All of them looked shaken. Their world of entitlement and privilege had come close to being toppled. Next time, they might not be so lucky.

There were seven of them left, a smaller and more exclusive club than they were happy with: Baxter, Palmer, Tulliver, Lippett, Haslam and Seward. They sat on old salvaged chairs or ammo boxes, each lost in their own thoughts or, perhaps, wondering whether to give voice to them.

From his desk, Everson looked around the room. The mutineers' stupid little act had almost cost him his men. He didn't want it to cost him his officers, too.

"Right. First things first. If anyone has anything to say about my leadership of the battalion since Captain Grantham's death, best get it off your chest now. I don't want another coup on my hands."

Palmer let out an awkward cough. "Everson, old stick, no one thinks anything of the sort." He looked around at his fellow subalterns. "Do they?"

There was a chorus of *nos* and *of course nots*. The position of battalion commander seemed to be a poisoned chalice. No one else wanted to oversee the decimation of a once-proud battalion.

"Have I lost them?" he asked.

"Just got to keep them busy, old man, that's the thing."

"How about an inter-company football tournament?"

Lippett sat polishing his glasses, breathing on the lens, watching them fog and rubbing them between a thumb and forefinger with a scrap of cloth before hooking the wire arms back over his ears again. The MO was considerably older than the young officers around him, and his rank of Captain purely honorary. Eager young bucks once, now cautious and fatigued. Old men before their time, their bright, once-flushed faces now drawn and pasty.

Lippett considered his words. "You're losing them," he said, "but you've not lost them yet. They need something concrete to focus on. Vague hopes of being spirited back home are no longer enough."

Baxter stroked his moustache, arched an eyebrow at Everson, and nodded with encouragement.

Everson stood up and braced his palms on the table. "You're right," he said with resolve. "We must move forward from this, carry the men with us. Our first priority is to relieve the tank crew and salvage the tank, if we can. That operation has been delayed far too long."

"Exactly! The ironclad is a great boost to morale. It scares the dickens out of the chatts. With that back in our midst, morale should soar."

Tulliver spoke up. "Well, the tank crew were still alive and camped by the crater as of my last patrol three days ago."

"But I thought the tank was at the bottom of the crater. How are we going to get the bally thing up?"

Everson smiled for the first time in days. "That's the easiest part," he said. "We'll use the captured Khungarrii battlepillars."

The battlepillars were great larval beasts of burden, giant armoured caterpillars larger than an elephant and up to thirty yards long.

"There are secondary objectives too," said Everson, his confidence growing with every moment. It was a relief to be putting a plan into action again. "On the way, I intend to leave a party of sappers at the gorge to investigate this mysterious metal wall that Corporal Atkins found."

Haslam, his curiosity piqued, leant forward. "Yes, what the hell is it?"

"That's what I intend we find out. Atkins reports that it's a machined face of metal in the gorge wall, perfectly flat, with no visible doors or windows. Indicative of some civilisation, perhaps. We won't know until we take a closer look at it.

"In addition, once we reach the Croatoan Crater, we can pick up Jeffries' trail. This is the closest we have come to him, gentlemen."

"But how do you know he was there?" asked Seward.

Everson fished in his tunic pocket and tossed onto the table a scrap of bloodstained khaki cloth with a button attached.

"This was found at the Nazarrii edifice by the crater. The button bears the Pennines' crest. Since Atkins and his men were the first Fusiliers to reach that place, this can only have belonged to Jeffries. He was there. I'd stake my life on it."

"You may well have to," warned Haslam.

"In the meantime, what of the chatts?" asked Seward. "Without the tank, we're still vulnerable to another attack."

"We've made progress there, too," said Everson. "I think we may be able to broker some kind of deal with the Khungarrii."

"How? We have one chatt prisoner and not an impressive specimen at that," said Seward, looking round the room to nods of amused agreement.

"It turns out that it's more important than we thought. It's one of their priest caste."

"Well let's hope we've got an ace up our sleeve, because we bally well need one."

Everson smiled. "Oh, we do, gentlemen. We do."

EVERSON MADE HIS way to the dugout where they held the chatt prisoner. Atkins and Evans stood to attention as he approached.

"I need to talk to Chandar," he said.

"Best take this, then, sir." Atkins handed the officer a PH hood. "Just a precaution after what it did to the rioters."

Everson nodded, took the proffered gas hood and pulled it on. He ducked his head and descended the steep steps. He never got used to the idea that the creature was not of Earth. There was no precedent in religion or science to explain it, yet here it was – or rather, here *they* were, for this, he forced himself to remember, was their world.

At the bottom of the steps was a bolted door with a small judas hole in it. They had erected it after the attempted mutiny, for the chatt's protection as much as that of the soldiers. He unholstered his revolver, and peered into the gloom beyond.

Chandar was one of the priest caste from the Khungarr colony of an arthropod race that called themselves the Ones, or the Children of GarSuleth, their insect deity.

Its only clothing was a woven silk garment made of a single, seamless piece of cloth that went over the left shoulder of its chitinous chest plate and wrapped around its segmented abdomen. Tassels hung from it, the knots scented with scriptural scent texts, like a prayer book or a rosary. Once white, like its carapace, the cloth was now stained and soiled.

Everson coughed. Chandar turned its head toward the door. Wet clicks issued from the mucus-slick maw between its mandibles. The smooth ivory white carapace of its facial plates caught the light of the hurricane lamp hanging from the roof beam. Its visage gave nothing away. Everson couldn't tell whether it was afraid, indifferent, or angry at its incarceration. On top of its cranial carapace, the remaining stumps of its antennae twitched and jerked, as if phantom feelers were still scenting the air.

Everson regarded it thoughtfully for a moment. "We need to talk," he said.

He heard an asthmatic intake of breath forced out over organs unsuited for human speech.

"If GarSuleth wills it."

"Stand back," he ordered as he slid the bolt and pulled open the door. It caught against the uneven earthen floor, and he had to jerk it several times to get it open.

The chatt waited patiently, and when Everson entered, sank down slightly on its legs. The vestigial middle limbs, little more than chitinous claws, splayed from its abdomen. It regarded the reflection of itself in the mica eyepieces of Everson's gas hood, as he looked back at himself reflected in its large, featureless black eyes.

Another intake of breath and its finger-like mouth palps moved within the arc of its mandibles like a loom, almost as if it were weaving the words out of its breath. "Ev-er-son?" it asked.

Everson pulled his gas mask off. It was a token of trust, but only a small one. The guards outside would kill it if it tried to escape.

A sharp acrid smell assailed his nostrils. His nose wrinkled. He almost wanted to put the mask back on. He looked around and saw a damp patch in the corner of the room. The thing didn't even know enough to use the bloody bucket.

"This One offers you a blessing in the name of GarSuleth," it said, refraining from the benediction spray that was the gift of all Dhuyumirrii, the chatt priest class.

Everson got straight to the point. "I need to know if the Khungarrii will attack again."

The chatt allowed its stunted middle limbs to fold inward against its segmented abdomen again. Its answer sailed on the top of a wheeze, the clicking of its mandibles punctuating the words. "Unless this One returns to Khungarr, it is a certainty." The tone was flat, emotionless. There was no emphasis. It was hard to tell whether this was a threat or merely a statement.

"That's what I'm here to discuss," said Everson, stepping into the small dugout, leaving the door open, as much to help ventilate the place as to suggest trust.

"This One wishes Atkins' presence," it said, shuffling back.

"No," said Everson calmly. "You will talk to me." He didn't wish his authority undermined by one of his own men. Not right now. This was something he had to do for himself.

The chatt blinked, but otherwise didn't move. Stalemate.

"God damn it," Everson wheeled round, the dirt scrunching under his heels as he pivoted. He called up the steps. "Atkins, get down here!"

It was as if the thing found some comfort in the Corporal's presence. If it made it talk then he'd have to put up with it.

Atkins thudded his way down the steps. "Sir?"

"Seems Chandar won't talk unless you're here," said Everson sourly.

Atkins' face flushed. "It's this Kurda thing, sir, some chatt sense of honour, as far as I can make out. Since I saved its life, it thinks we have a connection."

Chandar looked from one to the other. "This One wishes to know what you have done with the collection of sacred salves recovered from Nazarr."

Everson turned back to the chatt. "They're safe for now. That's all you need to know. You are in no place to make demands."

Nictitating membranes flicked over the black orbs of its eyes. "That is where you are wrong," it said, its mouth palps quivering as it spoke. "It appears that this One is in exactly the right place."

Everson indicated the earthen walls surrounding them. "You're in a prison cell."

The chatt's vestigial limbs opened and closed in what might have been a shrug. "This One is exactly where GarSuleth wants this One to be."

"Why are they so important to you? What do they contain, exactly?"

"Quite possibly, your salvation and this One's substantiation." The wheezing chatt said. "There has long been a debate in Khungarr that has consumed every generation, concerning the nature of what the aromatic scriptures refer to as the Great Corruption. At present, Sirigar, Liya Dhuyumirrii of Khungarr, seeks to join the disparate olfactions of the Shura in order to consolidate its position. That One's interpretation of the perfumed prophecy holds you Tohmii to be the embodiment of the ancient scriptural evil. Your actions in attacking Khungarr have only strengthened that interpretation, along with Sirigar's standing within the Shura. With the defeat of the Great Corruption, that One's power will be assured. Thus has Sirigar ordered your herd to be culled."

"You mean it's using us as a unifying threat?"

"Yes. However, there are those in the Shura that believe that Sirigar's interpretation is false and merely a political expediency. Those Ones believe that references to the Great Corruption refer not to an external physical threat, but warn against a theological dilemma that would see our own beliefs diluted to serve a baser purpose. We believe it refers to Sirigar's debasement of the Scents of GarSuleth.

"The only way to challenge and defeat Sirigar is in ritual debate before the Shura, the Supplication of Scents, but we must have arguments and commentaries to back up our claims. We had been diligently searching the Aromatic Archive of the Fragrant Libraries for such truths when Jeffries destroyed them. Irreplaceable scents that have been Khungarr's guide and strength for generations are gone forever. And with them this One's chance to defeat Sirigar."

"And you think this collection of lost scents will provide those answers?"

"Yes. It is this One's fervent hope that the scent texts discovered in Nazarr with Atkins will provide the scriptural proof this One's olfaction has been seeking. They could hold the scriptural arguments necessary to absolve the Tohmii of their apocalyptic role."

Everson paced back and forth, absorbing the information. "So you're saying our only hope of survival is to aid you in your religious insurrection to unseat Sirigar?"

"It is."

Having just put down a mutiny of his own, the irony was not lost on him. At least now he knew just how valuable the collection of stone jars was. That was worth knowing, and the jars themselves worth holding to ransom.

"Right. And how likely is this to happen?"

"That would depend on the contents of the scriptures."

"Don't you know what they are?"

It indicated its antennae stumps. "This one is unable to read the scents texts since Sirigar had this one's antennae broken."

Of course. With no feelers, it was crippled and scent-blind, effectively an invalid in their culture.

Everson exchanged looks with Atkins, who shook his head and shrugged. He hadn't really expected the NCO to have any answers. After all, this was his call. Everson returned his attention to the chatt. "You're not making this easy for me, are you? You want me to let you walk out of here, taking all those jars with you. Even supposing they provide whatever it is you need, there is no assurance that you can even dispose of this Sirigar."

"This is true."

He stopped pacing and turned to face Chandar. "Yet you expect me to trust you?"

"If GarSuleth wills it."

Everson considered the implications, and then shook his head. "No. While it is clear that these jars are of great importance, I'm not willing to let them out of my possession. Not without knowing what they contain. Not without guarantees. Quite honestly, your continued presence here is problematic."

Chandar cocked its head to one side. "So is yours, if this One does not succeed."

The thing was wily. It might act helpless, but its immobile features hid a cunning intelligence. It had the perfect poker face. Everson paced the small cell while the arthropod watched impassively. The thing had him over a barrel, but he wasn't going to let it know that. It had dealt its hand and it was a strong one.

His own hand was not so strong, but far from useless. He didn't trust it. To that end he had put plans in place, a fallback position, but for now he would let it return to Khungarr, although he'd be damned if he gave up the one advantage they appeared to have.

He approached the chatt, staring straight into its black eyes. "Very well," he said with deliberation. "I'll let you return to your colony."

Chandar became quite animated, clicking its middle limbs together. "GarSuleth wills it," it said. "In sending the sanctified odours of GarSuleth you will have demonstrated that you urmen are part of GarSuleth's will, that you possess a fraction of his essence, a fact Sirigar denies."

"That's not my problem. You say your olfaction means us no harm. Well, we want proof. Until there is some sort of deal struck between the Khungarrii and the Pennines, the scents will remain in our possession. You can take one. One jar, as a sample. The rest remain here."

Everson ushered Atkins from the dugout and made to follow.

"But this One cannot read the scent texts," said Chandar.

Everson turned and regarded it coolly. "Then you had better choose carefully."

CHAPTER FOUR

"The Clays of a Cold Star..."

"CORPORAL ATKINS TOLD us to wait here," Norman snapped at Nellie Abbott.

Nellie arched an eyebrow and stared him down, arms folded. The FANY, dressed in her calf-length brown skirt and brown jacket, stood her ground, short curly hair framing a plain face. Some of the men assumed her hair was cut short in support of women's suffrage. The truth was she simply found it more practical.

"I don't care what Corporal Atkins said. And, frankly, I'm surprised you do. You never did before," she retorted. "They should have been back here days ago. That's what Lieutenant Tulliver's message said. Something must have happened. We've waited long enough. We'll have to go down without them. The *Ivanhoe's* down there. Alfie and Lieutenant Mathers are down there, too, in case you'd forgotten!"

It had been a week since they watched, horror-struck, as the tank tipped over the edge of the Croatoan Crater, the Sub and Alfie inside, to be lost in the jungle-filled depression below. There had been no sign of fire, no billowing smoke and no string of explosions from the dozens of shells the tank carried, so there was every hope that it was still in one piece.

Since then the remaining tank crew had been without the tank's addictive petrol fruit fuel, whose vapours had heightened their senses, and they had begun to exhibit withdrawal symptoms. Some had suffered more than others had, although they all felt sorry for themselves. Tempers grew short, then the cramps came, and the cold sweats, then the shaking, and finally a fever took hold.

Jack, the brawny gunner, trembled but never groused, never uttered a sound, though his pain showed in his eyes.

Cecil, the youngest, whimpered and called out in his delirium. Although he was the one who had taken most against Nellie, it was him who sought her out for comfort now, glad, as he said in the midst of his fever, that they now had a lady to take care of them.

Norman rolled, groaned and complained, as if playing out the most prolonged and dramatic death scene of his far from distinguished stage career.

Reggie, polite as ever, apologised profusely throughout his withdrawal for every cross word and whimper and every request for succour.

Wally, the bantam driver, took himself off away from the others and suffered stoically, his pain private.

Through it all, Nellie dutifully took charge of them, bathed their brows, gave them water, hushed them and soothed them. She wondered if, down there, Alfie was going through the same terrors. The mechanic was not quite the beau that Edith took him to be, but she had to admit, to herself at least, he had potential. He had an easy smile, a shared enthusiasm for motorbikes and engines and a willingness to accept her for who she was. Although Edith thought she could do better, Nellie found that she did not want to. Now Alfie was down in the crater, and she didn't know whether he was alive or dead. She would move heaven and earth, or at the very least a truculent tank crew, to find out.

They would have to go down there. To that end, she conceived a plan while the others were ill and set about putting it into practice. It would give them something to focus on while trying to deal with their petrol fruit addiction.

Atkins had charged Napoo, the Pennines' urman guide, with her wellbeing. He was a grizzled, weather-beaten man, his skin criss-crossed with scars. The clothing he wore was of animals' skins and he was partially armoured with plates of hard-won chatt carapace. He was older than any of them, and that spoke of a certain tenacity and wisdom, especially on this world where nothing seemed to survive for long.

He hunted and kept them fed, a task made easier by the destruction of the Nazarrii edifice not too far away. The collapse of its subterranean levels had disturbed the warrens of some burrowing animals Cecil called snarks. Napoo took great delight in catching them by the dozen.

He took a great many to the nearby Gilderra clan as gifts, as Nellie determined they would need their help. The Gilderra saw this as a turn in their fortunes, for which the *Ivanhoe* and its crew were responsible. The crew had killed the Dulgur for them that haunted the Nazarrii ruins, and now animal life returned to the area. However, so, too, had the patrols of Zohtakarrii chatts, in whose territory the tank crew found themselves. Although the patrols did not venture too close to the crater, or the ruins of the Nazarrii edifice, Napoo had no doubt that the chatts had scented them on the wind and knew they were there.

During their recovery, the tankers had meekly allowed Nellie to take charge while their senses returned to normal, only to find that, having been under her care, they now found themselves susceptible to her natural authority as a nurse. All except Norman. In his withdrawal, she had seen him exposed and vulnerable. She had seen beneath the actor's mask that he chose to show the world. It embarrassed him, and he resented her for it.

"Why should we listen to you?" Norman asked petulantly. The tanker glared at her, his lip curled with bitterness, his hands shoved deep in the pockets of the dark blue coveralls the tank crew wore over their regulation khaki uniforms.

"Because she looked after us," said Cecil. "Because those are our mates down there. And the *Ivanhoe*."

"*Oh, Nellie, lady, be our mother!*" Norman retorted in a sing-song tone.

"Leave the lad alone, Norman," said Jack.

"Cecil's right," said Nellie. "We've been sat up here for nearly a week. We're not going to give up on them, or the *Ivanhoe*."

"Says you, but how are we supposed to get down there?" said Norman.

Nellie sighed. "The Gilderra have vine rope. We have been trading snarks for rope while you have been... recovering."

Realisation dawned. Wally stepped forward to hug Nellie, but caught sight of the look in her eye and thought better of it.

"We can really do this?" asked Cecil.

"Yes, we can," said Nellie, with relief.

Napoo scowled his disapproval. His only words on the subject were the last warning Chandar gave them regarding the Croatoan Crater. "Nothing must enter, nothing must leave."

THE NEXT MORNING Nellie looked out across the wide expanse of the crater. The morning sun was just beginning to light the lip of the far side. The alien sun steadily devoured the crater's shadow, raising a curtain of vapour that swept towards them, like a creeping barrage of mist.

It took three of the crew to drag the thick vine rope to a sturdy tree. They hauled it round the trunk and struggled to tie it securely.

Jack braced his foot on the trunk and gave the rope several violent jerks. The knot tightened and held. He gave a satisfied grunt and followed the rope back to the coiled mound by the crater's edge.

Despite his misgivings, Napoo had been charged with Nellie's safety and had made rough sacks to carry food supplies, amongst which were dried snark meat, fruit and a little edible fungus.

There were also several gourds of water. Napoo had his knife, Jack, Wally and Norman had their revolvers and Cecil and Reggie carried a couple of Enfields left by Atkins and his men.

"So," said Reggie, looking round at the others. "This is it. Do or die."

Wally took a deep breath. "Well, I wouldn't have put it quite like that."

Napoo's hand clasped Nellie's shoulder. "You should not do this."

"Napoo. Our friends are down there. And there are supplies in the tank, guns and food that we can use."

She took hold of the vine rope, heaved a loop of it from its coiled bulk and dropped it over the edge. The rope unspooled under its own weight with a speed she didn't expect. Seconds later, it snapped taut from the tree.

"Well, I was expecting to say a few words before we launched it," said Norman with a sour face.

Nellie sighed with relief and brushed her hands against each other. "Well, it's done now. I'm sorry."

"No need to stand on ceremony, then," said Jack brightly. "At least you saved us that. Norman's speech would have turned into an oratory anyway."

Norman gave him a petulant sneer.

"Well, I ain't going first," said Cecil.

"Manners dictate ladies first," said Reggie, "but in this case I don't think it wise."

Jack stepped forward. He had been a boxer and was by far the heaviest of the crew, his brawny frame filling his coveralls. "I'll go first," he volunteered. "If it takes my weight, the rest of you'll have no excuse."

"At least we'll have a soft landing if it doesn't," said Wally with a grin.

They clustered at the edge; Nellie looked along the crater lip to the place where the tank tracks ended and then dismissed them, focusing her eyes on the rope, almost aa thick as her wrist, that hung over the edge.

Jack took the rope in both hands and stood with his back to the lip.

"Cecil, you next; then Norman, Wally, then Reggie."

"Why does Reggie get to go last?" asked Cecil.

"Because he's got manners," said Jack.

"Manners?"

"Yes. He's a gentleman. He won't look."

"Look where?"

"Up."

"Up?" Cecil looked at Nellie. "Oh!" Jack clipped him round the back of the head before the growing leer could smear itself across his face.

Nellie, although quite used to the company of men, blushed and averted her eyes. So used to being treated with filial affection, she often forgot her feminine aspects. It was sometimes a shock to be reminded of them, and her brothers had the bruised arms to show for it.

"Nellie, you next and Napoo can come down last. We'll secure a position below," Jack told her.

He walked backwards, feeding the rope through his hands until he got to the edge. He leaned out slowly and began to walk down the steep camber of the rock face.

"It's like Jack and the beanstalk, ain't it?" said Cecil.

Nellie watched with dread. All of a sudden, she wasn't sure she could do this. But she had committed them to this course of action. She couldn't back out now, could she? For a brief moment, she thought of falling back on her womanhood for an excuse, and instantly despised herself for it. Of course she could do this. She could do anything they could do. And what's more, she bloody well would.

One by one, the men disappeared over the edge. She fixed her eyes on the rope. It jerked spasmodically as if it had a life of its own.

Nellie wiped sweaty palms on her skirt.

"Do not look down," Napoo said gravely.

She turned her back to the edge and grasped the rope as

she had seen the others do. One foot after the other, she took hesitant steps backwards until the ground gave way beneath her heel.

From below, she heard Norman yell out "Rock" as something careened down the crater side, impacted with the scree slope and skittered down into the jungle.

Her face creasing into a frown, she stepped backwards. Her breath came in short, sharp pants. Inside she was screaming. She bit the inside of her mouth hard, to stop it from escaping.

Planting one foot below the other, she slowly fed the rope though her hands as she stared at the crimson rock in front of her. She could hear Napoo climbing onto the rope above her.

As she descended the near-vertical wall, the panic and terror within transmuted into exhilaration. She was doing it. Carried away with the audacity of her actions, she glanced down, and immediately wished she hadn't. The ground seemed so very far away.

When she couldn't move, she started to panic, only to realise that her skirt had caught on some thorny shrub clinging to the crater side. With every inch she descended, her skirt rode up. She tugged at it in an attempt to free it, and the thorns held it fast. She tugged it again. The skirt ripped, and the momentum sent her twirling round in a vertigo-inducing spin, holding onto the rope by one hand. She managed to find the cliff face and braced her feet against the rock again to stop the spin and steady herself. It took a moment to recover her composure and, holding the rope tightly in both sweat-slicked hands, she continued her slow walk down the rock face. She had read of mountaineers doing this for fun. She couldn't think why.

After what seemed like an age, she reached the top of the scree slope. There, she could take more of her weight on her legs; she realised how much her arms hurt, muscles burning with effort.

It wasn't until she made her way down the slope, still holding the rope for balance, and found the others staring at her that she realised the extent of the torn skirt. It had ripped right up above the knee. Exposed as it left her, it did seem to allow her a good degree more movement.

"Lads," said Reggie. "Lads! Turn your backs. We're not brigands, you know."

They turned round, some faster than others, earning Cecil another clip round the ear from Jack as his gaze lingered longer than it ought to.

Reggie climbed out of his coveralls, leaving him in his greyback shirtsleeves, regulation khaki trousers and puttees as he held them out behind him towards Nellie.

She reached out and took them with gratitude. "Thank you, Reggie, that's very decent of you."

By now, Napoo had reached them. "Napoo, could you?" Nellie indicated that she needed a screen from the men. The urman grunted and stood in front of her, glaring at the backs of the tank crew.

Nellie quickly slipped off her ruined skirt, stepped into the coveralls and buttoned them up. The sleeves and legs were too long, but she just rolled them up.

"There," she said, arms spread as she modelled her blue coveralls. "What do you think?"

Cecil whistled, and – sensing Jack behind him – flinched involuntarily.

Jack laughed. "You'll do."

As THEY DESCENDED the scree slope, the cries of unseen creatures echoed through the canopy rising before them, underscored by arboreal creaks and groans in the undergrowth ahead.

It wasn't hard to follow the tank's trail. Churned earth, shattered rocks, broken boughs and the exploded smears of creatures not quick enough to escape from its headlong rush marked its path. Following the ironclad's furrowing, they headed into the jungle, where everything seemed draped with large pallid creepers.

"Lieutenant!"

"Alfie!"

They called out at regular intervals, but there was no reply.

Norman spotted the first piece of wreckage, tossed aside in the undergrowth like abandoned farm equipment.

Nellie let out a gasp.

"Don't worry, said Reggie kindly. "It's just the–"

"Steering tail. I know," said Nellie. "I just wasn't prepared."

Attached to the rear of the tank, the steering tail had broken loose. Its great quarter-ton iron wheels lay on their sides, embedded in the ground. The boxes and packets of supplies it carried lay strewn back along its path, some lying pawed and torn open by curious scavengers. The steering tail's hydraulic fluid had long since leaked from it, pooled, and sunk into the ground.

Norman inspected the wreckage. He shook his head. "No way can we save this. Always thought the thing was a waste of space. Only ever worked on solid ground. It's good riddance, if you ask me."

With all the caution that this world had taught them, they advanced slowly along the *Ivanhoe's* path, feeling naked and vulnerable without the ironclad shell that they had taken so much for granted.

Nellie's every step along the way was an agony of emotional turmoil; wanting to press on, but fearing what they might find.

"There!" cried Cecil.

In the arborous gloom of the forest floor, the huge bulk of His Majesty's Land Ship *Ivanhoe* squatted half-hidden in the undergrowth, at the edge of a clearing of its own making. It had come to rest surrounded by the tangled vegetation it had dragged along with it. Facing the tank crew, its drivers' visors down, it looked like some antediluvian beast asleep in its den.

Nellie felt a flood of relief. She wanted to rush towards it, but Napoo put out an arm to stop her.

Instead, Jack took a tentative step forward. "Lieutenant?" he called out. "Alfie!"

There was no answer.

Nellie found herself praying under her breath. "Oh, please, oh, please..."

A lingering aroma of petrol fruit vapour hung about the ditched ironclad. Nellie was quick to notice that Jack inhaled deeply once he recognised it.

"Is that the fuel?" she asked, her nostrils flaring as she sniffed the air.

Jack gave a guilty start and avoided her gaze.

With a wave of his arm, he gestured for Norman, Reggie and Wally to circle round to the starboard side. Nellie, Jack, Cecil and Napoo edged around the port side.

The tank's two six-pounder guns hung, dejected but intact. Miraculously, the tracks were still in place, although they were gummed up with torn and shredded foliage. It seemed that the jungle undergrowth had absorbed most of the impact of its crash.

From round the far side, Nellie could hear the soothing tones as Wally tutted and talked to the iron behemoth. "What have they done to you, eh?"

At the front of the port sponson, Jack peered in through the vertical slit of the gunner's sight alongside the lifeless gun.

"Well?" asked Nellie.

Jack shrugged. "Can't see a thing."

They edged along the sponson, past the machine gun toward the rear. Jack held up his hand. They stopped as he peered round the back of the sponson to the entrance hatch, before swinging round out of sight, his revolver raised. A heartbeat later, his head reappeared back round the sponson and jerked them on.

There was a squeal from above. Startled, the soldiers glanced up, guns at the ready. Something small and furry fell out of the trees above, hitting branches as it fell, to crash limply into a small grove of black saplings at the edge of the clearing, where it lay still.

Distracted by the poor dead creature, fallen from some nest, it was a moment before Nellie recognised the saplings themselves. "Corpsewood! Be careful."

They knew the plant well enough, having used it to kill the Dulgur's young that ate Frank, their other gunner. It generally fed on dead animal matter, but would feed on the living where it could. They made sure to give it a wide berth.

Nellie heard a despairing groan from inside the tank. Up in the driver's cab, Wally had found Mathers' body slumped in the starboard gangway. The Lieutenant's revolver was still in his hand. There was a small entry wound in his right temple, but its exit had blown away half his skull. Blood, bone and brain matter splattered the white-painted interior and blood had pooled below him and dried on the wooden planking.

The Lieutenant's death shocked the crew; not so much the fact of it as the manner. They hadn't expected suicide.

They lifted Mather's body from the tank with as much dignity as they could, given the cramped space, strapping the Subaltern's turtle-shell helmet to his head to keep what was left of his skull intact. Suicide or not, he was their commander, and as such he deserved their respect. Not wanting to leave his body to predators and scavengers, they used the entrenching tools from the *Ivanhoe* to dig a shallow grave at the edge of the clearing.

Wally collected the Lieutenant's paybook, a couple of letters from his inside pocket and the metal identity disc from around his neck.

They laid the body in the grave and Norman said a simple, improvised prayer. They stood for a moment round the fresh grave, lost in their own thoughts. Then they buried him, enclosing him in the clays of a cold alien star. At the head of the mound of fresh dirt, they marked his resting place with hastily-cut boughs lashed into the form of a cross and hung Mathers' splash mask from it.

Despondent, the tankers mourned the loss of their commander, but Nellie could not mourn. All she could do was hope.

"Where's Alfie? Where is he?" she asked each of them in turn, trying to hide her rising panic. They shook their heads and would not meet her eyes. "He could be out there, injured," she insisted. She wanted it to be true, although she knew there were other, more likely possibilities on this world, possibilities about which she didn't want to think. "He could be out there. We have to find him, Napoo," she said, desperation seeping into her voice.

Napoo regarded her solemnly. "I cannot give you that hope. On this world, the likelihood of an injured man not falling prey to a predator is small." He bowed his head and turned from her.

Unwanted tears pooling in her eyes, Nellie watched horrified as pale tendrils unfurled from the stems of ebony corpsewood and felt their way towards the body of the small fallen animal before burrowing into its flesh, almost as if to illustrate Napoo's point.

It wasn't the only thing attracted by the small, broken carcass. From a puckered fruiting body, a fibrous white fungus spread slowly, weaving a cobweb of filaments across the soil as fine white mycelia quested through the humus towards it. The fungus wasn't fast enough. The corpsewood was already desiccating the carcass.

Nellie turned her head away, unable to watch.

Around the tank, the creaking continued, punctuated every now and again by sharp reports that they initially took for gunfire.

Moving so slowly she wouldn't have noticed had she not been still, it was possible to see the large pallid creepers that draped everything, gradually entwining themselves round the trees, seeking to choke and leach the life from them.

As she watched, it became clear to Nellie that there was a battle going on here, a battle she and the others were ill-equipped for. Two sets of competing flora were in a struggle for dominance: the forest and something else. Down here, the trees were engaged in a slow war and they seemed to be losing. Nellie felt uneasy being caught in the middle of it.

* * *

A SHOUT FROM Napoo roused her from her maudlin thoughts. He had found footprints.

They were human-like, but they weren't the distinctive hobnailed bootprint of the Tommy. These were smooth, less defined and deeper.

"Someone else has been here," he explained. "They arrived here. See? Lighter." He pointed out the shallow footprints across the clearing. "They left carrying something heavy."

Nellie stared at them. "Alfie?"

A continuous cracking sounded through the clearing. This wasn't the slow vegetable conflict she had begun to realise was all about them. This was something altogether faster and heavier. Something that was crashing through the undergrowth towards them, and gathering pace.

"Into the tank. Look lively!" cried Jack.

Without waiting to see what was coming, they scrambled through the sponson hatches, Nellie and Napoo with them, the urman more than a little unwillingly. Once inside, they slammed the hatches shut and sat panting in the dark.

The crashing stopped. There followed loud low snorts and several heavy thudding footfalls. A low wet sniffing proceeded around them. The tank juddered as something large butted it.

The tank's crew glanced at each other in the semi-dark, came to a silent consensus, then loaded the guns and machine guns and flung themselves to the pistol ports, peering out, looking for their assailant.

"We can't drive this, there aren't enough of us," said Wally, scrambling into the driver's seat, trying to ignore the dried viscera that once belonged in Mathers' head.

"Yes, there are," said Nellie.

"But you're a woman," said Norman.

Nellie raised her eyebrows. "Yes. And this is the starboard track gear. This is the first speed. This is neutral," she said, showing him the gear levers.

Across the starting handle, Reggie grinned.

"Do you want me to tell you how the differential works?" she asked defiantly.

"I can see why Alfie likes you," said Reggie.

"All right!" said Wally. "Start the engine. Norman, get up here. I need you to operate the driving brakes."

It took four of them to turn the giant starting handle between the Daimler engine in the middle of the cramped compartment and the differential in the rear. The engine coughed unwillingly once or twice until it caught and roared into life, and the electric festoon lights flickered on.

Nellie couldn't stop the broad grin from spreading across her face as she took hold of the gear lever and waited for Wally's command. The thrill was muted when she saw the love heart hastily drawn in the grime of the engine casing. The heart she had once drawn for Alfie. She tried to ignore the dried blood at her feet. Was it Mathers' or Alfie's?

Napoo sat by her feet, hunched by the sponson door, his hands over his ears. She wanted to comfort him the way he had her, but she had a job to do.

She heard the two bangs from the wrench Wally wielded to communicate above the engine's roar and put the lever into neutral. The tank began to turn clockwise, presenting a broadside to the creature.

Cecil struggled to bring the six-pounder on the port side to bear on the thing as it paced round the tank. He squeezed the trigger. The loud report filled the compartment, contained and echoing off the metal walls.

Nellie gasped at the noise, loud even over the roar of the engine directly in front of her. It was beginning to get hot in there. She could feel the perspiration prickling her hairline. And that smell. Was that the petrol fruit fumes? She wondered what effect it would have on her.

The tank rocked again under the beast's charge.

To Nellie's left, Cecil let loose a burst of machine gun fire, the cartridge shells clattering to the floor and rolling out through a slot in the gangway.

The engine spluttered.

Jack leapt forwards and began working the manual pump for the starboard petrol tank by the commander's seat. Reggie did the same on the other side. The engine coughed a couple of times and died for good.

"We're out of fuel," he said in disbelief, his voice loud in the sudden silence.

Outside, they heard a thrashing in the undergrowth and a howl of frustration and pain that receded into the distance.

"It's gone," said Wally.

Nellie breathed a sigh of relief, her ears ringing. "Is this – is this what it's like all the time?" she asked Reggie, not sure whether she was drunk on the exhilaration of battle or the fumes.

"Mostly?" asked Reggie.

"Mm-hmm."

Reggie shook his head. "It's worse."

They clambered out of the dead tank. The ground was churned where the ironclad had turned. Black ichor dripped down the side of the sponson. It looked like Cecil had hit the creature. Jack grinned and rubbed his finger knuckles across Cecil's head as the lad beamed with pride.

They had used the last of *Ivanhoe's* fuel to fend off the attack. It had survived the fall into the crater, but without fuel the *Ivanhoe* was twenty-eight tons of scrap.

"So what do we do now?" asked Reggie.

"We find Alfie," said Nellie decisively. She looked around at the crew, an iron determination in her gaze, almost daring them to challenge her. None did. Even Norman, if he had anything to say, kept it to himself.

Taking what supplies they thought useful from the tank, they took a last look at the *Ivanhoe* and set off into the crater to find Alfie.

* * *

In the shade of the abandoned ironclad, the pale feeding tendrils of the ebony corpsewood saplings inched towards Mathers' freshly dug grave.

The fungus, too, stretched out a fine filigree of threads towards it and this time reached the prize first, its mycelia spreading out over the mound, like a hoarfrost blanket, as they began probing down through the newly turned soil for the freshly buried remains...

CHAPTER FIVE

"One Grim Shadow..."

"It wants what?" said Everson in disbelief as he looked up from the daily reports.

Sergeant Hobson stood before the desk and winced in apology. "Petrol fruit fuel, sir. The chatt asked for it quite specific, it did, sir."

"Did it now?" Everson sighed heavily and strode impatiently along the familiar trench route to the chatt's dugout cell. He was trying to impose his authority after the mutiny and he resented the fact that he was here on terms other than his own. He saluted the guards, descended the dugout steps and peered into the makeshift cell. Chandar stood in the middle, facing the door, as if it expected him.

"Petrol fruit?" demanded Everson.

"This One had been thinking," said Chandar.

"Evidently." Everson slid the bolt on the door and dragged it open. "So enlighten me."

"The urman called Mathers, he ingested the liquid. He was able to see what no urman ever could. He was able to read the odorglyphics, divine the sacred scents. He sensed the prophecy of the last of the Nazarrii."

"So I believe."

"You said this One had to choose which scent to take. It is this One's belief that this liquid could help restore this One's ability to read the scents. This One could divine which would be most useful to this One's interpretation, one that will be of benefit to us both mutually, Khungarrii and Tohmii alike."

Everson considered the proposal before shaking his head. It was a big risk. "I don't know. It's made our men mad, killed others. We have no idea what effect it would have on... one of your kind."

Chandar hissed. It stepped forward, arms out, its two long fingers on each hand flexing, pleading. It swallowed a great gulp of air and regurgitated it into words: "For too long the Odours of GarSuleth have been denied this One. This One will take the chance. Would you not do as much for your clan, for the Tohmii?"

Everson pursed his lips. He had to admit it could be a solution to their stalemate, and he couldn't see any other way forward. He just wasn't very happy about it. "Very well," he said. "But only under medical supervision. I don't want anything happening to you."

As THE CHATT watched from across the cell, Captain Lippett poured a measure of petrol fruit fuel into a small canteen sat on a small Tommy cooker, under which he had set a short candle stub.

"I'm not going to let you drink it," he told the thing. "This stuff has killed people. If you must persist in this madness, then breathe slowly and deeply as it vaporises."

He turned to Everson. "I don't know what help I can be if anything happens. Dissecting them is one thing, keeping them alive is another."

"Well, I hope it won't come to that, Doctor."

Atkins arrived with a selection of stone amphorae and clay vials rescued from the ruined edifice.

Chandar studied the sealed containers. "This one. This. That one."

Having made its choice, Atkins placed the selected jars on the floor.

"I want everybody out before I light this," said Lippett by the Tommy cooker.

Everson and Atkins withdrew from the cell.

Nurse Bell stood by with a tray of medical supplies Lippett thought they might need if the worse came to the worst. Her lips curled in disgust. "What's it doing?" she asked.

Atkins shrugged. "It seems to think that the petrol fruit fuel will restore its ability to smell."

Edith's eyes narrowed. "Is that possible?"

"With them? Hard to say. Damn near killed me, though; drove Mathers mad and made his crew paranoid."

Despite her revulsion, she forced herself to watch, lost in thought, as Lippett lit the candle with a Lucifer and stepped sharply from the cell.

Everson pushed the door shut. He watched through the judas hole for a moment as Chandar arranged the jars in front of him. The small candle flame guttered under the bowl of liquid, casting high shadows and imparting an almost demonic quality to the chatt.

Chandar began fingering the knotted tassels on its silk wrap as if it had never seen them before. It lifted another tassel, looking at it. Then another.

It breathed deeply of the vapours rising from the bowl and reached out for one of the amphorae. With its two fingers and thumb, it drew the stopper from the jar and swilled the contents. It tilted its head back, its gaze following the imperceptible whorls and eddies of the rising vapours, as if watching the emergence of an invisible genie from the bottle. Occasionally it swirled the contents of the bottle to refresh its perception. It stoppered that bottle and repeated the same performance with the other two.

Slowly, it rose up to its full height, its mandibles clicking as its mouth parts smacked rapidly in its own speech. It seemed excited. It turned to face Everson, almost belching out the words "It is GarSuleth's Will," before staggering sideways and collapsing against the wall.

Everson yanked the cell door open and Lippett was first in. He blew out the candle and handed the bowl to Atkins. "Dispose of this," he said, "out in the open."

Nurse Bell hung back, unable to bring herself to enter.

"Nurse, we have a patient," Lippett chided.

Hesitantly, she entered the dugout cell. Everson pushed in past her.

Chandar stretched out an arm towards Everson. "This One has been blessed. GarSuleth speaks to it once more." In its excitement, its speech dissolved into the harsh smacking and clickings of its native language.

"It was a success, then?" Everson said.

Chandar cast its arms open, its vestigial limbs following suit. "It was... different, strange. This One saw nuances and connections it had never noticed before. It will take practise, but in time this One could once more sense the text as this One has always done. Perhaps better." It picked up a jar. "This," it said. "This One will take this scent back to Khungarr. It contains the Commentaries of Chitaragar. Khungarr has not possessed this essence for generations. The original has long since evaporated. Only fleeting notes of it exist in other distillations."

It reached out to Everson, grasping his sleeves with its long fingers. Everson fought against the reflex to pull away.

"This One shall return to Khungarr," it said. "It is GarSuleth's Will."

The Chatt had put the ball back in his court. He couldn't allow the threat of the Khungarrii to loom over them for much longer.

Everson knew he had to keep his word and let the chatt go, but he didn't trust it, not completely.

"Then I want someone to go with you to make sure you stick to your side of the bargain," he said.

"Very well," it said.

Now all Everson had to do was find a volunteer.

* * *

PADRE RAND HAD already forgiven the man who hit him. However, since the assault, the visions he suffered had begun to plague him with greater frequency, fraying the edges of his faith. They were shades of the vision he had experienced in Khungarr, when along with Jeffries, the chatts forced him to undergo a cleansing ritual. Since then they haunted him, just beyond the edges of his perception. He would wake up in a cold sweat, the visions receding faster than he could recall them, leaving only the memory of terror.

A pulse of pain built and flared, hot and sharp in his skull. He touched his bandaged head as his vision darkened and the world tilted. He reached out to balance himself against the wall of the trench; in the momentary blackness that swallowed him, he felt something waiting for him, in the heart of the pain. Then, just as suddenly as it had appeared, the pain faded and his sight returned to normal.

He looked around as he recovered his composure, to see if anyone had noticed, but there was no one else in that stretch of trench. He was distressed to find the vision plaguing him even during his waking hours. Was there to be no relief from it?

He prayed to the light for guidance, but he knew what he had to face was hidden in the dark.

"I BELIEVE YOU need someone to accompany the chatt to Khungarr," the Padre told Everson.

"How did you know about that?" Everson asked.

The Padre was in an aid post, sat on a barrel, having his wound redressed by Nurse Bell. The bruising on his still swollen temple was now turning a dull green. It throbbed.

"Secrets of the confessional," said the Padre, glancing absently at Nurse Bell. "Never mind how I know, John. Is it true?"

"Yes. If there is a possibility of some armistice with these creatures, then it's a chance I have to take. I need someone who can be diplomatic, who can advocate for us. I can't pretend it won't be risky. I can't assure the safety of anyone who goes."

From the moment he heard of Everson's dilemma, the Padre knew with certainty what he had to do. He had been looking for a sign. Surely, this was Divine Providence at work. A return to Khungarr. There, where it all began, he might uncover what dark revelations his vision harboured. He drew himself up, grimacing as his head pounded.

"Then I will go," he said. "As commanding officer you can't go yourself; you can't send a soldier, you can't spare the officers. I'm the logical choice. They might hold you responsible for the damage caused to their edifice, but a priest? I might be more acceptable as an observer."

"I'll go with him," said Edith, taking a step forward before she knew she was saying it.

The men stared at her.

"What, might I not know my own mind?" she countered. "I'm concerned about the Padre's injury. He's not yet fully recovered. At least if I am with him, I can take care of it."

"It's not necessary, Nurse," the Padre protested.

"Nurse Bell–" Everson began.

"What?" Nurse Bell glowered. "You let Nellie go off to find the *Ivanhoe*. I've faced many fears since we arrived here, Lieutenant," she said, "and become the stronger for it. And both the Padre and I have been to Khungarr before."

"As prisoners," Everson reminded her gently.

"Then let me go back of my own free will, face my fears, and do my job!"

Everson raised his eyebrows in appeal to the Padre for support, but the chaplain seemed just as taken aback by the strength of the young woman's conviction.

Everson sighed with exasperation. "Nurse Bell, if you're convinced the Padre needs medical supervision, then yes, I agree."

"I beg your pardon," said the Padre.

"You're letting me go?" she asked with disbelief.

"Yes, although any more outbursts like that and I might change my mind."

Nurse Bell's face flushed.

Everson clasped the Padre's hands. "There's not a lot I trust on this world, but I trust you, Padre. I need you fit and well."

The Padre smiled faintly. "I tend to put my trust in the Lord, John, but I'm sure He won't take it personally."

EVERSON COULDN'T SPARE the men to escort them across the veldt, but then he didn't need to. They had the captured battlepillars. It would be much quicker and safer to cross the veldt on one of those.

In the aid tent, Edith hid the small jar containing the Commentaries of Chitaragar in her haversack of medical supplies. They hoped that the scents and aromas of the various medicines and unguents would disguise any tell-tale signs of the potential heresy they were effectively smuggling into Khungarr. Everson also provided her with a bottle of distilled petrol fruit fuel, for Chandar's personal use.

Atkins and his section escorted the chatt to the old Poulet farmhouse where the battlepillar was waiting, a sapper sat in the howdah at the great beast's head.

Everson shook the Padre's hand. "Good luck, Padre. And thank you."

The Padre nodded towards the camp. "Don't forget, John: they're not soldiers, they're men."

Everson nodded, then turned to Nurse Bell. "Look after him. And yourself. I don't want another Edith Cavell on my hands."

"I will, Lieutenant. Thank you," she said.

The Padre and Nurse Bell climbed a ladder to a large cradle slung along the side of the beast.

"I don't want them to come to any harm," Everson warned Chandar as the chatt clambered aboard the cradle.

"They will be safe under this One's protection."

EVERSON STOOD ON the OP platform of the Poulet Farmhouse and watched the small party as even the huge battlepillar was gradually swallowed by the immensity of the veldt before them.

Hobson appeared beside him and watched in silence for a moment.

"Do you trust 'em, sir? The chatts, I mean."

"Chandar? Maybe. The rest? Not as far as I can throw them, sergeant," Everson said.

"Glad to hear it, sir," said Hobson, walking along behind him as they strode down the communication trench and up the crude earthen steps onto the ground towards the hospital tents.

"This is why I want insurance."

Everson entered the Aid tent, and Stanton the medical orderly stood to attention. He returned the salute crisply and got down to business. "I'm given to understand you used to work in a cotton mill in the chemical labs before the war, Stanton."

"Sir."

"Then I have a job for you. I need your expertise, not as a medical orderly but as a chemist."

"Sir?"

"You remember the Khungarrii attack on the trenches?"

"Of course, sir."

"The poppies out beyond the front line disorientated the chatts somehow, threw them into confusion. Maybe it was something in their scent."

"Excuse me, sir, but poppies don't smell."

"Maybe not to us, Stanton. But one cannot doubt their effect on the chatts. We all saw it and were able to take advantage of it. Maybe there is something in the poppies against which they have no natural defence, because it's alien to this world. There has to be a way we can harness that effect deliberately; enhance it, strengthen it, turn it into something we can use against them."

"Like a gas, sir?"

Everson nodded his head with approval. "Yes. Something that we can use to de-louse on a large scale. Do you want to have a crack at it?"

Stanton's eyes widened and he stood straighter, taller. He pushed out his chest. "Me, sir? Just give me a chance, sir."

"Then you've got it, Stanton," said Everson, handing him a scrap of paper. "The men on this list have chemical or horticultural experience that might help. See what you can come up with."

Stanton took the paper and saluted. "Yes, sir."

"The Padre was right," Everson confided in Hobson as they left the tent. "I'd forgotten that they were men before the war. Appealing to their sense of duty wasn't enough. I have to appeal to the man."

"Very wise, sir," said Hobson.

Several electric blue flashes crackled and bloomed briefly above the trenches within the support ring, accompanied by too brief a scream.

"What the hell?"

Everson had seen the phenomenon before in the presence of Khungarrii electric lances. Was it a raiding party? And if it was, how the hell did they get past the sentries? Shouts of alarm went up from various quarters. Everson drew his Webley and weaved his way through the trenches towards the disturbance.

Everson and Hobson met near the fire bay with several other soldiers also converging on the scene.

Hobson nodded at them.

"Trench clearance formation," he hissed.

After the mutiny, only those on sentry duty had magazines and loaded rifles. The others had to make do with their bayonets.

Hobson peered round the sandbag traverse. "Clear," he hissed back.

The clearance party slipped into the unoccupied fire bay as Everson moved to enter the next.

He peered cautiously round the separating traverse, his revolver cocked.

A soldier lay splayed on the floor of the bay, his body wracked in spasms. He kicked and thrashed spastically, his boots scraping against the duckboards. Wisps of smoke rose from the soles. A Corporal was knelt beside him, trying to place an old strip of leather belt between his teeth. "Bite down on this, now, Tonkers. Bite down, that's it."

There was no sign of any chatts, although shards of a chatt's clay backpack lay strewn about the bay and an electric lance lay against the firestep. Everson jerked his head and Hobson sent a couple of men peering over the revetments.

"All clear, Sarn't," they reported.

Everson stepped into the fire bay.

"What happened here?" asked Everson urgently.

He noticed the Signals brassard on his arm. The NCO looked up. It was Corporal Riley.

"Sorry, sir," said the NCO with a disarming shrug. "Didn't mean to alarm you. Just an accident, sir. Tonkins here'll be all right," he said. The signaller's fit seemed to be passing. The Corporal held him, all the while talking to him in a low voice. "You'll be all right, lad."

"Stretcher bearer!" Everson hollered.

"No, it's all right, sir. He'll be right as ninepence shortly. It's not the first time."

Everson looked at Hobson, who dismissed the soldiers back to their posts. He turned his attention to the fusilier on the ground. His tone softened a touch. "What do you mean, it's not the first time? What's wrong with him?"

"One moment, sir." The corporal called out. "Buckley!"

A soldier swept back the gas curtain, stepped smartly out and saluted the Lieutenant. The sandy-haired lad had shiny red cheeks that looked as if they'd been polished, like an apple. "Sorry, sir. Didn't see you there."

"It's all right, Buckley," said the Corporal. "Give me a hand with Tonkers here."

Buckley helped the Corporal get Tonkins to his feet and the pair half-dragged, half-carried the dead weight of the still twitching Fusilier into the dugout.

Corporal Riley reappeared, holding the gas curtain aside. "If you wouldn't mind, sir?"

Everson and Hobson entered the dugout. It was crammed with crates and boxes of stores. The place served as office, workshop and storeroom for the few signallers that had been stranded with them. The three men from Signals kept the telephone and heliograph communications working with the observation posts. Three more were up on the Hill OP.

Large reels of copper wire lay against the walls, like huge cotton bobbins. There were lengths of cable, batteries, boxes of signal flares and several heliograph machines on closed tripods. In the corner lay a collection of semaphore flags. On a bench, several wooden-boxed field telephones sat in various states of disassembly, and an assortment of salvaged Morse code keys lay amidst scattered screwdrivers, wire cutters, wire strippers and other tools. However, what caught Everson's eye was the untidy heap of the chatt clay backpacks and electric lances. Some were broken, some merely cracked, and quite a few were intact, although they were in marked contrast to the ones that stood neatly against the opposite dirt wall.

Tonkins lay on a rude bed in an adjoining room. He seemed more peaceful now. The spasms and twitches had stopped.

"Corporal Riley, just what the hell is going on? What just happened to Tonkins?"

Riley cleared his throat. "What do you know about telephony, sir?"

"That it's a damned nuisance when the wires get shelled or cut."

Riley's cheeks reddened. "Tell me about it, sir. We're the ones who have to go out and fix it. Only just finished repairing the lines after that damned mutiny. 'Scuse my French, sir."

"Riley," said Everson, beginning to lose patience. "What have telephones got to do with that chatt electric lance out there?"

"Well as far as we know, the electric lances are charged by the chatts themselves, kind of like an electric eel. They generate their own charge. The clay pack is kind of like a battery, storing and amplifying this charge, which they release through the lance."

"And the field telephones?"

Riley picked up a wooden box and sat it on the bench with a thump. "A field telephone, sir. Type C Mark II, using two cells, electric, dry, charged by a magneto via the crank handle.

"We managed to recover a lot of these here backpacks after the chatt siege, and Tonkins there said, 'well if all they need is a charge, why can't we just fit 'em with a magneto?' He's been tinkering all week, and we think we've got it licked."

"Licked?" Hobson nodded toward Tonkins. "You call that licked?"

"Oh, aye, we're learning all the time."

"And what exactly have you learnt this time?" asked Everson.

"This time?" Riley rubbed the back of his neck as he gave it some thought. "Not to connect a wire straight into the conductive slime, for one. And if you do, wear gum boots, feet, for the use of."

Riley picked up one of the smooth crimson clay backpacks. It had a number '5' scratched onto it. Everson glanced around. He couldn't see numbers one to four; although he had a suspicion that number four lay outside in pieces. The clay container was curved in the inner surface to sit flush with a scentirrii carapace, but Riley had rigged it with some 1908 Pattern leather webbing and empty sandbags for padding, for a more human fit. Near the top of the clay container, inserted in a carved round hole, was a crank handle Everson recognised as coming from a field telephone.

"Buckley, come here, I need you," said Riley.

Buckley shot a nervous glance at the prostrate Tonkins.

"Never mind him, lad. Probably picked up a cracked one. You'll be all right if you wear gum boots for the test."

"Will he?" asked Everson confidentially.

"Probably," said Riley with a shrug. "Anything has to be better than earthing through bleedin' Army-issue hobnailed boots."

"Hmm."

A sour-faced Buckley picked up a pair of trench waders and pulled them on before lifting up and shouldering the backpack. They had reconnected the electric lance to it with a length of rubber-insulated cable in a braided hessian sheath.

Riley picked it up and handed it to him, then bent forward, inspected the backpack and tugged on the webbing. "You'll do," he said finally, giving him a shove through the gas curtain.

"After you, sir," he said with a sweep of his arm. Everson ducked his head and stepped out into the trench. Buckley waited, holding the lance awkwardly. Hobson joined them and Riley brought up the rear smartly, stepping over to Buckley and standing behind him.

"If you wouldn't mind, gentlemen?" he said, indicating that the officer should take cover. Everson and Hobson stepped back by the sandbagged traverse.

"Well, on guard, lad, on guard!" said Riley, noting Buckley's less than enthusiastic posture.

Buckley took a step forward, taking a stance as if the lance were a rifle and bayonet. Riley tapped Buckley once on the shoulder and began to wind the magneto's crank handle that now protruded from the clay pack. A quiet whirr built as the spindle inside the magneto revolved faster and faster. For a moment, it seemed as if nothing would happen. A nervous Buckley fidgeted as he gripped the lance.

Everson and Hobson exchanged concerned glances.

Riley gritted his teeth and wound the handle furiously a while longer. Then he let go and tapped Buckley on the shoulder. Twice. This time, a brilliant blue-white arc of energy blasted out across the fire bay, exploding against the far sandbag traverse. The sandbags erupted. Scorched, shredded hessian and dirt showered down on them.

When the dust settled, Buckley was still standing and the chatt device was still in one piece.

Riley turned and grinned. "Well, that went better than expected, eh?"

WHEN THE BATTLEPILLAR reached the edge of the forest, the driver would go no further. The Padre, Nurse Bell and Chandar dismounted and, under the chatt's guidance, proceeded on foot. From here on in, they were on their own.

They walked for several hours through the forest until Chandar directed them to stop by a grove of trees. There they waited.

Several hours later, a patrol of chatt soldiers, scentirrii, led by none other than Rhengar, the Khungarrii general, appeared. Its antennae waved, sensing something.

Chandar stepped forward and greeted them, its arms open wide as it breathed its benediction over its fellow chatts.

"Where have you been?" wheezed Rhengar. "Was your undertaking a success? This One has waited here every spinning at the appointed time. This One had given up hopes of your return, Chandar."

"GarSuleth has willed it, Rhengar."

Rhengar and Chandar fell to speaking rapidly in their own language, with many glances toward the chaplain and the nurse. The Padre got the feeling that Rhengar didn't approve of their presence. Eventually the two chatts reached some agreement and the party headed on into the forest, the scentirrii, their antennae twitching, escorting Padre Rand and Nurse Bell along a path only they could detect.

In a way, Padre Rand felt that he too followed such an invisible path, guided by a Divine hand; from his comfortable parish of St Chad's in Broughtonthwaite, to the trenches of France, where he lost the trail, like a path petering out on featureless moors. It was only once he found himself here, on this world, that he found his path again. Here, where he thought himself lost from God's sight, that still, small voice could be heard if he but listened, for the men of the Pennines were themselves God's creations, even if nothing else in this world was. A spark of the Divine existed in each one of them, so even out here, in the shadow of death, there was a light to mark the way. He drew comfort and strength from that. Like Daniel in the lion's den, he felt a calmness, as though he was at the centre of a storm. He walked erect and with a feeling of peace he hadn't known for a long time. But he knew this was only a moment of clarity, for even Our Lord had His Gethsemane.

Nurse Bell walked close beside him, but whether out of fear or concern he couldn't say. Maybe both. It wasn't surprising. He had surprised himself by volunteering for this, just as she had surprised him by offering to accompany him. Her Christian charity touched and partly shamed him. In coming here, he had an ulterior motive. Bell could have none, other than his welfare at heart. He did wonder briefly whether that made her the better person.

Nevertheless, he offered up a silent prayer of thanks for her presence. At least now, he would be forced to go through with his plan. Alone, he might not have had the strength. His resolve might have failed as it had before. His faith was gaining the fervour he once held, but it still felt fragile.

"You are one of the Tohmii's dhuyumirrii?" wheezed Rhengar, waving its mouth palps behind its mandibles.

"A priest, yes," said the Padre.

"You do not worship GarSuleth." There was no intonation in its voice. There never was with chatts. It took them enough effort to form the words in the first place. He wasn't even sure if they had emotions as he experienced them.

"No. I do not."

Rhengar fell silent, clicking its mandibles together in a thoughtful manner as it walked.

The Padre wondered whether he had gone too far, spoken out of turn and offended them.

Chandar caught up with them and limped alongside. "They are scentirrii," it explained. "They are not bred to question."

"Stop," said Rhengar, coming to a sudden halt.

The group of scentirrii stopped with him. Rhengar turned towards the Padre and Nurse Bell. "You go no further," it told them.

Nurse Bell stepped forward, affronted. "But you said–"

"You will be killed." It signalled to the scentirrii guards. They turned and advanced towards them.

The Padre wheeled on Chandar in disbelief. "You told the Lieutenant that we would be safe."

There was no time for the crippled chatt to reply. The scentirrii closed in about them. The Padre gathered Nurse Bell to him, putting his arms around her. She looked up into his eyes, and then turned to face the chatts with defiance as the Padre rattled out a hasty orison under his breath.

The gathered scentirrii opened their mandibles and hissed as one...

INTERLUDE 2

Letter from Lance Corporal Thomas Atkins to Flora Mullins

1st April 1917

My Dearest Flora,

Off to get the Boojum back tomorrow. Don't worry, I know where we left it. Not only that, we get a ride there, too. Should be a cushy number, which would be a first for this place. Just a case of 'there and back to see how far it is,' as Dad says. Porgy's happy and you know how workshy he is, so that bodes well. Pot Shot says it's going to be like riding elephants from the Raj. Not sure what I think about that. I know Mam will worry about me getting airs and graces what with riding round like a maharajah, though. Perhaps I should get Pot Shot to send her one of his pamphlets about how all workers deserved to be treated like that! Not that I'm complaining. I may even get used to it. Gutsy's not happy though. He's never been a good traveller, unless it's by Shanks's pony.

The Padre is going to visit the locals, with whom we've been having a little difficulty. You could say it's raised a bit of a stink. I thought the French could be a bit off, but this lot take the biscuit. Still, with a little bit of luck it might all be sorted out by the time we get back, and we'll all come up smelling of roses.

Ever yours
Thomas.

CHAPTER SIX

"I Knew That Sullen Hall..."

EVERSON CALLED THE officers together for a briefing in the Command Post. They had to be ready for whatever might happen next and he was trying to prepare them as best as possible. Unfortunately, most of them were like Palmer, good solid officers who could take orders, but not the initiative. Tulliver, on the other hand, he felt had too much initiative.

"So you've let the chatt go?" said Palmer.

Everson shook his head. "Not exactly. We've come to an agreement. Right now, we have something they want. We're holding the sacred scent texts we found to ransom until we get the deal we need."

"Which is?"

"Basically? They leave us alone, we leave them alone. If Chandar can convince its colony that we are not this Great Corruption their high priest speaks of, then there's a good chance that can happen. From there, we'll have to have further negotiations."

"But to send the chaplain and a nurse back with it!"

"Chandar wanted someone to speak our case to the Khungarrii council, the Shura. Padre Rand volunteered. He felt they might listen more to a priest than a soldier. I think he may be right."

"And the nurse? Good God, man."

"The Padre sustained a head injury during the mutiny. Nurse Bell feels he may still need medical care."

"I can confirm that," said Lippett. "It does mean that I'm short of two nurses thanks to your plans, Everson. Damn fine nurses, too."

"I thought you didn't approve of women on the front line, Doc."

Lippett shifted in his chair. "I didn't, but since those three arrived, they've done their damnedest to make themselves indispensable, blast them. You make sure that Abbott and Bell get back, John, or it won't be me you have to answer to, it'll be Sister Fenton; and I, for one, wouldn't want to be in your shoes then."

"Point taken."

Seward still wasn't convinced. "If this gambit of yours fails, Everson, the Padre and the nurse will be killed," he protested.

"And many of us shortly after," said Everson. "They knew the risks, Seward, and if the Padre can tip the scale with a few impassioned words rather than bullets, then that suits me."

"And if he doesn't, the chatts will come for us again?" asked Haslam.

"Without doubt," Everson told them candidly. "But we'll be ready for them. We already have battlepillars. We have several platoons of urmen that Sergeant Dixon has trained. In addition, Corporal Riley in Signals has had a breakthrough with the electric lances. We are adapting, gentlemen."

"And what about the gunpowder experiment?" asked Seward.

The huge tarpaulin-covered heaps of manure were a source of contention for the sanitation parties.

There, Everson had to admit defeat. "The dung and the charcoal are no problem and, with the men, there is no shortage of urine for saltpetre, but we're still looking for a source of sulphur. We've had a production line of jam tin grenades being made and when we run out of Ticklers' tins, Houlton of 'A' Company has found a substitute casing in some sort of fruit gourd."

"Hand 'gourd'-nades, eh?" said Palmer with a chuckle.

Everson's shoulders dropped with relief as a ripple of light laughter washed round the dugout. He knew these officers well. Once they'd found the humour in a subject, it spoke of a certain acceptance. He had won them round. All he had to do now was to rescue the tank, to bring their defences up to full strength.

"Palmer, I'll leave you in charge of defences. Keep a tight rein on the NCOs. I don't want them using my absence for personal reprisals. The ringleaders, and those caught for offences, have been punished. That's an end to it. And for God's sake, see what you can do with that Kreothe carcass up the valley. It's beginning to rot and the stench is frankly appalling. It'll bring every scavenger for miles down here."

"Actually, they don't seem to care for it," said Palmer. "It seems to be doing a damn fine job of keeping them away."

Lippett coughed. "Actually, I wouldn't mind studying this aerozoan Kreothe before you do anything. Portions of its body seem to be decaying into some sort of gelatinous matter. Some of the men are calling it 'star jelly.' They've reported a sulphurous smell associated with its decomposition and, if that's the case, it might solve our gunpowder problem."

"Are you sure?" asked Everson, intrigued.

Lippett shrugged. "No, but it bears further investigation, don't you think?"

"Very well, I'll leave that in your capable hands. Communications. Tulliver, you're going to have to be our line of communication to camp. You'll be our lifeline and our eyes, so yes, you'll get to fly."

Tulliver needed to hear no more. He rocked his chair onto its back legs and beamed at the rest of them, like a man who had just got a two-week pass.

"I'll be leading the salvage party out to the Croatoan Crater to recover the tank. On the way I'll leave a party to take a look at this mysterious 'wall' that Atkins found. I must admit, I'm eager to see it myself."

"Maybe take some men from Signals, see if they can pick up anything with their Iddy Umpty gear, hear anything inside," suggested Baxter.

"My thoughts exactly," said Everson. "We'll also take a couple of Riley's jerry-rigged electric lances, too. Give them a proper field trial." Everson looked round the room. "That's all, gentlemen. You have your orders." He gathered up his papers to indicate that the meeting was over. "Dismissed," he added lightly.

As they left, Everson fingered the khaki scrap and button in his pocket. The metal wall and the tank were certainly priorities, but he had one more objective for this trip, and that was to find Jeffries' trail.

TULLIVER STRODE ACROSS the parade ground from the briefing with a spring in his step and a grin smeared across his face. He was walking on air. He felt he barely needed his bus to fly, but fly it he would.

He felt no need to stick to the trenches, even though they felt familiar and comforting to most of the men. Those of a nervous disposition didn't have to face the alien landscape about them, and it helped hold their nerve. It felt like home.

Not to Tulliver, though. Up there, that was his home and that was where he was going. That new predator up there would have to watch out; next time, he'd be ready for it.

AT DAWN THE next day, the tank salvage party – a platoon of Fusiliers and a platoon of Karno's army, drilled and trained urmen outfitted in an odd combination of part-worns, carapace chest plates and steel helmets – fell in around the two captured battlepillars that Everson hoped would be able to haul the tank to safety.

The Fusiliers had outfitted the captured Khungarrii larval beasts of burden for their own use. Several people-carrying panniers had been slung along the sides of the beasts, chatt-style. Unlike the chatts, the Fusiliers had modified them to ride at varying heights, allowing for a wider field of fire by the pannier occupants, fore and aft, without their neighbours obstructing their view or aim. They had also constructed a less ornate, more functional howdah for the 'drivers.' One had been a drayman before the war, so it stood to reason in the minds of most that his be the unenviable task of controlling the brutes.

The private saluted as Everson passed. "Woolridge, isn't it?" asked Everson.

"Yes, sir."

Everson's face softened. "Your father was an Everson's drayman, wasn't he?"

"That were my uncle, sir."

"Ah. Right."

Everson looked up at one of the beasts. "What do you think to them?"

"Big Bertha and Big Willie, sir? They seem docile enough, sir. They're easy to command now we've got the reins figured out."

"I certainly hope so." Everson nodded his approval. "Carry on, private."

It was more than a mere battlepillar omnibus, however. Lieutenant Baxter and his Machine Gun Section had mounted a Lewis machine gun tripod to a small chariot-like basket just forward of the driver's howdah. They had also turned the section of the fuselage salvaged from a downed 1½ Strutter from Tulliver's squadron, with the observer's seat and the Scarff-ring-mounted Lewis machine gun, into a tail-end machine gun emplacement down the creature's armoured back.

Everson saw Hepton, pushing through the milling soldiers assigned to the salvage operation as they checked their gear and bartered for final supplies from mates, but ignored him. Everson couldn't bring himself to like the man. He had been foisted on them to record the battle for Harcourt Wood for the folks back in Blighty. He was only supposed to be with them for a day or two. In the end, he had got rather more than he bargained for, and so had Everson. Hepton had been a constant irritant ever since. He turned his attention to the supply manifest that Sergeant Hobson had handed him.

Hepton spotted him. "Lieutenant, you weren't thinking of going without me, were you?"

Everson looked up from his clipboard. "As a matter of fact, yes, I was."

Hepton pulled a face of mock hurt and put a hand to his heart. "You wound me, Lieutenant. It's my job. I'm authorised by the War Office to make you look good for the folks back home. You want to look good, don't you? All I'm looking for is a little excitement, a little action."

"Exactly the things I was hoping to avoid," said Everson.

Hepton smiled his greasy smile and shrugged. "In that case, I'll settle for a spectacular otherworldly landscape. Can't say fairer than that, eh?" he said with a wink, rubbing his hands together.

Hobson tapped Everson on the arm and drew him aside. Hepton, hands behind his back, proceeded to rock back and forth on his heels, pretending to inspect the battlepillar in whose shadow they were standing.

"It might be better to keep him where we can see him, sir," said Hobson in a low voice. "He's a troublemaker, by all accounts. If we leave him here – well, the devil makes work, sir," he said in a low voice.

"Is that your considered opinion, Sergeant?"

"It is, sir. The chap's a malcontent, a real four-letter man, sir."

Everson *hmphed* his agreement.

"Hepton?"

The kinematographer turned at the sound of his name.

"Very well. We move out in ten minutes. You have five to get your equipment together."

A straight razor grin sliced open Hepton's face. "You won't regret it, Lieutenant, you won't regret it." He turned and began to wade back through the crowd, waving and calling over the men as he went, "Jenkins, Jenkins, bring my things. Over here, man. Hurry."

Everson blinked. "Did you give him permission to use one of my privates as a batman?" he asked Hobson.

Affronted by the question, the NCO frowned. "Certainly not, sir."

"Damn the man."

THE NCOS BARKED their orders and the men began to embark the battlepillars. They climbed the ladders, one section to a pannier. Six panniers each side, the rear two panniers filled with supplies and equipment. They also carried drums of spare petrol fruit fuel for the tank strapped to the back of Big Willie, and two of the experimental magneto-powered electric lance backpacks and various sets of telephonic equipment.

"Careful, don't drop anything, lad," cautioned Corporal Riley as Buckley hauled the gear up into the pannier with Tonkins' help.

The battlepillars moved out up the hillside towards the head of the valley. The Khungarrii reprisals against the Pennines had also displaced clans of nomadic urmen in the process, some of whom sought the shelter and protection of the British Tommies. NCOs had drilled and trained their men into platoons to replace those of the 13th Pennines who were wounded, missing or dead. The training had worked, mostly. Many of them stood their ground when the Khungarrii laid siege to the trenches, and the jeering from the Fusiliers that assaulted them during their training had turned to respect in most cases. However, many would not board the battlepillars, preferring to run alongside or scout ahead. Everson watched them with an odd feeling of nostalgia. Seeing the urmen in their mixture of native and British equipment brought a Colonial air to the whole endeavour.

1 Section was in the first of Big Bertha's starboard panniers. Gutsy was leant over the side of the basket. The undulating movement of the battlepillar didn't agree with him.

"He was like this on the boat over from Blighty," said Porgy cheerfully. "As green as the meat he sells."

Gutsy straightened up and whirled round with a raised finger to contest the slur, but he clamped his lips tight as his cheeks bellowed out. He leant over the side of the pannier and threw up again.

"And that," said Porgy to the section replacements who had edged to the far end of the pannier, "is why he's called Gutsy."

The canyon was less than a day's travel by battlepillar. It was a lot quicker than walking and, by comparison, quicker than the tank or a Hom Forty. The battlepillars' size also deterred the more opportunistic scavengers and predators, and they reached the canyon by late afternoon without incident, much to Hepton's disgust.

As eager as he was to see the mysterious wall, Everson erred on the side of caution. The canyon was a good place for an ambush.

"We'll make camp here for the night," he ordered. "We'll go down into the canyon in full light."

Knotted ropes were thrown over the sides of the panniers and the men shimmied down, thankful for the solid ground – Gutsy most of all, although it took him a few minutes to find his land legs, much to the amusement of the others.

NCOs began barking orders and the men fell to their appointed tasks. Woolridge saw to the battlepillars. They seemed content to spend the night tethered side by side, nose to tail, like horses. Two sections established a secure perimeter and others unloaded supplies while the men set up their bivouacs.

Gazette set about starting a cooking fire for their section. Porgy, however, slunk off before someone volunteered him to collect firewood.

Half an hour later, he crept back to the fire, a grin on his face and patting a couple of webbing pouches.

"I'd stay clear of 4 Section, if I were you," he said slumping down on his bedroll. "They're in a bad mood. And it'll be even worse tomorrow morning."

"Oh, bloody hell, Porgy. What've you done now?" asked Pot Shot with a sigh.

"Just relieved them of their last gaspers in a game of 'Housey'," he said pulling a battered cigarette packet from his webbing. "Fag, anyone?"

THE NEXT MORNING, the battlepillars descended out of the early morning sunlight into the cold shadow of the canyon, past the still-inert deadly blister-like blue-green hemispherical growths scattered over the surface of the canyon walls.

Atkins and his men had found to their cost that these bloated alien lichen contained reservoirs of some acidic substance. They ate away at the rock itself, absorbing the minerals and leaving the shallow circular pockmarks that scarred the rock all around them.

The battlepillars moved down into the canyon as it twisted and jinked down through the rock strata. Round a bend and high up on the cliff face, at the top of the scree slope, Everson caught his first sight of the mysterious metal wall.

The wall was embedded in the rock, as though the rock face had crumbled away to expose it. A glimmer of dawn light caught the face of the brushed silver metal, suffusing it with a warm crimson glow.

The working party began to disembark with their equipment. By the time they returned this way, he hoped the working party might have some answers, but Everson couldn't resist seeing the thing for himself. He summoned

Atkins to accompany him up the scree slope, eager to inspect this mysterious wall up close.

Everson laid a hand on the sheer metal with a sense of wonder. It was flat, smooth, and warm to the touch, despite the chill of the morning air. "Intriguing," he said as he considered the conundrum in front of them. It seemed so much at odds with what they had experienced of this world so far. When they first arrived, there had initially been hopes of civilisations with gleaming citadels. Their first encounter with the chatts and their earthen edifices disabused them of that romantic notion. This, however; this was different. "You're right. This isn't natural," he said as Atkins scrambled up the last few feet of scree to meet him. "So the questions are; what is it, who built it and why?"

"I don't know, sir. We came across it tracking the tank. We couldn't dent it, or scratch it, not even with a grenade, and as you can see, no markings, no doors, no windows, no features of any kind. Nothing. It might as well be solid for all the good it did us."

Everson took off his cap, smoothed his hair back and, slipping the cap under his arm, pressed a cautious ear to the metal.

"And no sound from within?"

"None we could hear, sir."

He stood back and replaced his cap. "I'm hoping the Signals chaps can pick up something we can't," he said, considering the wall.

He was silent for a moment, then let out a sigh. "But right now we have more important objectives to achieve."

"The *Ivanhoe*, sir?"

"Yes, I want to get it back to the camp as soon as possible. If Chandar's scheme fails, we're going to need it." He paused, considering the wall a moment longer, then clapped his hands. "Right," he said and began to pick his way down the scree slope, sending rocks skittering down as he picked up speed and momentum.

Atkins followed unsteadily, and more carefully, so as not to dislodge rocks onto his superior.

"Sergeant Dixon, you and your work party see if you can't clear some of this scree by the time we get back, so we can get a proper look at this thing."

"Right you are, sir."

"Riley!" Everson called as he reached the bottom. The Signals Corporal turned from overseeing the unloading of gear from one of the panniers on Big Willie.

"Sir?"

"See what your man makes of that by the time we get back," invited Everson, gesturing towards the wall.

Riley turned to Buckley and put his arm around his shoulders. "Buckley, I'm leaving you here with this sorry bunch of reprobates and a Moritz station. See what you can pick up. And don't get into trouble while I'm gone."

"No, Corp."

"Good lad."

Everson wasn't unduly concerned about leaving the two sections of working party at the canyon. They had urmen Karnos to guard them, and Tulliver would be flying over three times a day. The party could signal the aeroplane if there were any problems or important developments.

With a last look at the wall, Everson ordered the battlepillars to move out, and they set off for the Croatoan Crater.

Alfie awoke with a start to find himself lying in darkness. "Lieutenant?" he croaked. His lips were dry and cracked, his mouth parched.

He felt around with his hand and was startled to find warm, damp earth under his hand, not iron plate. He wasn't in the tank, then. He lay still for a moment, trying to collect his thoughts. All around him, with his petrol-fruit-muddled senses, he could *see* the faint ambient sounds of animals' noises bursting and fading like Very lights. He felt a vague craving for the fuel. He didn't usually feel that unless he'd been away from the tank for some time. How long had he been here? Where was he?

He could make out a soft, low horizontal glow of light, as if from under a door. He raised himself up on his elbows to get a better look. His head began to pound and his right leg jangled with pain. He let out an involuntary cry.

The hide draped across the doorway as protection against the elements swept open, and the shock of radiance caused Alfie to cry out again, throwing up an arm to block the light.

The silhouette of a man resolved itself against the flare. It spoke. It took a moment for Alfie to make out the words, as his fuel-addled brain interpreted them as the bittersweet flavour of marmalade and the childhood feeling of the tassel ties on his mother's front parlour curtains against his skin.

"...name is Ranaman, shaman of the Ruanach clan."

In the light, Alfie could see he was no longer wearing his coveralls. His right leg had been crudely splinted. Lengths of wood had been strapped against it, and they had unwound and used his puttee to bind it.

He tried to move, thinking about escape, but his leg was bound tight; and if that didn't stop him, the pain surely would.

The man, clearly an urman, knelt before Alfie and bowed until his forehead touched the earth. The youth who entered behind him did the same.

God, not again, thought Alfie. They revered him. The crew of the HMLS *Ivanhoe* had met such reactions before. Lieutenant Mathers had decided in the past to take advantage of it and of the urmen they met. It started out as a scam, growing into a mad scheme to build a colony of the British Empire here on this world. Urmen had bowed before them, thinking them gods, or the heralds of gods. Some, like the Khungarrii, thought the tank to be Skarra, the chatt god of the underworld. The crew didn't disabuse them of it; it had got them food and women. Alfie's opposition to this madness had almost cost him his friendships. He had never agreed with Mathers' scheme, but now it might save his life.

"Where am I?" he asked.

"Croatoan's Barrow," said Ranaman, hardly daring to look up. "After his battle with GarSuleth, defeated and cast down, here fell Croatoan. To be thus conquered broke his heart in twain, and he was dragged into the underworld to be punished by GarSuleth's brother, Skarra. And here the Ruanach stand vigil, as our ancestors did before us, keeping watch over his heart, awaiting his return and eventual triumph over GarSuleth."

The crater, thought Alfie. They must mean the crater.

"Where are my friends?" he asked in a deep imperious tone, one that he'd heard Norman adopt on occasions like these.

Ranaman cocked his head to one side and frowned. "Friends?"

"Others. Like me."

The youth shook his head, puzzled. "There were no others. There was only you. You were alone. You appeared before Tarak on his vision quest to become a man, a warrior."

The words spilled from the youth's mouth in a torrent of nervous energy...

Tarak was not yet a man but no longer a boy. He was in the process of becoming. Or dying. That was always a possibility. It was his time, and he had undergone the rite. He had ingested the venom of the hurreg and had then been ceremonially cast out of the enclave. Now he must circle the Barrow and seek out his vision. If he survived, he would return to the enclave a warrior.

His skin burned, his eyes itched from the poison, his palm felt slick around the handle of his knife and otherworldly visions came and went. He heard a tortured screech that made him wince, followed by a roar so terrible that it silenced the jungle. There followed an impact he felt through the soles of his feet.

Fearful, he headed towards the sound. He stumbled through the undergrowth until he saw it, resting where it had fallen, as Croatoan had once fallen from the sky.

He watched as if in a dream as an opening appeared in the sky rock and an urman like himself – no, not like himself – stepped out and fell to the ground. Tarak watched, trying to decipher the vision.

There was a deep growl and something dropped from a low bough and landed on all sixes, ready to leap on the sky-being.

Though the hurreg poison seared his joints, Tarak leapt on the creature's back with his knife firmly in his fist. He felt the warm pelt beneath his flesh, smelled the damp fur and thrust the blade in. The creature bucked and writhed, trying to throw him off, but he pressed his thighs against its flanks, tightened his hold on the shaggy fur with his other hand and drove the knife in again. And again. Its legs crumpled beneath it. Tarak pulled back on the horns, exposing its throat, and slipped his knife across it. The creature shuddered beneath him, blood pulsed out of the ragged slit. He held it until it had stopped, then let the head fall. Ordinarily he would have taken it back to the enclave as a gift from Croatoan and returned a hunter. But he had something more important to bear.

He looked at the sky-being.

He stood up and circled the great iron rock from which he'd appeared. Never had anyone in his clan had a sign like this, though many had sought it. This was his omen, given to him, but he had no idea what it meant. Ranaman would know.

He hoisted the sky-being over his shoulders and began his triumphal return to his enclave, not as a boy but as a man. As a warrior...

"TARAK IS TO be envied," announced Ranaman proudly as the young man finished his tale. "But his fortune is the clan's fortune. Your arrival when the Torment of Croatoan is nigh, when the earth erupts with his pain, is a great omen!"

"And if the boy's vision proves false?" Alfie's voice quavered, looking at Tarak.

"Then he will be cast out as punishment for bringing a Dulgur, an evil spirit, amongst us. He will die and his spirit will not join the ancestors in the Village of the Dead. His body will be left to ward off other Dulgur."

Tarak looked alarmed and glanced at Alfie for confirmation that he had done the right thing.

God damn it. He couldn't risk harm to the lad who'd saved him.

Very well, he would play his part. As much as it stuck in his craw, he would have to play the game for which he'd held Mathers in such contempt. He needed to buy time. He had to stay alive until the crew of the *Ivanhoe* could find him. He couldn't be sure that they would look, but he had faith in Nellie.

"The man Tarak has acted truly," intoned Alfie, cringing inside as he spoke.

Ranaman nodded in approval. He bowed before Alfie. "The one who was sent before has gone to prepare the way."

"The one who was sent before?" asked Alfie, confused.

"He, too was garbed as you are."

Alfie looked down at his khaki uniform. Another soldier? There was only one man he knew who had been as far as this. Jeffries. If the rumours were true, the man could beat Mathers at his own game.

"Where is he, this other one?"

Ranaman looked at him blankly, as if Alfie should have known. "He communed with the ancestors and joined them in the underworld."

Jeffries was dead?

"Soon you must do the same to make possible Croatoan's return. The ritual must not fail."

A chill froze halfway down Alfie's spine. Dear God. He'd always known Mather's deception had been a fool's game, and now it was going to kill him.

He was going to be a human sacrifice.

CHAPTER SEVEN

"They Were Only Playing Leapfrog..."

THE PADRE BLINKED and looked up. They were alive. Around him, the gathered scentirrii stepped back and parted.

"I thought they were going to kill us," said Edith in a low tremulous voice, checking her hands and face for acid burns.

Trembling with fear and relief, the Padre turned to Chandar for an explanation.

It spread its vestigial middle limbs. "They cannot hurt you," it said. "They have received this One's blessing. They have merely scented you. If you are not scented, you will be killed. Now you will smell Khungarrii. You will be safe."

The precaution proved well founded. As they journeyed, they met more scentirrii patrols and parties of worker chatts in the forest. They noted their approach with a cautious waving of antennae, and then ignored them.

Ahead, dominating the large managed clearing, was the mound-like Khungarrii edifice, rising hundreds of feet from the cinnamon earth, like a cathedral tower. The last time the Padre had seen the edifice, a large section had been destroyed by Jeffries, blowing up a stolen dump of grenades, mortars and other weapons. It had since been repaired and once again stood pristine and whole above the forest. Unadorned and functional, the structure bore no ornate inscriptions or decorations, no carvings, but was speckled with a thousand points of light as the sunlight caught flecks of mica bound into the dirt walls.

Scattered around the perimeter of the edifice were the peculiar funerary mounds of large clay balls, each sphere containing the body of a dead chatt, waiting to be rolled into the underworld by Skarra, the dung-beetle god of the dead. There were a good many of them – no doubt due in part, the Padre realised, to the actions of the Pennines.

Ahead of them, columns of worker chatts, djamirrii, and Khungarrii urmen, carrying the day's harvest in baskets or on litters, streamed into the edifice through great open bark doors some fifty or sixty feet in height, bound into the edifice itself by root-like hinges and framed by great earthen buttresses.

The Padre noticed that the shantytowns that had once clung to the midden heaps against the edifice had been swept away. The free urmen who had dwelt there under sufferance, scraping a subsistence from the scrap heaps of Khungarrii society, were gone; the first victims of the reprisals after the Pennines' attack to rescue the Padre and some twenty-odd Fusiliers and the three nurses captured by a scentirrii raiding party.

He felt Edith's small hand slip into his, giving reassurance and seeking comfort in equal measure. His hand closed about hers and together they walked toward the cavernous entrance of the edifice.

INSIDE, THE GREAT cathedral-like entrance hall bustled with activity. Chatt workers and djamirrii assessed and sorted the continual influx of the day's harvest; battlepillars berthed against earthen jetties to be unloaded. The place seemed half port, half market.

Edith could remember arriving at Calais on the boat from Dover to scenes such as these. She had been a very different woman back then. The sharp formic smell of the place, of the chatts, made her want to flee. She had to force herself to walk on.

The scentirrii led them up inclined passages lit by niches of bioluminescent lichen to the higher reaches of the edifice, to the network of sacred chambers where the dhuyumirrii conducted their ritualised business.

The scentirrii left them by a circular portal, a door grown from a tough fibrous living plant. Chandar breathed a mist at it, and the plant matter recoiled from it, dilating open. Rhengar ushered them through into an ancillary chamber. They had barely arrived when the circular door shrivelled open again. Two scentirrii stepped through, followed by a tall, regal dhuyumirrii wearing a similar over-the-shoulder arrangement of many-tasselled silken cloth to the one that Chandar wore, with the addition of a light, finely spun cloak. They had both seen this creature before.

"This One is Sirigar, Liya-Dhuyumirrii, High Anointed One of the Khungarrii Shura," it said, surveying the chamber. It had chosen to speak in English, something it was not wont to do. It was making a point.

Chandar bent its legs, sinking into the chatt submissive posture.

Sirigar looked down on it. "So you have returned, Chandar?"

"This One went to observe the battle at the direction of the Shura and was captured. This you know," said Chandar.

"And they let you go?"

"They wish to bargain."

"The time for bargaining is long past," said Sirigar. "And these creatures?" it said, indicating the Padre and Nurse Bell. "What are they doing here? This One could smell their stench the moment they entered Khungarr. Your fascination for them is unbecoming, Chandar, maybe even heretical."

"The Shura has not declared it so, yet," said Chandar.

Sirigar hissed and turned to inspect Edith, who shuddered in spite of herself. Sirigar's mandibles opened wide, as if to suggest that it could take her head within them and crush it. Warm breath washed over her as moist labial folds opened, exposing its glistening mouth palps. Its long segmented antennae waved above her head.

She held its gaze, defiance and terror wrestling within her, conscious of the contents of her haversack. In moments like this, she thought of Edith Cavell and found a well of courage within her which, while not inexhaustible, saw her through the moment.

Sirigar hissed and withdrew, immediately losing interest in her.

"They... they are emissaries. They cannot harm us. They have been anointed with the blessing of GarSuleth," Chandar gestured toward the Padre. "That one took the Kirrijandat, the rite of purification–"

"So did their Jeffries," said Sirigar, loading every word. "And look at the ruination that he visited on Khungarr. They are the Great Corruption. Their presence here sickens this One. Yet again you have exceeded your bounds, Chandar."

The Padre saw his chance. He had expected to persuade them, but to have the opportunity presented to him like this seemed heaven-sent.

"Jeffries was not one of us. You cannot judge us all by him. We are not answerable for his sins. I will take the rite again!" he declared.

Edith stepped forward. "Padre, no. Remember what it did to you the last time."

The Padre remembered very well. The rite was one that new immigrants to Khungarr were required to undergo as a test of loyalty and faith. It was seen as a symbolic washing away of old lives and old beliefs. He would be lying to himself if he said he wasn't afraid, but he was more fearful of the shadow it had cast over his life since he first experienced it, of the night terrors that hid in the dark corners of his mind during the day. This was why he had returned.

He clasped Bell's hand in his own and flashed a beatific smile. "I survived last time, I will do so again," he reassured her.

Sirigar regarded the Padre, its large dark eyes unblinking. "Very well, undergo the Kirrijandat. It will not save you.

When the Shura stands behind this One and decrees your herd to be the Great Corruption the perfumed prophecies speak of, you will be the first of the Tohmii to die. You and your djamirrii."

Sirigar turned and directed its ire at Chandar. "Despite knowing what they are, you dare bring them here, when the Great Corruption has already tainted Khungarr and may even now threaten the very future of the colony itself–"

Sirigar glanced at the Padre and lapsed into its own tongue; a guttural stream of harsh smacks, clicks and snips. Chandar countered him, both creatures swaying and moving with each exchange, until Sirigar, rearing up on its legs, let out an aggressive hiss. It swept from the chamber, its scentirrii following. The plant door contracted shut behind it.

Both Padre Rand and Edith held their breaths for a heartbeat before exhaling with relief. They were still alive, and the seditious scents they had smuggled in had not been detected.

Chandar turned to the pair. "This One has bought some time, but precious little. Your submission to the Kirrijandat has bought more. But unless this One succeeds before the Shura then it will have been to no avail. Sirigar will consolidate the Shura behind it and your herd will be culled."

The Padre and Nurse Bell exchanged anxious glances. This was becoming more dangerous than either of them had realised.

"You can't leave Nurse Bell here while I undergo the rite," said the Padre. "Not now Sirigar knows where she is. Not when you know what she carries."

"This One agrees," said Chandar. "This One will make sure that your djamirrii is kept out of the way and hidden from Sirigar's spies."

Chandar addressed Nurse Bell. "Rhengar will escort you."

"Where to?" she asked.

"The safest place in Khungarr."

* * *

Chandar escorted Padre Rand through the high, domed cathedral-like Chamber of the Anointed Ones. Set in the walls of the great circular hall were large alcoves, decorated with hieroglyphs impregnated with sacred scents. Chatt dhuyumirrii occupied many of the alcoves, facing the walls, their antennae waving over the glyphs. The susurration of chatts at prayer filled the space, their clicking mandibles sounding, to the Padre's mind, like a women's knitting circle making socks for soldiers.

They continued down a passage, past the alchemical chambers where the chatt apothecaries distilled and stored the sacred scents. Here had been the Scentorum, the repository of all their knowledge. Jeffries had destroyed it; thousands of years of accumulated scent scriptures and commentaries boiled, burned and vaporised in the conflagration, generations of knowledge gone. It had been an act of desecration akin to the burning of the library at Alexandria. The chambers had since been rebuilt, but many ancient scent texts had been lost forever.

The Padre was here to rectify that, if his mind survived the rite.

They left the Scentorum behind and proceeded to a string of small chambers barely big enough to stand erect in. They reminded him of confessionals.

Two acolyte dhuyumirrii nymphs approached, guiding them towards the ritual chamber. The Padre paused for a second. If he was going to back out, now was the time. God knows he wanted to. But this wasn't just about him anymore.

"You will be safe in here. No One will harm you while you are undergoing the rite," Chandar told him. "Not even Sirigar."

With a deep breath, he ducked his head and entered the small chamber. A large clay oil burner moulded up from the floor dominated it. The Padre sat as the acolyte poured viscous oil into the burner, then lit it with a taper before retiring from the chamber.

"GarSuleth guide you," said Chandar as the plant door expanded to close off the chamber.

As he breathed in the fumes, the Padre began to pray. "Our Father, who art in heaven, hallowed be thy name–"

Under the influence of the alien fumes, the prayer became a mantra, the words warping, shifting, slurring, as the alien vapour enfolded his mind.

"Our Father, give us this day our hallowed Earth which art our English heaven, forgive us our daily trespass and deliver us from this evil kingdom. Forgive us our sins and lead us not into the earth. Lead us not into temptation, but into glory. Thine is the power to grant this. Amen."

He began to feel hot and faint. His fingers reached for the dog collar around his neck and pulled it free. "No, let this cup pass from me," he gasped. He struggled to get up, but his limbs wouldn't obey. He slid to the floor, staring into the guttering flame of the oil burner.

The vision came and he was powerless to stop it...

CHATTS MADE EDITH'S skin crawl. It was a base, primal revulsion, something she had no control over, no matter how much she tried to rationalise it. She wished that Chandar had blessed her again; frankly, the chatts' ability to affect your mind like that revolted her, too, but the mild euphoria had helped last time. However, both she and the Padre needed their wits about them here. So why, she wondered, did the Padre feel the need to undergo that rite again? What was it he was trying to prove?

She didn't know, but she couldn't wait to be out of here. She'd thought she could face it and conquer her fear of chatts, but it was proving harder than she'd expected. When she first signed up to be a VAD she had little knowledge of what it might entail. Oh, she had some romantic girlish notions about mopping the brows of wounded heroes. Experience disabused her of that: maggots in wounds, the telltale smell of gas gangrene, suppurating sores; all these she had faced and conquered, until now she was able to deal with them as a matter of routine. But the chatts still made her squirm.

Rhengar led her down through narrower utilitarian tunnels. Here, the lichen light became less frequent. Despite promises of safety, Edith began to feel uneasy.

"Where are we going?" she asked.

"You are a nurse," it replied.

"Yes," she said cautiously.

They arrived at a small, unremarkable plant door at the end of a passage.

"Do you have a patient you want me to see? Are they in here?" she asked.

"Here, yes," said Rhengar.

Edith suddenly became afraid. She wanted to turn and flee, but where was there to flee to in this nest of insects, when every denizen could be turned upon her in an instant with an insubstantial chemical alarm?

She gripped her haversack tighter and tensed as Rhengar breathed on the door. It opened, and Edith found herself pushed through.

"No, wait," she pleaded, but Rhengar was already striding back up the passage and the plant door was blooming shut.

Oh, how she wished Nellie were here.

Edith found herself confronted by a small chatt, its carapace a smooth pale white. It wore no silk garment like Chandar and its caste, or like the scentirrii. It stepped forward as its antennae investigated her. It seemed satisfied that all the required scents and aromas were in order and scuttled off down a ramp, stopping only to see if she was following.

Very well, she thought. She straightened her back, lifted her chin and turned to face her fate with a very English decorum.

As she descended, the passage opened out. The gloom beyond was filled with the scuttling and clicks of hundreds of chatts. As her eyes grew used to the low light, she was able to make sense of the space. She realised with a shiver of revulsion that she had been here before. It was the Khungarrii nursery.

No wonder Rhengar thought she would be safe here. It would be the last place Sirigar would think to look. It was also the last place she wanted to be.

She looked around and saw no signs of the battle that had raged there months before as a platoon of Pennine Fusiliers fought their way out of the edifice. The great hole in the wall, where the *Ivanhoe* had smashed through, had long since been repaired, as if they had never been there.

Around the walls of the chamber were recesses where the grubs pupated into nymphs. Only a quarter of the cells were sealed and occupied. The rest lay open and empty. Running across the floor of the chamber were long sinuous channels where urmen women and nursery chatts fed blind, wriggling grubs.

She noticed precious few eggs about the nursery. Surely, these things should be like factories. But there was no time to contemplate the problem, as her guide walked on down a large side passage. It curved and Edith could make out something huge and worm-like at the end, to which chatts were attending.

As she came closer, she realised that it was only part of some larger creature; the rest lay in a chamber beyond. Edging alongside the worm-like protuberance, she entered the chamber. Her mouth went dry and she could feel her heart pound in her chest. Occupying almost the entire space, as though they had built the chamber around it, was what she guessed to be the Khungarrii Queen. Its abdomen was a pulsating sac, twenty or thirty feet high, and grossly distended, to the point where the taut, glistening pale skin verged on translucency. Whatever limbs the Queen once possessed had withered or been swallowed by its vast bulk. Atop of that, dwarfed by its body, its head and thorax were of normal chatt size, making it all the more grotesque. It was incapable of moving, grooming or feeding itself.

To that end, the chamber wall ran with a spiralling gallery, and slung across the huge corpulent form were bridges and gantries, so that its attendants could groom every inch of its body. Even now, chatts scurried across it, licking up sweat. While others laboured in trenches dug beneath the vast bulk, removing excreta, a continual procession wound up the spiral gallery to a gantry level with the Queen's thorax and head. There, attendants supplied the Queen with an endless supply of bowls of some sort of substance which they first masticated and then fed to it, like some sort of royal jelly.

However, this obese creature was more than just an egg-laying machine. It controlled the state of the colony through unspoken chemical decrees. Above the Queen, in the roof of the royal chamber, were a cluster of vents that drew the royal scent commands up into the edifice, where they were circulated on the air.

Edith stared up in horror at the creature.

The whole machinery of attendance ground on around her, with chatts ignoring her, until one touched her on the shoulder, making her yelp in alarm. It directed her back to the tunnel where the appendage from the distended belly ran.

She realised what was wrong. There should have been a steady stream of nursery attendants carrying eggs from the ovipositor, the egg-laying tube, to the nursery chamber, but there were none to be seen. Was that what Sirigar had been referring to when it was talking about the future of Khungarr?

A chatt spoke, struggling with the language, its exalted position not needing much interaction with urmen.

"Queen. Ill. Sickness. No eggs."

Whatever was wrong, it was beyond their abilities to heal, and they were desperate. That was why she was here.

That changed things. With a patient, Edith was able to focus. Slowly, the terror she felt being surrounded by these creatures receded. She had a job to do. This was why Chandar hadn't blessed her. In a euphoric state, she would have been in no position to help.

"Light. I need light," said Edith, sharply.

The chatt chittered a command, and within moments, a blue-white light bobbed toward them. It made Edith think briefly of Tinkerbell. Her aunt had taken her to see a performance of *Peter Pan and Wendy* many years earlier with her young cousins. And she'd clapped; how she'd clapped to save poor Tink. If only saving the Queen were as easy, she thought.

Edith rolled up her sleeves as a dozen or so more chatt attendants arrived clutching bunches of luminous lichen, their light bathing the tunnel.

She set about examining the appendage. The tube was inflamed and swollen, with several large sores, two of which were open and suppurating. The translucence she'd found so awful also proved to be a great aid, almost like an x-ray. She could see that the tube was swollen and not allowing the eggs to pass. They were backing up, impacting on the side of the canal. Somehow, they would have to be released.

She knelt before the opening of the ovipositor and gently inserted her hand, feeling her way up the inside of the lubricated tube. Her shoulder was almost touching the ovipositor sheath by the time she felt the constriction. The swelling had all but closed off the canal. Slowly, she withdrew her arm to find it coated with mucus. She tried to hide her disgust as she flicked creamy opaque strings of it at the tunnel wall before hurriedly wiping her arm down with a length of silken cloth provided by the chatts.

After her internal exam, she returned her attention to the infected wounds. If the infection had got into the bloodstream, then there was no hope of saving the creature.

"Water!" she demanded. "And bandages." They brought water and more fresh silk almost immediately. She sluiced out the sores as best she could.

The open wounds needed debriding, the dead infected matter cutting away, but she had no knife, no scalpel, no way to do it. She looked around and met the inquiring eyes of the chatt. She looked at its mandibles. They would have to do.

"Here!" she said pointing at a wound. "Here!" she mimed snipping mandibles. The chatt understood, and under her direction, it chewed away at the dead matter.

When she was satisfied that the wounds were clean, Edith opened her haversack, sorted guiltily past the sacred scent and petrol fruit juice, to retrieve two precious ampoules of iodine. She broke one into each wound.

Next, she pulled out sealed bags of dried moss. It had been a method she had learned in London, before she came out to France, where they used sphagnum moss as an absorbent surgical dressing for wounds in war hospitals. Here on this world, it proved a Godsend, once they had located a suitable source.

She packed the wounds with the moss and bandaged them using lengths of silk that the chatts provided. She hoped that it would bring the ovipositor swelling down enough to allow the passing of eggs. The dressings would have to be changed every couple of hours. That, for now, was all she could do.

Tired, she found a nook out of the way of the constant scuttling, crawled into it and hugged her bag to her. The ability to sleep anywhere, at any time, was a skill the Fusiliers had long since mastered, and one she had soon acquired. Despite her unfamiliar surrounding and the constant, unsettling chittering, she fell quickly and deeply asleep.

SHE WOKE SEVERAL times throughout the night; or at least, she assumed it was still night. Down here, in the bowels of the edifice, it was hard to tell. She changed the dressings on the wounds and found that, whatever the hour of day or night, the level of attendance to the Queen did not drop.

The chatt who had conducted her attended her closely. It watched her, intently, so she taught it as she went along, seeing it not as a repulsive chatt, but another creature wanting to care for others. On the other hand, it would probably kill her if it looked as if she was harming the Queen in any way. They probably all would. She tried to push that thought to the back of her mind.

The dressings seem to have done their work. The wounds were less inflamed and the tube was looking less swollen. As to what had caused the wounds, she couldn't say, but she did wonder how such injuries were possible in a place where the Queen was cosseted and cared for every hour of the day. If Sirigar did not cause this, it had certainly gained great capital from it, seeking to blame the illness and possible reproductive crisis on the 'Great Corruption'. If the Queen had not responded to Edith's treatment, the chances of the Pennines' survival would be very bleak indeed.

She turned her attention back to the task in hand. Had she done enough to ease the egg blockage?

Parting the fleshy sheath, once again Edith eased her hand into the ovipositor canal. Gently but firmly, she pushed her arm up inside. There had been some improvement. She could pass her hand beyond the swelling now. At full stretch, she could feel an egg with the tips of her fingers, pressing against the wall of the canal. She struggled and flexed, trying to get another inch or so of reach. After a minute or two of frustration, her fingers finally curled round the far edge of the egg and she managed to retrieve it, scooping it slowly down the canal. Almost immediately, another slid down. Matters would improve as the swelling reduced.

When she delivered the pearlescent egg to the waiting chatt, a wave of excited chittering passed round the chamber. It almost sounded like soft, polite applause.

Edith glanced up along the ovipositor, over the vast, throbbing, translucent abdomen to the small thorax and head high above her, and saw the Queen staring back down at her over its vast bulk.

As soon as Edith delivered them, the chatts took the eggs to the nursery chamber, each one carried away with awe and reverence.

It might be days before the infection was gone, but she showed the chatt what to do. Its slender arm and longer fingers might be better suited to retrieving the eggs than hers.

In response to some unspoken command, Edith found herself manhandled, despite her mild protestations, from one chatt to another and guided swiftly up the incline of the spiral gallery until she reached the audience gantry. There, ushered by the arthropod attendants, she stepped out to come face to face with the Queen itself; with the greater part of its obscene bulk hidden below like an iceberg, the portion Edith faced looked natural, or as natural as these creatures ever could.

With feeble arms, it beckoned Edith closer. She took a faltering step toward it. The Queen leaned forward, waving its long antennae at her as an attendant tried to feed it from a bowl. The Queen chittered at it. It froze, not comprehending its instructions. The Queen spoke again, more forcefully this time. With reluctance, the attendant turned and proffered the bowl to Edith. Unsure as to the etiquette of the situation, Edith pointed to herself.

"Me? You want me to eat?"

The chatt offered the bowl again. There was no mistaking the gesture. Those chatts nearby halted briefly in their tasks to watch.

"It is an honour no urman has ever been given," said the chatt, watching her.

Edith looked at the grey, glutinous and masticated jelly in the bowl. It didn't look at all appetising. She could feel her stomach rebelling just looking at it. Seeing no way to decline politely, she smiled weakly at the Queen, cupped her hand and slipped her fingers into the warm gelatinous mess.

The Queen watched expectantly.

Edith took a deep breath and spooned her fingers into her mouth. She gagged a little at the thick and slimy texture, and had to force herself to swallow it. It was curiously filling, and it was a struggle to finish the bowl. She could feel it rising back up her throat and she swallowed hard, determined to keep it down.

The Queen watched in approval, unblinking.

Unsure what to do next, Edith gave a little curtsy. Another attendant ushered her away along the gantry as others resumed the chores of feeding and cleaning their Queen. Her royal audience was over.

Edith reached the other side of the royal chamber and looked back. They had forgotten her presence already. Down below, chatts once more resumed the collection of eggs.

A chatt led her down another passage to another circular plant door. The chatt breathed on it and the circular plant portal shrivelled open to reveal Rhengar.

"Come," it said before stopping. It looked at her, tilting its head to one side like a curious dog, its long antennae waving in an agitated manner. Then it did something Edith had not expected. It knelt before her, touching its head and thorax in reverence.

CHAPTER EIGHT

"Shall They Return..."

PADRE RAND VACILLATED all night. It had just been a dream, a hallucination, nothing more. How could it be anything else? Then he looked around at the small chamber, here in an edifice of arthropods on an alien world. The comfortable boundaries of what was and was not had shifted. Anything seemed possible. Here, so far from Earth, God had spoken to him, as He had to His people of old. He had asked something of him and the Padre wondered if he would find himself wanting.

He hadn't truly understood the function of the rite last time. The Khungarrii called it the Kirrijandat, the cleansing, a ritual ordeal meant to be a symbolic pupation for urmen, a casting off of old ways, a rededication. If he wanted to, he could see it as a re-baptism, a Confirmation. But for God to ask this of him? Now he comprehended the night terrors. But if it was the Lord's will, then so be it.

The plant door dilated open and Chandar waited outside the small chamber.

The Padre got to his feet with a groan as he felt pins and needles prickle his feet and calves.

He nodded to the chatt. "It's done," he said.

"This One has spent the night meeting with members of the Shura. They are willing to consider a supplication of the scents," said Chandar as the Padre joined him. "Sirigar now knows that this One has something of importance to say, but does not yet know what. Many of the Shura are convinced by Sirigar's words, that the Queen's illness is the taint of the Great Corruption spread by the Tohmii. Singar will call for the scentirrii to march once more and eradicate your clan for good."

"Where's Nurse Bell?" the Padre asked.

"Your djamirrii is safe. Do not forget she carries hidden about her the sacred salve that will be your salvation and the liquor that might be this One's. This One has sent for her."

Chandar led the way along an inclined passage, taking them up into the further reaches of the edifice. Streams of chatts went about on unknown business: scentirrii and dhuyumirrii, mostly, with the odd workers and urmen. Two tassel-robed dhuyumirrii approached from the other direction. One bumped into the Padre, and a small vial dropped to the floor in the collision. It shattered and oozed oil.

"I'm terribly sorry," the Padre said, almost as a reflex. "Here, let me–"

He looked around, but they had slipped away.

Chandar let out a long, low, wet hiss.

The Padre, wheeled round to see several worker chatts step out of the passage shadows, blocking their way. "What's going on?"

"Sirigar is trying to prevent our appearance before the Shura," wheezed Chandar.

"I thought I was marked with Khungarr scent, I thought you said they couldn't harm me."

"Normally, no," said Chandar, eyeing the workers. "But the scent can be masked. A stronger chemical decree can negate it."

The shattered vial. One smell being used to hide another, thought the Padre.

The workers began to circle, their long mandibles snapping together rhythmically.

"It is how this One became crippled, when Sirigar once before thought this One a threat to its plans," said Chandar as they watched the worker chatts advance,

Chandar hissed, expelling its euphoric benediction in the hope of stalling the workers. It failed.

Several workers leapt upon it, barrelling it into the ground. The Padre thought he heard a carapace crack.

Another lunged at him. He had done a little boxing in his youth, and now he put up his fists for the first time in years. He swung a right uppercut under the guard of its open mandibles, connecting with the soft mouthparts. They mashed satisfactorily under his knuckles. The chatt stumbled backwards, its mandibles slicing empty air.

"Hah!" cried the Padre.

His initial spark of triumph was soon doused as another chatt sprang at him. The Padre was thrown off balance and the pair crashed to the ground. It crouched over him, its splayed long-fingered hands pressing down on his chest.

"Dear God in heaven preserve me!"

Its smooth facial plate was vacant of any expression. Mucus dripped from its mouthparts onto his face as it opened its mandibles and placed them either side of his head. As the pressure on his temples began to increase, the Padre screwed his eyes shut and prayed.

Without warning, the crushing pressure eased and the weight from his chest lifted. It was a moment before he dared open his eyes. His attacker was crouched motionless before him. The others likewise had abandoned their attack and were sunk low in submission, their mandibles open, their antennae waving gently, rhythmically, in unison.

The Padre heard a woman's cry.

Nurse Bell. Dear God, no. They'll take her as well. He wouldn't let that happen.

"Padre!"

"Bell, run!" he called out. "Run! Run!"

He scrambled back away from the now-motionless chatts until he was against the wall of the chamber.

Chandar lay against the other side, its head slumped on its chest plate, its mouth palps hanging limply, bubbles frothing through them as it breathed. A thick bluish fluid oozed from wounds in its soft abdomen, where one of its vestigial limbs had been ripped off. Its claw lay discarded on the floor nearby.

The Padre and Chandar exchanged weary, pained glances, each alive, but neither knowing how.

Rhengar entered the chamber, and several spear-carrying Scentirrii filed out either side of it.

"You. So it's come to this, has it?" said the Padre with bitter recrimination. "Assassination?"

Rhengar regarded him blankly. "Yes."

Breathing heavily, the Padre braced himself, glaring at the chatts' general with outright defiance. He'd given these creatures the benefit of the doubt. But now he realised he'd let his Christian nature be swayed by these soulless things – for how could they be anything else on this world?

"Come to finish the job, have you?" he said brusquely. "Then do it, but spare Bell. She's just a nurse. You know 'nurse'?"

Rhengar crouched by the shard of vial on the floor, waving his antennae over the fading evaporated spill.

"The musk of the Sanfradar, a predator. It breaks into edifices to devour the young. The workers reacted instinctively. They thought you were a danger. They would have torn you to pieces."

Dazed, the Padre leant against the chamber wall until the place stopped spinning, the chatt workers' confusion now his. "Then why didn't they? What stopped them?"

"I did, apparently," said Nurse Bell, stepping from the safety of the passage shadows into the chamber, a shy smile of embarrassment on her face.

"You did? But how?"

She strode over to him. "Padre, you're hurt."

He obliged by bowing his head and smiled apologetically. "I think I banged my head again. I'm all right."

"I'll be the judge of that," she said, gently examining his head. "Nothing's got through your skull yet." She looked him in the eyes. "Has it?"

The Padre met her gaze. "I'm fine," he said.

Rhengar gave orders to the remaining four scentirrii, who stood guard round the chamber while Nurse Bell went over and knelt to examine the injured chatt.

"Is it safe?" it asked, the words coming in pained gasps as it struggled to regurgitate enough air for speech.

She continued to examine his abdomen. "It's safe," she said. "But you're not." She turned to Rhengar. "We must get Chandar somewhere I can treat its wounds."

Rhengar stooped to pick up the wounded chatt and directed them down a maze of side passages that eventually led to a chamber. It left two of the scentirrii outside as guards; the others it dismissed. It set Chandar down and looked at Nurse Bell.

"Chandar must speak before the Shura soon, if you wish to save your clan."

She wasn't going to be bullied. She didn't even look up from her examination of Chandar's abdominal wounds as she spoke. "I'll do what I can. I'm not promising any more."

She bound Chandar's wound where his vestigial limb had been, winding the silk bandage around his abdomen. She was able to disguise most of the bandage with Chandar's own ceremonial silk shoulder throw, as she wrapped its excess around its abdomen.

"There," she said, sitting back on her heels.

"It is done?" asked Chandar.

"Yes, for the moment, so long as you don't exert yourself."

The Padre, who had been watching her work, finally spoke. "You said it was you that saved us."

"I'm rather afraid it might have been," she said with an apologetic shrug as she got to her feet. "The Khungarrii Queen gifted me with some sort of royal jelly, anointing me with her own scent. From what I gather, it's rather like getting the keys to the city."

"An anointed urman," said Rhengar. "This One cannot recall such a thing. However, the royal odour is unmistakable. Every Khungarrii knows it. But we must keep it secret a while longer."

"Why?"

"It strengthens this One's position, but only if this One can successfully couple it with this One's argument," croaked Chandar as it struggled to its feet. It held out an expectant hand towards Bell. "Do you have it?"

She nodded and fished in her haversack, bringing out the small stone amphora holding the sacred scent she had brought with her from the camp. Chandar took it with reverence. Edith pulled out another small jar. "Lieutenant Everson told me to give you this when it was time. I think it is. It's petrol fruit liquor."

Chandar took the bottle and uncorked it. Tilting its head back, it opened its mandibles and poured the liquor through its mouth parts.

"What is this?" asked Rhengar.

"It revives this One's ability to scent."

"How is that possible?"

"It is GarSuleth's Will," replied Chandar. "And yet more proof, if it were needed, that our olfaction is right."

It tucked the amphora of sacred scent into the abdominal wrap of its garment, hobbled over to a small opaque roundel of plant matter, and breathed on it. Much like the door, it contracted open, revealing a view looking down on the Shura chamber.

"You may watch from here until summoned. Whatever happens, do not leave this chamber until you are sent for," warned Chandar as it turned and limped for the door, escorted by Rhengar.

* * *

The Padre looked down into the chamber. It was a sunken amphitheatre. At one end, a raised dais was dominated by a shallow ceremonial bowl about six feet across, a low flame burning underneath its centre. High above it, around the walls of the chamber, were window apertures that funnelled light onto the empty space at the centre of the chamber. Around it rose earthen tiers, which were steadily filling as chatts filed into the chamber. The space buzzed with the low burr of ticking and scissoring mandibles. Judging from the tasselled silk they wore, the Padre assumed they were all dhuyumirrii, like Chandar.

From an opening between two stands of tiers, Sirigar entered, wearing a light silken cloak that billowed out as it walked, its deep hood covering its head and antennae. Two acolyte nymphs followed, swinging burning censers.

The assembly fell silent as it strode to the centre and cast its gaze across the serried ranks of dhuyumirrii, almost as if challenging them to question its authority.

Chandar entered the amphitheatre, hobbling towards the imperious figure of Sirigar, whose presence dominated the chamber. Chandar cut a poor comparison, with its limp and its broken antennae; if the Padre had been a betting man, he'd put his money on the thoroughbred, not the nag.

Chandar had explained the nature of the debate. It would have to openly challenge Sirigar's stance and Sirigar in turn would defend it. But debate among the Khungarrii could go on for hours, if not days, requiring not just mental but physical stamina. Statements were accompanied by stylised movements, punctuating argument and proposition, counter-argument and denial. When they were last here, the Padre heard a disparaging Jeffries compare them to dancing bees. No blows were landed, though in the far distant past perhaps it had been a more bloody affair that had become ritualised over time.

The Padre hadn't quite appreciated what Chandar had meant until he saw it.

"Are – are they fighting?" asked Nurse Bell, dismayed.

"After a fashion," said the Padre.

As challenger, it was Chandar's place to begin by proposing the statement to be debated. It stepped forward in a low lunge, pushing its arm out, as if physically delivering the challenge, its blow not striking, but the proximity of the blow to the defender no doubt signalling the strength of feeling on the subject. The heel of its hand stopped inches from Sirigar's facial plate. It seemed more oriental martial art than debate.

Shifting its centre of gravity, Sirigar stepped back gracefully, then responded, symbolically brushing aside Chandar's opening statement with a sweep of its arm and a rapid statement of its own.

As the ritual debate progressed, there seemed to be an element of chess to it; forms of statement and response with which both debaters were practised, perhaps restating old arguments or theological positions, familiar forms of attack and response. The Padre noted that one tactic was to lure your opponent into a physically and maybe philosophically weak position while you considered your next point. Sirigar, once it discovered Chandar had been weakened by injury, forced it to maintain a stressful position. Chandar began to lose its concentration and its theological points were blocked, struck down or conceded, one after another.

Nurse Bell watched in frustration. "What is Chandar waiting for? Why does it not produce the amphora?"

"It seems to be more complicated than that. There's a ritual formality to the proceedings. I think it has to bring the argument round to it. Sirigar seems to be countering and blocking that line of enquiry. Chandar has to find new ways to introduce the point."

"I didn't realise it would be like this. It shouldn't be doing this with its injury. I thought it would just be talking."

Sirigar was well versed in the arguments that kept it in power, and practised in deflecting challenges, but it had grown too confident. In a devastating series of attacks, it forced Chandar to recant and concede. However, it was a feint, drawing Sirigar onto ground where it was less certain in order that Chandar might bring in its new evidence. Chandar, it seemed, was more cunning than the Padre had given it credit for. Chandar was rallying, building a convincing argument-attack, batting away Sirigar's increasingly feeble and desperate counterpoints.

From the reaction of the watching Khungarrii Shura, the Padre and Nurse Bell could see a change in fortunes as Chandar went on the attack. Sirigar fell back, apparently unable to defend his position.

"Yes!"

"What's happening?"

"I think Chandar is about to make its point."

Weakened by its exertions, Chandar stumbled up the steps to the ceremonial bowl, the flame guttering beneath it. It grabbed the edge of the bowl and felt inside the robe for the amphora, the Commentaries of Chitaragar, ignoring the spreading blue stain soaking through its bandage.

Sirigar, unwilling to admit defeat, cried out harshly and several scentirrii with spears stepped into the amphitheatre. Even as the scentirrii moved forward to stop it, under the caws of protest from the ranks of the Shura, Chandar poured the sacred scent text into the bowl. The scentirrii rushed the steps, seized it by the arms and dragged it to its feet.

The oil ran slowly down the curve of the bowl toward the heated centre.

Chandar was taken down the steps towards a crowing Sirigar, its arms thrown open as it gnashed its mandibles together, addressing the assembled chatts.

Unseen, the oil pooled and bubbled in the bottom of the ceremonial crucible, boiling and evaporating into the air, carrying its message up on warm currents to the domed roof, where it cooled and sank down over the gathered dhuyumirrii.

The Shura fell silent as antennae twitched, absorbing the delicate notes of the ancient aroma, as shifting layers of subtext from the long-lost scent scripture revealed themselves.

The Great Corruption so feared by the Khungarrii was not the Pennines. They had been used unscrupulously by Sirigar to further its power. The danger the Commentaries forewarned against was the corruption of their own faith by those who would use it for their own ends. The tide turned against Sirigar. Here was the proof that it had tried to deny, incontrovertible and damning.

Sirigar whirled round in confusion as his support fell away, until it too sensed the top notes of the ancient commentary, warning against false dhuyumirrii, and let out a harsh venomous hiss of frustration.

"By God, I think Chandar's done it!" said the Padre, turning round to Nurse Bell, but she was fleeing from the room. The scentirrii stood aside for her, but stopped the Padre from following.

EDITH COULD THINK only of her patient. She raced along the passages and before she realised it she had entered the amphitheatre. She barely noticed the reaction of the Shura about her as she rushed to Chandar's side.

"Let me see," she said to Chandar, examining the sodden bandaging.

Chandar brushed her hand aside. "Not yet." It raised its head, looking past her. "Look," it wheezed.

Edith looked. Around her the entire Shura was sunk on their legs, looking down at them, at her. The Queen's scent, she realised. She had been Chandar's final proof.

"You are blessed. Untouchable. Even Sirigar dare not move against you while you exude the Queen's scent."

Chandar steadied itself and addressed the Shura.

"The Shura has seen how they have been misled, and if further proof were needed that these urmen were not the Great Corruption we long feared, behold, this urman djamirrii, anointed by the Queen herself. How is that possible if they were ever such a threat? The true threat has been amongst us all this time. The Shura's attention had been falsely turned outwards, when the real threat was within." And it pointed at Sirigar.

Sirigar sank into a crouch. The evidence of its treachery was inescapable, permeating the very air around it.

Rhengar stepped from the shadows, and at some chemical command, the scentirrii seized Sirigar and led it away.

It was only once Chandar had the Shura's assent and had been instated as liya-dhuyumirri, the position held by Sirigar, that it allowed Edith to escort it back to the chamber to treat its wounds once again.

"What will happen now?" she asked.

"Now? The Tohmii will uphold their end of the bargain. They have been absolved. A chemical decree has already been disseminated throughout Khungarr. This view will become the established view. This will always have been the view."

THE THREE KHUNGARRII battlepillars had been decorated with lengths of coloured, scented silk and bore a multitude of silk pennants. There was an air of pilgrimage about the procession as it headed to the Pennines' camp, accompanied by grating dhuyumirrii chants and the beating of chest carapaces.

The swaying of the battlepillar's howdah unsettled Edith's stomach and she grasped the sides to steady herself as it rocked from side to side. Despite the little fluttering of girlish glee, Edith had to keep reminding herself that none of this was for her benefit, favoured by the Khungarrii Queen as she might be. No, this was in celebration of the long-lost ancient texts in the Pennines' possession, which would now be returned to the care of the Ones. It was part of the agreement made with Everson, in return for some kind of Treaty between the Pennines and the Khungarrii. She looked out happily across the veldt. She hadn't felt this relaxed since they had come to the planet. For once, the alien sun was shining and all seemed right with this world.

* * *

THE PADRE DIDN'T feel quite so ebullient. Thoughts of his vision churned away at his guts like three-day-old army stew. Like the men, he knew that being out of the line was temporary. At some point, courage or not, they would march back up the line towards the mud, shelling and shooting. He, too, knew that the terrors of his vision, and the choice he would have to make, were still waiting for him out there somewhere. But now, for Nurse Bell's sake, he smiled and allowed himself to be distracted.

TULLIVER'S SOPWITH SWOOPED low over them several times in their progress across the veldt, adding to the carnival atmosphere with its rolls and loops.

Delighted, Edith leaned out of the howdah and waved joyfully at the flying machine as it performed its daring aerobatics.

Beside her, Chandar watched the aeroplane with keen interest...

LIEUTENANT PALMER STOOD on the observation platform of the old Poulet farmhouse. He handed the binoculars to Sergeant Hobson, who stood beside him. "What do you make of it, Sergeant?"

Hobson peered through the glasses at the approaching procession. "A white flag of truce. I can't tell if the Padre or Nurse Bell are there."

The battlepillars didn't present a huge threat. The Machine Gun Section could cut them down before the chatts came within the range of their own electric lances.

Still, their appearance sent a ripple of unease along the line, men shuffling nervously on the firesteps. But this was a delicate time; Palmer didn't need nervous or trigger-happy troops. Those not on sentry duty were confined to the support and reserve trenches. Nobody wanted an incident.

The battlepillars stopped several hundred yards beyond the wireweed, along the line of the old Khungarrii siege, and upwind of the poppies that spread like a bloodstain across the scorched cordon sanitaire.

"Learnt their lesson, then?" said Hobson. "Bloody good job, too."

"Quite," said Palmer.

The white pennant flapped and snapped above the lead battlepillar as it chewed the tube grass.

Lieutenant Palmer, Sergeant Hobson and a small party walked out to meet them under a white flag of their own. Nervous, Palmer glanced back at the lines, like an unconfident swimmer too far from shore.

A faraway muffled cry rang out from the trenches and a shot cracked across the veldt, echoing off the hillsides.

There were angry chitterings and hissings from the chatts.

Several arcs of blue-white lightning leapt from electric lances towards the Fusilier party.

Palmer threw himself down on the ground and drew his Webley. Hobson hit the dirt beside him.

"What the hell's going on, Sergeant?" he yelled, picking himself up. "The men had strict orders!"

There was a deep, wet roar and a woman's scream. More shots. Roars. The keening cry of injured scentirrii. The brief buzzing crackle of electric lances.

Palmer froze as several hundred pounds of fur, muscle, fangs and claws leapt out of the tube grass at him.

A bright, white-blue, erratic bolt of lightning arced through the air, blasting the animal, earthing through it as it crashed gracelessly to the ground with a dull thud and a snapping of bone. The smell of charred meat, burnt fur and voided bowels filled Palmer's nostrils.

Hell hounds. They must have been stalking the battlepillars.

Rolling away from the smouldering corpse, Palmer got to his feet, seeking another target. He turned and emptied his revolver into another hell hound as it slunk through the tube grass toward the chatt party.

By the time the gunshots and electric bolts had died out, the ground was littered with hell hound dead.

Life had been difficult for the veldt predators since the arrival of the Pennines. The Fusiliers had decimated them, driving their packs further and further out into the veldt, and the recent harvesting of their natural prey by the airborne Kreothe had forced the packs into desperate actions to survive. The battlepillars were much too large to be brought down, but their passengers were a different matter.

Miraculously, there were no casualties on either side. Between them, the Fusiliers and chatts had made short work of the hell hounds. Perhaps this was the first sign of an entente cordiale?

PALMER AND HOBSON approached the battlepillars. The scentirrii watched them intently, waving their long segmented feelers in their direction and tracking them with their electric lances and spears.

Nurse Bell climbed down a rope ladder from the battlepillar's howdah and graciously accepted the Padre's hand as support as she stepped down onto the ground. The chatts around her all sank down and bowed low, their feelers almost touching the ground.

Palmer glanced at Sergeant Hobson, who just shook his head. The sergeant had ceased trying to figure this world out, and just got on with it.

"That's quite an effect you have on the chatts there," said Palmer, intrigued.

Nurse Bell blushed. "Long story."

He stuck out his hand and shook the chaplain's. "Padre."

"It's done," the Padre said. "Chandar has carried out its side of the bargain." He nodded toward the encircled system of trenches and Somme soil. "We're still on their territory, so there are things to be worked out, but generally a state of truce now exists between us."

"It is as your dhuyumirrii says," agreed Chandar. "Now you must keep Everson's side of the bargain. The sacred scents must be returned home to the Ones."

Palmer nodded to Hobson. The Sergeant sent a runner back to the lines.

Bearers brought out several ammunition crates carried on long poles thrust through their rope handles. They carted them over with less respect than they deserved, but more than the Army Service Corps usually mustered for items in its care.

Palmer opened the crates to show the repository of sacred knowledge, the ancient amphorae and jars packed with dried grasses. Chandar and the others touched their heads and thoraxes in signs of reverence. Chanting in veneration, the dhuyumirrii took up the crates and bore them like tabernacles before loading them into the battlepillars' panniers for the journey back to Khungarr.

"So that's that, then," said Palmer with relief as they watched the procession depart, banging their carapaces and chittering like a tiding of magpies.

"Oh, I doubt it, sir," said Hobson.

"What do you mean, sergeant? There's an understanding between us. We're at peace with them now."

"With respect, sir, we've *made* peace, yes. Now we have to *keep* it. We've still got to live with them, and I don't think that's going to be as easy as it sounds."

Edith strode into the hospital tent to find Captain Lippett. She had debated with herself all the way back from Khungarr whether to bring this up, but while there was a possibility of helping those under her care, she decided she would try. She took a deep breath.

"Doctor Lippett," she said. "I'd like your permission to start medical trials of petrol fruit liquor on the blinded men."

Lippett arched his eyebrows. "You do know that Lieutenant Everson has specifically passed an order forbidding its use for human consumption, Nurse?"

The words tumbled out before he could silence her again. "But Doctor, consider the anecdotal evidence of the tank crew and the efficacious effects of the liquor on the chatt. I think it could help those poor men blinded by chatt acid. It may not return their sight as they were used to it, but in time, might they not learn to see again in a different way?"

Lippett's stern gaze held her like pins splaying open a dissection specimen. She knew it, she'd gone too far. Perhaps it was a pity after all that her newfound status didn't extend beyond the chatts.

Lippet smiled faintly. "I must admit, Nurse Bell, the same thought had crossed my mind, too. Perhaps we should see about setting something up."

Humming gaily to herself, Edith sauntered into her tent with the lightness of soul of one who had just crept in late from a jolly good evening out.

She didn't care that the entire Khungarrii colony would now fall at its feet when she passed. Her exalted position didn't matter a jot. She had been away too long and had work to do.

SERGEANT DIXON LOOKED up at the canyon wall and sized up the pile of scree at its base. The metal wall stood bright and impervious above him in the rock. A challenge.

He turned back to his men. "Lambert. Bring me the guncotton and a number eight detonator."

Dixon and his men scrambled to the top of the scree slope where it met the metal wall and, several yards below, they packed the guncotton into the rocks as deep as they could, running a cable along the top of the slope to a large boulder that would shield them from the blast.

Sergeant Dixon blew his whistle.

Below, everyone moved back round the turn in the canyon, where they would be sheltered from blast. Two whistles indicated everyone was in position. There was one long whistle, and then Lambert pushed the plunger on the detonator. It sank with a ratcheted whirr. There followed the briefest of delays. The explosion echoed off the canyon walls, filling it with smoke, dirt and falling debris.

Then they waited for the raining clinker of rocks to stop and for the dust to clear...

CHAPTER NINE

"And There His Foot-Marks Led..."

EVERSON STOOD BY the lip of the Croatoan Crater. Across the far side, over a mile away, waterfalls half hidden by diaphanous mists plunged silently into the sunken world below. Nazhkadarr, the Scentless Place. The place that should not be, Chandar had called it.

He leaned forward and peered over the edge. To his right, the forest around them tumbled pell-mell into the crater. To his left, he could see the crumbled lip where the tank had gone over. He saw the gouged ruts it had made as it slid down the steep crater wall toward the dark hole in the jungle canopy.

Of Nellie Abbot, Napoo and the tank crew there was no sign. When the Fusiliers' battlepillars reached the crater, he had expected to find them waiting. His first thought had been some sort of attack, but their camp had not been disturbed. Then they found the vine rope slung over the crater side.

Again he found his plans frustrated. Why did they have to fight for every bloody inch on this planet? This was supposed to be a simple operation; salvage the tank and pick up Jeffries' trail. Now, even if they found the tank and managed to salvage it, there was no one to man the bloody thing. He'd gambled everything on this.

"God damn it!"

He kicked out in frustration. His boot clipped a small stone, and it skimmed over the ground, bounced once and skittered over the edge of the crater.

"I thought you said you'd ordered them to wait for the salvage party?" Everson snapped at Atkins, regretting it instantly. He watched the Lance Corporal shuffle uncomfortably.

"I did, sir, but Nellie, that is Driver Abbott, seemed very concerned about Lieutenant Mathers and Private Perkins, sir. We should have been here days ago. If it wasn't for–"

"The mutiny, yes, I know. So they've gone down there?"

Atkins sighed. "Knowing Nellie, sir? Yes."

Nellie Abbott. She had a stubborn attitude forged in suffrage. Which might have been fine if you were chaining yourself to the Town Hall railings. She might have had a point and he might have agreed with her, but out here? Couldn't the damn woman just do as she was told for once?

Even Nurse Bell, who wouldn't say boo to a goose the first time he met her, had become headstrong. What was it about this place and women?

The urmen treated their women as equals, sharing the work and the danger. Was that what happened when society started fraying at the edges? Wild Women?

Only Sister Fenton seemed to maintain a sense of propriety and decorum. Her exterior was stern, proper and unassailable. They had a saying in the hospital: 'Laugh and the nurse laughs with you, if Sister enters you laugh alone.' She could keep the girls in check, if she wished, but she seemed inclined to give them their head. Frankly, she was just an enigma.

"Bugger," said Everson on reflection.

Atkins peered down into the crater. "As you quite rightly say, sir, bugger."

"OH, THIS IS marvellous," crowed Hepton, framing the sunken lost world of the crater, with thumbs and forefingers. "Jenkins, bring my equipment over here at once. We've got to get this before the light goes. Jenkins, where the bloody hell are you man?"

Private Jenkins staggered up, carrying not only his own battle order kit but the tripod for Hepton's camera and several canisters of film. Shining with sweat, he dropped them on the ground, gasping.

"Careful with them, lad! Bloody expensive things, they are. I'll have your guts for garters if you break 'em."

Hepton panned his imaginary camera across the scene again to find Corporal Riley and Tonkins having a pissing contest over the lip. The awe-inspiring sight was clearly lost on the two soldiers.

"Philistines!" Hepton muttered.

Mercy was sat on the lip of the crater, feet hanging over the edge, oblivious to the height and happily tossing small stones into the jungle canopy below.

Porgy watched Hepton set up his camera. He took his cap off and preened his hair. "Think I'll try my luck, see if he wants a grin and a wave for the folks back home."

"What?" said Porgy, at their sceptical looks. "It's a chance to be famous, innit? When his film gets shown in all the picture houses, yours truly is going to be a matinee idol. The shop girls are all going to want my autograph."

Pot Shot shook his head. "I've seen the size of your 'autograph', it's nothing to write home about."

Atkins made his way over to his section.

"What did the Lieutenant say?" Gutsy asked.

"Might have to send people down there after them."

"By 'people', you mean us?"

"Probably," said Atkins. "That's the way our luck runs. In the meantime he wants us to set up a rear guard by the ruins, against any Zohtakarrii patrols, so look sharp."

* * *

Using the vine rope that had been left there by the tank crew, 3 Section, led by Corporal Talbot, descended into the crater to salvage the tank, Walker, Hardiman and Fletcher, going down first to secure the ground and cover the rest of the party. Hume, Owen, Banks, Preston, Cooper, Mitchell and Jackson climbed down after them and waited on the scree as the others advanced into the jungle.

The trail left by the tank was obvious. Not even Hardiman could miss it.

"Keep your eyes peeled," said Talbot as they edged down the verdant tunnel the ironclad had left in its wake, wary of every crack and rustle. If the tank crew had been here, they weren't here now. Anything might have happened. Wise to the ways of this world, Preston and Mitchell kept their rifles pointing up, scanning the canopy overhead. The whoops, squeals and shaking branches set them on edge.

They found the tank in a crushed bank of tangled foliage, broken saplings and trampled shrubbery. Anything that stayed still here was soon strangled by the ever-present pale creepers, and the tank was no exception as the thick, pallid creepers spread their grip over the ironclad.

"We've got it!" Corporal Talbot hollered back to Walker at the jungle's edge, who relayed the news back up to the crater rim.

"Below!" came the reply as several hundredweight of rope and chains tumbled down over the edge, snapping and unspooling as they crashed down the crater side.

"Jesus!" yelped Fletcher as the chain whipped down past them in a flurry of dust and gravel. "Nearly took my bleedin' head off!"

While half the rest of the section set to work with their entrenching tools, hacking the tank free of the creepers' unwanted embrace, Talbot, Hardiman and Walker set about hauling the heavy lengths of rope and chain towards the tank and securing them.

The all-clear was relayed up to the top. The drums of petrol fruit fuel had been unloaded from the battlepillars and stacked by the crater ready to refuel the tank, and the ropes had been connected to the battlepillars' jerry-rigged harnesses.

From his howdah, Woolridge urged Big Bertha and Big Willie to take the strain. The great ropes thrummed taut as the huge larval beasts edged forward towards the prospect of food at the forest's edge.

In the crater, the chains clinked as the slack was taken up and took the weight of the tank. The remaining creepers, unwilling to give up their prize, clung desperately to it, like a mother at a railway station whose son was setting off to war. But in this case, as with that, the army's pull was relentless. It ripped the tank from the creepers' grip, and those that didn't release their hold were wrenched from the ground by their roots as the ironclad machine was dragged inch by inch from the crushed and broken tanglewood that had saved it.

"Whooooo!" Owen waved his battle bowler as the *Ivanhoe* advanced foot by foot through the pulverised bower, back along its own track towards the jungle's edge.

When, with agonising slowness, the tank began to crawl up the scree slope, Talbot pushed his steel helmet back on his head. "You know, I never reckoned this would work, but they're only bloody doing it."

Fletcher clapped him on the shoulder and grinned. "That'll be a tanner you owe me, then."

ATKINS AND 1 Section took up position in the ruins of Nazarr to defend the approach to the Croatoan Crater, along with the men of 2 Section. The ruins had collapsed inwards on the subterranean tunnels, leaving obstinate pinnacles of wall standing here and there. Had it not been for the exotic vegetation already reclaiming the barren ground, it could have been any small Belgian village bombed to buggery by German shells.

"We're so close I can feel it," said Atkins as they kept watch on the jungle beyond the ruins. "We should be down there, going after Jeffries."

"You're certain Jeffries knows a way home, then," asked Gutsy.

"Not certain, but he claimed to have brought us here. I just want to get back to Blighty, and if there's the slightest chance he knows how, then I think we have to take it."

"I thought you said he was just a bloke," said Gazette. "Are you telling me you believe all that magic stuff now? You're not starting to believe your own press, are you, Only?"

"Blood and sand, of course not!" protested Atkins. "You know what happened. I told you. I didn't start those bloody rumours about me battling black magic. In case you forgot, it was believing those tales that got Chalky killed. Whether that diabolist gubbins has any truth to it, who knows? All I know is I didn't see any."

"You have to admit, that mumbo jumbo stuff does seem to follow you around though," Porgy chipped in. "There's that thing with the chatt, Chandar, too – all that Kurda stuff about how you two were connected by some web of fate or something."

Atkins rolled his eyes. "Give me a break. Look, I'd just like my soddin' life back, all right? My life, to do with as I please, not have all these people with expectations, telling me what I should be, and what I should be doing."

"Shouldn't have joined the army, then," said Mercy with a smirk.

"So you don't put much store in Mathers' mad prophecy, last time we were here, then," asked Pot Shot, mischievously. "*In the spira when the Breath of GarSuleth grows foul,*" he intoned portentously, "*the false dhuyumirrii shall follow its own scent along a trail not travelled, to a place that does not exist. Other Ones will travel with the Breath of GarSuleth, the Kreothe, made not tamed. Then shall Skarra, with open mandibles, welcome the dark scentirrii. There shall emerge a colony without precedent. The children of GarSuleth will fall. They shall not forsake the sky web. The anchor line breaks.*"

The rest of the section just looked at him as if he'd gone doolally.

"I memorised it," said Pot Shot warily.

Atkins raised his eyebrows with disbelief. "You memorised it."

"I thought it might be important."

"And is it?"

"I couldn't say," Pot Shot admitted with a lop-sided grin and shrug. "I don't know what any of it means."

His mood lightened, Atkins shook his head softly, smiled, and cuffed the lanky Fusilier around the head with his soft cap. "Daft ha'p'orth."

A thing the size of a man's forearm, like a corpse rat crossed with a spider, skittered out of the undergrowth.

Almost preternaturally fast, Gazette swung his rifle round, following the movement, before dismissing it.

"What the fuck?" Another ran through Porgy's legs.

Then a gaggle of the critters scuttled out of the undergrowth.

Atkins's eyes narrowed as he stared into the gloom of the forest surrounding them. Something had made those things funk it. Another gesture and the rest of the section sought hasty cover behind the lip of the old Nazarrii edifice ,scrambling at their chests for their gas hoods.

Hood in hand, Atkins called out. "Don't fire unless you have to. We may have to repel more than one attack until they can haul the *Ivanhoe* up."

"And then they'll be in for a surprise," said Porgy, his voice muffled by the layers of chemically impregnated flannel.

Atkins removed his soft cap and tugged the hood over his head, tucking it into his collar. The world yellowed and cracked, filtered by the mica eyepieces. He could feel his forehead begin to prickle with sweat under the thick cloth.

For a moment there was only silence and tension. Sweaty palms gripped barrels. Eyes scanned the wall of forest from behind dirty lenses of the gas hoods.

Zohtakarrii scentirrii swarmed out of the forest like cockroaches, leaping from the cover of the trees with angry, rattling hisses. Those with swords and spears bounded like grasshoppers, covering the space between the forest and the ruins in seconds.

One launched itself over the shattered wall. Atkins, braced against a large block of rubble, thrust up with his bayonet, slipping the seventeen-inch blade up into the soft abdomen, and used the chatt's momentum to swing his rifle like a pitchfork. He threw the chatt over his head, pulling the trigger as he did so. The chatt flailed through the air and fell against the rubble blocks, where its carapace cracked and a thick dark ichor seeped out of its broken body.

Gazette settled down into cover and picked off charging chatts with mechanical precision, flanked by Pot Shot and Porgy.

The ruins, though, were in danger of being overrun. Further afield, Atkins heard the sound of shooting. The chatts were flanking them and attacking the main rescue party. And he and his section were about to be cut off from the rest of them.

"2 Section! Fall back and give covering fire!" yelled Atkins.

They didn't have to be told twice. The section retreated to the rear of the ruins to give covering fire to Atkins and his Black Hand Gang.

ON HEARING THE first shots, Everson barked orders. "Stand to. Fix bayonets. Gas, gas, gas!"

There was no gas, of course, but the hoods protected against the chatts' acid spit and the command had been drilled into the men. Everson saw no point in changing it.

Everson turned to the Fusilier astride the battlepillar as it and its partner continued their obstinate plod forward, each footfall hauling the tank nearer. If they could get the tank to the top, then it could turn the tide for them. They might not be able to drive it, but its machine guns and six-pounders would bring much needed support. They had to cover Woolridge and his battlepillars for as long as possible.

He called up. "Woolridge, whatever happens, keep pulling. We need that tank. We'll buy you as much time as we can."

Woolridge waved his acknowledgement from Big Bertha's howdah. Ferris and Carlton manned the battlepillar's forward machine gun. Merrick and Bailey took the rear.

Woolridge saw Atkins and the two rearguard sections retreating towards the main party across the no man's land of scrub, with the lines of chatts advancing behind them.

"Covering fire!" he yelled.

Ferris and Carlton opened fire, their elevated position giving a good beaten zone. The Lewis gun chuddered out in short bursts, shattering carapaces and felling advancing chatts.

The rest of the platoon, having taken cover, yelled encouragement as Atkins' men pelted towards them, some helping injured or blinded comrades.

They reached the safety of the firing line, hurdling over the crouched soldiers.

Big Bertha and Big Willie were now advancing beyond the front line towards the chatts, as they continued to haul their ironclad load from the crater. For Woolridge to do his job, Everson couldn't afford to lose ground to the enemy.

There was nothing for it; they would have to attack and defend every yard they could. Their only problem was lack of ammunition. Whatever they faced today, even if they were to repel it, they would still need to conserve ammunition for whatever happened afterwards. To be out here this far from the trenches without ammunition would leave them effectively defenceless.

Everson summoned the nearest private. "Ellis! Tell the NCOs. On my order, we're going to advance towards the enemy. Single-round fire."

"Sir." The Fusilier dashed along the line as the first wave of chatts sprang towards them.

Everson blew his whistle and the sections stepped out from behind cover.

The skirmish line advanced: the bombers, flanked by riflemen, took advantage of the close bunching of chatts as Mills bombs arced through the air to explode in balls of fire and red-hot shrapnel, throwing limbs and razor-sharp shards of carapace whirling though the air.

"It's pig-sticking time, lads!" howled a Corporal, and the air was filled with cries and roars honed on English training grounds under the eyes of disdainful NCOs.

The Tommies charged with bayonets and crashed against chatt carapaces in close quarters fighting, too close for electric lances to be effective, fighting to hold the line. Everson slashed and parried with his sword, taking out his frustrations with every cut and thrust.

Atkins swung his rifle and bayonet, countering parries and thrusts from spears and swords, his khaki tunic becoming mottled and moth-eaten as drops of acid spit burnt themselves away against the thick serge. Chatts swarmed around them, like ants on jam. Again and again he stabbed, countered, swung the stock of his Enfield into the horned and nubbed carapaces, blocked blows with the barrel. As one chatt fell, another took its place. Under his gas hood, Atkins howled with frustration and rage, and the muscles in his arms began to burn with the effort.

The Fusiliers advanced past Big Bertha and Big Willie. Arcs of electric energy blistering the air around them as the chatts' lancers found their range.

The left flank of the line began to weaken and the Tommies were pushed back, but wheeled round to protect the straining battlepillars.

Below, in the crater, the sound of gunfire and screams echoed off the walls. The working party paused.

"Jesus, what the hell is going on up there?" said Mitchell. "Sounds like an attack."

"I don't know. But I'm not going to be stuck down here," said Cooper. He scrambled up the scree slope, stones slipping out from under his feet as he climbed.

"Cooper, who said you could leave your post? Get back here!" ordered Corporal Talbot.

Cooper ignored him, reached the vine rope by which they'd descended, and began to climb, hand over hand.

"What are you going to do?" Owen asked Talbot.

Talbot's shoulders dropped in defeat. "Nothing," he said. "Leastways, not yet. I've got his name, and he's climbing towards a fight, ain't he? He's not deserting."

"I don't know what's going on, but maybe we should all be up there, Corp," said Fletcher.

The tank groaned and clanked, clawing its way up the scree, like a faithful hound attempting to scramble up to help its master.

"Maybe we should, but our orders were to see to the tank. That's our job."

WOOLRIDGE JABBED THE driving spikes between the segmented plates behind Big Bertha's head, urging the beast forward.

"Come on, girl, come on," he urged, willing the larval creature on.

It wasn't lost on Woolridge that even as the others were forced back, he was slowly advancing towards the enemy, as the battlepillars hauled the twenty-eight-ton tank up the steep incline of the crater wall. To stop now would be disastrous. He knew that whatever happened, he must keep hauling the tank. But he also knew he'd need another fifty or sixty yards to do it. Yards that were slipping away as the chatts advanced, although the Pennines were making them fight for every inch.

In front of him, in the forward machine-gun basket, Ferris swapped out the last circular forty-eight-round ammo canister from the forward Lewis gun and swore.

"We're out of ammo!"

Woolridge dug the driving spikes in again, pulling on the reins. Big Bertha reared up off the ground as the advancing wave of chatts rushed towards it and Big Willie, before crashing down again, crushing half a dozen chatts, their smashed carapaces crackling under Bertha's bulk like brittle sheets of cellophane.

Several chatts sprang up onto Bertha's panniers, and from there scrambled up the sides of the beast.

Ferris was hit by a bolt from an electric lance. He went into spasm, lost his balance and slipped down Big Bertha's face. His webbing caught on one of its barbed mandibles; as he struggled to free himself, the battlepillar's mandibles scythed shut.

Cooper had almost reached the top. Even Talbot found himself willing the man on. There was a blue-white flash from beyond the lip, and the rope he was climbing dropped into the crater. Cooper's body plummeted down the crater wall, hit an outcrop and pinwheeled out into the air.

"Cooper!"

He hit the top of the scree slope with a sound like a wet sandbag. His limbs flopped at sickening angles. The broken body tumbled down the crater side until it slid to rest against the port track horn of the *Ivanhoe*. The track plates rolled implacably forward, crushing the body beneath its port track before anyone could reach him; the sound of splintering bone and bursting organs was mercifully lost amid the creaks and screeching of shifting iron plates.

The chatts advanced along Big Bertha's back towards the driver's howdah. Woolridge cycled the bolt on his Enfield and fired, sending the first chatt spinning off to the ground. And the second.

There was a loud wrenching and tearing followed by a snap as the load bearing fibre of the tow ropes finally tore, under assault from chatt mandibles. Released from tension, the ropes snapped through the air, hurling chatts from the battlepillar's back.

Free of its burden, Bertha lurched forward. Woolridge almost lost his footing. He grabbed the side of the howdah to steady himself. He caught sight of the chatt with its electric lance a second before his world was filled with an agonising white light that faded into a consuming blackness.

LEFT TO BEAR the entire load alone, Big Willie began to lose the battle. The weight of the tank dragged the battlepillar back towards the edge of the crater, leaving a great furrow in the ground.

Electric lance fire burnt through the great ropes and Big Willie was suddenly released from its harness, but its freedom was short-lived. Stray electric lance bolts licked its armoured sides, earthing through it, burning carapace and scorching soft tissue. Thrashing in pain, its rear end crashed against the stock of fuel drums, sending them toppling over the crater edge, like skittles, where they bounced down the side in a succession of hollow, discordant notes.

TALBOT WATCHED AS the tank reached the top of the scree slope and abutted the crater wall. The track horns caught the camber of the wall and began to creep the chassis up the steeper slope.

There was a lurch and the tank rolled back several yards, sending the Fusiliers scurrying out of the way. A huge length of rope dropped, piling up on the driver's cabin between the track horns like a great fibrous stool.

The tank remained still for a moment, and then with a despairing groan of tortured metal, the *Ivanhoe* rolled back down towards the jungle, picking up speed in a cloud of dust and chippings.

Watching with horror, Talbot flinched at every sound.

With their arms windmilling, the salvage section ran down after the runaway ironclad, as if they had a chance of stopping it.

EVERSON HEARD THE grating, metallic crash and the rumble of the tracks, and knew that the tank was gone again.

And with it, the Pennines' resolve. They found themselves pushed back by sheer weight of numbers until they had their backs to the crater's edge. They were surrounded. Trapped.

The chatts closed in around them, bristling with spears, swords and electric lances, mandibles clashing. But they didn't move in to drive them over.

"I think they want us alive," said Atkins.

"Works for me," said Porgy in ragged breaths.

Pot Shot eyed their scything mandibles. "Probably prefer their food live, knowing our luck."

A large scentirrii stepped forward. It wore a blood-red silk surcoat and its mandibles seemed larger and stronger than any Khungarrii. Its antennae waved. "You are prisoners of the Zohtakarrii."

The Fusiliers didn't move, but waited on a command from Everson. He knew they would fight to the last if he ordered them, but what would they be fighting for? Perhaps Bains had been right. This world wasn't about King and Country and Duty. It was about survival.

"Lower your weapons," he said, his voice laced with regret. He stepped forwards and offered his sword in surrender.

TALBOT AND THE others strained their ears. It had gone quiet up above. That wasn't good.

"D'you think they're dead?" asked Hume.

"If they are, then we're up shit creek," said Mitchell. "We're trapped down here."

"Maybe they've been captured."

Talbot cupped his hand round his mouth and called up. "Sir! Lieutenant Everson!"

There was no reply. Fletcher grimaced and shook his head.

"Anyone! Hello?"

"We can't just stay here."

"Doesn't look like we have a choice. We were ordered to watch over the tank and that's what we'll do until an officer tells us otherwise. It'll give us shelter, and maybe there are rations and ammo in there."

With many hopeful, but unfulfilled, glances to the top of the crater, they walked back into the tank's bower. It was dispiriting to find the ironclad embedded in the vegetation pretty much as they had first found it.

"Might as well be on the bloody Somme. A day's misery and no ground gained to show for it."

"Home from home, then, ain't it?"

"Corp!"

"What?"

Banks pointed into the undergrowth. Something was moving. They backed away, raising their rifles.

An officer, sallow-faced, unsteady on his feet, stumbled out of the undergrowth, his hand out searching for support to steady himself, but the branches and saplings bent under his weight and left him staggering. His skin and uniform were grey, dusted with a powder, motes of which swirled about him in the air as he moved.

"I recognise him," said Walker straining his neck as he peered into the gloom. "It's Lieutenant Mathers, the tank commander." He lowered his rifle and stepped forward "Are you all right, sir?"

Mathers lurched forward as if concussed and suffering from commotional shock, his mouth moving as he tried to speak.

Walker and Mitchell dashed to help him. "It's all right, sir, we've got you."

Mathers looked up at them. They could see, now, his eyes were rimed with grey powder.

Mitchell saw a gaping hole in Mathers head, filled with something soft and spongy extruding from the shattered cranial cavity. Not brain. He'd seen men with their brains hanging out, and this very definitely was not that.

Mathers' mouth still moved, as though he were trying to dislodge some obstruction in his throat.

"Here, corp, I don't think 'e's well."

Walker slapped him on the back to see if it would help. Clouds of powder billowed into the air. Walker and Mitchell coughed thick phlegmy coughs as they inhaled it, drawing it deep into their lungs.

Hardiman backed away. "That ain't dust, it's growing on him. Look. He's covered with it."

A network of fine grey filaments had spread across Mathers' pallid skin and uniform, like a gauzy shroud.

Walker and Mitchell's coughing fit dissolved into desperate asthmatic gasps as they clawed at their throats, eyes wide with panic.

Mathers stepped clumsily toward the others, his mouth opening and closing like a goldfish, as something swelled inside it. There was a soft pop and a cloud of spores exploded from his mouth, enveloping the soldiers.

They tried very hard to scream.

CHAPTER TEN

"A Fear That is Weird and Grim..."

THE AIR OF the Croatoan Crater was humid and thick with cloying scents and the heady smell of decay. Under her coveralls, Nellie's skin was slick with sweat as they moved through the jungle, following Napoo in Indian file.

"Wherever Alfie is, he can't be far. Why, this crater can't be more than a mile wide," she said, more to convince herself than anything.

"If he's still alive," said Norman, avoiding her gaze.

Nellie's eyes narrowed. "Of course he is. He must be." But there was a note of uncertainty in her voice.

A string of muffled cracks reached them through the jungle foliage.

Reggie cocked his head. "Is that gunfire?"

Norman listened for a moment. "No," he said dismissively. "That's them whip things up in the trees, is that. Gave me a heart attack first time I heard them. Thought we were being sniped at."

They pushed on, ignoring the faint firework crackle. Cecil approached Nellie, barely able look her in the eye as he mumbled, "I got scratched," and held out the back of his hand to her.

She suppressed a smile. When she took his hand to inspect it, his face flushed with embarrassment. She cleaned it, bandaged it and packed him off to rejoin the others.

"If the rest of them get cuts or scratches, tell them to see me immediately," she said.

Cecil nodded dumbly and hurried off to lose himself in male company.

Over the next few hours, Reggie and Wally came to her individually with cuts, grazes and sheepish glances. Cecil regarded them jealously. Nellie knew the smallest cut on this world could lead to Lord knows what kind of infection. She patched them up from her dwindling medical supplies and they were pathetically grateful for her ministrations. Without their commander, without their petrol fruit juice, without the *Ivanhoe*, they seemed a little less than themselves. A little lost.

As Napoo followed the trail, the jungle folded in on itself, forming a living labyrinth, as if to protect itself against the parasitic creepers that spread everywhere and sought to engulf it.

They threaded their way through the labyrinthine alleys of giant trees, buttress roots and tangled undergrowth, sharing them with things that scuttled and oozed briefly across their path. In there, the air was close and stale.

They eased gingerly between groves of giant thorns where the high pitched whines of insects made them flinch and duck just as much as any whizz-bang or Hun bullet.

"Reminds me of moving up communications trenches to the front," said Jack without a trace of irony.

Here, however, the revetments reached to the sky. The sunlight, such as it was, came in momentary shafts of light, or glittering chinks in the leafy cover high above.

Even used to the cramped space in the *Ivanhoe*, the jungle was getting to some of them. Their petrol-fruit madness may have faded, but there remained a lingering paranoia. That could be a healthy thing on a world where everything was out to get you, but it didn't do much for your peace of mind. Cecil whimpered, his eyes darting about in terror.

Jack laid a large hand on his shoulder, offering comfort, but even that made him jump. "Easy, lad."

Napoo led them on between the trees and thickets, following a seemingly invisible trail, at times clambering over huge boughs or ducking under trailing creepers until, eventually, crawling through a spiny bower, they came to the end of the labyrinth and stepped out into open jungle.

A slight breeze rippled through the undergrowth.

"Fresh air!" declared Reggie with the manner of someone stepping off a train at a country station. He mopped his face with a handkerchief and puffed out his cheeks, before taking off his turtle helmet to wipe his balding head.

A rushing gurgle through the trees told of a river nearby, its cold current sucking the air towards it. They headed down towards the sound over damp rocks. The air felt cool and refreshing against Nellie's clammy skin.

Cecil cried out and tugged at the sleeve of Jack's coveralls. Jack turned.

Standing behind them was a figure both familiar and horrifying.

Jack frowned at the apparition. "Lieutenant Mathers?"

The others stopped their scrambling and looked back, drawn by the impossibility of its existence.

Bewildered, Reggie lost his footing and slipped on his backside.

"It can't be."

Mathers was covered with a fine cobweb of grey filaments. The hole in his head bulged with some sort of soft, grey puckered growth. His left arm had begun to lose its form as man and uniform were being absorbed by the malevolent mould.

Wally, stepped forward, hand extended. "Lieutenant?"

Norman pulled him back. "Wally, don't."

"But it's the Sub!"

"No, no it isn't. Look, man."

The figure moved its mouth as if trying to speak, or draw breath. It stumbled towards them, clumsily, its arms outstretched to counterbalance its awkward leaden gait.

Nellie stood transfixed, as from its mouth a spongy growth began to swell. Stretching the jaw open unnaturally, it emerged obscenely from between grey cracked lips.

Cecil fired his Enfield twice, hitting the mouldering cadaver in the arm and chest. Plumes of dust puffed from the dry wounds. It reeled with the bullets' momentum, but continued towards them.

Filaments, questing mycelia, spread out from Mathers' feet towards them. The threads probed outwards, creating an expanding carpet of living fibres.

This was no longer Mathers. His cadaver was merely a host, ambulated by whatever foreign fungus now possessed him, seeking nothing more than to reproduce and spread its spore. If they succumbed to it, their fate would be that of Mathers himself, and right now that thought horrified Nellie more than anything else she could imagine.

"Back!" called Napoo, dragging Nellie away. "Back! It is Dulgur. Evil spirit!"

She stumbled away, unable to tear her gaze from it as the fruiting pod extruding from Mathers' mouth continued to swell, its puckered skin now taut and shiny. As Mathers lumbered towards them, the pod burst, like a puffball, ejecting a cloud of spores.

The tank crew backed away from the drifting spore cloud, tripping over roots and dragging each other in an effort to remain out of its reach. Even as the breeze snatched the spores away from them, other pods were fruiting across Mathers' body.

"Keep away from it!" yelled Nellie.

Mathers advanced, his lumbering steps pulling the spreading filaments behind him, like a bridal train, a counterbalance to his unsteady gait.

Norman fumbled in his haversack, pulled out a Mills bomb and slipped a finger through the ring of the safety pin. Jack's powerful hand closed round his.

"Don't. If it goes off it'll scatter that stuff and put us all in more danger."

Fire wouldn't work for the same reason, spreading what spores survived on currents of hot air. There didn't seem to be anything they could do to stop it that wouldn't make the situation worse. Nellie felt a nauseous wave of panic rise like bile.

Then she heard the rushing susurrus in the background.

"The river," she ordered, in a tone that brooked no dissent.

Wally and the others didn't need telling twice. She was startled at how readily they obeyed her.

Their hobnailed boots slipped and skidded on exposed roots and rocks, damp and slick with reddish algae as they headed down toward the sound of rushing water.

Mathers followed at a plodding but relentless pace.

Nellie could feel the moisture in the air and the greasy wet stones beneath her feet. Flat, wet leaves slapped against her face as she raced on to the river's edge.

She was brought to an abrupt halt as Jack thrust out an arm to stop her. She looked down. Another step and she would have tumbled headlong into the river. Half-hidden by foliage, the rocks dropped away into the torrent.

Powered by the waterfalls that plunged into the crater, the river rushed past below, foaming and tumbling as it roiled over smooth, waterworn rocks.

"It's too fast and deep to cross," called Norman above the water's roar. "We're trapped."

Nellie looked around. Humid spray hung in the air, a rainbow struggling to materialise within it. It would dampen the spores, stick them down. It gave them a fighting chance.

"We have to get it into the river!" she yelled.

They hunted round for anything they might use. Jack pulled experimentally at a thick green branch growing across the path. He hauled it back to the side of the trail and let it go. It sprang back into the path with a satisfying whip. He grunted with satisfaction.

Norman pulled a long length of fibrous creeper from the undergrowth. Unspoken, a plan materialised.

Mathers, his grey dusty pallor glistening with a dew of condensation, came on, step by jerky step, having built up a stumbling momentum, a fruit pod swelling and ripening on his gnarled arm, like a blister.

Jack watched it from the shadows of the undergrowth, his muscles aching, his teeth clamped together as he held back the supple branch. "Come on, you bastard, hurry up," he hissed.

Wally stepped out of the undergrowth by the river's edge just long enough to shout, "Oi, Sub!"

Jack watched as Mathers turned his head and took a step past him towards the sound, another spore pod fruiting from his mouth.

Jack let the branch loose. It whipped forward, hitting Mathers in the small of the back with enough force to wind an ordinary man. Mathers stumbled forward. Reggie and Napoo, hidden either side of the trail, pulled the length of creeper taut, catching him just above his calf-length boots.

Mathers toppled forward, but there was nothing for him to catch hold of. Arms flailing, he tumbled forwards through the thin foliage and down into the raging torrent below.

The spores were instantly drowned by spumes of water as the current carried him spinning slowly out from the bank, the train of filaments billowing out around him like some obscene Ophelia. His mouth opened and closed, one arm raised above the water as he was swept along into the white water rush.

Nellie hurried along the bank, following his progress until she reached a rocky promontory. Below them, the water tumbled recklessly over a lip, not into some pool but into a huge crack in the rock, a fault in the ground that swallowed the torrent whole; she could hear its roar echo as it fell away into blackness. She watched with a mixture of pity and horror as the figure of Mathers, half-lost in the churning waters, rushed over the edge and into the yawning dark.

The men took it hard, losing Mathers again, and it was all Nellie could do to chivvy them on as Napoo picked up the trail of Alfie's abductor.

* * *

MOTES OF GREY mould danced in the air as spore-rimed eyes followed their movement.

With an unsteady, barely coordinated gait, the fungus-ambulated things that had been Corporal Talbot and his party set off in slow, inexorable pursuit as a filigree of mycelia spread across the ground at their feet.

SERGEANT DIXON LOOKED up at the canyon wall. He was less than impressed with the results of the demolition blast. It had cleared perhaps another twenty feet of scree, exposing only more wall of the same featureless metal. Not a scratch, not a dent. No sign of a hatch or window.

He scrambled up to inspect his handiwork with Lambert and stood at the base of the wall. The newly exposed metal was the same colour, same smooth texture. Whatever this stuff was, it was like nothing he'd ever seen before.

They could blast all week, but he suspected the result would be the same, even if they cleared all the scree.

"We could try knocking," suggested Lambert.

"What do you think we just bloody did, private?" said Dixon curtly, surveying the scattered scree and newly-exposed metal. "Where's the Iddy Umpty bloke?"

Lambert fetched Buckley to the top of the scree, loaded down under the weight of several wooden boxes and haversacks.

"You're next on the bill. Show us what you can do, lad."

Buckley produced two copper plates each about a foot square, connected by wires to a listening set in one of the boxes. Normally they'd bury the plates in the ground to listen for German telephone communications, but now he set the plates against the metal wall.

"I need quiet," he said.

Dixon glared at him, took in a lungful of air until Buckley thought he'd pop the buttons on his tunic and bellowed, "Quiet!"

The order found itself repeated several times as it echoed off the canyon walls. Below them, the men stopped what they were doing and stood in silence.

"Quiet enough for you?"

Buckley smiled weakly. "Much obliged, Sarn't."

He put the earphones on his head and his forehead creased as he strained to listen...

News of the armistice between the Pennines and the chatts who'd plagued them for the last four months spread, and the air of relief in the trenches was palpable. Jubilation broke out in spontaneous displays of bonhomie as the soldiers celebrated in their own meagre ways; rousing choruses of *When this Bloody War is Over,* the more generous breaking out what little luxuries they had managed to save; tins of Ticklers – once despised, now prized – some shared their last hoarded gaspers, passing each one out as far as it would go, every inhalation so cherished and savoured they might have been the best cigars from the most exclusive gentlemen's club.

Even Sister Fenton, as stern and taciturn as she was, cracked a smile, so her patients claimed.

Impelled by his newly-remembered vision, Padre Rand anxiously made his way through the trenches looking for Lieutenant Tulliver. It was frustrating, therefore, to find himself stopped and congratulated every other fire bay or so; his shoulder patted, his back slapped and his hand shaken, even though he protested with all modesty that really he'd had nothing to do with the current situation and had merely been an observer. But they would have none of it and he was forced to bury his impatience deep down, for in their faces he saw the respite from their tribulations that he had long prayed for and took comfort in it. How might his vision shape their future? If it came true, could he shepherd them back to the Promised Land that was England?

The Padre eventually found the pilot in the Command Post with Lieutenant Palmer, sharing what they called mock coffee. It was hot, brown and came from some sort of bean, which was about all it had in common.

Tulliver raised his tin mug in salute, as he entered.

"The man of the hour," said the young pilot.

The Padre shrugged it off with a brief smile. "The Lord works in mysterious ways, Lieutenant. I believe you're due out on another reconnaissance flight."

"That's right, Padre, up with the angels. Want me to put in a word for you?"

The Padre smiled. "That won't be necessary. I want to accompany you. I need to get my report to Lieutenant Everson. There are things he needs to know. I'm sure he'd want to be apprised of the situation on the chatt front."

Tulliver drained his tin mug and put it down. "Well, I've no doubt you can patter out the prayers, and God knows a spare few might come in handy, but how good are you with a machine gun? There's something up there, and it's hunting me. I need someone who can watch my back."

"I've done a little hunting in my time," the Chaplain said. "I really must insist, Lieutenant. I don't want to have to take it up with a higher authority." He glanced at Palmer.

"I think you'll find I'm the highest authority round here," said Tulliver, tapping the RFC patch on his breast, a wry smile playing round his lips.

"Mine is a little higher, I think," retorted the Padre.

Tulliver glanced at his dog collar and grinned. "Touché, Padre," he said, scraping his chair back and standing up. "Very well. I'll be wing, you be prayer. Because God knows, we'll probably need both."

THE SOPWITH 1½ Strutter climbed away from the trenches.

Wearing a leather flying helmet and goggles and an army warm he'd borrowed from Lieutenant Palmer, the Padre –

who had never been up in an aeroplane before – experienced the exhilarating terror of take-off and marvelled as the world fell away and he saw the landscape spread out below him. He briefly wondered if this was the view that God had of the world, before remembering with a flush of shame that this wasn't God's world. It wasn't their world. It was no man's world. He turned around to look out across the veldt towards the great forest in the distance where he knew Khungarr lay, and took a last look at the small island of humanity dug in on its circle of Somme mud. How tiny and frail it looked. And how all the more remarkable it was for that. The experience would have been quite serene, were it not for the loud, determined roar of the engine and the fine spray of lubricating oil, hazing both pilot and passenger.

Tulliver banked the aeroplane and they flew beyond the hills sheltering the camp towards the plateau and the scar running across it that was the canyon. The two sections of Fusiliers waved as Tulliver and the Padre flew over. Tulliver waggled his wings in response. He pointed down over the side of the plane. The Padre peered over nervously. A bright glint momentarily blinded him as the sun caught the metal wall.

THE AEROPLANE DRONED on out over the Fractured Plain. Tulliver was constantly vigilant for landmarks. This was one. On a world where compasses didn't work – the damn thing just spun in circles – landmarks were vitally important to flying.

Thirty minutes later and he could make out the Croatoan Crater in the distance. He flew low over the surrounding forest, the whipperwills snapping away from the canopy, and suddenly there it was, the sunken world.

He'd judged his approach perfectly. The discoloured strip of vegetation in the crater aligned. In fact, from a landmark point of view, it was as good as a compass. It pointed perfectly towards the plateau and the canyon with its metal mystery.

He banked round and found the ruins of the ancient edifice and clearing where he'd left the tank crew and where the rescue party should be camped. But he could see neither.

He came round again, lower. He noticed one of the battlepillars grazing idly and he knew it by the crude roundel daubed on its side. He made out scorch marks on the earth, and small craters left by grenades. Here and there were dead bodies in khaki, one being torn at by a pack of small creatures. A battle, then. One that didn't go well for the Pennines, by the look of things.

He came round again and let off a burst with his forward machine gun, the line of bullets stitching the ground. The creatures scattered back into the forest.

What had happened here? First the tank was lost, and then the party sent to salvage it, and Lieutenant Everson along with it. Had it been chatts? He had to head back to camp and inform the others that the rescue party had been lost.

He pulled up and caught sight of a small shadow rippling over the face of a mountainous cloud. Was that the creature that had been shadowing him like a hungry shark, or just a phantom, a fleeting shift of cloud? He wanted to be sure.

He pulled back on the stick and climbed up into the canyons between the clouds, looking for his elusive prey. He glanced back. The Padre had turned round and was gripping the Scarff-ring-mounted machine gun as if his life depended on it, which it very probably did.

He'd played games of hide-and-seek like this for fun in the French skies over Fine Villas, and with altogether more deadly intent over Hunland. He flew through bottomless passes and towering white rifts. Ragged wisps of cloud blew past like minute-old Archie, but there was no sight of his nemesis. It could, of course, be hiding inside the clouds. That was always a possibility. But he wasn't tempted to look.

He heard the abrupt chatter of the rear machine gun and turned to look over his shoulder. The Padre pointed up and behind the aeroplane. Tulliver banked to get a better look.

Jabberwocks, fiercely territorial flying raptors with long necks, wings like a stingray and razor sharp talons and teeth, had spotted his bus and seen it as potential prey. They could shred the Sopwith, with its wooden frame and doped canvas, in a minute.

Tulliver pulled the nose up sharply. The world dropped away as the bus climbed. The jabberwocks pursued tenaciously, but their raucous cries were soon lost and they fell away, seeking easier quarry.

Tulliver pushed the bus higher. The air up here was cold and clear. Flocks of cloud lay below them, like grazing sheep. He'd never flown at this altitude here before; twelve thousand feet, close to the bus's operational ceiling. He looked down at the ground and felt that delicious thrill of flight, of being this high with nothing between you and the ground but the wooden seat you sat on.

And then he frowned. What the hell? What was that? He tried to rub his goggles clean of their mist of oil then, frustrated, pushed them up. He felt the altitude's cold bite into the exposed skin and the sting in his eyes. He had to squint against the cold, the air speed and the oil.

From this altitude, things always took on a different perspective, a bigger picture. The patchwork of fields over Kent, say, or the blasted pockmarked landscape of the Somme. But he'd never seen anything like this. What the hell was that? Below them, the landscape was–

The engine spluttered. He adjusted the throttle and the mixture, but it coughed and died anyway. There was a brief silence and then the weight of the nose pulled the plane down into a dive. The wind began to shriek through the wires.

The Sopwith started to corkscrew as Tulliver struggled with the stick. He had to pull out of the spin, level it out. If he didn't, the speed would rip the wings off and they'd fall the rest of the way in a folded mess of wood and wire.

Slowly he regained control of the aeroplane and brought it down in a long slow spiral, losing height and speed. The whole thing left him shaking and exhausted. He tried the engine again, but it coughed and spluttered, reluctant to catch.

"If you've got a good prayer, Padre, now's the time!" he yelled as he tried to restart the engine again.

He began looking for a place to land. Two thousand feet, now. Over to his left he could see the crater several miles away. The landscape below was filled with forest, with here and there little oases of meadow and heathland offering hope of a safe landing, but he was still too high and too fast.

Ahead loomed a towering hill of earth that Tulliver recognised as a chatt edifice, like that of Khungarr. Unfortunately, the large managed clearing around it was also now the nearest landing space. After what had happened to the salvage party, it wasn't his preferred course of action, but there was no choice.

The engine caught. It coughed and spluttered, one of the cylinders missing intermittently, but with life enough for Tulliver to control his descent over the tree tops into the clearing. It was a bouncy landing and even before they had stopped, chatt scentirrii were racing toward the Sopwith in their curious springing gait. By the time they had taxied to a stop and Tulliver had switched the engine off, they were surrounded.

Ignoring the agitated chatts, Tulliver sat in a state of utter funk, still shaking, his heart pounding, and tried to compose himself. That had been a bloody close thing. No need to let the Padre know, though. He pulled off his helmet, goggles and scarf, and left them in the cockpit as he climbed out.

"Sorry about that, Padre," he said brightly as he helped the pale-faced chaplain clamber shakily from the aeroplane.

"I think we have other more pressing concerns now," said the Padre, eyeing the nervous-looking chatts that had now ringed the aeroplane, armed with spears and electric lances.

"Really? Right, then." Tulliver turned and addressed the suspicious chatts. "Take us to your chieftain," he said in a loud, slow voice. He turned to the nearest chatt. "And make sure you take damn good care of my bus, or there'll be hell to pay."

If it knew what he was saying, it gave no sign.

As they stepped away from the Sopwith, the chatts closed in about them. Tulliver put his hand down and checked the reassuring weight of the Webley in his waist band under his tunic before allowing himself and the Padre to be escorted into the edifice.

They were conducted through dark passages illuminated with niches of luminescent lichen. One of the scentirrii exhaled on the barbed circular plant door and it shrivelled open.

"I've seen places like this before," said the Padre quietly. "It's a gaol chamber."

"Ah," said Tulliver, and then he scowled. "I thought I told them to take us to their chieftain."

They were ushered through the dilated doorway. The barbs around the rim of the contracted plant looked like fangs around an orifice – he had seen too many ugly things on this world to call it a mouth. Once inside, the door cycled shut.

They stood inside while their eyes adjusted. There was no luminous lichen here.

"Tulliver?"

It was a voice the pilot knew and often resented, but he was more than happy to hear it now. "Everson!"

"What the bloody hell are you doing here?" said Everson, stepping forward. "And more to the point, what the hell are you doing bringing the Padre?"

"That was my idea, Lieutenant. I twisted his arm, as it were."

"Well that was a bloody stupid thing to do, Padre, if you don't mind my saying." His voice softened. "I trust your mission was a success, then."

"Yes," said the Padre. "Although as to the exact nature of the armistice, that will be down to you and Chandar to negotiate."

Everson gestured at the earthen wall of the chamber. "Well, looking at the sterling job I've been doing here, we'll be in for a rough ride, then." He changed the topic. "How did you–"

"We were forced down, Lieutenant," said the Padre, patting Tulliver on the shoulder "Took some skilful flying to find somewhere to put us down in one piece."

Tulliver shrugged. It was actually a brilliant piece of flying, even if he did think so himself.

"What happened to you?" the Padre asked.

"Ambush," replied Everson. "They seemed to know we were coming." There was a shuffling and the odd cough in the gloom behind him. "Corporal Atkins and the men from his section are here, along with Hepton and Jenkins, Tonkins and Riley from Signals. The others are in chambers nearby. We can shout. Well we could, until the chatts got wise and got one of their dhuyumirrii to douse them with that benediction of theirs. We've not heard a peep for hours."

"So what next?"

The door began to dilate open again.

"I think we're about to find out," said Everson.

EVERSON, TULLIVER, THE Padre, Hepton, Atkins and his section were escorted under guard up a spiralling inclined tunnel that led them up into the heights of the edifice. They came to a large plant door, with scentirrii guards either side.

"About bloody time," murmured Everson. "Now maybe we'll get some answers."

The guards turned and breathed on the door in unison. It shrank away from their breath and opened.

Everson and his men were ushered into an airy chamber. Light came through a large window at the far end.

Silhouetted against the light was the figure of a man. He was standing by the window looking out over the unfamiliar forest landscape, his hands clasped behind his back, master of all he surveyed. This was no urman. This man was at ease in his surroundings, in control of them. This man wielded power, but what kind of man could wield power in a chatt edifice?

Everson made out the familiar outline of a fitted tunic and fitted calf-length boots.

An officer.

He must have known they had entered, yet still chose to stand there. There was only one officer he knew audacious enough to do something of this kind, one man who had the absolutely bloody gumption to treat them like this and expect to get away with it.

Jeffries.

Jeffries, wanted for the double murder of two debutantes back in Blighty. Jeffries, the infamous diabolist. Jeffries, the man who claimed he was responsible for bringing the Pennines here with some black magic ritual, using the Somme as a blood sacrifice. Jeffries, who had almost set them to war against the Khungarrii the moment they arrived. And a man for whom they had been searching for the past four months in pursuit of a way home.

Everson snorted with derision as anger boiled up within him.

The man turned.

"Gentlemen, welcome."

CHAPTER ELEVEN

"He Shook Hands with Britannia..."

IT WASN'T JEFFRIES. "I have been waiting for this meeting for such a long time. It's good to see some familiar faces. Well, I say faces," said the stranger with a dismissive wave of his hand. "I mean uniforms. I don't suppose you have any cigarettes? I would kill for a cigarette."

Atkins felt his fingernails bite into his palms as he clenched his fists in frustration. He could almost weep at the injustice of it. For a brief moment when he saw the silhouetted figure, hope burned bright hot and white within him, like a star shell illuminating No Man's Land and casting shifting pools of light on the darkest parts of himself, parts he would rather remain hidden beyond the barbed wire of his conscience.

When he and Everson faced Jeffries down in the Khungarrii edifice before he escaped and vanished, Jeffries claimed they couldn't kill him as he was the only one who could return them to Earth.

Earth. Just the mere thought of the word was enough to make his eyes sting with tears. Not because of Earth itself, but for what it held. Flora. His love, his shame. Seven months pregnant with his child, by his reckoning. Although that wasn't why he was ashamed. He loved her. She had been his brother William's fiancée. But William had gone missing on the Somme. His betrayal wasn't just of William, but their families, and God knows, every bloody soldier in Kitchener's Army. He was the man they all despised, the unknown man who'd take their sweethearts while they were at the front. "*You were with the wenches, while we were in the trenches facing an angry foe...*" That was how the song went. He'd sung it in the dugout enough times, and each recitation twisted the knife more.

The thought of her made his very being ache at their parting. His one driving thought was to return to her, to do by right by her, to make up for all the wrong he had done.

But it wasn't Jeffries. He had wanted it to be true, but then he would have to face the possibility that Jeffries might have lied. He was terrified the truth would leave them marooned on this world forever, like the Bleeker party. Those twin urges, wanting to find Jeffries and *not* wanting to find him, kept his hope alive.

It wasn't Jeffries. And some small part of him was relieved.

"AND JUST WHO the hell are you?" asked Everson, angry for letting himself be duped, if only for a moment.

The man stepped away from the glare of the window and into the chamber. Two stately red-surcoated Chatts stepped out of the shadows to attend him, their antennae waving in agitation at the Tommies' arrival. The man, however, seemed quite at ease with their presence.

Everson could see him clearly now. He, too, wore a uniform. It was grey.

"How is this possible?" wondered the Padre in hushed tones.

Everson shook his head.

"Jesus!" muttered Gutsy in astonishment. "It's a bleedin' Hun."

"A bloody Alleyman, here?" said Mercy, shaking his head. "And I thought we had the worst of it with Jeffries. Aren't we ever to be rid of the bastards?"

The Alleyman ignored them, addressing himself to the officers. He had a proud bearing, born of Teutonic aristocracy. His uniform was immaculate. His hair was black and slicked into a centre parting, and he had a peculiar little bow of a mouth that gave him a petulant look. He clicked his heels together. "My name is Oberleutnant Karl Werner, late of the Jasta Bueller." He held out a hand.

"You're a German pilot." Tulliver's eyes lit up and he shook the hand enthusiastically. "Lieutenant James Tulliver, 70 Squadron." Then he studied his host, somewhat aggrieved. "And, if I'm not wrong, I shot you down when we first arrived here."

The German laughed and clapped his hands on the top of Tulliver's arms. "Yes. Yes, you did." He smiled broadly. "You're a good shot," he said. "But not too good, I think. As you can see, I am still here."

The silent chatts observed the polite introductions intently. Their antennae waved as they communicated with each other using senses beyond the ability of the Tommies to understand. Everson found himself unnerved by their scrutiny.

Reluctantly, Everson put out his hand and introduced himself. "Lieutenant Everson, acting commander of the 13th Battalion of the Pennine Fusiliers. Your English is very good."

Werner shook his hand. "My aunt married an Englishman. He has a leather goods business in Suffolk. I used to stay there. Before the war."

"This is Padre Rand, our chaplain."

Werner nodded and shook his hand, "A pleasure, Father."

Padre Rand returned a polite smile. "I must say, you're the last person we expected to find here."

Everson turned and indicated the Fusiliers behind him.

"And this is Lance Corporal Atkins and his Black Hand Gang."

Werner's glance swept up and down the NCO, unimpressed. "Yes, I did ask to see the officers only, but obviously the *insekt menschen* can't tell you apart. Never mind; you're here now, Corporal."

"Bloody cheek," muttered Mercy.

Pot Shot rolled his eyes. "Officers, same the world over."

One of the flanking chatts spoke in its peculiar breathless, halting way. "What is Black Hand Gang?"

Werner pursed his lips as he searched for an appropriate term that they would understand. "I suppose you would say 'dark scentirrii'," he suggested, looking to Everson for confirmation.

Everson nodded irritably.

The chatt seemed satisfied and resumed its silent conversation.

Atkins felt a knot tighten in his stomach, and shot an accusing glance at Pot Shot. The lanky Fusilier's eyes widened and he spread his hands in protest.

Hepton pushed his way forward, an obsequious grin on his face, and grasped Werner's hand in both of his without being offered.

"Oliver Hepton," he said, pumping the pilot's hand. "Official War Office kinematographer, at your service. Pleased to meet you, Oberleutnant. What a moment! If only I had my camera."

"A photographer?" Werner pulled Hepton to one side. "You have a camera? Equipment?"

"Well I did until your chatts took it from me after they captured us," replied Hepton. "I hope it's being taken care of, that's all. It's very expensive." This last remark was addressed rather loudly at the uncomprehending chatts.

"My what?"

"Chatts. It's what the men called these insects. Chatts, after the lice that infected their uniforms in the trenches. Lice? Pop, pop, pop?"

"Ah, yes. Tommy humour, no? We must talk more."

Hepton beamed in triumph.

He was interrupted by Everson, irritated at Hepton's derailing of the conversation. "Look, this isn't getting us anywhere. What do you intend to do with us, Oberleutnant?" he demanded.

Hepton scowled but kept his eye on Werner.

The German took a deep breath and smiled at them, the expansive genial host. "All in good time, Lieutenant. All in good time. You're the first human company I've had in a long while. I'd like to savour it. Can we not converse as gentlemen? Perhaps your men are hungry."

He turned to the two inscrutable chatts and mimed eating. Moments later, several chatt nymphs with translucent carapaces came through from adjacent chambers, carrying gourds and platters.

Mercy leant over and whispered loudly to his mates. "So how come we're still living in trenches and he's living it up like a bleedin' lord? There's no fucking justice in the world."

"Have I not been telling you that?" said Pot Shot wryly.

There were no tables in the chamber. Mercy was considerably less impressed when the nymphs poured the contents into two long chest-high troughs set into the curved walls of the chamber, one of water, the other now containing some kind of sloppy fungus.

Gazette watched the chatt servants retire from the chamber, his sniper's eye mentally fixing them in his sights.

"Please, don't stand on ceremony. Help yourselves," said Werner to the Fusiliers. "It is *insekt futter*, foul stuff, but nutritious nonetheless. I'm sure you've eaten worse in the trenches."

Atkins glared at the Hun and then at the troughs. "No thanks to your lot – and never like animals."

Werner laughed, amused. "It's how these creatures eat," he explained, throwing off the accusation. "They don't use crockery and cutlery. They don't even use their hands. They eat directly with their mouth parts. They have the manners of pigs, these *insekt menschen*. Have you seen them eat? They slice with their mandibles and scoop it straight into their mouths with their – what do you call them?" he put the back of his hand to his lips and waggled his fingers.

"Palps," said Everson.

"Ah. Palps, then. Yes."

Everson gave a weary nod to Atkins, dismissing him, while the officers continued their conversation at the other side of the chamber.

The men went over to the troughs. They were at an awkward height, too high to eat from comfortably, even if they felt like it.

"A Hun," said Tonkins in awe, as they huddled round the troughs, glad to have some space away from the officers. "I've never actually met a Hun before."

"Never met a live one, you mean," said Riley.

Gutsy grumbled. "Just let me at the Bosche bastard."

"Keep your voice down," said Atkins. He picked absent-mindedly at the fungus, but kept his eyes on the officers across the chamber. "What the hell was all that about dark scentirrii?"

"Ignore it," said Pot Shot. "It doesn't mean anything."

Atkins wasn't so sure. He remembered Mathers' prophecy, and tried to dismiss the unwanted implications.

"What do you think they're talking about?" asked Riley, watching the officers.

"A way out of here, with a bit of luck," said Mercy, through a mouth full of half-masticated fungus. He looked up to see Gazette staring at him. "What?"

"God, doesn't anything put you off eating?" asked Gazette.

"Gutsy's farts?" Mercy shot back, spraying him with a soggy shrapnel of fungus. "Besides, do you know when we're going to get another meal?"

It was this attitude, of getting what you could where you could, that made Mercy such a useful asset to the section, not to mention the platoon, but in this case, Gazette was prepared to make an exception.

"Suit yourself," said Mercy.

EVERSON HAD BEGUN to tire of the social niceties. "What are you going to do with us, Werner?" he asked.

Werner looked affronted. "Me, Lieutenant? Nothing." He waved a hand at the two chatt attendants. "My hosts merely extended me the privilege of a little company. After all, I did let them know you were coming."

"You told them about us?" repeated Everson.

"Of course. They might have killed you all otherwise. After the unique manner of my arrival, the *insekt menschen* were on the look out for more like me. I told them of your existence and I told them you were coming. What are you even doing out here, Lieutenant, so far from your nice cosy trenches?"

"We lost... something. In the crater," said Everson. Ironclads were still supposed to be secret; tankers often referred to themselves as the Hush Hush Crowd, such was the clandestine nature of their training. However far they were away from Earth, Werner was still a Hun, and he didn't want to give any information to him that might profit the enemy.

Werner looked rueful. "Ah, the crater. Then I'm afraid it is gone for good. The *insekt menschen* are very zealous. They do not allow anything out of the crater and they certainly do not let anything in. They believe it is an evil place. When they knew you were headed towards it, they became very agitated, hence their attacking you like that. You were looking for some lost men, I think?"

"Yes," said Everson, warily. "Have you met a man calling himself Jeffries? An English officer."

Werner tapped his lips with a finger, frowned and shook his head. "I think I would have remembered an officer."

"You'd have certainly remembered him," Everson admitted with a grimace.

"What about soldiers?" asked the Padre.

Werner shrugged. "The *insekt menschen* have brought in one or two patrols, or deserters, maybe? I had to question them, see if they were useful. But to be honest, even if they were, the treatment of the *urmenschen* they keep as slaves here is brutal. I wouldn't hold out much hope for them, Lieutenant."

Werner shuffled uncomfortably, noticing black looks from the men by the troughs.

"There was nothing I could do," he said diffidently.

"So that's why we're here," said Everson, scarcely able to maintain an even tone, nodding towards the inscrutable chatts watching them silently. "So you could tell them if we're useful or not?"

There was an embarrassed silence.

"And what will you tell them?" asked Everson bitterly.

Werner lowered his head. "I regret, Lieutenant, that I cannot save you."

"Cannot, or will not?" he demanded. "Surely you can't side with these chatts against us? We're human."

Werner shook his head, heaved a sigh and corrected him. "You're British, Lieutenant," he said. "These *insekt menschen* may be uncivilised, but they do understand the nature of a territorial dispute. I told them you were my enemy when they found me. Your battalion is your downfall. These creatures see your numbers as a threat to their territory and resources."

"So you're working with them?"

"Don't be so high and mighty, Lieutenant," said Werner with disdain. "You had your battalion. I was on my own. These creatures saved my life. They raised me above the *urmenschen* that cling so desperately to existence here, and I agreed to help them. They are searching for something. I merely offered my services."

"As what?"

"A Luftstreitkräfte."

Werner ushered them out onto a balcony beyond the window. Looking down, Tulliver noted that the urmen shanty town that existed on the slopes of the Khungarrii edifice didn't exist here. The edifice was fortified, as if they expected a siege. Below, he saw a large courtyard, still under construction, judging by the chatts scurrying over the partially built walls. There within it, tethered, patched and inflated, was a silver-grey German kite balloon.

Tulliver remembered seeing one when they first arrived on this world, its winch line severed the moment they vanished from Earth. He had a vague memory of it drifting off when they appeared here. He'd thought nothing of it at the time, having an Albatros to deal with, and a world of strangeness since then.

"They might not understand our flying machines, but it didn't take long for them to grasp the principle of the balloon. Even now they are constructing their own."

"For what purpose?" asked Everson. "Are they at war?"

"In a manner of speaking. I told you they fear the crater. To them it represents some great evil, and they seek to arm themselves against it. They see the balloon as a useful instrument in their eternal vigilance. They stand guard at the edge of the crater like the angels at the gates of Eden, no, Padre?" he said, turning to the chaplain.

Before the Padre could reply, they were interrupted by a creaking sound and the fibrous door to the chamber shrank open. Werner's disappointment was evident. Even more so when two armed scentirrii stepped through. Four more waited outside. "No," he protested to his attendants. "They've only just arrived."

"Come," ordered the scentirrii. It waited for a moment then repeated the command, belching the word out. They were a lot less articulate than the Khungarrii. The scentirrii motioned towards the door with their spears, while guards outside wore clay battery packs and held electric lances similar in design to those of the Khungarrii.

"Come." It hissed again, raising itself up on its legs threateningly.

"Food was lousy anyway," muttered Mercy, spitting a half-chewed gobbet at Werner's feet as they passed. "Hope it chokes you."

Werner wore a look of pained exasperation.

Everson was still trying to finish his conversation with Werner, glean what further intelligence he could. "What happened to them, to the men they captured, damn it?"

Werner shook his head and waved his hand dismissively. "I do not know, but I'm very much afraid you will find out."

"No. Not me, I can be helpful," cried Hepton desperately, as a scentirrii prodded him with a spear.

Atkins looked at him with disgust. When another scentirrii manhandled him, he took the opportunity to accidentally plant his elbow into Hepton's solar plexus.

Hepton doubled over, winded, struggling to draw breath as he glared at Atkins through watering eyes.

"Sorry, Hepton," said Atkins.

A scentirrii attempted to seize Tulliver by the arm.

Werner stepped forward. "No, he stays," he said, appealing to his two chatt attendants. "He stays. He flies – like me." He stuck his arms out like wings and mimed flying, as you might to a child.

The scentirrii waved its antennae towards the chatt attendants, then shoved Tulliver out of the pack toward him, causing the flying officer to stumble.

"Hey!" Tulliver brought his arm back, preparing to swing for the chatts.

As the others were being herded out of the chamber, Everson stepped forward, appearing to help Tulliver, although it was more to gently restrain him from fighting back.

"No," he said in a low voice, looking over Tulliver's shoulder to where Werner stood. "Stay here. Find out what you can. And if you get a chance, escape. Get back to camp, let them know what's happened."

Tulliver's eyes flashed at the chatt that stood over them, but he nodded imperceptibly. He stood up and swept back his fringe as Everson allowed himself to be taken from the chamber with the others.

WERNER CLAPPED TULLIVER on the shoulder. "Don't worry, my friend. They'll be taken back to their cell," he said. "But come. We have so much to talk about, you and I."

At first Tulliver had been elated to find another flyer, someone who understood what it was like to be up there. He'd longed to talk shop, as if he were back in the officer's mess, but now the feeling had soured.

"I should very much like to see your machine. A Sopwith 1½ Strutter. Yes? With synchronised gears for your forward machine gun. You finally caught up with us."

"Maybe I'll take you for a spin," said Tulliver bitterly.

They moved round the chamber, unconsciously circling each other as if they were two thousand feet over the Somme, looking for the advantage. The chatt attendants watched, conferring with each other.

Tulliver looked up with a dawning realisation. "Your aeroplane," he said. "It still flies, doesn't it?"

Werner's broad smile was all the answer the pilot needed. It hadn't been his imagination. There *had* been something up there. Not a creature at all. It had been Werner keeping an eye on him all this time. He must be a damn good pilot.

"Yes. I have been watching your progress for months," admitted Werner. "Flying high over your trenches, catching glimpses between the clouds. And I shadowed you of course, discreetly. Tell me, with your squadron, did you ever play hide-and-seek in the clouds?"

Tulliver knew the game well. Every flyer did. It was good practice for dog fighting. "You're not too good at it," said Tulliver. "You became careless."

Werner shook his head. "Careless? No. I got lonely. I think part of me wanted to be spotted."

He wandered back to the window, and stepped out onto the balcony beyond, beckoning Tulliver to join him

It was easy to believe, standing high on the side of the Zohtakarrii edifice and looking out over the forests and the plains beyond, that you were Master of the World. It felt like you were flying, until you looked down.

"Magnificent view, isn't it?" said Werner with a sigh. But he wasn't looking at the landscape. He was looking up. "A whole new sky, new horizons." For a moment he seemed lost in melancholy. When he spoke again, he had recovered his bravado. "My Albatros is far superior in speed and performance to your heavy Sopwith, Tulliver. Had I not been so disorientated when we appeared here, then the story might have been very different, no?" He mimed planes with his hands, his right swooping up under his left, towards its palm, illustrating some manoeuvre. "I think you took advantage of the situation, my friend. After you shot me down, Herr Tulliver, I barely managed to pull out of the spin and make a safe landing.

"At first I was furious. I couldn't understand what had happened. Can you imagine my amazement to find that I was no longer in France? Yes, what am I saying? Of course you can. But you had men and defences at your disposal. I was a downed airman in a foreign land." He made a sweeping gesture at the forest surrounding them. "A foreign *world*.

"A patrol of *insekt menschen* found me. They saved my life and I repaid them with the only thing I had to offer."

"Your Albatros."

"They had never seen a flying machine before. They were amazed. And they have been able to produce a passable petrol substitute. Not long after, they found the kite balloon and I was able to direct their repair of it. They have done a fine job, do you not think?"

"It's hardly an air force, old chum," said Tulliver. "If that's what you promised them, then they're in for a surprise."

Werner turned and appealed to the pilot. "Ah, but they have constructed their own; and now they have your machine, too."

"Maybe, but they don't have me," said Tulliver.

"Pity. I should have liked to fly with you."

"You could leave them at any time," challenged Tulliver. "Why stay?"

"Why does the falcon not leave the falconer? Certainly I may leave, Lieutenant, but where to, and to what? I have seen you in your trenches. I have watched your vain attempts to tame this planet, watched your little huts go up, seen you grub fields and grow crops. And I have seen it all ruined. Here at least, I am safe. Here, I am–"

"Kaiser?"

Werner clucked his tongue in reprimand. "Able to fly. Able to fly, Tulliver! And I have flown high and far." He lowered his voice and stepped closer. "And I have seen things, Tulliver, up there where the air is thin and cold. There is a mystery to this planet." Werner stepped back and examined Tulliver's face. "You have seen it also, I think, have you not? It is what the *insekt menschen* search for. You and I might be the only people on this world to have seen it."

"Seen what?" asked Tulliver. He remembered his own brief glimpse of the world spread out below him, before his engine cut out.

"Marks. Marks on the landscape. Intersecting lines, miles long." He waved a hand towards the watching chatts. "You can tell them this, you can confirm what I have seen."

Tulliver wasn't sure what he had seen, it had been so brief, but his reaction now was one of scepticism. Markings on a geographical scale? And then he was struck by a thought. Wasn't that how Jeffries was supposed to have performed his Somme ritual, within a pentagram scored across the front lines by artillery fire? Tulliver should know. It was he who unknowingly took Jeffries up artillery spotting for it. He'd just been another anonymous spotter at the time.

Tulliver shook his head "I'm not sure what I saw. It was only for a brief moment. I couldn't confirm anything."

"The *insekt menschen* are searching for proof of their god's existence. I think I might have seen it. They believe it created this world for them, and that its mark upon it might be visible. The Albatros is only a single-seater. I cannot show them what I have seen. I have been trying to use a camera salvaged from the observation balloon, along with a number of unexposed plates, but I can't develop them."

"Then why on earth did you take them?"

"I thought perhaps someday..." He waved a hand. "That's why I need your help. You are the answer to my prayers, Tulliver. You can verify my findings." Werner paused, searching Tulliver's face. "You don't believe me." Werner shook his head. "You should see for yourself."

"Why, what was it, what did you see?" urged Tulliver.

"Fly with me. I will show you."

Tulliver was almost taken in by his earnest plea. "Free my friends and I'll consider it."

"I can't do that."

"Those are my terms. You have influence with these chatts. Let the Fusiliers go free and I'll help."

Werner's whole posture sagged. "It is not possible."

"Why?"

"Because they are earmarked for the pits!" he declared. "They're dead. If you won't help me, then perhaps your kinematographer, what was his name, Hepton. Perhaps he will help. He seemed very eager to save his own life. If you care so little about yours, you can join your friends!"

That was when Tulliver saw the truth. Across the side of the edifice, all the other balconies were scentirrii watch posts. He glanced back into the chamber. This wasn't a private chamber with its own balcony, like some hotel in Paris. It was unadorned and functional. The chatts weren't his attendants, they were his gaolers. This chamber was as much a cell as the one Everson had been kept in.

Tulliver's eyes narrowed with suspicion. "The chatts didn't save your life, did they? They spared it. In return for what? What do you owe these creatures?" he asked.

"Nothing," said Werner. But his face told a different story. The mask of geniality and charm had slipped to reveal someone who had been playing a game for far too long and had grown weary.

"But I am afraid, Tulliver. If I am right, then this world is a hell like no other, and no human god created this place."

INTERLUDE 3

Letter from Lance Corporal Thomas Atkins to Flora Mullins

5th April 1917

My Dearest Flora,

Today I spotted someone I thought knew. It would have been nice to catch up again, but it wasn't them. Still, maybe we'll meet up somewhere down the line. I remember bumping into William once down the reserve lines, when he was stacking artillery shells and I was on a ration party. We both had to do a double take.

We haven't made it to the tank yet (story of my life, that). We made some new friends along the way though, and took a bit of a detour. Still, I suppose we are still getting to see quite a bit of the local countryside, and at least we've got a roof over our heads for a while.

However, as Pot Shot will keep harping on, someone will have to pay the piper soon, so expect us to have to sing for our supper. They won't get much of a song for it though, because the food is nothing to write home about, so I won't. That never seems to stop Mercy. He'll eat anything (and he did). You should have seen Gutsy's eyes light up when he found out. "In that case, I've got some nice calves' trotters and scrag end of mutton I could sell you!" says he. What larks.

Ever yours
Thomas.

CHAPTER TWELVE

"Keep Your Head Down, Fusilier..."

ALFIE HAD HEARD estaminet tales about the poor buggers found guilty of desertion and sentenced by court-martial to death by firing squad.

He had a mate who had stood guard with one on their last night. 'Prisoner's friend.' Filthy job, he said. You needed a heart of stone. Young, he was, too; barely nineteen. Only been at the Front for a month before he funked it. But he wouldn't sleep. Couldn't sleep, probably. The lad's moods would swing wildly. Sometimes he'd sit with quiet resignation, constantly asking the time, for they all knew that when dawn came he was to be shot. Other times he wept and cried and wailed and begged and pleaded, every shred of dignity gone, dissolved in streams of tears and snot. In the end they got him drunk. So drunk, as it happened, that he could barely stand the next morning when they led him out to the firing squad. They literally had to drag him. When they tied him to the post, blindfolded him and pinned the white rag over his heart, he'd pissed himself.

Then again, half the firing squad were more than a little squiffy themselves, having been given tots of rum to stiffen their resolve. Didn't do much for their aim though, his mate said. Sergeant had to come over and finish the bugger off with his revolver.

Sat here in the dark of the urman hut, the pain in his leg flaring and a great knot of anxiety and terror churning in his belly, Alfie knew how the poor sod felt. He could feel the vomit burn up his throat, but he swallowed it again. He wouldn't give them the satisfaction of knowing he was afraid.

The urmen were going to kill him. They'd said as much. He was to be sent to converse with their dead or some such. Bit of a one-way conversation, he thought.

He never reckoned he'd end his days as a ritual sacrifice, even if that was what Jeffries had planned for them with his diabolic battlefield rite back at Harcourt Wood. Funny, he thought. Perhaps that's all they'd been all along; sacrifices. The top brass seemed willing to sacrifice everyone on the altar of Victory for a few hundred yards of muddy corpse-ridden field. Ah, the good old days. He let out a bitter laugh. Jesus, who'd have thought he'd be longing to be back on the Somme.

His thoughts turned to Nellie Abbott. He smiled to himself, but it was wistful, full of regret for the time they would never spend together. He thought of her out there, with the others. At least she'd be safe. Oh, bloody hell, what was he thinking? She didn't just sit still. She'd come halfway across the planet to find him before. What on Earth made him think she'd stop now? He didn't know who to feel sorry for most: him here without her, or his crewmates with her cajoling and barracking them into action.

But what the hell could he do? How far did he think he could get with a broken leg, even if he did escape?

Ranaman entered the hut with Tarak, interrupting his thoughts. "The time of Croatoan's Torment approaches," the clan chief said. "We must ease his suffering with your passage."

Alfie pushed himself back up against the wall, and his broken leg protested with another burning jolt of pain. He clenched his teeth and sucked air in through them, hard. Not because of what Ranaman had said, but what the urman was holding. It was a rifle. No, not a rifle; an old-fashioned musket.

"Where did you get that?" he asked in spite of himself.

"It is a holy relic. It is the Key. Our ancestors said it opens the door to the underworld."

"Well that's one way of bloody putting it," said Alfie under his breath.

He brandished the ancient firearm at Alfie, who flinched, half expecting it to go off, until he realised that Ranaman was holding it all wrong. He was holding it like a swagger stick, something with which to point. His finger was nowhere near the trigger.

Besides, Alfie found himself thinking, wasn't sacrificing done with a special sacred knife or something? What did they do, cut your heart out and hold it aloft, still beating, dripping with hot blood?

All of a sudden, a firing squad didn't seem that bad.

He determined to look for any opportunity to escape. At least then, if he were going to die, it would be on his own terms.

But no, if he did, the boy Tarak would pay the price. There had to be another way. If there was, though, he couldn't see it.

Ranaman nodded and Tarak took Alfie's arm, pulling him up without concern for his beside manner, or the suffering of his patient. Alfie sucked down the pain again as the young urman put Alfie's arm over his shoulders and helped him out of the hut.

He stepped outside into a small stockade settlement of wooden huts, flanked by Ranaman and Tarak, and a collective gasp arose from the rest of the clan as they saw their sky-being. They stood around swaying gently and muttering chants and litanies under their breaths, or making signs. They were elated. A litter stood adorned with great fragrant blooms.

He'd seen scenes like this several times, with the rest of the *Ivanhoe* crew dressed in their raincapes and chainmail splash masks, pretending to be priests, servants of Skarra the dung-beetle god of the underworld, as they tricked gullible urmen clans. He'd always had a bad feeling then, but he'd never expected to bear the full brunt of their come-uppance. That just wasn't bloody fair.

What Alfie wouldn't give for Norman and one of his music-hall magic tricks, or for the *Ivanhoe* to come crashing through the undergrowth like a wrathful god.

As the rest of the clan watched, eyes wide in awe at the sky-being, Tarak helped him onto the litter. This was his doing. He was responsible for bringing this fortune upon the clan. The pride was evident in the young urman's face.

"For me? You shouldn't have," said a resentful Alfie.

Four urmen picked the litter up to a great shout from the rest of the clan.

"So," said Alfie, though clenched teeth and pain. "Where are you taking me?"

"To Croatoan's Heart," said Tarak, as if that explained everything.

"Right," he said, none the wiser.

Holding his useless musket aloft, like an army band major, Ranaman led the procession out of the stockaded village. Two urmen with burning torches joined him. Behind them came urmen with metal-tipped spears and metal swords, then Alfie in his litter, while the rest of the clan fell in at the rear, blowing horns and banging hollow gourds.

The urmen in front chanted as Ranaman led them along a narrow, but well-worn path. Tarak walked proudly beside the litter, where every misstep of the litter bearers transmitted itself to Alfie's broken leg, amplifying every jolt and jar.

"Oi, take it easy," he berated the litter bearers. "Bloody hell, I got a smoother ride in the *Ivanhoe,* and that was with bleedin' Wally driving!" Another jolt of pain seared up his leg. "Jeeeesus!"

The urmen with spears cut their way through the writhing lianas crossing their path. Great fleshy plant pitchers turned as they passed, as if watching them.

Tarak pointed above the trees ahead of them, where a tall minaret pierced the sky. "There. The Heart of Croatoan," he said, proudly.

"Great." Alfie smiled weakly, his mind racing, as every jar and jolt of the litter carried him nearer to his death. If he closed his eyes, he could see Nellie standing, feet astride, hand on hips, scolding him. *"Alfie Perkins, don't you dare sit there and accept your own death. You've got a brain. Use it."*

There had to be a way out that would save him and the lad.

The procession filed into a clearing, dominated by an ancient domed building, from the centre of which rose the minaret, a hundred feet into the air. Worn and weathered, the building had seen better days and had fallen into some disrepair. It had been built from clay brick, which lay exposed where the painted clay daub had crumbled away. Only a few stubborn patches remained. Around its circumference, small, regularly-spaced, unglazed windows were set into it; like loopholes, Alfie thought.

The men carrying his litter placed it on the ground and Tarak hauled Alfie to his feet.

Ranaman's warriors unbarred the great wooden door, while urmen holding torches entered ahead of the chieftain, their chants echoing round the space within.

Tarak held onto Alfie's arm tightly, as if aware that his life depended on him. Alfie tugged it experimentally. The youth did not look at him, but his grip tightened, perhaps fearing Alfie was about to fall, or escape.

Ranaman reappeared and approached the pair. He placed a paternal hand on Tarak's shoulder and spoke to Alfie.

"You fell, as Croatoan once did. It is a powerful omen. Today you will talk with our dead. And from you we will learn their will."

Alfie blanched. How would they do that, exactly? Through some sort of divination? Perhaps it wasn't his still-beating heart they were after; maybe it was his entrails. Alfie felt his stomach lurch. The day just gets better and better, he thought.

They escorted him inside. It was gloomy and bare, lit by a circle of flaming sconces. At the centre of the domed temple, beneath the minaret, was a boulder the height of a man, a fracture down its middle cracking it in twain. There was enough space between the two halves that a man might walk between them. This was the Heart of Croatoan, Alfie assumed. A broken heart, as Ranaman had told him.

Alfie's heart felt like breaking, too. It was beating hard, loud, and far too fast in his chest. He could feel its pulsing echoes in his neck, his leg and his ears. He could feel panic tightening its grip on him, but it was a fear he knew. It was an old friend to a soldier.

The clan filed into the temple behind him, moving out around the edge of the space, encircling the broken rock in the centre, their shadows dancing on the floor beneath flickering sconces.

His chances of taking them on and getting out of there alive were slim now. Even Alfie could see that. Nonetheless, he strained his ears, hoping to catch the clanking rumble of the *Ivanhoe*, but heard nothing.

Just him, then.

Damn.

Two urmen stepped forward and took him from Tarak. The lad smiled at him as they took his arms and began to drag him towards the fractured rock. He cried out in pain, but his agony was lost in the rhythmic chants echoing around him. Shafts of light from the minaret focused on the rock, like spotlights on a Zeppelin.

He struggled to look back over his shoulder at Tarak who, not comprehending his situation, looked on proudly, his chest falling and rising as he joined in with the chant.

Ranaman waited for him in the space between the rocks.

"No, wait..." said Alfie, seeing reddish stains on the surface of the boulders, thinking they were signs of previous sacrifices. Then he realised the rocks, the Heart of Croatoan, were composed of iron. This must have been where they got their knives and spearheads. The lad Tarak thought the ironclad *Ivanhoe* was the same thing. Another sky rock. Alfie groaned. Hoisted by his own petard.

Ranaman walked between the two halves to the back of the temple. Two warriors held Alfie by the arms, his back to the rock. He couldn't see what Ranaman was doing. He had a sudden urge, a need to know. He tried to twist his head to see over his shoulder, but all he could see was the rock.

Panicking now, Alfie was turned round so he was facing the narrow gap between the rocks. As he was turned, he caught sight of Tarak watching with a fierce pride. The flanking warriors took Alfie's arms and held one hand on each half of the shattered boulder.

Ranaman returned through the cleft towards him, carrying a large ornately carved wooden box; the kind, Alfie thought grimly, that you would keep a ceremonial dagger in.

The chanting rose to a crescendo and then ceased.

"The time has come," Ranaman called out.

He opened the box and Alfie steeled himself for death.

GAZETTE HAD HIS ear to the wall of the gaol chamber by the door. Denied the use of his keen sniper's eye, he'd resorted to his hearing. He'd had his ear there for a while and his greasy ear prints stained the gritty hardened earth of the wall. "They're taking another lot," he said.

The others rushed to the wall of the chamber, pressing their own ears to the hardened earth.

Everson heard sounds of scuffles and angry protestations as scentirrii dragged other Fusiliers from their chamber.

"Get your hands off me, you filthy chatt!"

"Knocker, no!"

There was a charged crackle, a stunned groan and a heavy thump.

"You bastards!" yelled Mercy, thumping the side of his fist against the wall.

The Tommies vented their anger with shouts and threats, but at length turned despondently from the wall, as the Padre offered up an Our Father, the quiet liturgical tone calming them. Porgy and Tonkins joined in quietly.

Everson looked around at them. If there was any bunch worth being stuck with, it was Corporal Atkins and his Black Hand Gang. They'd had more experience of this planet than most others had and were still alive to tell the tale, which gave them the edge.

Right here, right now, they could do nothing but wait. Wait for the right moment, the right opportunity to act.

They had examined the cell from top to bottom. There was no air vent through which they could escape. The only light came from the garde l'eau in the floor that projected out over the wall of the edifice. Even if they could enlarge the hole, there was a hundred-foot drop to the ground.

The living plant door was cultivated for the purpose by the chatts. Barbed thorns covered its surface, its roots bedded deep in the walls round the chamber's circular opening. They knew from experience in Khungarr that it could fire its barbs in defence. There was no hiding place within the round bare chamber from them.

To pass the time, the Padre telled away at his Rosary in a Morse code of *Hail Marys* and *Our Fathers*, like a spiritual Iddy Umpty man seeking Divine orders from HQ.

Hepton, sensing the hostility from the rank and file, had removed himself and sat across from the men, from where he shot them the morose glances of a beaten cur.

Riley kept up a cheery disposition, keeping young Tonkins' mind occupied with a series of trench anecdotes.

Gutsy picked his teeth with the point of a sharpened lucifer he had saved for just this purpose. There seemed to be nothing else to do in the gaol chamber.

"Pity we haven't got that pet chatt of yours, Only," he said as he winkled out a nub of chewed fungus and flicked it toward Hepton, who glared at him. "He could have talked to them for us."

"He was never my pet," said Atkins with more bitterness than he meant. "And I don't think it works that way. These

Khungarrii and Zohtakarrii, they're like rival colonies or something. Like Britain and Germany."

"And we're in Germany?" said Porgy, trying to get his head round the analogy.

"Ain't that just our bloody luck?" chipped in Porgy. "And a bloody Jerry in charge, too."

"Bugger me if that's wasn't a turn-up for the books. Makes you wonder who else is wandering about out there."

The door puckered and shrivelled as it opened. The Fusiliers stood, tensed, fists clenching, glancing from each other to their NCO and officer for the order.

Two scentirrii armed with electric lances stepped through the door, with four more outside, scotching that idea. Everson shook his head and indicated with a hand down by his hip that they should stand down. They were ready for a fight, but with the release of an alarm scent, the whole population of the edifice would come down on them. Now wasn't the time.

Werner walked through the door.

"What do you want, Fritz?" rumbled Gutsy, slapping a meaty fist into the palm of his other hand.

"Private." Everson's rebuke stilled the stocky butcher, but his eyes still burned with contempt.

Werner waved the insult away with a magnanimity he could well afford.

Everson greeted him curtly, the same question on his own mind. "Well, Oberleutnant?"

"Nothing from you I'm afraid, Lieutenant. I wish to speak to your kinematographer."

"Me?" said Hepton warily, adjusting his glasses on his nose and risking a shufti at the Fusiliers.

"Yes, it appeared you were worried about your equipment."

Hepton glanced cautiously at Everson, who just scowled.

Hepton stepped forward hesitantly, expecting a trick.

"Yes. Is it all right?"

"As far as I know. There is, however, something you can do to secure its continued safety."

That caught Hepton's interest. "Yes?"

"You see, I need your expertise, Herr...?"

"Hepton. Oliver Hepton."

"Herr Hepton, I need you to help to develop some photographic plates."

"Plates?" Hepton looked from Werner to Everson.

Everson watched the exchange impassively. Hepton was an odd cove. On the one hand, the man was a coward and a cad. On the other, he was prepared to take the most outrageous risks to get his precious moving pictures. The canisters of undeveloped kine film he carried around, of the Pennines on this world, were his fortune. If they got back to Earth, they would make him tremendously rich. He needed them. He also needed Everson and his men to keep him alive until then. But Hepton was a survivor. He hedged his bets and covered his arse. His only loyalty was to self-preservation, and now was no exception.

Hepton turned to Everson and tapped his nose. "Don't worry; I'll keep my eyes peeled. See what I can find out," he said in a conspiratorial whisper loud enough for those Fusiliers nearby to hear.

He didn't fool Everson. Still, the chances were that Hepton would procure some information as security against his own survival. That might prove useful.

Hepton didn't wait for Everson's permission but stepped forward to join Werner, who nodded curtly at Everson before turning and leaving the chamber. Hepton followed, looking back as he stepped through the door to give a shrug and sheepish grin, as if to say, 'What else can I do?'

"Be seeing you – Kamerad," growled Gutsy.

Hepton looked away with a guilty start as he followed Werner from the gaol chamber.

The Scentirrii retreated and the plant door shut again.

"The jammy bastard," was all Pot Shot could say.

* * *

Tulliver was dismayed to see Werner return with Hepton. The kinematographer sauntered into the chamber with the air of one whose fortune had turned at the expense of others and who didn't care.

"Lieutenant!" Hepton said brightly when they met again. "It seems I have a commission." He clapped his hands and rubbed his palms together. "Shall we get started?" He turned to Werner. "Where is my equipment? You said it was safe."

"It is being held by their apothecaries," said Werner.

An escort of scentirrii took them up an inclined passage to the higher reaches of the edifice. A faint thrumming sounded through the passages as the ventilation system sucked fresh air deep into the core of the colony.

Despite his revulsion at the situation, Tulliver felt a rising sense of expectation. He was, he hated to admit, intrigued by Werner's mystery. Perhaps, he reasoned, there were bigger things at stake here than political enmity.

The scentirrii brought them to a small, unassuming chamber. They ushered them inside, going no further themselves. Werner strode past them with all the confidence of one who has rights and access.

Beyond was a succession of further chambers, occupied, Tulliver found, by a different class of chatts. These had plainer, pallid carapaces, as though they had never left the dark recesses of the edifice. They wore plain white silken tabards that almost touched the floor. Each wore a small pouch at its hip, slung across its thorax by silken rope. They were clearly akin to the dhuyumirrii caste of the Khungarrii.

There was a groan of despair from Hepton, as he spotted his precious equipment in the corner of one chamber. He dashed over and fell upon it, with all the fear and relief of someone inspecting a child for injuries after an accident, checking the camera box, his tripod, his haversack of film canisters, wincing at each scuff and scratch.

He pulled out a wooden box from a haversack and swore under his breath. The brown glass bottles that had contained the remains of his photography fluids had cracked and one had shattered completely. The chemicals had drained away, staining the wood. There was precious little remaining. Certainly not enough to develop anything. Hepton sat back on his heels, crestfallen, sure his fate would now be to join the rest of the Fusiliers below.

"It's cracked. There's nothing left," he rasped. "Not a drop."

"Let me see," said Werner brusquely. He took a bottle from him, held it up to the faint lichen light and peered through the brown glass. It was empty apart from a residue at the bottom. He unstopped the bottle and wrinkled his nose, recoiling from the lingering acrid smell of the chemicals.

Hepton flinched. "It – it's not my fault. You can't blame me. We were attacked by your chatts." His voice trailed away.

Tulliver caught sight of the chatts, who stood regarding them, as they themselves might watch ants. He had been in the officers' pow-wows and briefings about the Khungarrii. There was no reason to believe these Zohtakarrii were much different.

"If *we* can smell it," he said, nodding towards them, "then what could *they* do?" He strode toward them, belligerently. "Here," said Tulliver, holding out the bottle toward one of them.

The chatt inclined its head in a questioning manner.

"Smell this. Can you make more? You know, more?"

The creature looked to Werner, who nodded his assent.

It hissed, reached out a long-fingered hand and took the cracked glass bottle with some reluctance, as if the act were beneath it, as if Tulliver had spoken out of place and dared to call their skill and sacred calling into question.

The chatt returned to its fellows and, holding the cracked bottle with its precious residue, they gathered round it, like Macbeth's witches, their heads bowed, their segmented antennae waving gently over the opening.

They were like the alchemists of old, thought Tulliver. Although their main occupation was the protection and interpretation of the sacred scents and prophetic perfumes, they could turn their skills to other things. After all, they had manufactured a fuel for Werner and his aeroplane. Developing fluid shouldn't be beyond them.

The chatts withdrew from the chamber and Werner followed. He beckoned Tulliver and Hepton. "Come."

In chambers beyond lay endless niches of stone jars and amphorae filling the walls, each containing scents and odours, elements and compounds, the contents of which Tulliver couldn't even begin to guess at, arranged by some system he could not comprehend.

Ranks of similar chatts worked on unfathomable tasks at rows of solid clay tables rising from the floor.

"It's like a scriptorium," whispered Werner. "Medieval monks making illuminated manuscripts, but with odours, aromas and scents."

The three chatts approached another, standing at a clay lectern, like a chief clerk or overseer. There was a brief consultation. The bottle produced much agitated waving of antennae and, in a disconcerting moment, all four turned their heads in unison to glance at the three men.

The clerk went over to the wall of the chamber, summoning an acolyte nymph with a few judicious clicks and hisses. The creature returned to the niches and carefully selected various amphorae, jars and pots.

The men had nothing to do but wait nervously as the chatts attempted to concoct an ersatz developing fluid.

Then they would see if it worked.

THE CHATTS CAME for the Fusiliers several hours later.

The plant door dilated open. The moment it did, the men were up on their feet. This was it. They had come for them as they had come for the others before.

A moment's luck, to a soldier on the front line, could be a matter of life and death. They all had their good luck rituals, however idiosyncratic. Gutsy quickly kissed his lucky rabbit's foot. Porgy had a collection of girls' keepsake photographs, his 'deck of cards'. He quickly selected one to be today's lucky Queen of Hearts and put her in his top pocket. Atkins' was no more ridiculous than most. He pulled out his last letter from Flora. For better or worse, he had come to believe that if he could still smell the perfume on the last letter she sent, he would be safe, and it had worked. Now the letter was months old and her perfume had faded. Mathers, with his petrol-fruit-enhanced senses, was the last to smell it. With a heavy heart, he slipped the fragile letter back into his tunic as the scentirrii herded them down the passage, past gaol cells once occupied by men of the rescue platoon, now ominously open and empty.

CHAPTER THIRTEEN

"Our Little Hour..."

UNARMED, APART FROM contemptuous glances and an anger that bristled like the scentirrii spears around them, the Fusiliers found themselves marched like POWs along a passage that spiralled down into the subterranean depths of the edifice.

"Another long bloody walk," Porgy muttered.

"It's not going to be Fritz machine guns and barbed wire at the other end, though, is it?" said an indignant Mercy.

Atkins took the feeling of fear expanding in his belly and, by a controlled application of hate, compressed it into a small hardened ball of dull nausea, as he had done many times going over the top to advance across No Man's Land.

The passage took them down into the bowels of the edifice, and Atkins became aware of a soft roar building on the persistent low hum of the air currents, beyond the Padre's muttered Rosary.

Gazette had heard it, too. "Sounds like a carpet slipper bastard."

It didn't make any of them feel easier. As they continued their descent, it rose to a crescendo, punctuated with a clashing rhythm of carapaces, a rhythm that they had heard before, albeit to a Khungarrii beat.

The scentirrii guards stopped and ushered them into a side passage off the main incline. It was dark and small, and they had to go Indian file, the scentirrii bringing up the rear.

"Anyone else feel like we're going up the commo?" said Gazette.

Nobody answered. They didn't have to. That's exactly what it felt like; the long march from the reserve area up to the front line along the shallow, narrow zigzag of the communications trenches. Each man retreated into his own world, his own private space, preparing himself as best he could for whatever was to come.

Atkins thought of Flora. Denied his usual ritual of the letter, he plucked a memory to savour, as Porgy might select one of his photograph cards; that last night, the memory of Flora naked in the firelight, in her front parlour, her skin suffused with a rose gold glow, her saintly smile full of wonder. He froze the moment, before the smile slipped and welling tears distorted the scene, before the memory of William tainted it. He couldn't have one without the other. The memories were entwined.

They emerged from the cramped dark tunnel into another chamber. Once in, Atkins heard a creak and turned to see a barbed plant door contract shut. There was no way back. There was only one other exit from the chamber. It was in front of them and another barbed plant door blocked that, too.

There, piled on the floor were their confiscated weapons; webbing, haversacks, gas hood bags, steel helmets, rifles, bayonets, Mills bombs, trench clubs and even Everson's sword, along with the kitbags containing the modified electric lance packs and Riley's Signals gear.

Atkins and the others looked to Everson.

"Arm yourselves. Take everything you can. I've a feeling we won't be coming back this way," he said.

The men set about putting on webbing and packs, a sense of anxiety and foreboding building as they did so, ameliorated by small personal victories. Gazette was reunited with his sniper's rifle. Gutsy found his meat cleaver; he picked up the instrument and hefted it, comforted by the familiar weight in his hand.

He took the startled and frightened young Jenkins under his wing, checking his equipment and webbing. "Stick to me like glue, lad. You'll be fine."

Jenkins tried to force a smile through his fear and only partially succeeded.

Everson found and holstered his Webley and picked up his sword.

By the time they had readied themselves, there was not much left on the floor; a bayonet, the odd battle bowler and several pieces of webbing lay unclaimed.

Mercy went through the webbing pockets pulling out spare ammunition and the odd grenade and redistributing them.

By the time they were fully and correctly attired, they felt whole again, each item adding a little to their fortitude.

When they were ready, Everson instinctively looked at his wristwatch. "Stand by," he said, for no other reason than habit. Whatever they were about to face, they were as ready for it as they would ever be.

Atkins felt he could almost be back in the trenches, staring at the hated ladders, waiting for zero hour. He stood by the living door, through which they could hear chanting and carapace-beating. It began to recoil and open, shrivelling back towards the walls of the circular opening.

A breeze blew down the tunnel towards them, carrying on it the sound of massed chatts... and something else: the smell of blood and shit and cordite.

For a few seconds, the men hesitated, though not from any sense of wind-up or funk. Atkins and the others turned their eyes to Everson, who stepped forward to the van. If they were going to go 'over the top,' they would go when he gave the order and not before.

Instinctively, Everson put his whistle to his lips and blew. Holding his sword and drawing his pistol, he began to walk down the tunnel and his men followed.

* * *

In the canyon, Sergeant Dixon balanced on a block of unstable scree and glared at the ruddy-faced Buckley, hunched over his precious wooden box of tricks by the metal wall, a hand cupped over one of the earphones clamped to his head.

They had tried repeatedly, at different times of the day, with the same result. Dixon shifted his weight. The rocks clattered under his feet.

Buckley turned and shot him a dirty look. "Shhh."

Dixon glowered but bit his tongue.

The signalman finally pulled the earphones down around his neck, looked up at Dixon and shook his head.

"I've not heard a peep, Sarn't. But maybe that just means they're not doing anything the equipment can pick up."

"Is there anything else we can do?"

"Well, I could try sending a telegraph. If there's anybody inside listening, they might pick it up. Unless you have any better ideas, Sarn't."

He couldn't see the point of trying, but Lieutenant Everson would want a full report on his return. It wasn't as if they had anything better to do. The mystery of the wall was fast beginning to lose its allure.

Dixon frowned. "No, I haven't. I just blow stuff up. Frankly, if I can't bomb it, mine it or call a barrage down on it I'm at a loose end, and any more cheek from you and I'll have your name."

Buckley looked up at the Sergeant, unsure if that was an order or not.

"Well hop to it lad, hop to it," said Dixon impatiently. "We haven't got all day."

That, though, was exactly what they did have, so Buckley busied himself connecting up a field telegraph to the wall and began tapping on the Morse key.

Everson and his men walked warily from darkness into twilit gloom, until the tunnel opened out into a deep trench leading out in to a large arena. It was surrounded by a wall some twelve feet high, beyond which were stands of chatts, mostly scentirrii. So large was the space that, unlike any chatt chambers they had seen, it needed columns and buttresses to support the roof.

At the sight of the Tommies in the mouth of the tunnel, the carapace-beating from the assembled chatts quickened aggressively. On the wall above, chatts armed with electric lances urged the soldiers out into the killing space.

The spectating chatts grew quiet with anticipation.

The bodies of Fusiliers and Karnos lay strewn about the arena, twisted and broken. Rifles lay scattered and discarded, along with several limbs, and shallow blackened grenade craters dimpled the arena floor.

The centre of the arena was dominated by a large striated outcrop of rock thrusting up through the floor at an angle, creating a small incline about twenty feet high with an overhang beneath its peak.

Lieutenant Everson, sword in hand, led the advance into the arena. Atkins, Mercy, Porgy and Gazette spread out in a line either side of him. In a second line, Riley and Tonkins advanced with their kitbags of electric lances and backpacks, flanked by Gutsy and Pot Shot. The Padre was unarmed and while refusing to carry weapons, had loaded himself down with the Signals gear and brought up the rear with Jenkins, the Linseed Lancer, with his small medical knapsack and more Signals gear.

As they headed for the outcrop, they saw, round the other side, the body of a huge pale toad-like beast, larger than an elephant. It lay slumped by the rock, glassy-eyed, its side torn open by shrapnel, its rib cage shattered, allowing its viscera to slop out onto the ground.

As Atkins watched, an urman stepped forth from the bloody cavity, stripped to the waist, covered in encrusted blood and gore. To the accompaniment of hundreds of scissoring mandibles, the warrior hefted the creature's heart above his head and threw it to the ground. Covered as he was with blood and viscera, it was hard to make out details, but Atkins could see that the warrior was bare-chested apart from some sort of harness. Around his neck, he wore a collar hung with small round adornments. The only clothing he wore were trousers tucked into knee-length boots, and he carried two long knives, their straight blades dripping with a dark ichor. He glared up at the watching chatts with contempt as he wiped the knives clean on his trousered thighs before thrusting them into loops hanging at his waist.

"Bloody hell," said Gutsy, aghast. "And I thought I was a butcher."

"We could do with a few men like that," said Pot Shot. "Let's hope he's friendly."

The warrior ignored them and began searching the bodies of the dead Fusiliers nearby.

"Oi, mate, fuck off!" warned Gazette, lifting his rifle and sighting him as they edged towards the outcrop.

Crouching over the body, the bloodied warrior turned his blood-grimed face towards the Fusiliers, white teeth clenched in a snarl as he glared at them with undisguised contempt. He continued to search the dead man, going through his pockets and webbing, extracting a paybook, bullets and a grenade, before ripping the identity disc from his neck, like a trophy.

Atkins' brow furrowed. Despite the warrior's savage appearance, there was a familiarity to the man's actions, and Atkins saw with growing horror that he had been wrong. They weren't knee boots. They were puttees. They weren't knives, they were bayonets. It wasn't a harness, it was webbing. This was no savage urman warrior. Dear God in heaven, this man was a Fusilier.

ABOVE, IN THE apothecary chambers, Hepton supervised the conversion of a small chamber into a makeshift darkroom. He filtered the diffuse blue-white bioluminescent lichen light by using the large translucent petals of a red flower. A dull amber glow now filled the room.

Chatt acolytes had laid out shallow bark bowls to use as makeshift developing trays on a plain earthen work counter.

Tulliver watched as Werner entered the dark chamber, accompanying a handful of chatt alchemists holding up an amphora, like a Eucharistic sacrament. They were followed by acolyte nymphs bearing a shrine the size of an ammo box. To them this was as much a religious ritual as a chemical reaction.

"Have they done it?" asked Hepton, the dull red glow lending an aptly Faustian cast to his features.

Werner merely shrugged his shoulders. This was out of his hands now.

THE CHATTS CARRIED the portable shrine to one end of the chamber. There, they removed three exposed glass negative plates from within, each held reverently by a nymph. They were about eight inches by five and wrapped in several layers of black silk cloth, like relics. These plates, the chatts believed, would provide physical evidence of the existence of GarSuleth.

"What are they?" asked Hepton.

"Aerial photographs," said Werner. "Taken from fifteen thousand feet."

"And what is it that they think they're supposed to show, exactly?" asked Hepton, a faint but supercilious sneer playing round his mouth.

"That their god created this world."

"Tall order," quipped Tulliver.

"And what happens if it proves nothing of the sort?" pressed Hepton.

"Then we're probably dead men."

The chatts no longer stood before a counter, but an altar. It had become not a darkroom, but a chapel. The senior chatt stood holding the amphora before the counter with its shallow trays. The nymphs approached in procession behind it, each holding its silk-wrapped glass plate like an offering.

"Right, let's do it," said Hepton. "Then I can get out of here." He went to take the amphora, but the chatt reared up on its legs, hissing venomously. Realising he had misjudged the situation, Hepton backed off.

"You must guide them only," said Werner.

Hepton was horrified at the thought. "Guide them? But look at 'em. How can I get proper results – and proper results is what we're after, if we want to live – with those things?"

"You will die if you try to do it yourself, Herr Hepton. It is a heresy. They are quite insistent on that," said Werner.

Hepton curbed his belligerence, but it still simmered beneath the surface as he directed the chatts to pour the sacred 'balm' in the shallow troughs, and then have an acolyte nymph uncover the first plate and place it in the solution.

There was a slight delay when Hepton suggested that they agitate the troughs and swill the liquid over the plate. Well, not so much a delay, Tulliver observed ruefully, as a complete theological debate. Was this merely a task that could be performed by an acolyte, or did the very transformative nature of the ritual require a greater degree of initiation and honour? After all, if this 'ritual' worked, it would make manifest the hidden hand of GarSuleth itself.

By now, Werner had to restrain Hepton to stop him interfering.

"But don't you see? If you leave it too long–"

Tulliver felt just as frustrated.

By the time the chatts had discussed the matter and decided that this was no work for a mere acolyte but an Anointed One, and with Hepton unable to intervene, the plate had been in the fluid too long.

It had turned black.

* * *

The blood-encrusted warrior strode over to the Tommies.

"God damn it, Everson. This is all your fault!" he screamed as he threw out an arm at the bloody aftermath around them. With his other he ripped off the necklace about his neck and thrust it out at the officer accusingly. Hung from it were the collected identity discs of too many dead men.

Shocked, Everson took them and stared at the man, whose face was so streaked with blood and dirt that he couldn't place him immediately. It didn't take him long, though; he hadn't exiled many men. "Rutherford? Dear God, man. What's happened to you?"

Rutherford looked at the officer with disbelief, his rage and invective spent. "*You* happened, sir. You exiled us, sent us out to die, that's what happened. We'd only been out a few days when a Zohtakarrii patrol captured us. Bains, me and the rest of them bought the urmen time to escape. Our uniforms saved us." He shook his head in bewilderment. "They said they were looking for us."

"Werner," Atkins realised.

Everson pressed the point. "The chatts saved you?"

"For this," spat Rutherford as he gestured towards the bloody carnage.

"Where are Bains and the others now?"

"Dead, for all I know, but that's what you wanted, isn't it, sir? You were too cowardly to sentence us to a firing squad, wanted to spare your conscience, did you? Well, just because you didn't order anybody to pull the trigger, doesn't mean you're not responsible for their deaths," he said with rancour.

Everson looked at the filth-encrusted Tommy, sure now of his actions. "This is the mutineer that hit you, Padre," he said sourly.

The Padre studied Rutherford's face. "No, no it isn't, John. He was there. He tried to stop the other fellow."

Everson reeled as if he had been dealt a physical blow. He looked at Rutherford aghast.

"Yes. Wilson. He framed me," said Rutherford simply, as realisation dawned on the officer's face. "I won't lie, I took part, but I wasn't guilty of the crime you punished me for. But that's Army justice for you."

Padre Rand stepped forward. "Son, this is not the time for recrimination–"

"Sir!" yelled Mercy, directing Everson's attention to the far side of the arena, where another gate opened.

"There's no time," said Rutherford. "Prepare yourselves, sir. God knows what the chatt bastards'll send out this time."

All enmity was swept aside in that moment. Survival was all that mattered.

"Make for the rock," ordered Everson. "It's our only defensible position."

The section advanced towards the outcrop, rifles pointed at the opening gate and void beyond.

Atkins deployed his men, using the outcrop as cover. He sent Gazette up the incline to its peak, where they could use his sniper skills. "What the hell is this place?" he asked Rutherford. "Is this their sport, pitting men against monsters?"

"After a fashion," Rutherford said. "They think it their holy calling to protect their world from the spawn that rises from the crater. They bring 'em here, and force urmen to fight against them so they can study the creatures, the better to defend against them in the future."

A high-pitched screech echoed round the arena and Atkins watched, tensed, as a huge squat creature lumbered out of the tunnel behind the open gate. A sulphurous stench accompanied it as it plodded into the ring. Moving on four pairs of short, thick legs, each wreathed in folds of tough leathery skin, it walked with a graceless movement, as if it were completely out of its element. Atkins could see no eyes, but the head bristled with long twitching hairs arrayed around a large maw. Scabrous growths covered its leathery back, and a heavy fanlike tail dragged behind it.

At the sight of the demonic thing, Padre Rand made the sign of the cross and offered up a hasty prayer.

The chatts wrangling the beast took their electric lances to it and it bellowed with pain and rage as they herded it into the centre of the arena.

It looked slow and clumsy, but Atkins didn't let his guard down. Some of the deadliest things on this world barely moved at all. He had no idea what defences this creature might have. None of them did. Neither, it seemed, did the damn chatts, which he supposed was the whole point of the exercise.

"Fire!" barked Everson.

A volley of rifle fire slammed into the creature. It screeched and retreated. The electric lances of the chatts behind it crackled pitilessly, driving it forward again. It bellowed in pain and confusion, its maw opening to reveal a gullet easily big enough to swallow a man and filled with inward-pointing spines.

Everson gazed round at the stands of chatt scentirrii. "They expect us to fight for our lives," he confided to Atkins. "They want us to fight. They've pitched us against this monster to study our strengths and weaknesses, but we're not going to give them the satisfaction."

"Then may I ask what you intend to do?" said Atkins, keeping one eye on the beast as it lumbered round the amphitheatre, snuffling blindly at the dead bodies.

Everson grinned. "Something they won't expect, Corporal. Escape."

The creature charged towards the outcrop with a territorial roar, building up a surprising momentum until, head down, it butted the rock. The outcrop shuddered under the impact.

"If you've got a plan, Lieutenant, I'm all ears."

"We need a diversion. We have to get the wall down, get that thing among the chatts."

"We've got Mills bombs."

"We'll never throw them that far."

From a trouser pocket, Rutherford produced a braided length of rope with a bark cradle. "Sling," he said.

Everson glanced at it. "Good man. Evans, give Rutherford a bomb."

Mercy handed over a Mills bomb from his webbing. "I've used a trench catapult to throw bombs, but a sling? Jesus. Isn't that a little dangerous?"

Rutherford just laughed as he fitted the bomb into the cradle, pulled the pin, whirled it around his head, and then let it fly. It arced up into the darkness and was lost until the wall of the arena exploded in a fireball and the faint whistle of red-hot iron shrapnel. The blast flung chatt bodies into the air, briefly silhouetted against the fireball.

Caught by the blast, a supporting column began to crumble, bringing down a section of the chamber's dome.

The section fired again, this time concentrating their volley to one side of the creature driving it away, towards the rubble-strewn breach. It scrabbled over the debris to escape the gunfire, causing panic among the chatts, their acid spit proving ineffective against the creature's thick hide.

In the confusion, Everson ordered Atkins and the Tommies across the arena towards the beasts' entrance. Going back the way they came would only lead them back into the edifice. Everson reckoned they must get these creatures in here through a dedicated entrance somewhere, without endangering the general population. Perhaps that way lay an exit.

Pot Shot hurled a Mills bomb at the gate. The explosion ripped the toughened gate from its root hinges in a plume of dirt and resinous sawdust.

Atkins and his section walked through the cloud, smoke billowing down the tunnel and swirling round their feet. Bayonets caught the pale blue lichen light as they advanced in trench clearance formation, ingrained in them at the training camps in France. They'd swept through Hun trench systems time after time, and it was reassuring that their training and tactics suited battle in a chatt edifice so well.

This was something they knew how to do, and do well.

* * *

Tulliver's mouth was dry with anxiety as they watched the third and final glass negative plate reverently slipped into the solution by the acolyte, almost as if it was being anointed or baptised. After a second failure the chatts seemed to decide that what the process lacked was prayer and began a clicking, smacking chant, almost as if they were counting: *one elephant, two elephant.*

The air of tension was palpable. Werner rubbed a finger inside the stiff Teutonic collar of his uniform.

Hepton fidgeted impotently as he watched the chatts wash the chemicals over the plate.

"I just wish they'd bloody well let me do it," he whispered. "I just wish–"

An image began to form.

Hepton, in an effort to preserve the image on the plate, stepped forward, only to be warned off by the chatts.

"Wash it!" he said. "Wash it. The other tray!"

The chatts understood and slipped the plate into the other tray to stop the process.

When the chatts saw the image, the chanting stopped. They stepped back in awe, touching the heels of their long-fingered hands to the bases of their antennae and then to their thorax.

"What is that?" Hepton asked, squinting at the negative image that had appeared. The man might be a photographer, but he had no experience in aerial photograph interpretation. The composition was odd, the angle oblique.

"Look. Lines radiating out across the landscape from two central points." Werner was triumphant. "I knew I was right."

Tulliver, too, saw the images he'd glimpsed all too briefly as his bus spiralled down out of control. "You were right, Werner. But what are they? The scale of those things; they're miles long. What does it mean?"

"They are the Threads of GarSuleth," hissed the chatt, beholding its new relic. "Divine proof that this One never thought it would see. These Ones are truly blessed. Our scentures tell us that GarSuleth came down from his Sky Web to spin this world for his Children, the Ones. You have seen them and by GarSuleth's Will have brought us this holy glyph. This is a most miraculous spinning. The elders must be told."

The discussion was interrupted by the arrival of several scentirrii, one of whom addressed Werner.

"The urman like you and its dark scentirrii have escaped. You know what you must do."

Werner looked shocked.

The news shook Tulliver as well. Not so much the fact that Everson and his men had escaped – that much he expected of them – but the fact that he was now stuck here, alone. No, not alone; with Hepton, which frankly was less preferable.

However, Hepton took it the worst. The man was torn. He didn't know what card to play. Where did his best chance of safety lie, with the Fusiliers or with Werner and the Zohtakarrii? Confusion and alarm washed across the man's face like a rip tide.

Tulliver looked at him in disgust. He had no sympathy for the man.

"You are to come with us," the scentirrii urged Werner. "You are to be the acid on the Breath of GarSuleth and strike down those who defy his Will."

Tulliver stepped forward and grasped Werner's forearm. "Werner, you can't do this."

"I don't have a choice," Werner said, averting his eyes as he pulled his arm free of Tulliver's grip.

"You always have a choice."

"And I choose to fly. I am sorry, my friend. I truly am."

Tulliver looked the German pilot in the eyes and saw that his decision was not without cost, but it was one he was willing to pay. Service to the chatts for the chance to fly.

"Fly with me," Werner appealed to him. "You and I, up there. The Zohtakarrii have only kept you alive because you are like me."

"I'm nothing like you, Werner. Nothing," said Tulliver vehemently.

After Werner had been escorted away, the two remaining scentirrii moved in to seize him and Hepton.

"Don't take me," Hepton wheedled. "I helped you. I can still help you. I helped reveal the Threads of GarSuleth. That must count for something!"

The feeling of impotence welled up in Tulliver again, summing up his whole time here on this world. It left him feeling grounded. Useless. He'd had enough of that with Everson. He'd never liked being helpless. That's why he joined the RFC. By God, not any longer.

He pulled the revolver from his waistband and shot the scentirrii.

Hepton looked on in horror as he saw his chance for salvation dissipating with the cordite smoke before his eyes. "What the bloody hell are you doing, man?"

"My duty," snapped Tulliver. "Move."

Waving the chatt apothecaries back with his revolver, Tulliver picked up the glass plate negative, wrapped it in its cloth and backed out of the chamber, Hepton accompanying him only with the greatest reluctance.

One chatt raised itself up on its legs and hissed venomously. Tulliver put a bullet through its head and it dropped to the floor before it could exhale its soporific benediction.

The others hesitated and sank back down again in a submissive posture, unwilling to risk their new relic.

Tulliver glanced at Hepton. "Come on. We're leaving."

"But my equipment!" begged Hepton.

"You want it, you carry it," said Tulliver still covering the chatts, who looked as if they were just waiting for a moment to strike. "But I'm not waiting."

Hepton hastily loaded himself up with the canvas bags of film canisters, and picked up his tripod and heavy wooden camera box and shuffled as close to Tulliver as he could.

Tulliver raised the wrapped plate to the chatts as a final warning. "Try to stop us and I'll smash your precious 'holy glyph' to smithereens."

CHAPTER FOURTEEN

"To Face the Stark, Blank Sky..."

EVERSON KNEW THAT the creature attacking the chatts would have set off their alarm scent and the rampaging monster would command their attention for only a short while. They had to take advantage of that.

He moved his men swiftly but cautiously up the tunnel, into a larger chamber with numerous broad tunnels leading off. The stench of urine, dung and musk hung heavily in the air. The space was filled with roaring, snarling and unearthly sounds that churned his insides and made him want to vomit. He felt glad that they didn't have to face what was down those passages, but they might slow the chatts down. He signalled to Evans and a couple of Mills bombs rolled down the passages. The tunnels shook and bloomed with a brief hellish light and a chorus of inhuman shrieks.

The section pushed on quickly, picking off any chatts that challenged them.

"Atkins, they must get the creatures in here somehow. That's our way out. Find it. We'll hold here. But we can't do it for long."

"Sir. Mercy, Pot Shot, Porgy: with me. We're looking for a big fucking entrance. Something you can drive a tank through. Put some jildi into it."

The phrase brought a smile to Everson's lips. It was one of Sergeant Hobson's little sayings from his time in India. Atkins could do worse than pick up a thing or two from his platoon sergeant.

Any major attack would come from the direction of the arena. Gazette, Gutsy, Riley and Tonkins covered the exit to the chamber. The Padre and Jenkins huddled against a wall.

"What about Tulliver and Hepton, sir?" asked Jenkins.

"Oh, I shouldn't worry about Hepton, Jenkins," Everson said, his lip curling. "As my father would say, he's one of life's floaters, that one. And as for Tulliver." He let out a sigh. "Hopefully he can take advantage of our diversion."

Everson shot another chatt. "Come on, Atkins," he muttered impatiently.

Rutherford sloped up the tunnel, panting, his bayonets dripping.

Without warning, a chatt appeared from a side tunnel. Jenkins, in a move so uncharacteristic it must have been from terror, roared to mask his fear and charged with a rifle at the thing, plunging his bayonet into it, cracking and splintering its chest carapace.

"Face, Jenkins!" yelled Everson in warning.

"Sir?" Jenkins turned as, with its dying breath, the chatt spat its acid. It seared the side of Jenkins' face with a sickening sizzle, blistering his cheek and ear, as skin and muscle burnt and dissolved. Turning, however, had saved his sight. He staggered back, screaming, as the chatt slumped to the floor.

Corporal Riley was first to reach him, emptying the contents of his water canteen across Jenkins' face, flushing away the remaining acid. "Stay still, lad." He cradled the man as he whimpered. "Tonkins," he called. "Morphine."

Tonkins fished in his haversack and came up with a tablet of morphine. Jenkins quietened down.

The others took the opportunity to pull their gas hoods on.

There was an explosion.

Mercy came haring down the tunnel, skidding to a halt.

"Sir, we've found it! Corp's holding it now."

"Move!" yelled Everson, waving his men past him up the tunnel.

The Padre led the way, and Riley and Tonkins took Jenkins between them, whimpering in pain.

It wouldn't be long before the place was swarming. Scentirrii were already running down the tunnel towards them as the dust settled.

Rutherford charged, screaming, bayonets in hand, and thrust them into the throats of two scentirrii before they had a chance to spit acid.

Gutsy swung his meat cleaver, Little Bertha, and split the head of another.

Everson ran the next chatt through with his sword.

Rutherford fought off two more scentirrii, swinging Jenkins' rifle, smashing in one facial plate with the shoulder stock, leaving the large black eye bleeding from its orbit, like a yolk from a broken shell. The other he caught against a wall and drove his hobnailed boot into its chest once, twice, three times to crush the carapace, driving shards into the vital organs.

Gazette knelt in the shelter of the tunnel giving covering fire for their retreat and picked off several more chatts with characteristic accuracy.

Atkins, Pot Shot, Mercy and Porgy were covering the exit into a large partially built courtyard. It may have been used for wrangling demonic creatures from the craters, but today it held something else. Something even bigger, tethered by ropes to the courtyard walls.

Atkins was elated and despondent at its discovery: the German kite balloon, patched, mended and inflated, with a new larger basket fitted below, a cradle adapted from a battlepillar. It floated above the courtyard in a serene silence, its mooring ropes reminding him of tentacles and its great grey bulk of the aerial Kreothe.

It called to mind Mathers' prophecy. '*The Kreothe, made, not tamed.*' If that wasn't a description of a balloon, he didn't know what was. What the hell did it all mean? What was the next line? He couldn't recall and grimaced.

Tethered by anchor lines it floated, giving them some cover from the battlements above. There was a large drum of rope for winching it up and down. That would have to go. A swift blow with Little Bertha saw to that. The huge sausage balloon rose slightly, tugging at its moorings.

Already chatts were rushing along the walls above. Bolts of white fire crackled down from electric lances, pinning them in the entrance. Behind them, Everson could hear the crack of rifle fire as Gazette held the rear.

Pot Shot picked off one or two chatts on the battlements. They tumbled to the ground, hitting heavily with wet cracking noises, their broken clay batteries shattering with blue flashes.

Porgy dashed out to secure the long basket. "All aboard!" he yelled.

They clambered into it. It was a tight squeeze and even Pot Shot complained as Gutsy eased his stocky form into the wicker-work cradle. Riley and Tonkins helped Jenkins in, the right side of his head livid and blistering, and sat him on the floor in a morphine stupor, where the Padre comforted him.

"Christ, we're never going to take off with you in it," said Porgy.

"You have to think good thoughts!" Gutsy declared.

"Bloody hell, then we really are in trouble!" Porgy said with grin.

From the basket, Atkins called to Everson, who was sheltering in the doorway with Rutherford.

"We have to go, sir. Now!"

"Come with us, Rutherford," said Everson.

"In that thing?" Rutherford shook his head with a regretful smile. "Not a chance. Besides, I can't. My clan is out there somewhere."

"We're your clan," Everson replied earnestly.

Rutherford shook his head. "Maybe, once, but I'd made my mind up long before the so-called mutiny. We're marooned here for good. You're on a fool's errand, sir. The sooner you realise that and start to live in the here and now, the better it'll be for you and the men. And even if there was a way, I can't go back home, sir. Not to Broughtonthwaite. Not after all I've seen; all I've done. I can't go back to some quiet little redbrick terrace after all this. No. I'll wish you the best of luck, sir. I hope you find what you're looking for. I intend to find my urmen."

The man had gumption, Everson had to admit that. And maybe there wasn't a way home, the Bleeker party certainly suggested that, but he wasn't willing to accept it until he had exhausted all the possibilities. He owed *that* to the men. Nevertheless, he held out his hand. Rutherford took it and shook it firmly.

"Good luck, Rutherford. I was wrong about you."

Rutherford held his gaze. "Yes, you were."

Everson ran for the cradle. Several pairs of hands helped him over the lip.

"Whoops-a-daisy, sir."

Once Everson was in, Rutherford untied the last of the mooring ropes. The large sausage-shaped kite balloon began to rise; Rutherford caught hold of the rope as the kite balloon drifted up over the courtyard wall. He planted his feet against the side and ran up the courtyard as the balloon rose.

Chatts swarmed along the wall to stop it. One raised an electric lance. Rutherford kicked away from the wall as he reached the top, swung back and knocked the chatt off the wall as the balloon drifted over.

It continued to rise, edging towards the trees. Rutherford slipped down the rope and hit the ground. He turned and gave a brief salute before racing for the tree line.

Mercy shook his head in exasperation. "Bloody hell, who does he think he is, Peter bleedin' Pan?"

TULLIVER, REVOLVER DRAWN, the glass negative under his arm, followed the first passage he could find heading down.

He knew he had to get off the main thoroughfares as soon as possible. He had their sacred relic under his arm, but he doubted that would keep them alive for long.

"Wait for me," demanded Hepton, staggering under the bulk of his kinematic equipment.

"If you can't keep up, get rid of it!" barked Tulliver sharply.

Hepton glared at him as if he'd asked him to leave behind his own grandmother.

"Suit yourself," said Tulliver, perversely satisfied to have earned one of Hepton's black looks.

He kept his eyes peeled and saw an urman slip into a small side passage. He followed. It seemed to be a series of 'belowstairs' passages, exclusively for urmen. That made things a little easier. Their scent would be lost among the throng, or so he hoped. The fact that Hepton was loaded down actually helped them. With urmen hurrying this way and that on various errands and with assorted loads of their own, none of them gave Tulliver or Hepton a second look.

They reached the ground level and the urman passage opened out into a larger tunnel filtering into the cavernous entrance chamber. Tulliver pressed his back against the wall and watched for a moment. It was obvious an alarm scent had spread. They were sealing the edifice. Scentirrii herded the urmen out of the vast space, leaving baskets and bundles of harvested foods abandoned. Tethered to their loading quays, battlepillars rippled nervously.

Scentirrii urged urmen to close the great bark doors.

"Just our rotten bloody luck."

Hepton had just caught up with him and was panting hard and trying to shift his load into a more comfortable position. Too bad.

Tulliver scowled at him. He'd have a better chance alone, and he was almost prepared to leave Hepton to his fate, but for the fact he needed someone to start the propeller. "They know something's up, they're battening down the hatches. It's now or never. As a favour to you, we're going to walk up there. That should allow you to catch your breath, but once I start running you'd better keep up."

Hepton swore under his breath.

Tulliver crept out, using stacks of abandoned foods and battlepillar jetties for cover until they neared the great bark doors. Hepton scurried along behind him, struggling to hold the tripod under his arms while lugging the camera box and knapsacks of film canisters. They had barely got two thirds of the way across the space when the two chatts at the door stepped forward with spears raised to challenge them.

Tulliver carried on walking, pointed his revolver and shot the pair of them.

"That's your cue," he said to Hepton, sprinting towards the closing doors.

As the kite balloon drifted up over the surrounding forest, Atkins spotted the Sopwith, with its unmistakable British roundels, and two figures running towards it, chased by chatts. "Tulliver!"

"I've got it," said Gazette. Resting his rifle on the basket and taking aim, he picked off the chatt scentirrii around the aeroplane. The figure of Tulliver looked up and waved his thanks.

Tulliver fired his last bullet into the body of a wounded chatt that rose to stop them, then stepped past and climbed up into his cockpit, yelling at Hepton.

Hepton staggered up to the Sopwith, as quickly as his forty-a-day body would let him. It hadn't been forty-a-day for a while, but the damage had been done and he was gasping and coughing like a mustard gas victim. But he still had all his equipment. Just. He stepped up and stowed the tripod and camera box into the observer's cockpit and was about to climb in himself.

"No," said Tulliver.

"What the bloody hell do you mean, no?"

"I mean I need you at the front to turn the prop over."

"I'm not a bloody air mechanic."

"No, and you're not bloody dead yet either, and you will be if I don't get my bus off the ground." He pointed towards the edifice, from where a number of chatts were running and leaping towards them, "Prop. Now."

Swearing, Hepton stepped down off the fuselage and hurried round to the front of the machine.

"Contact!" yelled Tulliver over the roar of the engine.

Hepton swung the propeller with both hands. It caught, and Tulliver ran the engine up. The bus began to move, pulled by the propeller's traction.

Hepton raced round the wing and heaved himself into the observer's cockpit as the plane picked up speed, bouncing along the uneven ground. He had barely strapped himself in when the Sopwith took to the air.

"OH, NOW THAT'S not bloody fair," said Porgy, peering over the edge of the basket in dismay.

Three smaller balloons of the Zohtakarrii's own manufacture rose out of chimney-like buttresses around the walls of the edifice. They were spherical and of some translucent skin stretched taut with gas. The balloons were tethered by long lines that played out as they rose into the air to meet the kite balloon's escape. Each carried a basket holding eight chatts, armed with electric lances.

Atkins remembered the line of Mathers' prophecy now, '*Other Ones will travel on the Breath of GarSuleth, the Kreothe made not tamed.*' The Breath of GarSuleth was a chatt phrase that could mean the wind. How did Mathers know? How could the Nazarrii, who made the prophecy and who died hundreds of years ago, possibly know?

Atkins looked back over his shoulder, to the open meadow, but could no longer see Tulliver, although he could hear the determined putter of the aeroplane's engine.

As if that wasn't bad enough, they were drifting back towards the edifice on the prevailing wind. The kite balloon was about as manoeuvrable as a bloody Kreothe, thought Atkins, his blood running cold.

The great earthen walls drifted past, too closely for comfort, and they passed by the great hollow buttresses from which the balloons had been raised; one of the balloons was above them even now. Pot Shot dropped a grenade down the chimney. The cap of the open buttress blasted apart, flinging rocky shrapnel and chatt body parts high into the sky and raining down against the sausage balloon.

The men in the cradle ducked and covered their heads as it pattered down past them. Then the concussion wave hit, buffeting the cradle and sweeping them clear of the edifice.

Even as the gap widened, one scentirrii leapt from a watch balcony across the void towards them, striving to catch a trailing rope. It missed and fell, its body racing its shadow down the edifice side until the two collided against the incline, where it slid for a second before tumbling off towards the ground.

Driven by an impulse greater than self-preservation, two more chatts made last-ditch leaps from the edifice as the kite balloon drifted beyond it

One leapt for the basket. Its long fingers closed about the lip, and it began to haul itself up. The moment its face appeared, Gutsy smashed it with his rifle butt, and it fell, flailing, to smack into the ground.

As the kite balloon drifted out over the forest canopy, the second chatt, hanging from a trailing mooring rope, attempted to pitch its spear into the balloon. It struck the skin a glancing blow before falling harmlessly away.

Tonkins cut through the rope with his bayonet. "Thank God the bastards haven't got wings," he said as he leaned over and watched the chatt drop. "They haven't, have they?"

The falling chatt didn't even have a chance to hit the ground. Its shadow, falling across the forest canopy below, triggered a whipperwill, which lashed up into the air, caught the body and snatched it out of sight.

After that, Atkins watched the shadow of the balloon nervously as it sailed over the forest, a trail of hungry whips snapping far below.

A crackle alerted Atkins to more danger. He looked up. A chatt balloon, its mooring now a smoking ruin, was now adrift. It was higher and floating in the same direction as the kite balloon, out towards the crater. The chatts fired their electric lances.

Atkins couldn't get a sight on the chatt balloon's occupants. The balloon itself made a better target.

He heard the roar of an engine and raked his eyes across the sky, looking for the source, but couldn't see anything. Then he heard the sickening stutter of twin machine guns and saw the Albatros diving towards them.

It was virtually impossible to move in the cramped basket now, as everyone crouched for what blessed little cover they could get. From the other end of the cradle came a shout. Atkins craned his neck.

Another aeroplane, this one theirs.

KNIGHTS OF THE air, jousting in single combat. It sounded romantic; Tulliver had thought the same when he volunteered. His flight commander had quickly debunked that notion. It wasn't a game. It was kill or be killed. There was no fair play. No chivalry. Shoot them in the back, from behind. Whatever it took. Up here, he owed Werner nothing.

Push forward on the stick, dive.

Werner's Albatros was in his gunsight. He fired.

Werner banked away sharply. The Albatros was faster and more manoeuvrable than the Strutter, but with its front-mounted twin Spandau machine guns, the Albatros could only fire head on. If they were to stand any chance at all, Hepton would have to use the observer's Lewis machine gun, mounted behind him. It would even the odds a little.

Seeing the two tethered chatt balloons rising above their chimneys, Tulliver pushed his stick to the side and banked, coming down on them from above. He strafed them with brief bursts of machine-gun fire. You were supposed to wait until you were almost on top of them, but he wanted to keep out of range of their electric lances. The petrol tank was between him and Hepton, and the whole plane was doped fabric and wood. He didn't fancy going down in flames.

As he pulled up, he saw the punctured balloons begin to deflate and sink towards the edifice on their leashes.

He heard the *pop-pop-pop* of machine gun fire. The threat of death spurred Hepton into action. The man had found some gumption. He was firing off at the Hun as the Albatros dived down on them from behind.

Left stick and rudder, Tulliver side-slipped away. Both planes were now trying to turn inside each other's circles so they could bring their forward guns to bear on their opponents. Diving and climbing, they spiralled, each pilot desperately trying to thwart the other, seeking the advantage for himself.

Werner levelled out and swept towards the kite balloon, firing incendiaries at it as it drifted out over the crater.

Tulliver pushed forwards on the stick and followed him down, all the while trying to centre him in his gunsight. He needed to be as close as possible to avoid hitting the kite balloon, but it was looming up fast.

Werner flattened out at the last minute and roared so low over the top of the kite balloon that it looked as if he might set down on it.

Tulliver could see the men in the cradle shouting and waving at him frantically. He was on a collision course. Wiping the fouling oil spray from his goggles, he nudged the nose forward, steepening his dive, sweeping under the kite balloon's cradle.

He hauled back on the stick and the bus raced up in a long climb. He swivelled his head about him, looking for the

Hun. He tipped his wing and, looking down, saw him below, readying for another run at the kite balloon.

Tulliver watched in horror as the balloon crumpled, flames consuming and shrivelling its skin, as it sank towards the crater.

RANAMAN STOOD IN the cleft between the two halves of Croatoan's Heart, holding the box. He nodded at the two warriors holding Alfie's arms and they released him. Alfie tensed himself for the inevitable. If they were going to sacrifice him, then he would go with as much dignity as he could muster. He wouldn't give them the satisfaction of screaming, or at least, he'd try not to.

"Now you are to commune with the ancestors," Ranaman demanded.

The urman withdrew another smaller box from the first and offered it to him.

Alfie's resolve collapsed in confusion. Would it spring open and douse him with a poison? Or did it contain some sacred creature that would kill with a lethal sting? If they wanted to kill him, he wasn't going to make their job any bloody easier. He refused to touch the box, and glared at the chieftain.

With a nod, Ranaman offered the smaller box again. "It is time. Channel the spirits of the ancestors."

Alfie looked again and saw that it wasn't a box: it was a large book, spine on. He almost laughed. It was the last thing he expected. It had been an easy mistake to make in the dim light of the temple. It was an old book by the look of it, too, a large leather-bound tome with iron clasps. Its cover had some sort of symbol cast in iron set into it. Water damage had wrinkled the page edges and there was a faint smell of mildew about it.

Seeing no alternative, he reached out and closed his hands about the book, trembling. What could be so bad about a book?

There was an audible sigh of relief from Ranaman as he let go. It was as if he had transferred some great responsibility and was now absolved of any further expectations.

Alfie turned to face the gathered clan. Ranaman had stepped back and joined the others, looking on with an awed, expectant gaze, expecting some miracle to occur.

He's going to be severely disappointed, thought Alfie as he frowned and turned his attention to the book. He opened it and riffled through the pages, a murmur of expectation rippling through the waiting clan. They watched him in amazement as he turned the pages.

Why the hell didn't they just read it themselves?

And then it struck him. They couldn't. He didn't even think they knew what a book was, let alone writing. They seemed to think it was some arcane object, imbued with great supernatural powers, a vessel through which someone with witchcraft could communicate with the dead. In fact, this book looked old enough for their ancestors to have written it. If he could read it, then he supposed he *would* be communicating with the dead, reading their thoughts. He'd never thought of it like that before, and now that he did, it sent a shudder down his spine. No wonder they thought it a great magic.

There was nothing else for it. He thumbed through the pages and stopped at random. Illegible, close, handwritten text filled the thick parchment pages. It hadn't occurred to him that the language might not be English.

He flipped through the pages, becoming anxious. He tried to look serious and portentous. He glanced up over the top of the book at the clan, who shuffled uneasily. Two men had stepped up behind Tarak, as if to make good on their threat, should Alfie fail.

He could brazen it out. Make something up. If they couldn't read, they wouldn't know, would they? Is that what Jeffries did, make something up?

He stopped and squinted at the writing. Something familiar. A word. Was it a word? He traced the writing with his finger, trying to spell it out. *C, O, M*. Something long. A, N. Something long, similar but not exactly like the other long letter. Company? Company, that was it. With that, the whole page seemed to unlock. He glanced over the page. It was English. Very old English, the *s*'s were *f*'s and the handwriting was hard to decipher, but he could read it. He breathed a sigh of relief before the thought, *how was it English?* crossed his mind, but the urmen were becoming restless. That was a question for another time. Here and there, he made out words: *White* and *Virginia* and *Roanoke*. On one page there even looked to be a date, *1588*. But that couldn't have been right, for any schoolboy who knew his dates of kings and queens knew that was the reign of Queen Elizabeth I.

Flanked by the broken halves of Croatoan's Heart, he began to read aloud to the assembled clan, hesitating as he tried to make sense of the unfamiliar script. Perhaps it had no more significance than the Bible readings he had heard the Padre give during Church Parade. He tried to sound solemn and authoritarian.

"The rituals are complete. One has gone ahead to scout the way for the company. They will go to seek the mouth to the underworld, there to descend to the enclave of the dead and petition for our Lord and Master, Croatoan, or else seek to destroy the false god and free him, restoring the Fallen One to his rightful place. Those that aid him, we have been told, will be granted great boons, and this new world will be theirs to dwell on, in the sight of Croatoan."

It wasn't merely the words that sent a chill down Alfie's spine. It was the fact that they were there at all. It was both an exciting and a horrifying discovery.

All at once, he was out of his depth. He had never felt at ease with Mathers' duplicity in pretending to be messengers of the gods. He was just a mechanic from Nottingham. All this occult stuff was fine, if fanciful, contained between the covers of Cecil's adventure story magazines. Give him his tank any day, its one-hundred-horsepower Daimler engine, its six-millimetre steel plate. He understood that. But this?

His brow creased as he gazed out over the pages of tightly-written text at the clan watching him beyond. Was it possible that these were the descendants of other earlier missing people? He looked up again at the people in shock, the book slipping from his hands, as the enormity of what he had just read sunk in.

It seemed a magical transformation *had* occurred with his reading. The tables had turned. He was no longer the magical being. They were.

"Who *are* you?" he asked, his voice barely a whisper.

Ranaman cocked his head and answered as if it were plain for all to see.

"We are the sons and daughters of Ruanach. Worshippers of Croatoan. We have long sought to ease his pain and we have been promised that Croatoan will return."

"Promised? Promised by who?" he asked, though he feared he knew the answer.

"The one who came before. Jeffries." Ranaman replied.

Ranaman stepped forward and took the closed book from Alfie, replacing it in its box, taking the responsibility from him once more, his part in the ritual done.

The hair on the back of Alfie's neck began to prickle. "But if we're not the first..." He tried to marshal his thoughts. "Your ancestors, did they not leave? Go back to where they came from?"

"Leave? Why? They sought a new world and were led to this place. They came a great distance seeking Croatoan, invoking his name. But he was tricked and defeated by GarSuleth and bound below in Skarra's realm and they were lost, our new world taken from us by GarSuleth and its children."

It wasn't just his neck that prickled now; it was the hairs on his arms, too, as if an electric charge were building.

The air grew warm.

The men groaned, the women wailed, and Ranaman cried out.

"The Torment of Croatoan begins!"

CHAPTER FIFTEEN

"I Feel Once Again as of Yore..."

THE ACRID SMELL of burning rubberised canvas filled Atkins' nostrils as charred scraps of material from the burning balloon swirled round the cradle, leaving a greasy grey smear across the sky as they sank down into the crater. Right now, it was a moot point as to which would meet them first, the fire or the ground.

"I'm not sure I like the Royal Flying Corps," Porgy confided to nobody in particular. "Have I got time to put in a transfer back to the Poor Bloody Infantry, sir?" he called over to Everson with a smirk.

"I think it'll be granted sooner than either of us would like, Hopkiss," said the Lieutenant grimly, gripping onto the sides of the cradle as they plunged towards the ground.

They were passing over the strip of discoloured vegetation. As the cradle twisted in the air, Atkins turned his head to keep it in sight, in an attempt to keep his bearings. Rising just above the treetops, near the centre of the crater, was some sort of narrow tower.

"Sir!" he said to Everson, pointing.

"I see it, Corporal."

The balloon's passing shadow triggered small explosions, like gunshots, as whipperwills snapped hungrily at it, like sixty-foot bullwhips. As they lashed into the sky, sections peeled back at their tips, opening like fleshy petals, to reveal flayed-red lamprey-like mouths, each one ready to tear and strip, snapping one after the other at the deflating balloon like chained dogs, before recoiling into the trees beneath.

Tonkins, the signaller, squeezed off several rounds at them, but they moved too fast and the bullets vanished harmlessly into the canopy.

"Never mind, lad," said Corporal Riley.

The burning balloon was out of reach for the moment, but as it continued its inevitable descent towards the crater's jungle canopy, it was clear it wouldn't stay that way.

Several of the ropes suspending the cradle from the balloon burnt through, and the cradle dropped a few feet with a jerk and tipped precariously, causing yells of alarm and consternation from every quarter.

Porgy's gorblimey slipped from his head.

"My cap!" groaned Porgy. "Bloody hell, the Quarterbloke'll never give me another one."

"Aye, the only excuse he'll take for losing it is if you lost your bleedin' head along with it!" agreed Mercy as they clung to the side of the swaying and now spinning cradle.

"Yes, well there's still a chance of that," retorted Gazette, as burning scraps fluttered down around them.

The canopy was rising up to meet them fast now. Something struck the underside of the balloon's cradle, and again, and again, and they realised that they were now within reach of the whipperwills. Sensing wounded prey, the things began lashing out with greater ferocity, tearing at the wattle cradle, their fleshy petals opening as they snapped their small razor-sharp teeth.

Gutsy swung his meat cleaver at them. Everson slashed out with his sword, severing several whipperwills' heads and sending them tumbling down to the treetops, only for their hungry brethren to snatch them out of midair.

A bigger specimen cracked up out of the canopy like a seaborne leviathan and tore at what remained of the blazing gasbag above. The flames licked at it and some sap or aqua vita within it ignited, fire consuming its entire length. It thrashed about the air like a fiery lash, until with a thunderous *crack*, it extinguished the flames and the scorched whipperwill crashed back into the leaves, leaving behind the faint smoky ghost of it hanging in the air.

Unable to keep the cradle aloft any longer, the remains of the balloon flapped and guttered, streaming ineffectually above them as men and cradle now hurtled down. They skimmed across the treetops, the drub of branches and leaves against the bottom of the cradle sounding like sticks against a railing.

"Brace yourselves!" shouted Everson.

Atkins hunkered down into the cradle as best he could. He looked at the wan faces around him. Eyes met his, the unspoken communion of the soldier about to go over the bags: "We'll be all right," "Stick by me," "See you in the Hun trenches." But they all knew it was every man for himself.

The cradle hit the canopy with a crash and capsized.

Atkins' world tumbled, like a broken kaleidoscope, a whirl of limbs and wattle, of green, russet, khaki and daylight.

Boughs slammed into his limbs and trunk, knocking the wind from him as he fell, buffeted and pummelled from bough to branch, towards the ground as he dropped through the trees. Thick broad leaves slapped and scratched him. He plummeted through an angry buzz of insects, sounding like the whine of bullets, hands and face stinging as he passed through. For a brief, blissful moment, as if in the eye of a storm, all sensation ceased.

A flare of heavy floral scent burst around him. Perfume. He thought of Flora. Lily of the Valley. Oh, Jesus, Flor–

Atkins slammed into the ground.

NELLIE ABBOTT HELD up a hand, halting the rest of the tank crew. Underneath her short mop of unruly hair, her nose wrinkled and her brow creased with concentration.

"What is it, Miss?" asked Cecil.

Irritated, she flapped her hand in his direction. "Shh!" she hissed, a little more harshly than she had meant to.

Cecil flinched like a scolded puppy.

Above the rustle of the leaves and the faint rush of water, a distant purr caught her attention and held it, as no other sound could.

Wally cocked his head and listened.

He sniffed. "An engine," he said.

"Two," corrected Nellie. "Aeroplanes."

"Two?" said Jack. "Are you sure? But we've only got the one."

"Well, there are two now," said Nellie, her mood defiant.

"Friend or foe?" asked Reggie.

"I don't know," she said thoughtfully. She looked up at the sky, shielding her eyes and squinting against the glare.

Ablaze and drifting down over the crater, the kite balloon was hard to miss.

She soon spotted another smaller balloon, higher and partially hidden by the smoke from the first, drifting in the same direction.

Above them, she saw what she was looking for, the small shapes spiralling higher and higher. She could just make out Tulliver's Strutter, but the other – was that a Hun? Her eyes widened with surprise before her forehead scrunched with doubt. But how?

By now, the others had gathered around her and the air filled with theories and observations.

"There's men up there," said Reggie, pointing at the balloon.

"It's a Hun observation balloon," said Wally. The bantam cockney driver clenched his fists, and his lips contorted into a snarl.

It was spiralling down rapidly into the crater. It was going to come down not a quarter of a mile away. She felt a surge of pity for the men trapped on it. The smaller, higher balloon was sinking too, but that would come down further away.

"Where the hell have they come from?" wondered Jack.

"Perhaps it's a way home!" suggested Norman.

Nobody spoke out in agreement, but nobody would gainsay it.

Nellie felt a blossoming of hope in her breast at the words. Home. Could it be?

There was only one way to find out.

A PALL OF smoke stained the air above the trees. Expecting Germans, the crew of the *Ivanhoe* approached the crash site cautiously.

"Stay by me," Jack told Cecil in a low voice, as he drew his Webley.

The young lad stepped closer, his eyes darting about as if he expected picklehaubed Fritzs to leap from every bush.

Norman and Reggie watched their flanks and Wally. Wally wasn't to be trusted around Germans. It was frightening that such a little man could have such a fury bottled up within him. They didn't want him killing them before they got whatever information they needed.

Nellie wasn't happy about bringing up the rear.

"I can kill if I have to," she told Jack, petulantly.

He studied her face.

"I don't doubt it," he said. "But we're soldiers. It's what we have to do." He bent his head and spoke quietly. "You shouldn't kill unless you have to. Knowing you've killed a man changes you." He tapped his chest. "Inside. It breaks something in you. Something that can't be mended. Bad enough it has to happen to lads like Cecil; I wouldn't want that to happen to you. I don't want that on my conscience," he said. He straightened up and added firmly, "You'll stay in the rear."

Nellie had no answer and relented. This was one area where she was relieved to forego responsibility. The weight of the revolver in her hand began to feel like a poisoned chalice, but she gripped it firmly nevertheless.

Ahead, somewhere through the undergrowth, there was a sound like a groan. Jack held his hand up and the rest of the party crouched down. He signalled the crew to spread out in a skirmish line, then stood and, looking right and left, waved them on with his revolver.

LIEUTENANT EVERSON LAY dazed against the bole of a tree, a large lump forming on his forehead, waiting for the world to stop spinning and his body to stop hurting.

The last thing he expected to see was Nellie Abbott walking out of the undergrowth with a look of shock on her face.

"Lieutenant Everson! What happened? How did you get here?"

He looked up and saw the coverall-clad tankers beside her. "The crew of the *Ivanhoe*, I presume," he groaned. "Don't you salute a senior officer?"

Jack shrugged. "Generally not, sir. Mr Mathers said it usually gets 'em shot."

"And where is Lieutenant Mathers?"

"Gone west, sir."

While not a shock, it was unwelcome news. There were precious few surviving officers as it was without losing another.

"Then who's in command here?" he asked. The men looked sheepish.

"I guess that would be me," said Nellie, stepping forward in her coveralls.

Now it was Everson's turned to look shocked. "You?" he said. He looked to the awkward tank crew. "You're taking orders from a woman now?"

Nellie's eyebrow arched.

Reggie intervened. "Begging your pardon, sir. We were in a bit of a state for a while, the fumes from the tank engine and all that. Some sort of neuralgia. We weren't quite ourselves. Miss Abbott saw us right. Showed us how we'd let Alfie down. We owed it to him, to find him, sir. We only did what was right. Orders or no orders, right is right. We were on his trail when we came across you."

"We saw you come down. How on earth did you end up in that thing, Lieutenant?" asked Nellie.

Everson's tone hardened. "We arrived at the crater. You weren't there," he said. "We were captured by Zohtakarrii and escaped in a captured observation balloon."

"So there are no Huns?" said Wally, disappointed.

"No," said Everson. "Well, one. I expect Tulliver's on his tail this minute."

Now fully aware of his surroundings, he looked around. "Where are the rest, Atkins and the others? They were in the kite balloon. Are they all right?"

Jack waved his arm. "Spread out, find them."

THE TANK CREW came back in ones and twos, with bruised and battered Tommies and scattered haversacks, gasbags, battle bowlers and rifles.

Corporal Riley and Tonkins had found themselves stuck in adjacent trees, having slid down a succession of broad flat leaves as though they were slides. Their electric lance kitbags were found nearby, their fall broken by the undergrowth.

Gazette had twisted his ankle and ended up entangled in a thicket, as if he'd been left hanging out on the old barbed wire.

They came across Pot Shot groaning in shrubbery.

"Bloody hell, I haven't taken a beating like that since the police set about us during the general strike!" he moaned as they hauled him out.

Gutsy had got away relatively unscathed, having had the benefit of the unfortunate Mercy as a soft landing as they came hobbling in together.

"Well, if it isn't Wendy and the Lost Boys," Gutsy said in clipped, bitter tones when he saw the tank crew.

Nellie threw him the kind of haughty look she usually reserved for her brothers. Gutsy, who had contended with

Mrs Blood's occasional wrath for over a decade, baulked nevertheless.

All were maps of contusions, scratches, bruises and livid welts from whip-thin branches, and all had run their gamut of swear words until there was nothing left but a weary acceptance of the discomfort and pain.

They found Padre Rand kneeling over Jenkins, the signals gear hung from various branches around them. The livid, raw acid burns on Jenkins' face were the least of his worries now. He screwed up his eyes in pain as he snatched short ragged breaths. Padre Rand barely had time to read him the Last Rites before Jenkins' breathing became softer and then, with one last gasp, stopped altogether.

ATKINS CAME ROUND, his head hurting, every limb throbbing and aching. He eased himself into a sitting position against a tree trunk, resting uncomfortably against the jumble of gear in his knapsack.

He was amazed to find himself still alive. His first thought now was of Flora, just as his last thought had been. He was still alive. He could still get back to her. But to do that, he would have to move.

He saw his rifle some yards away, and levered himself to his feet. The action set off a ferocious pounding in his head. Spots danced before his eyes as he steadied himself. He heard voices calling. He tried to call out, but his mouth was parched and he couldn't find his water bottle, so he started towards the sounds.

Ahead, white petals drifted down from a tree bough, spinning round in eddies and carpeting the ground beneath the tree. Limping towards it, he realised they weren't petals, but pieces of card. He could see photographs on some. A slipknot of fear tightened round his stomach. He dropped to his knees and brushed his hand through the fallen photogravures, turning them over. They were photographs of girls, every one, some smiling, some demure, full figure, portrait, occasional French nudes and music hall singers. He knew them all.

Several more fluttered down from above.

Not wanting to, but needing to know, he looked up. He dearly wished he hadn't.

Fifteen feet above, a body lay face down, splayed awkwardly across a couple of boughs with an arm outstretched, as if reaching for the fallen cards. Pallid whipcord creepers had wrapped themselves around the neck, biting deeply into the skin. The eyes were wide and bloodshot; the fleshy parts of the face were dark purple and bloated with settling blood, distorting the once pleasant features into a grotesque caricature as it stared down through the foliage at him.

Atkins' voice was quiet but heavy with sorrow, regret and guilt, all bound up in a single word. "Porgy."

Try as he might, he couldn't reach his mate's body. Unwilling to abandon him, he set about collecting up the fallen photographs, Porgy's 'deck of cards'. As he did, Atkins felt the tears come, stinging the welts on his face as they tracked down his cheeks. Being alone, he let them fall.

He wasn't sure how long the voices had been calling. He cuffed his eyes dry and shook off his despondency enough to call out hoarsely, "Here!"

The rest of the section and the tank crew arrived in short order. It took five of them to cut Porgy's body free and lower him gently to the ground, as Atkins watched, numbed.

Nellie sought to comfort him, putting a hand on his arm.

"Only–"

Atkins shrugged it off, rounding on her.

"Where the fuck were you?" he spat at her. Shocked at his own vehemence and anger, he watched Nellie open her mouth to say something, but he wasn't listening. He didn't want to listen. He knew it wasn't her fault. But he couldn't stop himself. As if Porgy's pointless, stupid death had given him permission, all the pain and self-doubt he had kept bottled up over William, over Flora, welled up in a way he hadn't felt since Ketch died. Atkins' brutal words had opened a sluice gate, and the rage and pain poured out in a torrent. "I told you to stay where you were. If you'd stayed at the top of the crater, like I said, like I ordered you to, we wouldn't be in this bloody mess and Porgy wouldn't be dead! But oh, no, Miss bloody high-and-mighty knew better. This is all your fucking fault!"

The tank crew gathered protectively behind Nellie, and Jack stepped up to Atkins.

"Are you looking for trouble, chum?"

"Jack, Only. Stop it," said Nellie as the men glowered at each other. "I have four brothers. I can fight my own battles, Jack. I don't need you to do it for me."

Atkins balled his hands into fists. He didn't care. He deserved it. He would take anything the burly tanker dished out; after all, he thought to himself bitterly, wasn't he the penitent Fusilier?

"Come on, then," he said.

The longed-for blow never landed. Everson stepped between them.

"That's enough," he said. "I've already had one mutiny. I won't have another. Is that clear?"

Jack lowered his fists and allowed Nellie to escort him back to the others, berating him as they went and giving his arm a solid punch.

Atkins continued to glare at the gunner's broad back.

"Is that clear?" repeated Everson.

"Sir," said Atkins, grudgingly, his hands relaxing.

EVERSON BREATHED A sigh of relief and gestured Gutsy over.

"Blood, take Lance Corporal Atkins over there, calm him down. Otterthwaite, get Hopkiss's identity disc and divide his ammunition and food. Then we need to organise a burial party."

Everson noticed the tank crew in a brief huddle. They pushed Jack from the scrum towards him. The gunner looked awkward and embarrassed.

"We don't think it's a good idea to bury them, sir. We should burn them."

"Burn them?"

"It's just that the sub – Lieutenant Mathers, sir–"

"I thought you said he was dead?"

"He was, sir."

"Was?"

"Some sort of fungus reanimated his body, sir."

Everson pinched the bridge of his nose and sighed. Was nothing ever straightforward in this place?

"And where is Mathers now?" he asked wearily.

"Sucked into an underground river, sir."

"Well then, problem solved. Private, we haven't the time to cut down wood and build a pyre to burn them. We bury them and move on."

Jack shuffled, unsure.

"That's an order, private."

"I DON'T LIKE any of this, Corp," said Tonkins, as he stood by the fresh shallow grave with his entrenching tool. "I wish I was back in the dugout, making repairs."

"Well, lad," said Riley, stood by another, ready to dispense his customary wisdom. He really wished he had a pipe to draw on. These things always sounded better when punctuated by puffs of shag and wreathed in a fog of fragrant smoke, but needs must. "It's like my old father always said: 'Hope for the best, expect the worst and take what comes.' After all, I put in for extra staff in my unit and Battalion sent me you. And look how that's turned out!" he said, slapping Tonkins heartily on the back.

Tonkins smiled broadly, nodded with relief, paused as a penny dropped and then frowned. By then, Corporal Riley was already halfway across the glade.

* * *

After the Padre led a brief funeral service for Hopkiss and Jenkins, Everson called Atkins and Riley together, along with Nellie who, although he didn't like it, seemed to speak for the crew of the *Ivanhoe*.

Hopkiss' death had hit the Black Hand Gang hard, Atkins most of all. Everson needed something to keep them occupied other than mere survival.

As he waited for them to arrive, he fished in his tunic pocket and retrieved the scrap of bloodstained khaki serge cloth, and the Pennine Fusiliers button that had once belonged to Jeffries. He played it through his fingers, rubbing a thumb idly over the raised Fusilier badge cast on it as he pondered. With his petrol-fruit-heightened senses, Mathers had been able to divine Jeffries by some sort of psychometry. He had said Jeffries' trail led into the crater. And here they were. If so, what did that make this, some kind of talisman, some sort of fetish? Did that mean it had some kind of eldritch connection with Jeffries? He shuddered and found himself stuffing the button away in his pocket again, as if to be rid of it, or at least put it out of sight.

"We need to decide our next move," he said as the others turned up. "It's clear we have several objectives. One, to find Private Perkins. Two, to see if we can pick up Jeffries' trail."

Nellie spoke up. "Napoo believes Alfie has been taken by urmen."

Hesitantly, Atkins chipped in, "If we're looking for urmen, sir, there was the tower we saw, towards the centre of the crater. That looked man-made. It should be easy enough to find."

Everson nodded, relieved that Atkins was engaged. "It's a start," he said.

Corporal Riley nodded in agreement. "Don't like leaving a man behind, if I can help it," he said.

Twenty minutes later, they moved off, heading for the centre of the crater and the tower.

* * *

TULLIVER SAW THE remnants of the blazing kite balloon crash slowly into the treetops, then lost sight of it as the bus continued to turn into its climbing spiral. There was nothing he could do for them. He silently wished them luck, pulled back on the stick's spade handle, hauled the nose up and raced after the Hun.

The Strutter was no real match for the Albatros as it was, but now Werner had the advantage of height and extra speed. And he used it.

The Albatros was now diving steeply on them from above. He would wait until he was almost on top of them before he opened fire. Tulliver had only moments to act.

He slide-slipped and plunged through an indolent cumulus as the mountainous cloud drifted by. The bright blue of the sky faded, and he found himself enveloped by a diffuse grey space. He kept his rudder as level as he could, or thought he had. He felt the negative plate at his feet slide across the cockpit. He was drifting, banking. Straighten up. Straighten up. The fog thinned to a mist and, through that, the ground gradually resolved itself.

He'd lost sight of the Albatros. Tulliver pulled up, climbing parallel to the great shifting white slopes of the cloud, the Strutter's shadow rippling over its bright surface.

The Albatros burst out of a cleft between two cloudy peaks above and he climbed after it, contour-chasing though the misty canyons of a morphing landscape, landing wheels scudding along their insubstantial surface, leaving whorls of mist in their wake.

He's leading me on a wild goose chase, thought Tulliver, as the Albatros stayed tantalisingly out of reach above.

They left the cloud behind as they continued to climb in a spiral. His ears crackled as the pressure changed, and the air got colder with the altitude. The sharp bite of the wind whistling through the wires was clean and exhilarating, at least to begin with. At this height, and at speeds of eighty to ninety miles an hour, the cold started to numb his extremities. Chances were his machine gun would freeze up, too, not that he had much ammo left. Still, he climbed hard on the Hun's heels. Now, if he could just settle the bastard in his gunsight.

There was a brief burst of tracer bullets across his top plane. Werner roared overhead, and waggled his wings once – twice. When he came round again, he was pointing down insistently.

Tulliver banked and chanced a look. Eleven thousand feet below, crisscrossing the landscape, were vast intersecting lines, scoring the landscape. He had seen a few of them in reverse on the negative plate down by his feet, but they didn't do the scale or the number justice.

Helped by the petrol fruit fumes from the engine, they were even harder to miss. The lines, however, weren't continuous. They were broken and faint in places, sometimes marked only by a slight change of colour or thickness of vegetation, sometimes vanishing under forests or hills and valleys, reappearing fractured, miles away, half-hidden but concomitant. They seemed to run for miles, disappearing off towards the horizon until they were lost in the haze of aerial perspective. On the ground, they would have been invisible, but Tulliver knew that the new aerial photography could reveal geological features that had long lain undiscovered. What they could be, he had no idea. Were they evidence of ancient earthworks or geological processes?

There did seem to be unpleasant associations with Jeffries' perverse appropriation of artillery to plot a pentagram on the landscape. Was this a pattern, too? There looked to be a geometric aspect to it all. Was this, as the Zohtakarrii claimed, proof of their world's creation? Were these the strands of the world as woven by GarSuleth for his children? From their reaction to the plates, they certainly thought so.

But the sheer scale of it. It beggared belief.

As he and Werner circled each other, it was clear now that the Strip in the crater was part of it, too, an exposed part of a line.

This was what he had glimpsed before. This was what Werner had tried to tell him about. There was more to this world than met the eye, the German had said. Tulliver had thought it mere hyperbole at the time.

Werner hadn't been trying to shoot him down at all. He'd lured him up here to show him, to let him see for himself, in order to corroborate it.

He turned to Hepton. Hepton had to see it, too. He couldn't fail to. But the kinematographer was sat huddled in the observer's cockpit, shivering, his hands cupped round his mouth, trying to blow on them to warm them. Tulliver pointed down, but Hepton wasn't interested.

Out of the corner of his eyes, Tulliver thought some of the lines shimmered. He couldn't be sure. Frustrated, he lifted his fouled goggles and looked again.

No, there it was. With his fuel-sharpened acuity, he could see an ephemeral energy flowing along the lines like water, towards intersections, building in intensity until a vast spastic column of lightning blasted briefly up into the sky. Across the planet's surface, lightning bolts jagged up into the atmosphere in an inverted lightning storm, with a noise like an artillery barrage.

The Strutter's rigging wires began to hum and sparks started arcing from one to another.

That wasn't good.

Then, with a roar like Wotan's furnace, a tremendous column of brilliant white lightning punched up from the ground into the sky between the Strutter and the Albatros, in a searing blast of heat and noise. It filled Tulliver's world, obliterating everything, leaving his ears ringing and his eyes blinded.

The concussive shockwave smashed into the fragile machines of wood and wire and fabric and sent them spinning out of control.

They were going down.

CHAPTER SIXTEEN

"Each Flash and Spouting Crash..."

TOSSED ABOUT BY the repercussing air, deafened and blinded by the brilliant flash of the blast, Tulliver struggled with the controls. It seemed a hopeless task. He could hear Hepton screaming incoherently behind him.

Dragged by the traction of the engine and the weight of its nose, the Sopwith fell from the sky. The struts groaned. The wires shrieked. Loose cotton drummed. Violent vibrations threatened to shake the bus apart.

Dear God, the engine was still going. He'd rip the bloody wings off at this speed. Hampered by a fog of afterimages, he groped around the dashboard and cut off the engine.

As his vision cleared, Tulliver was terrified to see the ground all around him, spinning like a dervish. He had to pull out of the spin; it was death if he didn't. He played the rudder bar with his feet and gradually brought the spin under control, praying the bus would hold together a little longer. He pulled back on the stick. The vibrations eased and the ground began slipping away beneath him; a flash of horizon and then everything was sky. He was out of the dive and gliding, several hundred feet up.

It was quiet without the engine. His hearing returning, even above the persistent ringing, he could hear the distant crumps as, far off, bolts of energy continued to strike skyward. Trembling and nauseous, he started the engine again and gripped the stick tightly in an effort to stop his hands shaking, biting the inside of his cheeks hard enough to draw blood in order to stop himself sobbing with relief. Not trusting himself or his bus to do anything else, he flew level for a while, to get his bearings.

Searching the landscape for the crater, he saw a telltale trail of smoke hanging in the sky and caught sight of Werner's Albatros spiralling down at the bottom of it.

He pushed the stick forward and dived after it, following it down; there was nothing else he could do but bear witness. It looked as if Werner had been trying to head back to the Zohtakarrii edifice, but lost control. Tulliver watched as his machine plummeted into the crater. Whipperwills snapped around it as it hit the tree tops. The Albatros stood proud on its nose for a moment before toppling over on its back. The canopy gave way beneath it, breaking its wings as it swallowed the machine in fits and starts, sucking it down out of sight beneath the waving boughs.

Tulliver felt a twinge of regret as the machine disappeared. Werner hadn't been a bad man, just trying to do his best with what he had. Tulliver suspected that under different circumstances, they might even have been friends.

As the terror drained from him, an almost divine elation at his survival replaced it. Had he not been flying at such an altitude, he would surely have crashed. Werner had been damned unlucky.

What was causing those vast electrical discharges, he couldn't say, but flying in these conditions was asking for trouble. Still shaking, he flew over the crater, the whipperwills snapping like ineffectual Archie as he looked for somewhere he might put down. He would have preferred landing outside the crater, but he didn't want his bus to fall into the clutches of the Zohtakarrii again.

He noticed the spindly tower poking through the tree canopy, swung round it and turned towards the Strip. After what Tulliver had just witnessed, it wasn't the best place to land, but it was the only place. Vegetation was thinner there. There were fewer whipperwills as well, and he couldn't yet see any build-up of energy along it.

Loath as he was to admit it, he would be glad to have his feet on solid ground again.

THE DIFFUSE FLASHES that lit the sky, and the loud but distant reports, startled the Fusiliers at first.

"Christ, they put the wind up me! For a moment it sounded like a barrage going off," muttered Mercy.

"Must be a lightning storm," said Gazette glancing up, unconcerned. "Good job we're in this crump 'ole of a place, if you ask me."

"It is the time of the lightning trees," growled Napoo. "It will pass."

They heard the putter of an engine and caught sight of the Sopwith as it flew low overhead.

The sight of the red, white and blue roundels cheered them, and several waved, glad to see it.

Everson was relieved to see Tulliver had survived. As the aeroplane came round again, he pointed in the direction of the minaret and, having seen him, Tulliver waggled its wings in acknowledgment.

THE TANK CREW and the Black Hand Gang still regarded each other with suspicion, neither fully trusting the other after the events at Nazarr.

"Well, they seem a little more normal to me," Gutsy said to Atkins. "Now they haven't been in the tank for a week, and those fumes of theirs have worn off. Maybe we'll get a bit more sense out of them. If you don't keep trying to punch them, that is, you dozy mare."

"Hmm," said Atkins, his mind elsewhere. The fumes had caused many problems, but part of him wished the tankers still suffered from its effects, and then maybe they might tell him if they could still smell the remnants of Flora's perfume on his letter. It was selfish, he knew, but since Porgy's death, it felt like a matter of self-preservation. Since he could no longer smell it, a sense of fatalism settled over him and he fought to shrug it off.

In the background, the star shell flashes of the electrical bolts continued beyond the rim, their thunderous crashes following more quickly in their wake.

EVERSON WAS STIFF and sore from his fall and still reeling from the shock of meeting Rutherford, as he watched the tank crew and Fusiliers anxiously. If he couldn't persuade these two sections to get on, what chance had he with the whole battalion? Maybe he was wrong, trying to hold the whole thing together. Maybe Rutherford was right; he should just let them all go their own ways and seek their own fortunes. He shook his head. Hadn't that been what he'd wanted to do in defying his father and volunteering? And look where that had got him. It might work for some, but for those that did prosper, dozens more would die. No, he had a responsibility to the battalion, the whole battalion. He couldn't afford to doubt that he'd done the right thing, otherwise what was the bloody point? No. He'd chosen his course. Onwards and upwards. There was no looking back now.

THEY HAD TO cross the Strip. Here, the soil was thin and dry, exposing weathered sandstone beneath. Networks of shallow roots laced the ground as plants tried to leech what nutrients they could from the poor shallow soil. Overshadowed by more fecund flora, the pale, hardy scrub clung stubbornly to the niche they had carved for themselves.

Napoo stooped, brushing sand away from the ground where the sandstone had weathered. He grunted, sat back on his haunches and rubbed his stubbly beard, perplexed.

Nellie noticed the urman's unease and walked over. It was worth taking notice of anything that caused him concern.

"What is it, Napoo?"

In reply, the grizzled urman swept his hand over the ground, brushing aside the shallow sandy soil to reveal a hard surface underneath.

Nellie's mouth formed a small 'o' of surprise. "Lieutenant! Only! Over here," she called.

Everson came over as she knelt by Napoo. Her forehead knitted to a frown as she swept her hand to and fro, brushing away further sand as she sought to clear more of the surface. She sat back on her heels, looking at the results of their work. A large, perfectly flat, brushed silver metal surface lay before her. 1 Section and the others drifted over to see what they had discovered.

"Well, I'll be damned!" muttered Everson. He looked up, abashed. "Sorry, Padre."

Padre Rand shook his head, dismissing the apology as unnecessary, seeming just as flabbergasted.

"I've seen this before," said Nellie.

"We all have," said Atkins. "We didn't make any sense of it last time, either."

"We haven't," said Reggie. "Where?"

"The canyon," said Nellie, "before the Fractured Plain, when Corporal Atkins came looking for you. Only that one was set in the canyon."

Norman shook his head. "We didn't see it."

"You must have," Nellie insisted. "You couldn't miss it."

Wally shrugged. "My eyes were on the road."

"And I was pounding away at some bastard insect men high up on the–" Norman paused. "The canyon wall you says?" A penny dropped. "Oh."

"Do you think there's a link then between that one and this one?" asked the Padre.

Here, Nellie was on less certain ground. "Well, it does seem... odd," she admitted. "Don't you think?"

"Oh, it's that all right," agreed Jack, stamping on it with his hobnails, with a sound of metal on metal. It was solid; there was no hollow note. "But everything about this place is bloody odd."

Almost as a reflex, Atkins swung his right foot, scuffing the hobnails against the metal surface with the memory of sparking clogs on cobbles. He'd done it since he was a child, running through the streets with William, and later with Flora, too. There were no sparks here, though.

Beyond the crater, another bolt of lightning crazed into the sky with a thunderous clap hard on its heels. Whatever it was, it was getting closer.

"Riley, what do you make of this?" Everson asked the signaller.

Riley pushed his cap back on his head, and then rubbed his palms together with relish. "Tonkins, get the listening kit out."

The kit was one of Riley's own devising, based on a captured German Moritz set, used to listen in on British communications. He placed copper plates against the exposed metal and connected the wires to the boxed listening apparatus.

Tonkins put the earphones over his head. After several minutes his eyes narrowed, then slowly widened. He beckoned Riley urgently. "Corp!"

Riley rolled his eyes in exasperation and held his hand out. "Well, hand 'em over, lad." Tonkins gave him the earphones and Riley placed them over his own ears.

"What's going on?" asked Norman as they gathered to watch the sideshow.

"The Iddy Umptys reckon they can hear something," Gazette whispered back.

"What, down there?"

Gazette nodded.

"Jesus!" Norman leapt back as if he'd stepped on a hot plate.

"Relax," said Gazette, unperturbed. "If it's like the one in the canyon, it's built like a brick shithouse."

"Quiet, back there!" hissed Everson.

Turning his attention back to the signalman, Everson looked on in frustration as a similar look of bafflement washed over the Corporal's face.

"Well, I'll go to the foot of our stairs!" exclaimed Riley. The NCO pulled the earphones down around his neck and looked up at Everson, baffled. "It's Morse code, sir."

"Morse–"

Riley scowled, held up a finger to shush him, and put the earphones back on.

His wide-eyed gaze met that of Everson's. "It's us, sir," he declared.

Everson was perplexed. "Us?"

"It's young Buckley, sir," said Riley.

Everson let this sink in for a moment. "You mean back at the canyon. How?"

"Same way we eavesdropped on German communications, I expect. Electric induction of some sort. There's a low electric current runs though the earth, a telluric current, you might say, but it should be too weak to transmit the signal this far, unless..." His voice trailed off as he deliberated.

"Unless what?" asked Everson impatiently.

"Unless these two places, this oojah, the strip, and the canyon wall are connected somehow, transmitting the signal like a cable."

Beside him, Tonkins nodded in eager agreement.

"Is that possible?"

Riley raised an eyebrow. "Have you taken a look around, lately, sir?"

"All right, point taken, Corporal," said Everson, taking it in his stride. "Can you send a message back?"

Corporal Riley gave him a black look for even doubting it. He hauled over a kit bag, set up the telegraph apparatus as best as he could and began tapping the Morse key on top of the wooden telegraph box. Then they waited.

"C'mon, Buckley..." muttered Riley, frowning intently as if trying to draw the message through the ground by willpower alone.

There was a tense minute until Riley yelled and punched Tonkins in the arm, before sobering up and reporting po-faced. "Sorry, sir. I mean, message has been received and understood, sir."

Everson was bewildered and surprised, but relieved. "So we have a line of communication."

There was a loud howl of interference. Riley let out a yelp and ripped the earphones from his head. "Jesus, Mary and Joseph!"

A moment later, a magnesium white light flared briefly, lighting up the jungle as another bolt of lightning ripped up into the sky beyond the crater, followed a couple of seconds later by a peal of thunder, causing the men to flinch and duck.

"Right, well, we'll try again after this damn freak storm has passed. Pack up again, Corporal, and prepare to move out."

As they headed towards the centre of the crater, Nellie caught up with Atkins and tried to set her stride to his, but he didn't slow his pace and she had to compensate by jogging intermittently to keep up with him. He might not want to talk to her, but she had one or two things to say to him. She glanced back over her shoulder. The tank crew were watching her, though trying not to look as if they were. Sweet, really. She turned her attention back to Atkins.

"How's it feel to be commander of a tank crew, then?" he muttered darkly.

"Don't be like that, Only. They're not bad men. They haven't been themselves; the fumes affected them. You should know that better than most."

"You disobeyed orders. You went looking for him."

"You'd have done the same," she said, scurrying to keep up.

"Yeah, well, I only hope you find him alive, that's all."

The resentment in his voice surprised Nellie, but he had just lost a good mate and she put it down to that. "I'm sorry about Porgy. Edith will be, too. She liked him."

"He isn't the first mate I've lost, and he probably won't be the last," said Atkins.

There was another flash and thunderclap, almost on top of one another. Atkins sighed heavily.

"I feel like my life's not my own anymore," he said. "I've had prophecies thrown at me, deciding my future. I've had that bloody chatt, Chandar, treating me like some kind of saint for saving its life and telling me I'm something of great significance. Half the men believe me to be some kind of St George, the rest think I'm a glory hound. It feels like everyone else owns a piece of my life but me. Nobody asks what I want."

"It's not just that, though, is it?" said Nellie. "There's something else troubling you."

"It's no business of yours."

"I'm not saying it is. But whatever it is, it's eating you up. It might help to talk to someone."

"You, I suppose?"

"No, but you need to talk to somebody. One of your mates, perhaps."

"No!" he said curtly. Then in a softer, reconciliatory tone, "They wouldn't understand."

"The Padre's a good man," Nellie suggested.

"I'll think about it," he said, head down, eyes fixed ahead, drawing the topic to a close. He stomped along in a sullen silence but, she noticed, his pace had slowed to match hers. It was enough.

THE DOMED BUILDING, with its narrowing finger of a tower, dominated the clearing. From within the structure came the sound of chanting.

Lieutenant Everson beckoned the men to remain in the cover of the undergrowth at the clearing's edge. There were sixteen of them, all told, but their ammunition was severely limited. He didn't want to get into a skirmish if he didn't have to.

He ordered Gazette to cover the doors to the building. A little persuasive fire might keep those within from breaking out, if necessary.

But he needed to know with what he was dealing. With another gesture, he ordered Atkins and Gutsy to advance and scout out the building.

Crawling on their bellies, they crossed the open space until they reached the wall of the building. Crouching with their backs to the wall, Atkins beckoned to Gutsy to stay where he was. Keeping close to the wall and below the loopholes, he made a circuit of the dome, checking for other entrances. He made his way round and came to the only entrance they had seen. The wooden doors were shut as he crawled past. The sound of chanting from within rose and fell like a liturgy.

When he got back round to Gutsy, Atkins jerked his thumb up. "Take a dekko through t'loophole."

Gutsy stood cautiously and peered through the hole. "Urmen. They've got the tanker," he hissed. "He's still alive, but I don't know for how much longer. There's loads of the buggers. Fifty, sixty maybe. Most of 'em had their backs to me, couldn't see much past 'em. Looks like some sort of temple. It's not looking good for Alfie. They had him by some altar thing."

"Bugger," said Atkins. "Stay here. See if you can tell what they're saying."

Atkins headed back to the cover of the undergrowth on his elbows. He slithered down by Everson.

"There's a large mob of urmen in there, all right, sir. Gutsy – I mean Private Blood – thinks they might be getting ready to sacrifice him. From my experience they have a tendency to do that," he offered, before nodding with respect towards their urman guide. "Napoo's mob excepted, that is."

Everson chewed his lip, looking at the building, considering his next move. "It's a defensible position."

"Only if they know how to defend it, sir. There's only one way in and out," said Atkins. "Seem to me that we have surprise on our side, and those loopholes can act just as much in our favour as theirs. Depends who gets to use 'em first."

Everson nodded approvingly. "I see your point, Corporal." He patted Atkins on the shoulder as he crawled back to where the rest had laid up.

"Jack and Pot Shot, take the door with me. Gazette, cover us from here. Riley, Tonkins. Miss Abbott, Padre, stay with him."

"What, we don't get to try out the electric lances, sir?" asked Tonkins, disappointment clear on his face.

Everson smiled. "Not now, private. I can't take the chance." He looked back at Mercy and the tank crew. "The rest of you, fan out and take up positions below the loopholes. Make sure you keep the next man along in sight and on my signal, stand to arms and cover the interior. Fire only on my orders. Napoo, you're with me."

They crept up to the edge of the undergrowth and Lieutenant Everson drew his Webley, its cord lanyard hanging round his neck as he ran across in a stoop to the doors. Napoo followed. He reached the entrance to the building and stood with his back against the wall by the door, and listened for a moment. Inside, the chanting continued unabated. Jack and Pot Shot joined him either side of the door. He watched as the rest of the section and tank crew slipped from the undergrowth to take up their positions at the loopholes. He could hear the familiar but faint jingle and clink of equipment, of men moving and trying to be quiet. He waited for it to stop.

Gazette signalled him from the undergrowth. Everyone was in position.

Everson looked across the doorway at Pot Shot, who nodded his readiness.

He took several deep breaths, steeling himself. He could order the men to do this from the rear, but he was too much the subaltern. He'd always led his men over the top. This time wasn't any different. Neither were the nerves.

* * *

NELLIE LAY IN the undergrowth with Gazette and the signallers. Although she had her revolver, Jack's words still reverberated in her head. She checked her First Aid bag again. Field dressings, iodine, and morphine. It took her mind off Alfie, if only for a moment.

She thought she heard something in the jungle behind them. Or rather, she didn't hear anything. The background jungle noise, which seemed so ubiquitous it barely registered at all. She only noticed it once it had stopped. Why had it stopped? She glanced back over her shoulder, eyes and ears straining.

EVERSON BLEW HARD. The shrill pea whistle split the air.

Pot Shot and Jack put their boots to the wooden doors, which crashed open. The large Tommies stood in the doorway, silhouetted in the rectangle of light, before stepping to the side and covering the urmen with rifle and revolver.

With a rattle of equipment and a cycling of bolts, the men outside stood to, the barrels of their rifles at the loopholes, as they had done hundreds of times before in the trenches, pointing in and covering the urmen inside.

The chanting churned into a jumble of screams and shouts of anger as the urmen turned to face the intrusion, raising swords and spears, ready to defend their sacred space.

Lieutenant Everson stood in the doorway. A couple of Mills bombs in this space and the urmen would be taken care of, he found himself thinking coldly. Instead, he fired his revolver into the roof.

The shouting and screaming died down to a ripple of sobs and muted wailing.

"I want our man and I want him unharmed. Do you understand?" Everson demanded, loudly and slowly. He indicated the loopholes around the circumference of the building and the bristle of rifle barrels and bayonets thrust though them. "We have you covered."

The urmen muttered darkly, restrained by uncertainty and fear, shooting nervous glances at the gun barrels.

"Where is Private Perkins?" he demanded again.

THE COMMOTION STARTLED Alfie as much as the urmen, but when he heard the barked orders and the cycling of Enfield bolts he at least knew what was happening, even if he never expected it. He felt a flood of relief to know that he hadn't been forgotten, and that they had come for him.

"Here, sir," he called over the heads of the urmen.

Alfie limped towards the Lieutenant. The crowd of frightened, angry urmen parted, allowing him to pass.

Alfie took in the rifle barrels at the loopholes. "I've not been harmed, sir. In fact," he said, "just the opposite." He hobbled forward on his splinted leg. The cheery grin of mustered bravado twisted into a grimace as pain lanced through him.

"Alfie! Thank God!" blurted Jack as he saw his crewmate.

Alfie hadn't parted on the best of terms with his crewmates. The last time he saw them they were so paranoid, they'd forced petrol fruit down his throat to try and make him see things their way. He hadn't expected to see them again, and now that he had, he wasn't sure how he felt about it. Anger, relief, and a bright flare of hope. Nellie. Was Nellie with them?

Everson shot a glance at the gunner over his shoulder and the man clammed up. It looked as if Alfie's answers would have to wait.

"It's all right, sir," said Alfie. He turned to face the urmen, who were looking from Alfie to Everson in muted awe. "You can put your weapons down," he told them. "I know these men. They are like me."

"Perkins, what's going on here?"

Alfie glanced back at the urmen. "Long story, sir,"

"Quick précis, then," said Everson, brusquely, eyeing the restive savages.

Alfie raised his eyebrows. "They worship Croatoan, sir," he informed him. "Seem to think he's condemned by that chatt god to the underworld to be punished. They believe the earthquakes and this storm, something they call Croatoan's Torment, are signs of his hellish punishment, sir."

Everson arched an eyebrow. "All right, Perkins, you've got my attention."

"Apparently it attracted Jeffries' attention too, sir. He's been here."

"Jeffries? How do you know?"

"They knew him. I thought they'd killed him, but now I'm not so sure. They wanted him to communicate with their ancestors, sir, the way they did me."

"Spiritualism, Perkins?" said Everson archly. "I hope you haven't been up to Mathers' tricks."

"No, sir!" Alfie protested. "They wanted me to read them something," said Alfie. "Only they can't read. Forgotten how, I daresay. To them it's like magic. So when I read it, they thought I was channelling the voices of the dead, as it were. I suppose in some way I was."

"Read?" said Everson. "What did they want you to read?"

"A book, sir. They claim their ancestors wrote it, like. And there's something else, sir. This book, if it was written by their ancestors," he said, indicating the urmen standing around him. They wouldn't believe his next words. He was not entirely sure he did either. "If that's the case," he said, "the urmen aren't native to this world. I think their ancestors came from Earth."

He pulled back, steadying himself, studying the officer's face, expecting some shared disbelief, that it came as a big a shock to Everson as it had to him, that there was, in all probability, no way home. That they were marooned here. But the revelation barely seemed to register with the subaltern. Everson's shoulders sagged, and a sigh escaped his lips, as if it was not the bad news he had been expecting.

Alfie looked at him in a disbelief that turned swiftly to anger. He felt the bitter betrayal of the soldier denied the full facts. "You knew!"

OUTSIDE, ANOTHER BOLT of energy crackled skyward with a flash and thunderclap. This time, there were scant seconds between them.

Croatoan's Torment had begun.

CHAPTER SEVENTEEN

"And Assemble the Engine Again... "

TULLIVER PUT THE Sopwith down on the Strip. To avoid any damage from whatever energies ran through the lines, he and Hepton pulled the bus into the lush undergrowth bordering the Strip and camouflaged it with large fronds.

Tulliver pulled off his helmet and goggles and leaned against the wing. The elation of survival was fading. He felt like he was going to vomit. He looked at his hand. It was still trembling, and his legs felt shaky.

Hepton walked round the machine in a fury. "What the bloody hell do you think you're playing at? You nearly got us killed up there. When I see Lieutenant Everson, I'll–"

"Mr Hepton."

"What?"

Tulliver's fist connected with Hepton's jaw, and the kinematographer went sprawling. The immense satisfaction it gave Tulliver far outweighed the pain that now ballooned in his knuckles, but at least his hand wasn't shaking anymore.

"I just saved your life. I won't feel obliged a second time."

Something the size of his leg, with nasty-looking pincers, scuttled towards the prostrate Hepton as he glared back up at him, rubbing his jaw. Tulliver swore under his breath, grabbed the man's arm and yanked him to his feet, while drawing his revolver with the other hand and shooting the thing.

Their eyes met and each could see that the other resented the action. Hepton yanked his arm from Tulliver's hand, straightened his glasses and tugged his officer's tunic down with nary a word of thanks. Tulliver didn't care. He wouldn't have accepted it anyway.

Hepton held his peace, and after retrieving his camera, kit and tripod from the aeroplane, let Tulliver lead the way towards the centre of the crater and the tower he had seen, where he hoped to find Everson.

As they pushed through the undergrowth, Tulliver felt things splinter and crunch beneath his boots. Occasionally there was a squelch or a pop. He didn't look.

They stepped through a curtain of hanging vines, and Tulliver stopped. There, hanging in the trees before him almost vertically, as if it were a carcass in a butcher's shop, was the burnt and broken wreckage of the Albatros. The top wing had been sheared off and Tulliver could see scattered sections higher up in the trees. The tail had been ripped off, and its lower planes hung awkwardly in a tangle of wire and snapped spars. Oil and petrol dripped and pooled on the ground beneath it. The engine casing and fuselage showed signs of recent fire, charring the struts and scorching the fabric. Tulliver ran up to the shattered machine. The engine had been driven back into the fragile space behind and he peered into the impact-crumpled cockpit. It was empty.

Tulliver felt a pang of pity, quickly subsumed by horror. Werner had been closer to the lightning bolt than he had, and now his machine had gone down in flames. The military hierarchy on both sides had decided, in their infinite wisdom, that fliers should be denied parachutes. It would, they thought, lead to cowardice and the abandoning of their machines in the face of the enemy. There were two stark choices faced by pilots in those situations. Jump or burn.

Tulliver, himself, had never been faced with that decision, but he'd seen men who had. He'd watched them slowly burn to death as their machines spiralled laconically to Earth and he'd seen them leap and tumble through the air to escape the ghastly pirouetting pyres that would have consumed them.

Jump or burn.

It looked liked Werner had opted to jump.

"One less Hun, then," said Hepton, appraising the wreckage.

Tulliver's eyes flashed with anger. Hepton avoided his gaze and clamped his mouth shut.

The feeling of the loss surprised Tulliver. He'd barely known Werner, but he had been a fellow pilot more than he had been an enemy. For a brief moment, he'd had someone else who could understand, someone with whom he could have shared his experiences.

The empty chair in the mess, the empty bunk in the hut, were constants in the life of a pilot, it seemed. Before, there would always be replacements. But not here. Now, with Werner's death, he felt the ache of loneliness again.

But Werner had wanted his secret shared, and the mystery of the planet penetrated. Tulliver felt the wrapped negative plate under his arm. He could do that much, at least.

"YOU KNEW?"

Everson shook his head emphatically. "Suspected," he said, fending off Alfie's accusation. He studied Alfie as the man glared at him. The revelation had obviously come as a shock to Alfie, as it had to him when he found out about the Bleeker Party. The man knew that others from Earth had been stranded here, but this new disclosure was a dark thought to which he had hardly dared give voice.

"For how long?" asked Alfie, aghast.

"Honestly? Not much longer than you," he said, aware of the urmen's constant scrutiny and that Alfie's own crewmate, Jack, guarded the door. "We'll get your leg looked at." He turned to the door. "Jellicoe, ask Miss Driver to step inside, would you. She has a patient. Order the rest inside, too. Leave two men outside on guard."

"Sir."

Ranaman stepped forward, holding his musket. There was a rattle of rifles from the loopholes as they targeted him.

"No!" said Alfie, hobbling in front of the urman. "He doesn't know what he's holding."

Ranaman bowed his head and offered the musket to Everson. Looking uncomfortable, Everson took it.

"Tell your people I need them to sit down on the floor," he said. "We won't harm them."

NELLIE ENTERED THE temple, the tank crew and Fusiliers filing in behind her and fanning out around the walls, covering the now seated and kneeling urmen. The Padre helped Riley and Tonkins dump kitbags containing the adapted chatt weapons and the knapsacks full of Signals equipment against the temple wall. Mercy and Pot Shot remained outside as sentries, along with Napoo, who wasn't happy about entering another clan's sacred space.

Unable to contain herself, Nellie rushed forward. "Alfie!" She honestly didn't know whether to hit Alfie or hug him. Oh, dash it, of course she did. She hugged him, briefly, aware of the eyes upon them, then stepped back and tried to assume some semblance of public propriety, all thought of the troublesome silence outside pushed from her mind.

As if her reaction had given them permission, the tank crew surrounded Alfie and Nellie both, covering up their emotions with hearty slaps and bonhomie.

Alfie met their gaze. Their eyes were free of the black oil-slick glaze of petrol fruit fuel. He looked around at his crewmates, and knew them all. Days without constant exposure to the petrol fruit fumes had restored their natural selves. He breathed a sigh of relief. These were the men he recognised, the men he trained with at Elvedon, the men he fought with in France, the crew of the HMLS *Ivanhoe*. These were the men he was glad to see now, not the paranoids that they had become under the influence of the alien fumes. "Thanks for not giving up on me," he said.

"If we're being honest," said Reggie, taking Alfie's hand in both of his with sincerity and speaking for them all. "We could say the same. We weren't ourselves."

Wally coughed politely, and the rest of the crew began to drift away. Jack put a large hand on Cyril's shoulder and steered him across the temple. "Come on lad, let's give them a minute."

"What for?" he asked.

Jack whispered something in the lad's ear and Cecil blushed fiercely.

Alfie and Nellie stood awkwardly for a moment.

Nellie punched his arm. "You idiot," she scolded. "You had us worried half to death!"

"Ow. We have to stop meeting like this," said Alfie, scowling and rubbing his bruised bicep. He took her shoulders in his hands, pushed her to arm's length, cocked his head and looked at her in the dark blue tanker coveralls. She looked more at home in them than she had done in the brown uniform of the FANY.

"There's something different about you," he teased. "New hair style?"

"Oh, you," she said, giving him a playful shove.

"Whoa!" he yelped, pivoting round his splinted leg and overbalancing.

She caught his sleeve.

"Better let me have a look at that leg," she said.

ATKINS WATCHED ALFIE and Nellie as she ministered to his injuries, envious of their reunion. Then, unable to look any longer, he turned away, seeing Jack approach. Judging from the tank gunner's bearing, this was trouble.

"Did you hear, Alfie? These savages are descendents of people like us from Earth. Can you believe it, that there were others marooned here before us?"

Atkins looked around at the tank crew. They were looking for reassurance, but the Fusiliers nearby didn't return their looks of confusion. Their glances slipped away. Embarrassed. Guilty. The solidarity of the two sections, which had been fragile at best, began to fail. Whether it was lingering paranoia from the petrol fruit fumes, or justified outrage at being lied to, Atkins wasn't sure.

Norman turned to Atkins, a dangerous edge to his voice. "What, this isn't a surprise to you, either?"

"Not exactly," he mumbled.

"You knew? You fucking *knew*? How long have you known?"

"A few weeks. Since the Nazarrii edifice," said Gutsy.

"But we were there. You kept it secret?"

"You see?" said Pot Shot. "I knew this kind of thing would happen."

Mercy's brow furrowed with annoyance. "Come on, you lot weren't exactly playing with a full deck out there, now were you?"

Norman ignored the barb. "Who the fuck else knows?" he demanded.

"Nobody," said Atkins. "Everson ordered us not to say anything to anybody."

"You're all missing the point," said Wally. "Everson knew, they knew. What else aren't they telling us?"

Everson, noticing the altercation, marched over sharply, his face stern and resolute. "Nothing. I just wanted to avoid exactly this kind of situation, until I was absolutely sure."

The crew of the *Ivanhoe*, subdued by the presence of an officer, were reduced to sullen glares.

"You would have been told," said Everson, "along with everyone else, when the time was right."

"When?" demanded Norman.

Nellie looked over from where she was resplinting Alfie's leg. "For goodness' sake!" she said in exasperation. "You know about it now. This is why Lieutenant Everson is searching for

Jeffries, to find a way home. We're all in the same boat, so stop it, all of you."

There was a stunned, shamed silence.

"Miss Abbott," said Everson. "I'd be thankful if you stopped telling my men what to do."

"I'm sorry, is it bad for their morale?" she asked in a scathing tone.

"It's bad for mine."

RANAMAN STEPPED FORWARD, a religious joy flooding his face, to address the urmen sat before him, like a congregation at a Sunday service, eager to bear witness to the unfolding events. He threw his arms wide and high.

"This is a day long to be remembered; that so many of the sky-being's brethren should appear together at such a time is an omen of great fortune not witnessed in generations. The words of our ancestors are fulfilled before our eyes. Did they not say that at the time of Croatoan's Torment a party would gather here to enter the underworld to abate his suffering? Already one has gone before to confer with the ancestors, those who dwell in the Village of the Dead in the hinterlands of the underworld. They who petition Skarra for mercy and await the day of Croatoan's release, when the Fallen One would be reunited with his broken heart once more. And now, my kin, the time of Croatoan's salvation is here!"

All around him, the urmen wailed in a ritual response.

Atkins heard the words with something akin to despair, and let out a low moan. He felt the weight of another prediction bearing down. It seemed that the more he struggled towards his goal of returning to Flora, the more the damned skeins of fate drew tighter in around him. Was there no way he could escape them? Besides, they promised only vague generalities, never specifics. Where was the one that could have prevented Porgy's death?

There was another flash. Atkins glanced up out of a loophole. Another discharge. Nearer, this time. He saw the perverse lightning bolt punch up, writhing restlessly into the sky. Then came the *crump* of thunder.

The urmen flinched as one, and some wailed and ululated, as if in grief.

"It's another–" Atkins groped for the word.

"Telluric discharge," Riley offered.

"–Telluric discharge, sir. Nearer, this time, by the looks of it."

"They are the Anguish of Croatoan as he is punished in the underworld by Skarra on GarSuleth's decree. His cries made manifest," declared Ranaman.

"Tell me what you know of Croatoan," asked Everson.

The chieftain's face beamed with pride as he spoke, white teeth against a tanned weathered skin. "We are the devoted servants of Croatoan. We have kept the faith of our forefathers." He turned and beckoned towards the fractured rock. "Come, I will show you."

Everson's eyes flicked around, "Atkins, with me. Perkins, you'd better come too. The rest of you, stay alert. Keep them covered."

Ranaman led the Tommies to the huge split boulder that dominated the sacred space. Crepuscular fingers of light shone down upon it from the slits up in the tower above. With its blood-coloured rust stains, Atkins could well believe it was the heart of some giant.

"Behold, the Heart of Croatoan. Long has it been in the care of the Ruanach. His heart was broken when he fell and will only be healed when Croatoan is released from his prison in the underworld. And now, with your presence, as foretold by our ancestors, that time is near."

"This temple marks the centre of the crater," said Everson.

"The very spot where Croatoan fell," declared Ranaman catechistically.

Everson stood close to Atkins and Perkins and, leaning in, spoke in a low voice. "This thing is composed of iron. Probably the remains of a meteor that hit the planet hundreds of years ago. It would seem that chatt and urman myth has some basis in fact." He looked up into the minaret above. The domed temple, with its thin, tapering minaret, might be a representation of the ancient event, the dome being the impact of the meteor, the minaret its fiery tail.

"Iron?" said Atkins, touching the boulder.

"The reason I suspect Perkins was spared," said Everson. "They mistook the crash of the *Ivanhoe* for another sacred rock falling from the sky." He raised a sardonic eyebrow. "You're the Man in the Moon, Perkins."

"Come," said Ranaman, leading them through the narrow cleft between the two halves of rock, towards the back of the temple. They could have walked round, but there seemed to be some implied ritual in passing between them, a significance of which they were unaware. There, from a niche in the wall, Ranaman retrieved the wooden casket.

"This great magic was left in our keeping also. Through it, our ancestors who sought out Croatoan communicate with us from the Village of the Dead. It has been a long time since our ancestors spoke to us. Then came the sky-being, Jeffries. He said he came from the place of our forefathers in search of Croatoan. He spoke to our ancestors and then passed beyond, following them into the underworld."

As he spoke, Ranaman opened the casket, revealing the leather-bound book. Everson lifted it out of its resting place and set it on a shallow facet of the rock so that it was illuminated by a pool of light from the minaret above. It was definitely older than the Bleeker journal, with heavy binding and thick wrinkled vellum pages.

His anticipation grew as he traced a finger over the Croatoan Sigil, cast in iron embedded on the front. He licked an index finger and proceeded to turn the pages. The book was another journal of sorts. Many early portions were in a script he couldn't read, but one that he recognised.

"It looks like the code in Jeffries' occult journal," said Atkins.

"Hmm," said Everson thoughtfully. Here and there, he recognised the Croatoan symbol again. He felt the hair on the back of his neck stand on end.

Near the beginning, there was a manifest. Those sections he could read spoke of a new Virginia colony and of Croatoan. It seemed that whatever befell the missing colony, stranger and more deadly things had befallen them here.

"So they *did* come from Earth," said Perkins.

"It appears so," said Everson uncomfortably. "They'd gone looking for a new world. It seemed the one that they found wasn't quite what most of them expected."

Other pages spoke volumes, more so because they weren't there. Someone had torn them out. Jeffries again, no doubt. All of which served to convince Everson that he was on the right track. He speculated on what information they might contain. There was no doubt that this book contained a factual account of the colony's day-to-day survival, among other, more esoteric, matters. He would have liked to study it more closely, but Ranaman took the book from him and clutched it to his chest.

As the urman led them back through the cloven rock, Everson wondered wistfully if the battalion's own War Diary would become such a relic in the future. He had a vision of some other snatched and stranded band of people, some decades or a century hence, arriving on the strange world in strange machines, coming across the Pennine Fusiliers' official account. He imagined them finding the remains of the trenches, reclaimed by the veldt, long overgrown and forgotten. Skeletons occupied the firesteps, standing to for eternity, their khaki uniforms rotting and their bleached bones intimately entwined with wireweed. In his mind's eye, he saw his dugout, half-collapsed and empty, a memorial, like Scott's Antarctic hut, and envisaged the strangers coming across the mildewed and foxed Battalion War Diary and looking at it in wonder and fear. He shook his head and dismissed the maudlin fancy. He didn't want that to become their reality.

TULLIVER CAUGHT GLIMPSES of the tower through the trees before him. The only sound breaking the silence around him was the crack and slap of the undergrowth and Hepton's inveterate cursing as he lumbered along, carrying his bags, boxes and tripod.

He squinted through the thinning canopy overhead. His petrol-fruit-enhanced eyes caught an area of the sky that seemed to shine a little brighter than the rest, as if it had been polished and worn through wear. Another bright flash arced its way into the sky. Interesting. It seemed his heightened senses could pick up a building discharge.

It was followed a few seconds later by a rolling boom, and in the distance, he could hear whoops and howls of alarm. However, around them, but for the persistent creep and creak of the parasitic creepers that pervaded the jungle, they were cocooned in an area of silence.

As they pushed on, Tulliver, curious, exercised his newfound skill, spotting other shiny patches of sky and finding that each built to a lightning bolt. So intent was he on honing this new skill that he stepped out of the undergrowth and almost onto the end of a bayonet, as Mercy and Pot Shot spun round to meet his unexpected arrival with cold steel.

"Halt! Identify yourself. Friend or – fucking hell, sorry, Mr Tulliver, sir!"

Something came crashing through the undergrowth, huffing and snorting. The two Tommies swung their rifles towards the sound.

"Christ, no!" said Tulliver, his hand pushing Mercy's rifle barrel down. "That's Mr Hepton." Then he sniffed and waved his revolver in the general direction of the noise. "Then again, kill him if you want. I shan't bloody blame you."

Hepton stumbled into the clearing and, upon seeing the Fusiliers, proceeded to divest himself of his baggage and equipment, dumping it on the ground at his feet.

"Where the bloody hell is Jenkins? He can carry this stuff now," he said, straightening up, arching his spine and pushing his hands into the small of his back as he recovered his composure.

Mercy and Pot Shot looked at each other.

Hepton stood there, waiting. "Well?"

"Jenkins is dead, sir."

Hepton threw his hands to the heavens and rolled his eyes in exasperation. "Bloody typical!"

"Where's Everson? I've something he needs to see," Tulliver asked, patting the wrapped package under his arm.

"This way, sir," said Mercy, leading him into the temple.

"Are you going to help me?" snapped Hepton at Pot Shot.

"Can't sir," said Pot Shot, straight-faced. "I'm on guard."

Muttering and huffing, Hepton glared darkly after the pilot before shouldering his load, unaware of the gossamer-fine white threads spreading silently through the damp soil and leaf mulch at his feet.

INSIDE THE TEMPLE, Tulliver saw Everson, standing at the centre along with Atkins, a tanker and an urman, lit by shafts of sunlight converging from slits in the tower above. They served to illuminate two halves of a huge boulder. Around them, a host of urmen sat or knelt, watching them with rapt attention as if trying to burn the moment into their memories.

The doors of the temple crashed open behind him as an irate Hepton dragged his equipment inside, almost tripping over an urman, who shuffled out of his way.

"Bloody fuzzy wuzzies!" he muttered.

Tulliver shook his head and ignored him.

The Lieutenant looked up from his rocky lectern. "Tulliver! Thank God. Is your machine safe?"

"As safe as it can be around here," said Tulliver, irritated that Everson's first thought was for his bus.

"What about the Alleyman?"

"Werner?" said Tulliver. "Crashed, but not before he showed me something I think you ought to see. It concerns the wall we found in the canyon. I've reason to believe that it may be part of something much bigger altogether." Tulliver unwrapped his package. "Werner told me he'd seen a pattern etched across the landscape. I think the canyon wall and the crater strip are part of it."

Everson raised an eyebrow. "Interesting. We've managed to send a Morse signal along the Strip back to the canyon earlier. They seem to be made of the same metal."

"Really? Thanks to Hepton, unbelievably, now you can see, too. Werner took this negative plate from thirteen thousand feet. We got the chatts to mix up some sort of developing fluid."

"It's not perfect. We didn't have anything with which to fix the image," said Hepton. "It's not my fault."

Tulliver passed the negative plate to Everson, who held it up in a shaft of light.

He frowned with concentration as he studied the image.

"What am I looking at?"

Tulliver took him through it, pointing out the tracery of geometric lines across the landscape, clearer for being reversed.

"They look like some kind of roadways across the landscape, or some sort of sacred geometry, perhaps; see how they radiate out from various points," he said.

"Reminds me of Jeffries' pentagram on the Somme, sir," said Atkins, peering at the pattern.

"That occurred to me, too," admitted Tulliver. "It's more than that, Everson. If you are right about the wall and the Strip, it would seem to indicate some sort of superstructure underpinning the landscape. The chatts believe it to be a kind of geomancy, divine proof that GarSuleth wove this world for them. And another thing, these reverse lightning bolts–"

"Riley calls them telluric discharges," said Everson.

"–these telluric discharges seem to emanate from points where these lines converge and intercept. Here and here, for instance," he said quickly pointing out nodes on the rapidly darkening glass plate. "If you ask me, there's a much bigger mystery at the heart of this than mere chatt theology. I'd stake my life on it."

"Hmm." Everson nodded thoughtfully. "The urmen believe these telluric discharges are the agonies of Croatoan, imprisoned and tortured in some chatt version of hell."

As they studied the image on the plate, Tulliver felt a faint tingling in his hands. He lifted his arm, inspected his palm, and turned it over. The hairs on the back of his hand stood on end, as if a static charge were building. He looked at the rocks and noticed out of the corner of his eye, in the cleft between them, the same kind of peculiar shine; as if the air had been polished to a high patina and worn thin in the process. He couldn't think of any other way to describe it.

"John," he said in measured tones, "I think you should step away from the boulders."

A faint intermittent buzz started to issue from the two halves.

"He's right, sir, better step back," said Riley, foregoing military conduct and grabbing Everson's braided cuff.

By now the other urmen were moving back, all except Tarak, who watched the proceedings with growing concern. Ranaman held the metal-clasped book, mesmerised by the sudden activity, as small writhing threads of white-blue energy began to spit between the two halves. As they built in power to a crescendo, crackles of energy leapt from the rock to the walls of the dome like Tesla arcs.

"The Heart of Croatoan begins to beat!" cried Ranaman, his voice filled with wonder and triumph, his hair now billowing out with collected static.

"No!" cried Riley, dropping to the ground. "Get down and for gawd's sake take off yer battle bowlers if yer wearin' 'em!"

Bolts of energy, attracted by Ranaman's proximity, leapt across the space and earthed through him, jerking him like a crazed marionette. He let out a strangled scream that cut off abruptly as the bolt vanished. He dropped to the ground, a broken puppet, as if it had been all that was holding him up. The book skittered between the two halves of rock.

There were moans and screams from the urmen, who got up and stampeded for the temple doors, knocking the crouching Fusiliers and tankers aside.

Tendrils of blue-white energy spat out from the split rock to lick the inside of the dome before dying down as if someone had turned a dial, leaving one or two stray arcs that still sparked and spat intermittently between the halves.

Everson looked back past Ranaman's body to the rocks. The fallen book lay in the cleft between them.

Everson made to go back and get it, but Perkins grabbed him.

"It's too dangerous, sir."

"We need the book, private!"

Tarak hesitated for a second, and then bolted past Ranaman's body towards the sacred rocks.

"No, son!" yelled Perkins.

Tarak knelt low by the rocks, stretching his hand out to reach the tome. Fingers flexed as he strained to reach for the book. Small arcs of energy snapped angrily about it, like electric teeth. Undeterred, Tarak edged into the cleft and grasped the book firmly. As he retrieved it, clasping it to his chest, a bolt of energy arced out and struck the book, propelling him back across the chamber.

Perkins began to drag himself on his belly and elbows across the dirt floor towards the urman.

Then, from outside, the shouts and screams began, accompanied by the sound of rapid rifle fire.

INTERLUDE 4

Letter from Lance Corporal Thomas Atkins to Flora Mullins

6th April 1917

My Dearest Flora,

Still no blessed tank. Would you believe it? We did meet up with the RFC chap, though. Not blagged a go in his aeroplane yet, then again, I've been a bit busy. Still, when all is said and done, we had a grand ride in a hot air balloon. You could see for miles. Who says the Army is all hard work and no play?

Having said that, we've come down to Earth with a bit of a bump now. The place where we are now is completely overgrown, it's worse than your dad's vegetable patch. I think we might have to do a bit of weeding.

Mind you, we do actually have all the modern conveniences – and your Mama worries about us poor lads at the Front. We have Electricity at the moment. All I need is a smoking jacket and an armchair while I read my book and look at photographs and I'll be right at home. I know my Grandma doesn't hold with it, and I can see why. I very nearly did have a smoking jacket! The Company Quartermaster Sergeant wouldn't have been too happy about that.

Ever yours
Thomas.

CHAPTER EIGHTEEN

"The Sullen Ghosts of Men..."

On the floor of the temple, Alfie shook the prostrate Tarak by the shoulders, as the indoor lightning played over his head. Splayed on his back, Tarak still clutched the book tightly to his chest.

"Lad? Lad!"

The youth groaned.

"He's alive. Nellie. Nellie!"

Nellie came over on all fours, the medical knapsack swinging at her side from one shoulder as she sought to avoid the tendrils of energy that spat from the rocks. Needing to do something, Padre Rand went with her on all fours.

Nellie checked Tarak's pulse and breathing. He was still alive, but unconscious.

She gently prised the book from the lad's grasp, and as she did so, she gasped.

The Padre made the sign of the cross. "Dear Lord, the poor man," he said under his breath.

Seared into Tarak's chest, from the iron design on the front of the tome, was the Sigil of Croatoan.

Staying low, Tulliver scrambled over to the temple wall and, with a wary glance back at the arcing rock, raised his head to look out through a loophole.

The clearing surrounding the temple was white, as if someone had draped a fine muslin sheet over everything. It was like a thick white cobweb. Through it, taut, swollen bulbs had fruited. It seemed as alien to the surrounding vegetation as that did to the flora of Earth, and that, thought Tulliver, was saying something.

The urmen, fleeing the electrical discharge in the temple, had run straight into the deadly carpet. The fruiting bulbs exploded, enveloping them in yellowish clouds. They coughed and choked, gasping for breath in the noxious plumes, clawing at their throats.

"Christ! Gas! Gas! Gas!" cried Gutsy, peering out of a loophole in the wall.

"It's not gas, it's spores," yelled Nellie.

By now, the Tommies were at the loopholes, peering out as stray bolts of energy crackled out at the wall of the temple around them. They fumbled at their chests for their PH gas hoods, pulled them over their heads and tucked them into their collars. With their circular mica eyepieces and short red rubber non-return valves, they looked as alien as anything else there.

The urmen of the Ruanach succumbed to the spore clouds and fell to the ground, where the gossamer fine carpet of mycelia advanced inexorably over their bodies, and the spores that they had inhaled sprouted from their mouths and noses, choking them.

The fast-spreading network of living threads made short work of their bodies. It desiccated them before the Tommies' eyes, and the mummified remains split open with dry cracking noises as more fruiting bodies rose from them.

Atkins hurried from one loophole to another. The carpet of threads was creeping towards the temple. "Whatever it is, it's surrounding us," he called out.

"I knew this was a bad place," said Napoo, a bandanna of cloth round his face against the spores.

Everson stood at the temple doors, revolver in hand. "Evans, Jellicoe," he called out. "Fall back! Get inside." Everson turned to the others. "The rest of you, stand to!"

Mercy and Pot Shot hared through the doors, slammed them shut and rested against them with relief.

"One minute it wasn't there, the next it's sprouting up through the ground. What the hell is that?" heaved Mercy through his gas hood.

Pot Shot turned towards him with an exaggerated movement so he could see him though his eyepieces. "Don't you ever get tired of asking that question?"

"Around here?" queried Mercy. "Half the time it's the only sane question worth asking." He arched his back, pushing himself off the door, and ran in a low stoop along behind the rest of the section and the tank crew at the loopholes, stopping only to duck and yelp as a venomous electrical tongue lashed out from the rocks, snapping indolently at the wall above him. He took his place next to them, and Pot Shot appeared by his side.

Outside, drifting in from the jungle, a yellowish spore mist was rising and a vague shadowy shape moved with it, coalescing into a ghost-like grey figure that stepped lethargically from the trees.

"Huns!" yelled Cyril, glancing back into the temple from the loophole. "It's bloody Huns!"

Risking a whiplash of energy, Jack launched himself up to the loophole and peered out across the shrouded clearing. "Huns?" Then he saw. It had been an easy mistake for Cyril to make. Too often, in a pale dawn, they had seen the grey-clad Huns creeping towards them.

This, though, was no Hun. Thin and cadaverous, its skin was grey and sunken, its ill-fitting serge uniform scarcely visible beneath a dusting of fine threads. Wrinkled, puckered growths, like some sort of cankers, distorted the shape of its head and right arm and half its chest. The figure moved clumsily, as if trying to maintain its balance was an effort. This was a misshapen travesty of a man, an obscene mockery of a Tommy.

Nellie recognised the sight, too.

"Mathers!" she cried though her gas hood. "But that's impossible. We saw him swept away."

"It's wearing puttees. It's not an officer," said Atkins, peering out. "That's Talbot, one of the tank salvage party."

"Jeffries has woken the dead to do his bidding!" cried Tonkins.

"Can he really do that? Bring back the dead?" asked Cecil, his voice tremulous with fear.

"It's the kind of diabolical thing he probably would do," said Mercy.

"Well, the last time we saw Talbot, he weren't actually dead," said Gutsy.

"Maybe so, but he doesn't look well," admitted Mercy.

"I'll give you that."

Mercy and Pot Shot fired at him. The bullets tore through Talbot's body, the initial force throwing his shoulder back and twisting him off balance momentarily as he recoiled from the impact, but he remained standing. Motes of grey spore dust swirled in the air around him from the impact.

Mercy looked back over his shoulder. "Well if he wasn't dead then, I'd say he is now."

"No!" came the muffled cry from one of the tankers. "It does no good. You'll just spread the spores. We tried it. You can't bomb them, shoot them, or burn them without spreading spores. There's no way to stop them!"

The gaunt, grey-faced soldier turned towards them and watched implacably.

"He's possessed by the same thing that Mathers was," said Nellie.

From out of the spore mist, other emaciated forms appeared to surround the temple, each one a shambling mockery of a Broughtonthwaite Mate, each one laced with a fine filigree of mycelia and deformed by cankers. It was the rest of Corporal Talbot's salvage party.

"Talbot, stand down!" cried Everson through his gas respirator.

The cadaverous Corporal and his grey men stood immobile. From their feet, thin, pernicious threads began to advance across and through the soil, joining with the carpet spreading from the dead urmen, weaving its way toward the temple.

ATKINS LOOKED ON with revulsion. Since he'd volunteered and been shipped over to France, death was something he'd lived with daily. For Christ's sake, his own pal had just died. On the Somme, you couldn't escape from death and decay; everywhere you looked there were bodies, English, Belgian, German, French. The stench of rotting corpses filled the air, but there was at least some comfort in that. As the old trench song went, '*When you're dead, they stop your pay.*' Dead was dead. But this? This was abominable. It appalled him. The fact that they knew these men repulsed him even more. There was Hume, Owen, Fletcher, Banks, Preston, Mitchell, Walker and Hardiman. It was like some sick joke Jeffries might play, reanimating the dead to serve his own evil ends. In some way he wished it were. But this was just nature, some kind of hellish mould that animated their bodies. It had taken them over, while all the time feeding on their flesh in order to sustain itself, even as it used them to migrate to look for new hosts, new food.

Now it had found them.

STANDING WITH HIS back to the wall, beside a loophole, revolver in hand, Tulliver glimpsed the shine in the centre of the temple again between the rocks. It grew brighter, shining as though the air was threadbare and worn.

"Down!" he warned.

Behind them, the two halves of the meteorite spat out bolts of energy.

"Jesus!" Mercy ducked as another buzzing arc of energy whipped the wall over his head and dragged itself upwards towards the apex of the dome. "Talk about a rock and a hard place – no offence, Padre."

The Padre, hunched against the wall, clutching his Bible, shook his gas-hooded head. "None taken."

"By George! It's stopping!" said Reggie, peering through his loophole at the surrounding white carpet.

The creeping deathly white shroud had slowed and petered out six yards from the temple, like melted snow. The grey mould-ridden men waited.

"Why, what's holding it back? They've killed enough urmen. What are they waiting for?"

Tulliver barked another warning. "Stay down!"

The Tommies hugged the earth as, overhead, bolts whipped and snapped.

"Bloody hell, it's worse than a barrage of whizz-bangs!"

Mercy shrugged. "It's all just stuff in the end," he said as he hunkered down on his haunches, his head under his arms as if he expected a rain of dirt and shrapnel, the default position for a soldier under barrage.

"Bloody good job we aren't wearing our splash masks," said Wally, as an arc of lightning brushed the wall above his head.

Outside, another flash went off. This time it must have been very near. The thunder was almost on top of them. Atkins felt it reverberate through the walls of the temple.

"Jesus, that was close!"

"Quite takes me back to the Somme," bellowed Gazette through his gas hood. "Ah, the good old days!"

Atkins saw the field of fungus convulse and shrivel in the presence of the lightning, and the grey men recoil. He looked at where the carpet of mould stopped, in a circle around the temple. He turned around and glanced at the Heart of Croatoan, the space between the two halves sparking half heartedly, as if the discharge was dissipating.

"It's the telluric energy," he said. "That's what's holding it at bay."

"And if we stay in here, the same energy might kill us," said Everson grimly.

AT THE CANYON, having sent, and received, a message from Lieutenant Everson in the crater, Buckley found himself regarded in a new light. The ability to press some technological advance on this world seemed like a triumph of sorts, as though they had managed to bend this alien nature to their will.

As a reward, Sergeant Dixon had him manning a permanent, if precarious, listening post atop the scree slope at the base of the exposed wall. For a job that required quiet, the last few hours of distant booms from beyond the canyon didn't make his job any easier. They echoed off the canyon's walls, rebounding in a constant barrage of noise and flashes.

Dixon tramped loudly and carelessly up the scree slope, hoping for more news. Buckley frowned at him and held up a finger for quiet. Dixon curled his lip and said nothing, waiting impatiently.

Without warning, Buckley ripped the earphones from his head with a yelp of pain as a high-pitched howl threatened to burst his eardrums.

Arcs of energy began to lash from the metal, rolling over the surface of the wall, spitting and hissing like an angry cat, until they danced and flickered out over the top of the scree slope, sending Dixon tumbling back arse over tit.

Buckley disconnected his equipment, lugged it behind a boulder, and prayed.

A bolt of lightning burst up the wall and exploded through the top of the canyon with a clap that echoed round it for what seemed minutes. It crazed briefly up into the sky, starkly illuminating the canyon, causing the blue-green lichen blisters scattered across the canyon rocks to burst in showers of glutinous acid that hissed as they etched speckled pits into the surrounding rocks.

Dixon looked up at Buckley, apoplectic with rage. "What have you done, lad? What the bloody hell have you done?"

"It wasn't me, Sarn't," said Buckley, looking down at the Sergeant in alarm. "It wasn't me."

THEY HAD TO leave the temple. Atkins watched the telluric energy flicker and spit round the walls above them, the arcs becoming weaker and fainter.

"Isn't there any way we can channel this telluric energy, direct it somehow?" he asked.

"I don't see how," said Mercy. "Even if we could get near the rocks, how do we move them?"

"We don't even know what generates it," said Pot Shot.

"Oh, that'll be you and your books again, will it?" snapped Mercy.

"This isn't getting us anywhere," Nellie snapped at them.

Tonkins said something, but the thick flannel of his gas hood muffled it.

Riley jabbed his elbow into Tonkin's ribs. "Speak up, lad. They didn't hear you through your gas hood."

Awkwardly, Tonkins raised his hand, cleared his throat. "It's only electricity," he said, emboldened by Riley's encouragement.

Fifteen pairs of blank mica eyes turned to stare at him. Their unblinking glares unnerved him until Riley urged him on, kicking his foot. "We – we don't need the rock for that," he added quietly.

Everson clapped his hands and pointed at the signalmen. "You're right, private. Riley. Tonkins. You wanted to test those electric lances in the field. Now's your chance."

"Well done, lad," muttered Riley with pride.

"They will work, won't they?" asked Tonkins.

"Our bits I'm sure about," said Riley shrugging heavily for effect to compensate for his gas hood as he dragged the kitbags towards them. "The chatt stuff, not so much."

They pulled the two jerry-rigged chatt backpacks from the kitbags, along with the electric lances attached to them by insulated cable.

"You can't be serious!" said Hepton. "You're putting our lives in the hands of a pair of Iddy Umpties?"

Everson turned on his heels. Even through his gas mask, his tone was hard. "Mr Hepton. Entire divisions have often depended on Signals. The lives of every member of this battalion have depended on Signals. Their work, under dangerous conditions, has saved countless lives, so if you have any complaints I suggest you keep them to yourself, if you get *that* message."

Tonkins ran a hand over the smooth clay battery backpack, checking for damage.

"You ready?" asked Riley, setting his pack between his legs and gripping it with his knees.

Tonkins nodded and did the same.

"Good lad."

They began cranking the magneto telephone crank handles set in the back; the clay battery packs whirred as the charges began to build.

"How long?" asked Everson.

"We're going as fast as we can, sir," said Riley, frantically turning the small crank handle. "Some chatts generate a natural bioelectrical charge that they can store. We have to do it manually."

Atkins peered out of the loophole and watched as the urmen bodies beyond desiccated further, crumbling to dust before his eyes.

Outside, the telluric discharges no longer preventing their advance, the grey men shuffled closer, dragging swathes of white filaments along with them as they moved. They stopped at the boundary where the mycelia had stopped, unable or unwilling to advance further. The inert carpet of fungus at their feet began to grow once again, its mycelia threading its way towards the temple.

"It looks like we're out of time!" said Atkins.

"Tulliver, anything?" asked Everson.

Tulliver glanced out of the corner of his eye at the boulders. He shook his head. "Nothing."

Without the telluric discharge from the meteor to hold it in check, the web of fungus continued its relentless advance towards the temple.

"Whenever you're ready, Corporal," said Everson impatiently, as he watched Riley.

The fevered whirr of the magnetos filled the air with an insect buzz as the two men wound the handles for all they were worth. Tonkins resorted to short bursts of frenzied turning, stopping once in a while for a few seconds to catch his breath.

"That should be enough," said Riley, standing up and trying to shake some life into his cramped hand. Beside him, Tonkins eased himself up onto unsteady legs, like a newborn foal.

"Right," said Riley, picking up the attached electric lances. "I'm going to need four volunteers, two to fire and two to wind the crank handle and recharge the battery. It's a bit like a Flammenwerfer, you see, where you have to keep pumping."

Everson flicked out a finger. "Atkins, Evans, Tonkins, Blood."

Mercy and Gutsy shouldered their rifles and fell in by the signalmen, taking Atkins' and Tonkins' knapsacks for them.

Riley lifted a clay backpack and slipped the webbing straps over Atkins' shoulders, and helped Tonkins follow suit. Atkins hefted the unfamiliar lance, connected by cable to the backpack.

"Atkins, Evans. I want you at the van," said Everson. "Tonkins, Blood, you'll have to bring up the rear."

Both men nodded with slow exaggerated movements from under their gas hoods to show they understood.

Nellie wrapped bandages round the face of the young injured urman to protect him from the spores. She called to the urman guide huddling sullenly against the wall. "Napoo," she asked. "Can you help the Padre carry this young lad?"

"His name's Tarak," said Alfie, through his gas hood.

Napoo, seeing the brand burn on Tarak's chest, shook his head and backed away.

"Napoo, it's not his fault. It was an accident."

"He is cursed!"

"He will be if we don't help him!"

Nellie gave the book she had prised from Tarak to Everson, who told Mercy to pack it in his knapsack.

The Padre and a reluctant Napoo lifted the now semi-conscious Tarak between them.

Either side of the temple door, the tank crew and the Black Hand Gang readied themselves.

"Walk and keep walking." said Everson. "Stay close, don't get separated. Hold your fire. Don't shoot at them, don't use bombs."

Mercy stood by the doors with Atkins.

"Check you can turn the crank handle," said Riley. "Never really tried it in battlefield conditions."

Mercy glanced around in his hood, and Atkins smirked under his. He could tell Mercy was embarrassed. He gave the handle a tentative crank.

"You'll have to do it faster than that!" scolded Riley.

There was a peculiar hacking from under Pot Shot's gas hood. He was laughing. "It's what your right arm's for!"

TULLIVER PULLED OPEN the temple doors. The sky outside, just beyond the crater, had worn through and seemed almost black. If he shifted his eyes, its normal colour reasserted itself, as if some after-image danced in the corner of his vision. "Wait!" he called out.

A tremendous flash of light and a deep sonorous boom that he could feel in his bones drowned out any response. It set off a frenzy of whipperwills somewhere overhead as a concussive blast of wind swept over the jungle.

Before them, the advancing carpet quivered and almost seemed to ebb, and the grey mould-ridden cadavers cowered from the harsh flash.

As the skyward bolt dispelled, the fungal carpet was briefly dormant.

"Now!" commanded Everson.

Atkins stepped from the temple and aimed the electric lance at the edge of the fungus now covering the clearing. He squeezed the chatt trigger pads and felt the lance kick and jerk in his hand, as the untamed bolt of lightning bucked and writhed, vaporising a patch of fungus. Fruiting pods had no chance to spore and surrounding mycelia shrivelled. He soon found that by varying the pressure on the trigger pads, he could vary the strength of the electric bolt.

"It's working!" yelled Mercy into his ear.

The Talbot-thing waved a hand and the clearing began to blossom with more swelling fruit pods.

Atkins fired again, moving forwards to clear a path out towards the surrounding jungle, sweeping the lance from side to side like a Flammenwerfer.

Following them, the rest of the party edged nervously along a narrow causeway of cleared ground through the deadly garden. Bringing up the rear, Gutsy turned the crank handle as Tonkins' bolts licked away at the ground, repelling the fungus threads trying to close in behind them, lapping at their feet like a rising tide, cutting off their path back to the temple.

"Keep cranking!" yelled Atkins to Mercy over his shoulder.

The grey fungus-possessed corpses kept their distance. The electric lance wasn't a useful long-range weapon, but it was enough to keep them at bay.

The tight knit group shuffled forward behind Atkins as he cleared a path, edging past the urmen bodies smothered by the thick blanket of mycelia, like the cobweb-cocooned bodies of flies in a spider's web.

But the time between recharges was getting longer, and the strength of the electric bolts weaker. Gutsy and Mercy were tiring at their crank handles, leaving the Tommies vulnerable. Everson ordered Pot Shot and Gazette to take over the cranking.

With a fresh charge, Atkins' lance spat another convulsive stream of electricity into the growing fungal mass as the Talbot-thing watched impassively, out of range.

Tulliver stumbled, and several hands caught him up before he fell. "Wait!" he cried.

Another telluric discharge, somewhere within the crater this time, ripped up into the sky with a blinding flash and a concussive wave of thunder that Atkins felt roll through him.

Around them, the fungal mat convulsed and the advancing mycelia shrank back involuntarily.

Atkins pressed home their advantage, white bolts of energy carving a path through to the forest. From there, with Pot Shot behind him cranking the magneto handle, he covered the rest as they made it to the comparative safety of the tree line; the Padre and Napoo helping the semi-conscious Tarak, Alfie hobbling along, aided by Nellie, followed by Jack and the tank crew; Cecil, Norman, Reggie and Wally, leaving Hepton to struggle alone, weighed down by his equipment. Mercy and Gutsy came next with Riley, who kept his eyes nervously on the backpacks. Everson followed them in and Gazette and Tonkins brought up the rear.

Even here, gauzy curtains of fungal threads hung from the trees, but they were thinner, as though the fungus had been conserving its energy for its assault.

"More spore pods," called Cecil as huge great plum-pudding-sized balls swelled in the fungus-covered undergrowth nearby. Atkins turned and swept a jagging electric bolt across them.

"It's at times like this I really wish we had the *Ivanhoe*!" cursed Alfie.

"I agree. But it's out of fuel and ditched," said Reggie.

"Fuel?" said Pot Shot. "I saw a stack of fuel drums go over the side of the crater during the Zohtakarrii attack. Rolled right over the edge, they did."

"Why the bloody hell didn't you tell us before?" asked Norman, aggrieved.

"I had other things on my bloody mind, all right?"

Atkins squeezed the trigger pads of his lance. The lance tip fizzled. "Pot Shot, stop gossiping and get cranking."

"You know I've already got a wife, don't you, Only?" he sniped as he set about the magneto handle with a will.

They advanced through the jungle. Shrouds of fungus hung from the boughs above them, where more fruit pods began to balloon.

"Overhead, Atkins," cautioned Everson.

"I'm on it, sir." Atkins brought his lance up. Behind him, Pot Shot's handle turning began to slow and he stopped again, shaking his wrist to try to bring some life back into it.

Jack pushed Cecil forward. "Take over, lad; give the mud-slogger a break."

Cecil stepped past Pot Shot, who nodded his thanks, and the young gunner whizzed the handle round. Hearing the hum build, Atkins held the lance firmly, squeezed the trigger pad, and played the arc of electric energy across the trees. Super-heated instantly to high temperatures, wood and sap exploded above them like Woolly Bears, even as the gossamer veils and fruit pods were vaporised. The Tommies ducked as hard wood shrapnel exploded around them like Whizz Bangs.

"Jesus! Watch it, Only. It's not us you're trying to kill!" yelled Gazette.

"Sorry!"

Atkins looked back and saw that the mycelia had reached the temple; the path by which they had made their escape was lost again under the tide of alien filaments that now covered the entire clearing.

Watching them, the Talbot-thing lifted its feet from the tightly knotted fungus fibres around it and, dragging a train of them behind it, began to lumber after them, the other grey reanimated Fusiliers turning to follow.

"Go on with the others!" Atkins ordered Tonkins, "I'll follow."

Atkins waited. Behind him, Cecil kept cranking the handle, building the charge. "Keep going, Cecil. I want to teach this thing a lesson." The whirring upped its pitch as Cecil redoubled his efforts.

Atkins fired. The lance kicked violently in his hand as a bright bolt of electrical fire snapped out at one of the grey mouldering dead, incinerating the puckered growth on its chest and flinging the creature backwards, where the carpet of corpse-fed filaments cushioned its fall.

The others halted their advance.

From under his hood, Atkins curled his lip with grim satisfaction. "That ought to buy us a minute or two. Come on, Cecil."

As he turned to leave, Atkins heard a whirring.

"Cecil, it's all right, you can stop cranking now."

"But I have," said the young tanker, standing by his side in his coveralls and gas hood.

The whirring noise continued. Was something wrong with the backpack? Atkins twisted his neck in alarm, trying to look over his shoulder for signs of damage, but couldn't see any, and with his gas hood on it was difficult to tell where the sound was coming from.

"Then what the hell is that... noise..." His voice trailed away as he turned.

Hepton stood with his box camera set on its tripod, cranking the handle and panning it across the shroud-covered clearing and its fungus-animated corpses.

Atkins didn't know what was worse, the fate of those Fusiliers or Hepton's exploitation of them. Did the man only have eyes for the main chance? Those were men out there, dead men who deserved better. Perhaps he should have left him to them.

"I can see the caption card now," bellowed Hepton cheerfully from beneath his gas hood. "Attack of the Crater Mass!"

Atkins shook his head in disgust and deliberately barged into the kinematographer with his shoulder as he pushed past, jarring the camera.

"I say, there was no call for that," said Hepton, looking up from the viewfinder. "I'm only doing my job!"

Atkins strode off after the others without looking back. Cecil followed, leaving Hepton alone.

Alarmed, the kinematographer hoiked his tripod and camera box onto his shoulder and hurried after them.

"Wait, don't leave me!"

CHAPTER NINETEEN

"What Dead Are Born..."

RAGGED WHEEZES AND dry gasps filled the air as men collapsed against tree trunks and rocks to catch their breaths; all except Napoo, who looked at the rest of them impatiently, as if they were dawdling children. Slowed down by Alfie and a dazed Tarak, Everson had let them rest only when he felt they were safe. Although here, safe was always a relative term.

Atkins' lungs burned with effort. Running and breathing in his gas hood, sucking in air through the thick layers of flannel and blowing out through the red rubber-titted non-return valve was hard work at the best of times. Couple that with your limited vision, the stink of the chemical-impregnated cloth and the stifling heat of the whole thing; it was a relief when he dragged the thing from his sweat-drenched head, before shucking off the clay battery backpack and lance.

They might have put some distance between them and the fungus, but neither could he hear the usual sounds of the jungle. They weren't out of the woods yet.

Riley and Tonkins began inspecting the chatt weapons, fussing over them as if they were old family heirlooms.

"They worked. We did it, Corp. We saw the buggers off!" said Tonkins, flushed and ecstatic.

Riley carried on checking the clay battery backpack. "I don't think so, lad. I think they're just moving at the pace of a Hom Forty, a bit like Buckley. Even he gets there in the end."

Keeping a discreet distance from Atkins, Hepton laid his camera and tripod down carefully, and then ripped his gas hood from his head before doubling over with a hacking cough.

Atkins eyed the man, his resentment smouldering like a moorland peat fire. "I can't tell whether the man's a coward or a cad," he muttered.

"Saved his neck again, eh, Only? You're a better man than me," admitted Gutsy, following his gaze.

Atkins felt his cheeks flush with shame and guilt. He knew he wasn't, and if he told Gutsy about Flora, he'd know it, too. He brushed the compliment off. "I don't intend to make a habit of it but, like it or not, he's one of us. Besides–"

"–it was the right thing to do, I know," said Gutsy. "You'll have to watch yourself. You'll put the Padre out of a job."

Hepton began patting his pockets, idly at first and then with increasing desperation. "Oh, for fuck's sake," he panted. "I've dropped my gaspers!" He looked around at the disinterested Tommies, a haunted look in his eyes behind his wire-rimmed spectacles. "Has anyone got a fag? Anybody? I'll pay."

If they had any gaspers left, they were keeping them to themselves.

"Bastards," muttered Hepton.

"Only." Mercy nudged Atkins and with a wink, nodded down at his tunic pocket. In it was a packet of Woodbines, crushed but serviceable. "Lifted them from him back in the temple."

Atkins shook his head. However incorrigible Mercy was, he took some small pleasure in Hepton's distress and allowed himself a smirk of satisfaction.

"See," said Gutsy, joining him, "there's hope for you yet." The large man nodded towards Everson. "Eh up, the Lieutenant wants you."

Lieutenant Everson was talking to Nellie and Norman from the *Ivanhoe*. He beckoned Atkins across.

"No rest for the wicked," groaned Atkins.

"Or NCOs," grinned Gutsy, tapping the stripe on Atkins' upper arm.

Atkins heaved himself up with a groan and walked over, smartening his tunic as he went.

"LIEUTENANT EVERSON, SIR," Norman was saying. "Me and the lads want to see if we can get the tank running. If there's fuel down here, then we're in with a chance."

"It'd offer us some protection from those things, at least," said Nellie.

"Possibly," said Everson. "Splitting up might make some sense. There's no point staying all together to be all caught in a spore cloud."

Atkins wondered whether it was really the tank or access to the petrol fruit fuel they were more concerned about. They'd become quite animated since they heard about the fuel. "Sir, we're down here looking for Jeffries. We're so close; we can't give up now."

Everson studied him for a moment, and then shook his head. "Yes, but I don't see how, Corporal. There's nothing we can do to those things that won't make the situation worse. I can see no other option other than to fall back. The tank would be useful. It would give us more protection down here."

Atkins knew Everson couldn't afford to lose either the tank or the aeroplane. Both were major advantages in their survival on this world. From what Miss Abbott said, the tank crew had overcome their addiction, and it would take a while for the substance to build up in their bodies again. It was a risk he seemed willing to take, at least in the short term.

Atkins, however, couldn't just cut and run. "But Talbot and his men, sir. Those things, those men, they should be... in their graves. Dead is dead. You're their officer, sir. We can't leave them like that. It isn't proper. It isn't right. It's an abomination worthy of Jeffries himself. We owe it to them to see that they're put to rest. They shouldn't be walking round like some... mouldy Lazarus. It ain't natural. What about their immortal souls?"

Everson looked to the Padre. The Chaplain raised his eyebrows, pursed his lips and shook his head. "They didn't say anything about this kind of thing in the seminary, but yes, if these poor souls can be put out of their misery and lifted to their Reward, then I think it behoves us to act, Lieutenant."

Atkins nodded. "It's the right thing to do, sir."

"Atkins, we can't defeat these things, we can't shoot, bomb, or burn them without spreading those spores and facing the same fate ourselves."

"I think I can help," offered Tulliver, "Those things don't react well to those telluric blasts and well, to be brutally honest, John, the petrol fruit fuel has sharpened my vision in some way. I can *see* where those charges will build."

Atkins saw the dark look cross Everson's face. Tulliver waved it away with an air of indifference.

"Yes, yes, I know you don't trust this petrol fruit stuff, but I'm the least of your problems. If I can get to my bus, I can lead you towards the next telluric discharge. This bizarre land storm is practically on top of us, so there should be another one or two from within the crater, somewhere along the Strip, surely? If we can lure them there, they'll be vaporised instantly."

Everson frowned and chewed his bottom lip. "That's a lot of *ifs*, Lieutenant. By all accounts, you barely survived one of those blasts."

Tulliver shrugged his shoulders. "But I did, and I've got the measure of them now; I know what I'm looking for. If we don't move soon, these telluric geysers will pass beyond us and we'll be back to square one. You have to make your mind up."

Everson considered for a moment. "Do it."

Tulliver grinned, and then paused. "I'll need someone to fly with me. I can't start the engine on my own."

"Take the Padre, I can't spare anyone else," said Everson.

"Come on, Padre. We'll make an angel out of you yet."

"You may well have your wings, Lieutenant. I'm not quite sure I'm ready for mine yet," said the Padre archly.

Tulliver tutted. "And you call yourself a sky pilot."

The tank crew and Nellie nodded and headed off into the jungle with Tarak, who had offered to guide them back to the tank, while Tulliver departed with the Padre, leaving Everson, the Black Hand Gang, Riley, Tonkins, Hepton and Napoo to await the coming of the grey men.

Mercy watched the two groups go off.

"So," he said cheerfully. "We're the bait, then."

WITH TARAK'S HELP, the crew of the *Ivanhoe* stuck to the edge of the Strip for as long as possible and avoided the labyrinthine groves. In the distance, through the trees, they heard the muffled roaring of the river as it headed for its underground fall.

Alfie felt an odd mixture of joy and anxiety when they finally came upon the *Ivanhoe*, like meeting an old sweetheart with whom he'd parted awkwardly. He barely remembered the crash over the edge of the crater, and didn't recall Tarak rescuing him at all, but there were many other memories, not all pleasant, that stirred at the sight of the ironclad.

Looking at his crewmates, the old concerns rose unbidden. For almost two weeks they had been without the balm of the sense-altering petrol fruit fumes, and until he saw the tank, he thought he, too, was over them. Now it sat there, he could feel the dull need deep in his bones.

The *Ivanhoe* was quite hidden, at first sight. The ubiquitous pale strangling creepers had overgrown and entangled themselves round the machine. Thin tendrils entwined the great six-pounder guns, quested their way in through the gun slits and loopholes and tried to force themselves between the iron plates.

The lidded eyes of the drivers' visors peered out of the fast-growing foliage as if it were some ancient forest spirit, waiting to be invoked and awoken.

Tarak started to bow before the tank, until Alfie hobbled over on his crutch to stop him, catching his arm under the urman's armpit.

"No," he said quietly. "We've had quite enough of that."

Tarak stood, confused, but obeyed. He touched the still-livid scar on his chest with bewilderment. "My clan..."

"They were killed," said Alfie softly. "I'm sorry, lad."

Tarak looked at him, uncomprehending. Alfie shuffled uncomfortably, at a loss for something to say.

Nellie interrupted the awkward silence. "Right," she said, rolling up the sleeves of her coveralls and taking charge. "We need to start cutting back this undergrowth and find those fuel drums. I do hope they're intact. Jack?"

"We'll find out," said Jack. "Norman, Cecil, with me. Let's hope that Fusilier was right."

Nellie, Wally and Reggie set to work hacking at the liana with the fire axe from the tank and their entrenching tools, while Tarak set about it with his short sword.

Even as they cut it back, the insidious pale growth sought to regrow. "Watch it," said Wally, ripping a thin stem as it sprouted along the track plates. "I reckon if you stand still long enough it'll have you an' all."

"What the hell is this stuff?" said Reggie as he tore his hand away from a few grasping feelers. "It spreads like some pernicious weed."

"We don't know. It appeared many spira ago," Tarak answered bitterly, punctuating his answer with savage swipes of his sword. "We call it GarSuleth's Curse. Ranaman believes," – Tarak faltered and swallowed – "*believed* that it was sent by GarSuleth in revenge for our faith in Croatoan. It chokes the trees we live off. It kills the animals we hunt. It poisons those things that eat it. It is of no use, yet it spreads like a plague and nothing is able to stop it."

There was a dull metallic rumble as Norman, Jack and Cecil herded five recalcitrant fuel drums towards them.

"We found these caught in the shrubbery," said Jack. "A little dented, but none the worse for wear. A few others were split, worse luck. Still, we have these. We have fuel."

"So the show will go on!" said Norman, clapping his hands together.

Jack and Cecil set about refilling the petrol tanks in the front track horns, either side of the driver's cabin, with the salvaged fuel. Alfie, his splinted leg proving something of a liability in the tank's cramped interior, directed Wally, Norman and Nellie as they set about restoring the compartment and stores to some semblance of order and checking the engine.

They were soon ready to depart. Alfie clambered in through the starboard sponson hatch. Tarak made to follow him, but Alfie held up his palm.

"You can't come with us," he said shaking his head. "There isn't room. You must make your own way now. You saved my life and now I've saved yours and where we're going you can't follow. But thank you for all you have done for me. For us."

The urman put an arm across the hatchway, blocking his way.

"GarSuleth has killed my Clan, the Ruanach," Tarak said. His eyes narrowed as his voice hardened. "He has snared them and cocooned them in that living cobweb for *food*." He looked down as his hand traced the raw, tender brand on his chest.

A voice called out from inside. "Alfie, get a move on!"

Alfie shook his head and was about to speak, when Jack's great arm brushed Tarak's hand aside. Alfie caught the urman's eyes. "I'm sorry," he mouthed as Jack pulled the sponson hatch shut. Alfie was quietly grateful that the decision to abandon Tarak had been taken out of his hands. He wasn't sure he'd have been able to go through with it.

He heard the urman bang on the iron plating. "I have been spared and marked by Croatoan to bring vengeance upon the children of GarSuleth," he declared. "Take me with you."

Alfie closed his ears to the pleading. He was doing the lad a favour. "Cecil, you'll have to be starboard gearsman, I'll tell you what to do," he said quietly.

Cecil's eyes lit up and he looked to Jack. Jack jerked his head. "Go on, lad, do as you're told."

Inside the cramped white compartment of the ironclad, Wally edged forward and took his place in the driver's seat. "When you've got it started, come up and sit with me," he told Nellie as he squeezed past her on the gangway. "I need a co-driver."

"Me?"

"You can drive ambulances, can't you?"

Nellie grinned, despite herself. Driving a tank. Since she had seen one, it was all she had ever wanted to do. She felt the same delicious thrill she'd felt when she rode her first motorcycle.

First, they had to start it.

Norman spat on his hands and grasped the giant starting handle at the rear of the compartment with the others. Norman had never quite accepted her as the others had, and held some deep-seated resentment to her presence. The great Daimler engine coughed and spluttered into life and settled into a steady roar. Nellie clambered forward to join Wally in the drivers' seats and tried to ignore the dried blood on the gangway and walls of the starboard bulkhead.

Wally ran the engine up and signalled the gearsmen at the back.

Norman and Cecil put their tracks into gear.

The crew exchanged wary glances as the fug of the petrol fruit fumes began to fill the compartment. Nellie held her breath for as long as she could, then took a deep breath, followed by a second, more contented one.

* * *

Like a blind and bound Samson, once the source of its power had returned, the *Ivanhoe* roared like a territorial beast, belching smoke from its roof exhaust as its track plates began to move tentatively, slapping the ground. The ironclad gained traction and rumbled forward, ripping itself free of the remaining tangle of undergrowth, shrugging off its now insubstantial chains.

Tarak watched the tank for a moment, touched the brand upon his chest once more in a silent oath, and then, as the iron behemoth moved off, he ran lightly up the back of the port track to crouch behind the raised driver's cab, like a barbarian astride a prehistoric mount.

"They're coming!" Atkins heard Pot Shot's warning shout. "They've bought it, they're following us." His gangly form came racing along the path, his lanky legs dwarfing Gazette's strides as the sniper tried to keep up with him. "And I bloody wish they weren't," he said as he passed Atkins.

"Shut up, you daft 'a'porth. They're just walking mushrooms."

"I hate mushrooms."

Atkins shrugged his shoulders in an attempt to make the electric lance backpack sit on his back more comfortably. It didn't work. Behind him, Mercy wound the crank handle to build the charge. Atkins could feel the whirr of the magneto in his chest as Mercy's efforts pressed it against his back. Atkins hefted the lance in his hands, his fingers fidgeting over the trigger pads. The end of the lance sparked. Mercy patted him on the shoulder. "You're good to go, Only."

The tide of grey filaments crept silently towards them, over the rocks and through the jungle floor detritus.

The grey dead men followed, their halting advance accompanied by the soft puffs of bursting fruit bodies and the muffled falls of creatures as they succumbed to the choking spore clouds, and whose desiccating bodies fed the ineluctable advance.

"Gas hoods!" ordered Atkins, pulling his own down over his head. He was soon cocooned inside the damp, close flannel hood once again, his vision, hearing and breathing impaired, the metallic copper tang of the return valve in his mouth.

He had a moment of doubt as the hooded soldiers with their blank eyes and red proboscises began to stumble forward in their masks. Napoo, bandanna tied over his nose and mouth, fixed him with an accusing glare, and Atkins felt abashed. Perhaps this had been a bad idea. Still, it was too late now. His repugnance for this stuff, and what it had done to decent men, drove him on. And, beyond all of that was the persistent thought of Jeffries, and above it all, Flora.

"We should be able to keep ahead of it," warned Everson, as they moved through the jungle ahead of the slow wave of mycelia as it burrowed through the decomposing humus beneath their feet. "But not so far ahead that we lose them," he reminded them.

"Shouldn't be too hard. They move like they were wading through Somme mud anyway," said Mercy.

Gutsy turned and watched their slow, implacable advance. "Still gives me the willies."

The Fusiliers moved on at a fast walking pace, checking every so often to make sure the things were still following them and that Hepton was still with them, refusing as he did to give up any of his equipment. They needn't have worried.

Atkins caught sight of something out of the corner of his eyes. He couldn't be sure whether it was really there or just a smudge on his mica eyepiece. He stopped and turned his whole head. Something grey slipped between the trees to their left.

"Blood and sand. They're trying to outflank us."

More glimpses of grey to the right.

He listened for the drone of the aeroplane, but it was difficult under the hood. They just had to stay alive until the next telluric discharge occurred. Atkins had eagerly acceded to Tulliver's plan since it meant Jeffries' trail would still be within reach. Now he was beginning to doubt the wisdom of it.

More grey figures appeared to their right and left, and with them came the grey-white carpet, as more fruiting bodies burst around them like a barrage and yellow-white clouds of spore blossomed like subdued trench mortar explosions. The cloud of spores billowed and settled, the turbid mist drifting around their legs in whorls and wakes as they passed.

It was the silence of the advance that unnerved Atkins. It lent an air of unreality to their predicament, as if he were watching it unfold in a picture house. He could almost imagine the melodramatic piano accompaniment.

Atkins heard the crackle and caught a brief flash against the tree trunks as Tonkins fired his electric lance. For a moment, the spore cloud parted and the creeping white carpet was repulsed, as if he had dropped soap into oily water.

He forged on, trying to stay ahead of the rising tide of spore cloud. "Have you charged me?" he bellowed at Mercy.

"What do you think I am?" retorted Mercy with a good-natured bawl. "A Lyon's Tea Room Gladys?" Mercy walked straight into Atkins' back as he came to an abrupt halt. "Oi! Watch it, Only!"

Atkins raised his electric lance. "We've got company."

"Bloody hell, how did they move fast enough to get in front of us?"

"Does it matter? They've got us surrounded."

Ahead of them, two more grey ambulated corpses emerged shambling from the woodland, a carpet of grey filaments laying itself down before them. Even with the cankerous growths and the blighted features, it was with horror and dismay that Atkins recognised one of them and let out a groan.

"Porgy!"

THE STRUTTER ROARED into the air, the landing wheels clipping the tree tops as Tulliver continued to climb. A few whipperwills cracked and snapped after it, but he left them behind as the aeroplane banked away.

Tulliver circled round the crater at a couple of hundred feet, out of range of the whipperwills. He could see the tower of the temple and the cobweb shroud of fungus threads draped over it. He pointed down for the Padre to see. It looked like a cobweb-covered bride cake. From the air, the extent of the fungus became clear, draping through the trees. The extent of its growth was far worse than it looked from the ground. He was glad the Fusiliers didn't know. In his head, he was already calling it the Havisham Effect.

In the distance, beyond the crater, great plumes of telluric energy blasted into the sky. He saw the shiny patches in the air, far off, as distant energies built, but nothing over the crater. He circled over the Strip again.

Every now and again, through thinner canopy, he'd catch flashes down below as the Tommies' electric lances flared. At least he knew where they were.

Oil spattered from the engine and built up on his goggles. He pulled them off as he scanned the crater jungle for any sign of imminent telluric build up.

As he banked round again, he saw it, out of the corner of his eye: a patch of air that shimmered as though worn through. It was on the Strip's edge.

ATKINS COULDN'T BRING himself to disassociate the thing before him from his friend. To him, this shambling grotesque was in some way still Porgy, and therein lay the danger.

"Porgy, it's me, Only," he shouted though his gas hood.

"Then do him a favour and fire!" yelled Mercy from behind him as the things that had been Porgy and Jenkins lumbered towards them.

The mould-ridden men showed no sign of recognition. Anything that was Porgy was long gone. The advancing carpet of fungal threads forced Atkins and Mercy back.

* * *

EVERSON HEARD THE drone of Tulliver's engine overhead, and could see him circling above through the leaves and waggling his wings. He'd found a telluric build up. If they were to have any chance of defeating these things, of staying alive, they had to follow him.

"That way!" he bellowed though his gas mask. "Atkins, Tonkins, break out, follow Tulliver! We may only have one shot at this."

Atkins tore his attention away from the shambling things that were once Porgy and Jenkins, and joined Tonkins as they concentrated their electric fire. Blue-white bolts danced and flicked across the white-carpeted ground, vaporising a path through the thick fungal shroud that surrounded them.

Behind them, fruiting bodies began to swell as the Talbot-thing and the others followed, now keeping their distance beyond the range of the electric lances, paralleling their advance as they spread out in a skirmish line behind them. Like beaters, thought Everson bitterly.

"There!" said Pot Shot, pointing in the sky, where Tulliver was circling tightly.

The Tommies forged towards the spot beneath him, and broke out of the trees onto the scrub-covered Strip.

As they set foot on open ground, Everson waved the aeroplane away. Tulliver waggled his wings in acknowledgement and side-slipped out of the turn.

"I guess this is the spot, then," said Everson.

From the edge of the wood, the Talbot-thing and its ghastly grey section appeared and staggered silently towards them.

Something in the air changed. Even under his mask, Atkins could feel it. At their feet, the thin rocky mantle began to crack, exposing the metal beneath as the telluric charge began to build.

Napoo, trusting to his nature and innate sense of survival, would not stay. He fled to safer ground beyond the Strip.

The grey-faced Fusiliers shambled towards the small group. The creeping wave of mycelia stopped, its advance stunted by the discharge, but the twisted Tommies kept coming. The fungus that animated them was drawing on more and more of their tissue to fuel itself and the bodies shrivelled with every step as it sought to reach fresher hosts.

"Hold your positions," yelled Everson.

Atkins and his Black Hand Gang shuffled nervously. They'd been here before, repelling German attacks on the trenches; you hold your nerve, try not to funk it. It didn't get any easier.

Small crackles of energy flickered about their feet.

"Hold it."

Hepton danced a jig as ribbons of energy snapped and flared around his boots. "Christ, talk about out of the frying pan and into the fire!" he said. "Are you trying to get us killed?"

"No, just you if we're lucky," muttered Mercy.

Discharges of blue-white energy rolled across the ground, building in strength.

"It's coming!" hollered Riley. "Hold steady, son," he said calmly to a fidgeting Tonkins.

Hepton broke and ran, lugging his tripod, camera and film canisters.

Energy began arcing up from the exposed metal around them, striking out at trees.

"Hold it," Everson called.

The Talbot-thing stopped and the others lurched to a halt alongside it.

It wasn't falling for it.

Atkins wasn't going to let this happen. This had been his idea. These things had to die, if only so the men themselves could rest in peace. He pulled off his gas hood and stepped from the defensive ring.

"Atkins, what do you think you're doing!" bellowed Everson.

Atkins ignored him and walked towards the grey men.

"Porgy. Porgy, it's me. Only! You remember me? Porgy!"

The ashen-faced soldier turned its head and stepped towards Atkins, pulling free of the mycelia that wove into the ground around it. The others began doing the same. The fungus, overcome by an imperative for survival, lurched towards him.

As energy began to build beneath his feet, Atkins could feel the thrum of it through his boots. About him, tongues of lightning lashed out at the trees.

The Tommies could hold their position no longer.

"Run!" yelled Everson. They didn't need telling twice. Atkins took one last look at the fungal effigy of Porgy staggering towards him, its grey skin almost shrivelling against his skull as the fungal canker that possessed it sought to extract every morsel of energy from its decaying host.

A huge bolt of telluric energy roared up from the ground, shattering the thin shell of rock over the metal below. The concussive wave threw Atkins and the others off their feet as a blast of heat washed over them. It threw everything into sharp relief, like all the Very lights in the world going off at once.

Atkins turned his head and squinted through his lashes against the light. He saw the silhouettes of fungal Fusiliers caught in the blast, consumed as the huge white beam jagged up into the atmosphere, like some electric beanstalk. Their faint outlines grew fainter and more indistinct against the increasing brightness until there was nothing left but a painful angry white light, spitting and crackling.

Suddenly that, too, was gone.

Ears ringing with the blast, half-blinded by the brilliance, the Tommies staggered to their feet. They wandered round dazed, waiting for their senses to return.

Where the blast had erupted, there was now an exposed circle of metal, one of those nodes Tulliver had talked about, a planetary junction, an intersection of geometric alignments.

Of the animated corpses, there was no sign. They had gone. Beyond the metal, the fungal carpet lay blackened and charred. It crumbled to dust with a soft satisfying crunch beneath the boot.

For minutes afterwards, the decaying afterimages of the men haunted Atkins, but eventually, they faded, too, as the ghosts of the dead ought to.

Atkins blinked away the last of the images and the tears that came with them.

"Goodbye, Porgy."

CHAPTER TWENTY

"Hellfire Corner"

AFTER THE TELLURIC blast, it took a while for Atkins' senses to return. His vision was mottled, and his ears buzzed with phantom swarms. Temporarily deaf and blind, he was not in the best condition to go stumbling round a cruel, capricious jungle. None of them were.

Gutsy, Gazette, Mercy and Pot Shot sat quietly, each lost in his own thoughts, waiting on orders and watching the exposed metal warily, as if no longer trusting the ground they stood on.

At least here, at the seat of the blast, the thunderous flash had panicked the animals into flight. It should be a while before they picked up the courage to return. The Tommies would be safe for the moment.

EVERSON LET EVERYONE take a breather while he took stock and decided on his next course of action. He turned his attention to the book they had taken from the Ruanach temple, as best he could with the fading afterimages obscuring and distorting his vision; the book that had come from Roanoke, all the way from Virginia.

He traced his fingers over the iron sigil of Croatoan on the book's cover. The crater had been caused by a meteor impact, and he had seen the proof for himself in the broken

Heart of Croatoan. It had clearly inspired the myths that had been woven into both chatt and urman mythology. For all the urmen's belief in Croatoan, the underworld and some Promethean punishment by a dung-beetle god, he couldn't bring himself to believe it, although some small part of him began to wonder. It was certainly enough to bring Jeffries all this way.

How many other groups of humans had been displaced from Earth? There were stories and legends of mass disappearances throughout history. What if all the urmen were merely descendants of displaced survivors, subsisting like Adam and Eve cast out of the Garden of Eden? And if they were, what did that say of the Pennines' chances? He coughed and dismissed the thought as best he could. There would be plenty of dark, lonely nights in which to dwell on thoughts of that nature.

He looked around at the jungle-filled crater and idly fingered the scrap of khaki and the Pennine Fusilier button. If he had petrol fruit liquor, could he, too, see Jeffries' trail as Mathers had done? He withdrew his hand quickly, overcome with an irrational fear that Jeffries might somehow sense him through it. If the chatts were insistent that nothing enters and nothing leaves this place, then returning might be problematic. Then again, so could leaving. They might as well try to find Jeffries' trail while they were down here.

RILEY AND TONKINS wandered idly over the metal, newly exposed by the telluric blast. The storm, or whatever it was, seemed to have passed now, and although the blasts continued, they had rolled into the distance beyond the crater.

Thinking aloud, Riley held forth on various electrical theories, wondering whether he could stabilise such power, to charge not just an electric lance, but also perhaps an electric cannon. Tonkins' only contribution to the discussion was, "I reckon you could have powered all the electric lights in London from that."

Riley mulled that over for a moment, before going to check over the electric lance packs.

HEPTON SAT BY himself, ignored by the others, his hands shaking, two fingers extended by force of habit as if holding a cigarette he wished he had, but didn't. He caught himself doing it and clenched his fist. It still trembled.

TURNING HIS MIND from Porgy, all Atkins could focus on now was Jeffries. Whatever Jeffries was after, whatever he wanted, he had come down here by himself to get it. By himself. Atkins held that thought for a moment and shook his head in disbelief as he recalled the men they'd lost getting this far. Jeffries had done it by himself. Whatever else he hated about Jeffries, the man possessed a self-belief and determination that he found hard not to envy. Whatever it was he was after, Jeffries was a driven man. But now, so was Atkins.

His mind turned to Flora. He would go to hell and back for her. Now it looked very much as if he would have to do just that.

Unfortunately, it meant taking his mates with him.

Talk to someone, Nellie had said. There was no one to whom he could talk. No one that would understand. His mates wouldn't. They thought he was a decent, honest chap. He'd gone out of his way to show that he was, to himself if to no one else, to prove himself penitent.

Silently, he renewed his vow to return home, and thought of those who wouldn't. Jessop, Lucky, Ginger, Nobby, Prof, Chalky, Jenkins, Porgy and, yes, even Ketch; he wanted their deaths to mean something.

He feared Everson might get cold feet. He hadn't come this far to give up now.

He approached Lieutenant Everson. "Sir, we shouldn't stay put too long," he advised, glancing warily at the surrounding scrub. "We're still going after Jeffries, aren't we?"

Everson was leafing through the ironbound tome.

"This mission has been a complete shambles, Atkins," he sighed quietly. "We've made peace with one colony only to start a war with another. Quite frankly, if I go back to the camp empty-handed, I think the men will lynch me."

"It won't come to that, sir. We have our second objective."

"Are the rest of the men up to it?" he said, glancing over to the weary Tommies. It seemed that he had asked much of them, over the past few months. Dare he ask more?

"They will be, sir. The Black Hand Gang hasn't let you down before. If that man knows the way home, I'd follow him into hell itself."

"Well, it looks as if that's were we're going. But I don't think we need worry. We've been there before. Remember Wipers?"

Atkins shuddered at the memory. "That I do, sir."

THERE WERE ENTRIES in the book that, if they weren't allegorical, very clearly pointed to a gateway, an entrance to the underworld and the Village of the Dead.

They moved off out along the Strip, that the Ruanach clan referred to as the Road of the Dead, heading towards the crater's far wall, every so often marking their route with a chalked 13/PF on a rock or tree trunk, for the *Ivanhoe* to follow.

Wearing the Lightningwerfer, as Mercy had christened the electric lance pack, Atkins took the lead with Mercy as his winder; Everson followed, with Napoo occasionally scouting ahead. Pot Shot and Gazette eyed the jungle either side of the Strip, while Riley and Hepton struggled along like pack mules under knapsacks and kitbags of gear, but at least the going was firm, and Tonkins with the second Lightningwerfer brought up the rear with Gutsy.

Knowing now what was beneath his feet as they walked, Everson thought about the wider context of the mysterious lines on the landscape. He knew there were megalithic roads that scarred the landscape of Britain, but nothing there suggested any kind of giant structure beneath the surface like here. Who built it, and what was it for?

Trees towered high either side of the wide ribbon of scrub, spreading their thin spindly foliage out over the Strip and dappling the scrub beneath with dancing shadows. The tough shallow-rooted plants clung fiercely to the thin soil, reinforcing the image of an ancient, overgrown, long-disused road.

As the crater wall rose up before them, the vegetation became thicker. A grove of gnarled scab trees stood in their way, choked with the pallid creepers that infested the crater.

Mercy and Gutsy whirred away on the magneto handles, making sure that Tonkins' and Atkins' electric lances were fully charged. Atkins would rather have his Enfield in his hand – he trusted it more than this alien device – but knew as long as the magneto didn't wear out and there were hands to wind, he didn't have to worry about ammunition. Here, though, the electric lances came into their own: they spat and burned through the snarl of plants, sending small ugly creatures scurrying for new cover.

As Napoo slashed away at the last of the lianas and vines and they broke through the last of the undergrowth, they saw the far wall of the crater, towering six hundred feet above them. They clambered over moss-covered boulders down into an old stone-strewn dell, where huge buttressing tree-roots supported trees that must have been centuries old. At the base of the crater wall, a vast yawning crack split the rock, its mouth barred by a writhing mass of the pallid creepers that reached out to choke the surrounding vegetation. The size of the cavern mouth dwarfed the Tommies; it could have taken three or four battlepillars abreast.

A single valiant shaft of sunlight shone down through the scab trees behind them, attempting to penetrate the gloom beyond the entrance, but it fell on nothing within that it could illuminate. The light was swallowed whole and snuffed out, engulfed by the immensity of the black void beyond, a void that seemed to brook no examination from without, forcing those who gazed into it to take what lay beyond on faith.

Looking into that black gulf for too long gave Atkins an unsettling sense of unease and nausea. There was nothing within the obsidian darkness on which to focus, and strange unearthly shapes and colours swam in his vision, until he was no longer sure whether they were a trick of the mind or not. It was only when he looked away that reality reasserted itself.

Impressive though the entrance was, it was certainly more natural than their imaginations had led them to expect. Atkins had envisaged demons with flaming swords guarding it, perhaps, or giant lintels carved from the rock face and inscribed with unspeakable glyphs, standing on weathered, ruined Doric columns of great size. Or something darker, exuding great age and malevolence: vast forbidding blackened doors of charred bone, and niches of skulls.

"So that's it?" said Mercy. "The gateway to the Underworld? Can't say that I'm impressed. I was expecting something a little more–"

"Fire and brimstone?" suggested Gutsy.

Mercy shrugged. "Well, yes, I suppose. A little less woodland dell, more *Welcome to Hell*, as it were. Although I'm not complaining. To be quite honest, I'm a little glad it ain't."

"Evil has a banality all its own," said Hepton, eyeing the entrance warily. "I wouldn't let your guard down." He made the sign of the cross and, a little self-consciously, Tonkins followed suit.

"Well, we're not getting through that stuff without a little help," said Gutsy, watching the slow-writhing creepers. He had a hand on Little Bertha, but knew it would be of little use against the mass of choking plant tendrils before them.

A bolt of blue-white energy blasted Pot Shot off his feet.

"Another telluric blast," yelped Tonkins.

They dived for cover. Atkins grabbed the dazed Pot Shot by his webbing and hauled him behind a buttress root.

"What hit me?" he asked.

"Lightning," said Atkins, his attention focused on the undergrowth around them. "Lucky for the rest of us you're the tallest. Makes you a natural lightning rod."

"Good job I wasn't wearing me steel helmet then," he said with a dazed smile.

Another blast followed, but it wasn't the thunderous concussive heaven-bound telluric bolt, nor was it the half-expected blast of sulphurous hellfire.

"What the hell is it?" asked Everson, his back to a boulder for cover, as he checked the chambers of his Webley.

Mercy peered over the top of a fallen tree, behind which he'd taken cover.

Another bolt of energy arced out from the undergrowth. It was the writhing, spitting Tesla arc of an electric lance. Another licked out across the open space, scorching the undergrowth in which they'd taken cover.

"Chatts!"

"Blood and sand!" cursed Atkins. "How? I thought they were afraid of this place. What the hell are they doing here?"

"One of their balloons must have come down, like us," said Gutsy.

"*Nothing must enter. Nothing must leave,*" Gazette quoted, laconically. "They've been abandoned. They know they're not getting out of the crater, so they've got nothing to lose. Makes them dangerous."

Another arc of energy spat across and hit a fallen log, vaporising sap and moisture in an instant and exploding the bole into a thousand fire-hardened shards of wooden shrapnel.

"Christ, you think?" yelped Gutsy, ducking as low as he could.

Gazette settled against a rock, nestled the stock of his Enfield into his shoulder and targeted the shadows in the grove of scab trees to the side of the cavern entrance. He squeezed the trigger.

Another bolt flashed from a different direction.

"How many of them are there?" bawled Pot Shot, pinned down behind a buttress root.

"I can't tell, they're leaping around, keeping us pinned down," replied Gazette.

"Where's Napoo?" asked Everson.

Atkins looked around. The urman had vanished. Gutsy jerked his head upwards; Napoo was edging round a scab tree, trying to get a better vantage point to spot the chatts.

Hepton flinched as the brief flash of another electric bolt threw his shaded funk hole into sharp relief.

There was a gunshot and a chatt fell from its perch, in a tree overlooking their position. Gazette cycled the Enfield's bolt and looked for another target.

There was another gunshot. A chatt staggered through the undergrowth towards them, its electric battery backpack spitting and fizzing. It stumbled a few steps before the pack emitted a brief whine and exploded, engulfing it in a ball of white heat that left its carapace charred and smouldering as it collapsed.

"That wasn't me," said Gazette.

There was a snap of dry wood underfoot and the shade of a grey ashen-faced man stepped into the dappled shadow of Hell's dell.

"It's another fungus-man," said Hepton, shrinking into the shadows as far as he could.

The figure stepped into the light.

"Fuck me," said Mercy. "It's the Alleyman."

"Werner," muttered Everson.

The German pilot looked the worse for wear. His smart uniform was scorched and his tunic unbuttoned, his face blacked with oil and soot; oil-filmed goggles sat atop his flying helmet and his smart polished boots were now scuffed and dulled by dust and mud.

"We meet again, gentlemen," he called out jovially.

"If you think we're surrendering to you and your chatts, you have another think coming," called Everson.

"On the contrary," Werner called back.

Another electric white-blue flash arced towards him out of the undergrowth, interrupting him. He flinched and ducked as it earthed yards away from him, blasting a chunk out of a young Japheth tree. The trunk gave way slowly with a creaking tear. Werner began running towards the Tommies. The tree crashed to the ground and Werner flung himself into the dirt. Using the fallen tree as cover, he scrambled over to them before peering back out at the undergrowth where the rest of the chatts were concealed. When he looked back, it was into the points of several rifles, fixed with bayonets.

Slowly Werner put his pistol down on the ground and raised his hands to shoulder height, not wanting to present more of a target to the remaining chatts.

"Tulliver said you crashed," said Everson.

"My machine crashed. I survived, which is more than can be said for my uniform," Werner said, indicating his torn and scorched tunic. "My tailor will be furious."

"They were firing at you."

"I knew my alliance with the *insekt menschen* was at an end when I came down in the crater, that I would be outcast and untouchable to them," he said with a shrug. "I no longer have my machine, so I am of no further use to them. They will not let me out of the crater now. They let nothing out unless it is to kill it. They would leave me here to die, and I do not want to die, Lieutenant."

"None of us do," said Everson.

"I am alone," admitted Werner. "You have your battalion. I wish to put aside our enmity. I wish to be... human again."

They ducked as another flurry of electric bolts crackled through the air. The remaining chatts had moved to cut the Tommies off from the cavern entrance.

Werner snatched up his pistol. Nobody stopped him.

Gazette squeezed off another couple of rounds. Normally, he'd look for a muzzle flash and target that spot, like any good sniper, but here the blue-white brilliance of the electric bolts left irritating afterimages blotting his vision. The chatts fired and moved, springing across large spaces with inhuman speed, never firing from the same place twice.

"You know what?" said Gutsy, shouting over the miniature thunderstorm that raged briefly around them, "I'm beginning to look back on the days when I could kill chatts in the hundreds using just a candle with some nostalgia!"

He pulled a safety pin from a Mills bomb and lobbed it into the writhing tangle of creepers that contorted around the cavern entrance. The explosion ripped and shredded it like barbed wire, throwing chatt limbs up into the air in graceless arcs.

"They will not let us go," said Werner. "Nor can they leave themselves. They are dead to the colony. All they can do is carry out their overriding chemical decree; nothing must enter, nothing must leave. They will die to fulfil that precept."

"Well I'm sure we can oblige," said Everson through clenched teeth.

"Are you really going to trust a Hun, sir?" asked Mercy, eyeing the German with deep suspicion.

"No, Evans," said Everson firmly. "I'm going to trust a gentleman."

TULLIVER CIRCLED THE crater, looking for signs of another telluric blast, but it seemed that the land storm was moving away.

He hadn't known about Werner's Albatros for long, but the sky seemed an emptier, lonelier place without it. As he spiralled down, he could see a haze of smoke hanging above the Zohtakarrii edifice. One of their balloons still floated above it on a winch line, on watch.

As he flew lower, he turned round and jabbed down with a gloved finger. He wanted the Padre to keep a look out for the Fusiliers. Behind his goggles, the Padre nodded in acknowledgement.

Tulliver spotted the deflated remains of a chatt balloon hanging ripped and torn in the boughs of a tree below. Then, out of the corner of his eye, towards the crater wall, he noticed faint patches of air shimmer briefly. They erupted with the brief short crackle of electric lances. It looked like the balloon's passengers had survived.

He flew lower, risking the whipperwills, but they seem to have been shocked into sluggishness by the sheer violence of telluric storm. He flew along the Strip towards the crater wall. There he saw more polished patches of air shine amongst the overgrowth round the mouth of a fissure, birthing more crackling arcs of electric fire. As he circled, Tulliver saw the Fusiliers pinned down by constantly-shifting fire. They couldn't get a fix on their enemies, but he could.

He brought the bus lower and flew along the Strip towards the fissure in the crater wall, waiting for the patches of strange air to appear again.

"Come on, come on," he muttered as the Strutter closed on the crater wall. Areas in the undergrowth began to shine, and he fired. From deep within the undergrowth, there came a brilliant flash and a rising puff of white smoke like a photographer's flash powder.

He pulled on the stick and banked away sharply, climbing away from the looming crater wall.

The Padre patted him on the shoulder and pointed down to the Strip. Tulliver followed his finger and then put his thumb up and let out a whoop of triumph.

Barely had the roar of Tulliver's Strutter receded when Atkins heard the slow, squeaking creak and rumble of the ironclad as it clattered along the Strip. As it approached, it ground the hardy growth beneath its tracks and ploughed over the shallow-rooted trees that had clung so tenaciously to life; surviving all that the alien world could throw at it, only to be crushed by something not of this world at all. To Atkins, right now, that felt like tit-for-tat.

The roar of the ironclad behemoth dropped to a throaty growl as the tank came to a halt, but it didn't stop completely. One track continued to run, turning the tank until it faced the cavern entrance. Astride the tank's roof, Tarak crouched defiantly behind the driver's cabin, at least until a belch of smoke from the roof exhaust set him coughing. He stepped sprightly onto the starboard sponson and leapt to the ground.

Napoo glared at the scorched brand on Tarak's chest, greeted him with a sullen growl of disapproval and turned away, wanting nothing to do with him. Not that Tarak seemed to care. He only had eyes for the cavern entrance.

"The way to the Village of the Dead," he said, brooding. "My clan passed this way not long since. Soon I will be reunited with them."

Werner witnessed the arrival of the *Ivanhoe* with a face that registered first horror and then incredulity as the land ship hoved into view and clanked to a halt.

"Mein Gott, is that what I think it is? I have heard of such a thing, but never have I seen one before. It looks like some kind of primordial beast."

"It is the hell hound of Croatoan," declared Tarak proudly, patting the sponson like the flank of a prized animal.

Looking at the ironclad in the confines of the jungle, Atkins had to agree. It was just as much at home here as on the battlefield of the Somme.

"That's what's going to beat the pants off your boys in the War, Fritz," said Mercy with a sneer.

The starboard six-pounder rose, paused and then fired, the report echoing off the crater side and the shell exploding in the middle of the writhing mass of pale creepers, sending a spume of shredded plant matter into the air.

"Now we'll show those chatt bastards," said Gutsy gleefully.

In the end, they didn't have to.

As they watched, the chatts revealed themselves voluntarily, stepping out of their concealment, surprising even Napoo, who had not known where they were. The tank rumbled closer, rolling past the Tommies, who came out from behind the shelter of their buttress roots and logs, falling behind the tank for cover, just in case the chatts were of a duplicitous bent. Even Hepton managed to unclench himself from the bole under which he had hidden in order to witness the scene.

The chatts divested themselves of their clay battery backpacks, put down their lances and weapons, and stood immobile before the tank. They performed a sign of reverence towards the *Ivanhoe*, touching the heels of their hand to their foreheads and then to their thorax.

"The Skarra thing still works, then," said Atkins with relief. "I still find it hard to imagine – a dung-beetle god of the Underworld. They must think their time has come."

"Felt that way myself, sometimes," said Pot Shot.

Atkins grunted in agreement. They all had, at one time or another. It made the chatts seem a little more human, albeit not enough for him to feel pity. Right now they were all that stood between him and Jeffries, him and a way home to Flora, for he felt sure that Jeffries had been this way. How could he have resisted?

As the tank brought its guns to bear on the chatts, they turned and, without looking back, walked on of their own volition and disappeared into the cavern, entering their underworld as ones already dead, almost as if it were an honour to be escorted into the underworld by Skarra himself. Dwarfed as they were by the scale of the entrance, their bodies looked more insect-like than ever and Atkins watched as the Stygian blackness within swallowed them,.

"Blood and sand, who would have thought it was that easy?" he said.

"They had us bang to rights, but they just gave up," said Riley, shaking his head, nonplussed.

"Well," said Gutsy, "they met their god of death, they must have–"

High pitched squeals of terror and agony rang from the cavern, the unearthly screams prolonged, magnified, iterated and reiterated by the vast chamber beyond.

"What the hell was that?"

"Sounded like the chatts," said Everson.

Something moved in the starless black expanse beyond the entrance. It was impossible to tell what, or how big it might be, or whether it was one thing or many, from the sound alone.

The tank engine revved, snorting like a territorial beast, and lurched forward, like a hound at the leash.

If they were expecting a demonic gatekeeper, they weren't disappointed. From the mouth of the cavern scrabbled a savage-looking creature of gigantic size, part insect, part reptile with razor-taloned feet and a wide mouth filled with sharp needle teeth for shredding and tearing. Caught between some of them were the mangled, crushed remains of the chatts. It took a mouthful of the writhing creepers and tore them from their roots. A heavily segmented carapace covered its back, and when it roared, a warm foul stench assailed the Tommies. Atkins felt his stomach heave at the smell.

"Well at least it's only got one head," said Pot Shot. "I was half expecting Cerberus."

Gazette let off five rounds rapid at the creature. They hit its carapace, but they didn't stop it. It turned in the direction of the petty annoyance and roared. The Tommies scrambled back for their recently-vacated cover.

The tank's six-pounders fired. One missed, hitting the crater wall, and the other glanced against the beast's carapace, blasting a hole in its side. It roared in pain. Now it was wounded and roused to anger.

From out of the sky, Tulliver's Strutter dived on the creature, incendiary bullets streaking through the air. The beast shook it head as if trying to rid itself of vicious insects. It reared up after the Strutter and swiped the air with its talons, but Tulliver had pulled the machine away beyond its grasp.

In that moment, Everson saw their chance: the belly of the beast wasn't armoured. The tank crew had noticed too, for the *Ivanhoe's* guns spoke again, carrying a message of death as two six-pounder shells hit their target squarely this time, in the soft underbelly, ripping open the flesh of the beast, disintegrating bone, eviscerating cavities and vaporising organs as the creature fell forward through a mist of its own atomised blood. Its jaw hit the ground, slamming its teeth together, and it released its last foul breath.

INTERLUDE 5

Letter from Lance Corporal Thomas Atkins to Flora Mullins

6th April 1917

My Dearest Flora,

Today I walked a Road of the Dead that leads to Hell. I thought I had walked one before. I thought it was in Belgium on the Menin Road to Ypres, paved with mud, corpses and crump holes.

But I was wrong. This is different. This is a more personal torment. Sitting here now, with this yawning abyss of darkness before me, I can't help but feel that with every step I have taken, my own good intentions have brought me here. Mea culpa.

I always told myself that you were the kind of girl that I would go to hell and back for, and I know William had said as much to you, too, the night before we left for training.

I have lived through hell on Earth once and not returned. Neither did William. For that, I am truly sorry, but now I have a second chance, a second hell. I hope with all my heart that this time I shall return to you.

Ever yours
Thomas.

CHAPTER TWENTY ONE

"A Forlorn Hope..."

HAVING LANDED THE Strutter on the Strip, just beyond the trees, Tulliver and the Padre walked in the dell, trusting that it would be safe now that the telluric storm, Croatoan's Torment, had passed.

Tarak was roasting meat over a fire. Napoo was still keeping his distance, not approving of the Ruanach's worship of Croatoan. Atkins' Black Hand Gang and the others sat round the fire eating, Everson and Everson mucking in with them, while Pot Shot and Gazette stood on sentry duty. The tank crew sat together by the *Ivanhoe*. Old habits were hard to break, Tulliver guessed.

Tulliver sniffed the air. "Smells good! What's cooking?"

Mercy was about to open his mouth when Atkins spoke up. "Don't ask; just eat it. You'll be better off."

Tulliver caught sight of the slain beast and was about to venture a query when he was distracted by someone calling his name.

"Tulliver!" cried Werner, striding towards the pilot and shaking the man's hand. Tulliver was taken aback. This was truly a day for dead men.

"Werner? How the devil did you survive? I saw your bus crash, I found the wreckage."

Werner shrugged with false modesty. "I managed to slow my airspeed almost to a stall, so when I crashed, the tree canopy cushioned the impact. I was lucky; I was able to climb out and down a tree while those whip creatures tore my aeroplane to bits. Still, any landing you can walk away from, am I right?"

"Well, yes," said Tulliver, still stunned at the sight of the German.

"Did you see, up there?" he asked earnestly. "I was not trying to kill you. Did you see what I wanted to show you, the *Heilige linien*? It is a big mystery, is it not?"

Tulliver nodded. "Yes it is, we both saw it," he said, indicating the Padre and getting caught up in Werner's enthusiasm. "The scale of it! It's unbelievable."

Everson patted the Roanoke journal resting on his lap. "We've learnt a lot about this world, and yet there is so much more that we don't know." He shook his head, daunted by the sheer scale of the task. "What is this structure that's buried in the ground, which covers hundreds of square miles and discharges telluric energy?"

"Well, I've no answers," said Tulliver, shaking his head, "but I do know we can use it to navigate by. It means I can fly further and higher. It gives us a network of landmarks, a vast geometric web, like roads or canals, to fly by. If one gets lost, one can simply follow one of these to a crossroads until you come upon some other landmark. We can map these lines, use them to explore."

Riley joined in. "We can send telegraph signals along them, carried on the telluric current that flows through them. That gives us lines of communication. We can stay in contact with patrols and exploration parties at much greater distances. There might even be a way we can tap the telluric current itself."

"All very admirable, gentlemen," said Everson, bolstered by their enthusiasm, "and with an armistice in place with the Khungarrii we may be able to do just that – if we can avoid colonies like the Zohtakarrii, that is. But I don't intend that we should stay here if there is a way home. We've come this far and discovered a lot about this world, but dare we go further?"

Everyone knew what he was talking about. It was hard to avoid it.

"It appears that Jeffries has descended into the chatt underworld to free the imprisoned demon, Croatoan."

"Tartarus," muttered the Padre, glowering at the pitch-black cavern. "The great pit, a hell for fallen angels."

"Quite. The point is–"

"We have no proof," said Alfie. "I know what the Ruanach say, but you pointed out that it's all just myth based on fact. This search for Jeffries could be a wild goose chase."

Everson nodded, frowning. "But surely we have to be certain?"

A high-pitched scream interrupted them.

"Nellie!" said Alfie in alarm.

"Yes?"Nellie said from behind, where she was applying a salve to Tarak's raw branded flesh. They had all been surprised that Tarak had hitched a lift on *Ivanhoe,* although Alfie was secretly relieved. Tarak was already proving himself invaluable.

"If it wasn't you, then who?"

"Over here!"

The cry came from a grove of trees by the side of the cavern entrance. It was Hepton. He staggered towards them, throwing an arm out towards the grove. "I was just, you know, call of nature. I think you ought to see." Something had clearly put the wind up him.

Pot Shot went to investigate; Atkins grabbed his rifle and caught up with him. They moved up past the body of the beast. Something glinted over to the side of the entrance, amongst some large boulders. Atkins nodded to Pot Shot and, cautiously, they made their way over.

"Ah," said Pot Shot. "Well, that's not nice,"

"Better call Everson," said Atkins.

BACK AT THE trenches, under Doctor Lippett's watchful eye, Edith had begun administering the first medicinal doses of petrol fruit liquor to a group of five chatt-blinded volunteers. For a couple of days now, they had been taking a measure three times a day at a controlled dilution.

Sergeant Warton, blinded in the Khungarrii siege, was one of the first to volunteer; the bandages were still round his head, covering his eyes. Edith took him for a short constitutional walk around the parade ground. She held onto his arm while he tentatively shuffled along, one arm out to warn him of any unexpected obstacles.

The weather was warm, and across the veldt, in the distance, there was a peculiar lightning storm. Edith could swear the lightning flashes were zagging up, not down.

The tattered Union Jack fluttered from the flagpole in the centre and Warton turned his head towards the sound.

"How are you feeling?" she asked.

"Not as peculiar as I expected," he said, a trifle amused.

He stopped and cocked his head. "I thought I saw something."

"Don't tease," said Edith, "it won't be working yet. And there's no promise it will," she added sternly.

"No, really," he said. He turned blindly and pointed out across the veldt, past the Khungarrii siege workings and their scattered grave balls. "There," he said.

Edith was glad he couldn't see the disappointment on her face. "There's nothing there," she said gently.

A second later there was. A bolt of lightning struck up into the sky, followed a few seconds later by a soft, muted rumble.

"And there," he said again, turning round and pointing elsewhere.

Moments later, another bolt struck skywards from the spot. Another muffled timpani roll.

Edith's eyes widened and she clapped her hands. "Again!" she demanded gleefully.

Warton smiled, bowed theatrically, and then correctly predicted several more flashes.

It was working. Already, the petrol fruit liquor was allowing him to sense the lightning bolts before they happened.

With time and training, wondered Edith, what else might Warton and the other volunteers be able to see?

EVERSON STARED AT the find. It was a totem, the body of an urman lashed with vines to crossed posts in the form of an 'X,' a warning to bad spirits. The man had been dead for about a month, from the look of him, although there wasn't much left after the jungle creatures had been at him. From what clothing remained, he seemed to be one of the Ruanach. The men stood around in solemn silence as it stared at them from empty sockets, its jaw hanging open in mockery of their slack-jawed surprise.

"Dear God," said the Padre, making the sign of the cross.

"It is Garam," said Tarak, reaching out to touch a scar on the arm. "He was Jeffries' guide. He was supposed to guide the sky-being on the first leg of his journey to the Village of the Dead. Garam never returned. We thought he had gone on ahead with Jefferies." Tarak's face twisted with fury at the sight of his kinsman. "That he should be placed here, like this, it is *jundurru*, bad magic."

It wasn't crucifixion that killed him, however, but the bullet hole in the centre of the forehead. But the most marked thing about it was the British Army Officer's cap that it wore, complete with a Pennine Fusilier cap badge. Someone was sending a message, and they'd hung it round Garam's neck to make sure it was received, scrawled on a flattened piece of bark; *"Everson, the Underworld is mine; the rest is yours – for the moment. Do not attempt to follow me – Jeffries."*

Everson gave a guilty start. How did Jeffries know he would find it? Almost on impulse, he reached up to the tunic pocket where he kept the fetish of Jeffries' button, but thought better of it and let his hand drop.

"Looks like we're on the right track, then," said Pot Shot.

"So it would appear," Everson took no joy in the fact, but at least now he had his proof. Jeffries had descended into the underworld to free his demon.

Everson knew what he must do. They should go after him. They had suffered the worst that War-torn Europe and this place could throw at them; how could this be any worse?

"And if indeed Jeffries has gone into the underworld, then that's where we're going. To Hell."

He was surprise by how certain he sounded. Still, that's what officer training was for. He summoned the signallers.

"Riley, I want you to see if you can send a message back to the canyon. Let them know what we're doing."

Riley nodded and went to collect the kitbag that contained the Signals equipment.

"Tonkins, stop stuffing your face. We've got work to do!"

Tonkins, who hadn't gone to view the grisly find, hastily finished chewing, wiped the grease from his mouth with his cuff and followed Riley out towards the Strip.

At the canyon, nobody was eager to go back up to the wall after it had lit up like a star shell, least of all Buckley, and certainly not Sergeant Dixon, but the lightning flashes and the thunderous booms were receding, and somebody had to do it.

Sergeant Dixon pushed out his chest and looked at Buckley with the curdling contempt that only an NCO could muster. "You will go up that scree slope and set up your Iddy Umpty equipment again. I don't care what might happen. So you can either have a thousand volts up your arse, or my boot; which is it to be?" he bawled, warm, thick spittle speckling Buckley's face.

Buckley grunted and heaved as he hauled the kit bag of equipment up the rocky slope to the base of the metal wall. Below, he heard the work party, building a defensive breastwork around the camp, break out into song in sympathy, relieved it

wasn't them. *"Send out me muvver, me sister and me bruv*
but for gawd's sake don't send meeee!"

At the top, Buckley touched the metal tentatively. It was warm, but then it always had been. There was no sign of melting or burning. It looked just as it always had, despite the lightning that had erupted from it.

With a sense of relief, he began setting up the telegraph again. At least he knew now that he'd get a few seconds warning if anything were to happen again, and to be honest being up here it was no worse, or more dangerous, than being in a listening sap out beyond the front lines. At least Sergeant Dixon wouldn't be looking over his shoulder every five minutes.

He put the earphones over his head and began listening.

He had been up there a few hours when the clicking began. He hastily scrawled out the message on a scrap of paper with a stub of blunt pencil.

He stumbled down the scree side, calling for Sergeant Dixon as he went.

He found Sergeant Dixon waiting for him as he reached the bottom. The NCO waited impatiently while he took a moment to catch his breath.

"Message, Sarn't," said Buckley handing the scrap of paper over. "From Lieutenant Everson, Sarn't."

Dixon studied the paper and fixed Buckley with a steely glare. "Is this your idea of a joke, Buckley? 'Go to hell'?"

Buckley looked alarmed. "What? No, Sarn't. No. It reads, 'Gone to hell.'"

ATKINS AND THE rest of his men got ready to move out. Atkins found himself both scared and elated. This was everything he'd been wanting for the past five months. At last, they were hard on Jeffries' heels, and perhaps a way home. It was a desperate hope.

"Mathers said this would happen," said Pot Shot, casually.

"Are you bringing that up again?" said Mercy.

"He did, listen," Pot Shot put on a solemn face, as if he were about to give a church reading. "'*Other Ones will travel with the breath of GarSuleth, the Kreothe made not tamed*'," he said. "Well that's them chatt balloons isn't it? '*Then shall Skarra with open mandibles welcome the dark scentirrii.*' Well, Werner said our Black Hand Gang were like Dark Scentirrii to them chatts. And Skarra welcomes us. These Nazarrii knew we were going into the underworld centuries ago. Don't you find that just a little bit spooky?"

"Blood and sand, Pot Shot. Will you shut up about that? Just for once, just once, I'd like to think that something I did on this hell of a world wasn't 'fated'." Atkins threw down his knapsack and stormed off.

"I was joking!" protested Pot Shot. "Only! It's just a bloody cave!"

If they really were going into Hell, or Tartarus, or whatever, then perhaps Nellie was right; he needed to talk to someone.

Padre Rand sat quietly by himself, reading from his Bible.

Atkins felt awkward interrupting him. He seemed lost in some private contemplation. "Padre, have you got a moment?"

The chaplain looked up, smiled, and lifted the small book. "Trying to find a little guidance," he said with a smile. "Atkins, isn't it? What can I do for you?"

Atkins approached the Padre, his hands wringing the bottom of his tunic. "I want to make a confession."

And it all poured out of him: his big brother William, his brother's fiancée Flora, and his own love for his brother's sweetheart, and the strength and companionship they'd found in each other when William was declared missing during the Big Push on the Somme. He told of the last few tormented months, of his guilt and shame, and of Flora's last letter and his hope for a return and reunion.

"Some men see this as a hell world, Padre," he said, in a voice almost devoid of hope. "I see it more as a purgatory planet. Once I have paid for my sins, then maybe I can leave."

Padre Rand listened quietly. "Do you truly love this woman?" he asked.

"With all my heart, Padre."

"Then so long as you seek to make it right, it seems to me that you are truly penitent and wish to do the right thing. God could ask for nothing more. I could give you a few Hail Marys and a bunch of Our Fathers to say in penance, but I can see you've been a lot harder on yourself than that. I can forgive you, Atkins, but more importantly, you must learn to forgive yourself. Go, and sin no more," the chaplain said in calm, measured tones.

Atkins didn't know quite what he was expecting. A lifting of a great weight, perhaps, and a buoyant and happy heart. What he felt, however, was the relief of sharing his problem and having someone actually listen, and that was enough for now. As the Padre said, the rest was up to him. At least now he could look forwards, knowing that he was doing the right thing, and not torment himself with the past.

On his way back to his mates, Atkins saw Nellie.

"I talked to someone," he said. "It helped. Thank you."

Nellie smiled. "I'm glad."

THE PADRE WATCHED Atkins go and felt a little ashamed. He wanted to promise Atkins that he would get back, but he just didn't want to make a promise that *he* might not be able to keep, and for that he was sorry. He felt a connection to Atkins. They were both, in some sense, lost; alone. They both carried a terrible private burden they felt they couldn't share. At least he had been able to help there. As for himself, that was a different matter.

The vision he'd first had in Khungarr revisited him now in all its glory. He'd wanted a sign that out here on this alien world, so far from His creation, God could hear him, and God did hear him. He had prayed that he might save his flock, the battalion, and see them returned safely home, like any good shepherd. God had answered and the Padre had accepted God's beneficence with tears of joy. But the price God was asking for their salvation would cost him every ounce of faith he had, and he had blocked it from his mind, shut it away, but the still small voice would not be denied, and it tormented his sleep. Seeking his vision a second time, it was now clear to him, although there were times when he wished it was not, for God had told him that in order to save the souls of these Pennine Fusiliers, then he would have to trust in God, and die a martyr's death. Only then would their souls be saved from this purgatorial world. It was a task worthy of any minister of God, but when that day came, would he have the strength, and the faith, to suffer the ordeal? That was the thought that haunted his quiet moments now.

EVERSON SAT, TRYING to appeal to the tank crew. "I really could do with the *Ivanhoe*," he said. "It's a scouting mission, nothing more."

"I'd like to help sir," said Jack. "But I'm sorry, we can't go in there. It's not practical. We don't know what's in there. I don't want the tank getting stuck or driving into an abyss."

"No. No, you're right, of course," said Everson. "I just thought I'd ask."

"Well, if you ask me, you should just let us blast the thing and close the cavern entrance off for good," said Wally.

"It may well come to that, but not today," said Everson.

Wally *hmphed* his disapproval and went back to greasing some engine part.

Jack tried to be a little more conciliatory, "Look, if it'll help, we'll come in as far as we can. Just to make sure there are no more of those creatures, if nothing else," he said, looking at the carcass of the giant beast. "But that's it. We'll wait for you."

"The Ruanach enclave is stockaded. We can hole up there," said Alfie.

"Fair enough," said Everson, getting up. "Thank yo[illegible]
He reached out and shook Jack's hand, before turning h[illegible]
attention to Tulliver.

"I need you to fly back to the camp and let them know what's going on. Tonkins is going to stay here with the tank crew at this Ruanach stockade. He can keep in contact with the canyon, and if there's any chance that we can use these telluric paths to communicate, maybe we can send messages, too."

"Are you sure this is the right thing to do, John?" asked Tulliver.

"No, but we've come this far. Do you want to come with us, Oberleutnant?" he asked the German.

Werner smiled politely. "What use is a pilot without a plane? No, I will stay here with Tulliver and soar with the angels, not consort with demons."

Everson nodded. "Very well."

He noticed Hepton skulking uncomfortably, like someone on the horns of a dilemma. The sight of the totem had put the wind up him. He knew the plan and wanted no part of it.

The kinematographer edged up to Everson. "I'm not a member of your battalion, Everson. You can't make me go. This may be an officer's uniform, but it carries no rank."

"Got some demons you can't face, Hepton?" Everson asked wryly.

"I don't want to go," repeated Hepton. "Tulliver can fly me back to the camp."

"The aeroplane only seats two. Werner is flying with him. If you want to go back, you'll have to walk."

"Go to hell," said Hepton,

"Oh, I intend to," said Everson.

THE PADRE WAS offering the Last Rites to all those who wanted it. Considering their destination, it seemed a sensible precaution. Pot Shot was first in the queue.

But I thought you weren't religious?" said Atkins.

"Look, if I'm really going to hell, then I'm going to hedge my bets. I want to enter in a state of grace, all right? All my sins forgiven. That way the devils have got nothing over me."

In preparation, Tarak had gathered some of the same sort of bioluminescent lichen that the chatts used, and he, Nellie and Alfie made torches for them, while the rest of the tank crew checked over the *Ivanhoe*.

When the hour came, the tank gunned its engines, belched smoke and lurched forward, slowly and implacably rumbling forwards to guard the entrance. If Skarra really existed, it was about to meet its mechanical match.

Everson drew his sword, took a deep breath, blew his whistle and began to walk past the slain beast towards the cavern entrance. The Padre had joined the scouting party, arguing that he was uniquely qualified.

Atkins and the Black Hand Gang fell in behind him, Atkins and Mercy carrying the Lightningwerfers. Riley followed, pulling a makeshift litter loaded with equipment. He turned and waved at Tonkin, who stood watching some distance off, alongside the *Ivanhoe*, with Tulliver, Werner, Hepton and Napoo, the urman guide refusing to have anything to do with the venture.

Tarak, however, would not be denied. He accompanied them, a look of grim determination on his face. He had a clan to avenge, and if he failed in that, he would join them in the Village of the Dead.

Close up, the size of the cavern entrance staggered Atkins; it was larger than he had thought. Staring into the vast starless space within, he felt gripped by a sudden wave of vertigo, but he carried on, one foot in front of the other. *If in doubt, walk forwards* was always the advice, and he clung to that now; that and the thought of Flora.

The Padre clutched his Bible to his chest and spoke the words of the twenty-third psalm under his breath, "*Yea, though I walk in the valley of the shadow of death, I shall fear no evil...*"

Everson took a deep breath as they stepped beyond the threshold into the Stygian blackness beyond.

"Abandon all hope, ye who enter here,' he muttered.

THE OTHERS WATCHED the cavern entrance until the figures of the Fusiliers were lost from sight, swallowed by the obsidian blackness beyond. As they began their vigil, Nellie wondered if they would ever return...

THE END?

GLOSSARY

Albatros: A single-seater German fighter biplane.

Alleyman: Mangled by the Tommies from the French, *Allemand*, meaning a German.

Archie: Slang term for anti-aircraft fire and for its aerial shell-bursts.

Battalion: Infantry Battalions at full strength might be around a thousand men. Generally consisting of four *companies*.

Black Hand Gang: Slang for a party put together for a dangerous and hazardous mission, like a raiding party. Such was the nature of the tasks that they were chosen from volunteers, where possible.

Blighty: England, home. From the Hindustani *Bilaiti* meaning foreign land.

Blighty One: A wound bad enough to have you sent back to England.

Boojums: Nickname for tanks, also a Wibble Wobble, a Land Creeper, a Willie.

Bosche: Slang for German, generally used by officers.

Bus: RFC pilot's slang term for their aeroplane.

Carpet Slipper Bastard: A heavy artillery shell passing high overhead, and thus with little noise.

Chatt: Parasitic lice that infested the clothing and were almost impossible to avoid while living in the trenches. Living in the warm moist clothing and laying eggs along the seams, they induced itching and skin complaints.

Chatting: De-lousing, either by running a fingernail along the seams and cracking the lice and eggs or else running a lighted candle along them to much the same effect.

Communication Trench: Trench that ran perpendicularly to the *fire trench*, enabling movement of troops, supplies and messages to and from the Front Line, from the parallel support and reserve lines to the rear.

Company: One quarter of an infantry *battalion*, 227 men at full strength, divided into four *platoons*.

CQS: Company Quartermaster Sergeant.

CSM: Company Sergeant Major.

Enfilade: Flanking fire along the length of a trench, as opposed to across it.

Estaminet: a French place of entertainment in villages and small towns frequented by soldiers; part bar, part cafe, part restaurant, generally run by women.

FANY: First Aid Nursing Yeomanry. The only service in which women could enlist and wear khaki, they drove ambulances, ran soup kitchens, mobile baths, etc. in forward areas.

Fire Bay: Part of a manned *fire trench* facing the enemy. Bays were usually separated by *traverses*.

Firestep: The floor of the trench was usually deep enough for soldiers to move about without being seen by the enemy. A firestep was a raised step that ran along the forward face of the *fire trench*, from which soldiers could fire or keep watch.

Fire Trench: Forward trench facing the enemy that formed part of the Front Line.

Five Nines: A type of German high-explosive shell.

Flammenwerfer: German fire projector or flame thrower.

Fritz: Slang term for a German.

Funk: State of nerves or depression, more harshly a slang word for cowardice.

Funk Hole: Generally, any dugout or shelter, but often referring to niches or holes big enough to shelter one or two men scraped into the front wall of a trench.

Greyback: A soldier's regulation grey flannel shirt, with no collars and tin buttons.

Guncotton: A service explosive commonly used for demolition.

Hom Forty: A French railway goods wagon, used for moving troops up to the front line. Very slow. Named after the sign on the side, *Hommes 40, Chevaux 8*.

Hush Hush Crowd: Nickname for the Machine Gun Corps Heavy Section, or Tank Section, owing to the secrecy that surrounded their training.

Iddy Umpty: Slang for Morse Code and, by extension, the signallers who used it.

Jildi: From the Hindi – get a move on, quick, hurry

Kite Balloon: A blimp-shaped observation balloon, carrying a basket for an observer but attached to the ground by a winch.

Land Ship: A tank.

Lewis Machine Gun: air cooled, using a circular magazine cartridge holding 48 rounds each. Lighter and more portable than the Vickers.

Linseed Lancer: Slang for a stretcher bearer of the *RAMC*.

Look Stick: Slang for a trench periscope.

Luftstreitkräfte: The German Airforce formed in October 1916, previously known as *Die Fliegertruppen des deutschen Kaiserreiches* – the Imperial German Flying Corps.

Mills Bomb: Pineapple-shaped British hand grenade, armed by pulling a pin and releasing the trigger lever.

Minniewerfer: German trench mortar shell.

MO: Medical Officer.

NCO: Non Commissioned Officer; a sergeant major, sergeant or corporal.

Neurasthenia: Contemporary medical term to describe emotional shell shock, less charitably seen as a 'weakness of the nerves.'

No Man's Land: Area of land between the two opposing Front Lines.

OP: Observation Post.

QM: Quartermaster.

Parados: Raised defensive wall of earth or sandbags along the rear of the trench to help disperse explosions behind the line.

Parapet: Raised defence of earth or sandbags at the front of a trench to provide cover for those on the *firestep*.

PH Helmet: Phenate-Hexamine Helmet. Early type of full-head gas mask. Not so much a helmet as a flannel hood soaked in neutralising chemicals, and a mouth tube and distinctive non-return red rubber valve for exhalation.

Picklehaub: German full-dress helmet and ornamented with a spike on top. A very desirable souvenir.

Platoon: A quarter of an infantry *company*, commanded by a *Subaltern*. Consisting of 48 men divide into four *sections*.

Plum Pudding: Nickname for a type of British trench mortar round.

Port: The left side of a vessel or ship.

Puttee: Khaki cloth band wound round the calf from the knee to the ankle.

RAMC: Royal Army Medical Corps, often summoned with the well-worn yell, "stretcher bearer!" Uncharitably also said to stand for Rob All My Comrades.

Red Tabs: Slang for staff officers, after the red tabs worn on the collars of their tunics.

Revetment: Any material used to strengthen a trench wall against collapse; wooden planking, brushwood wattling, corrugated iron, etc.

RFC: Royal Flying Corps of the British Army.

Sap: A *communications trench* that runs out from an already existing trench to an emplacement, kitchen, latrine or stores.

Section: A quarter of a *platoon,* usually consisting of 12 men in the charge of an NCO.

SMLE: Short Magazine Lee Enfield. Standard issue British rifle, with a 10-round magazine.

Sponson: The side-mounted gun turret of a tank, taken from the naval term. The Mark I 'male' tank had no central-mounted roof turret, like later tanks, but two side-mounted sponsons, one on either side. Each sponson was armed with a six-pounder gun and a Hotchkiss machine gun.

Stand To: Stand to Arms. Highest state of alert when all men should be ready for immediate action, weapons at the ready. Occurred regularly in the trenches at dawn and dusk to repel any attempted attacks.

Starboard: The right side of a vessel or ship.

Subaltern: Or Sub; a commissioned officer under the rank of captain; first or second lieutenant.

Tankodrome: A tank park and workshops behind the lines where maintenance and repairs can be carried out.

Toffee Apple: nickname for a type of British trench mortar bomb.

Traverse: Thick sandbag partition built in trenches to prevent enfilading enemy fire and to limit the effect of any explosions. In *fire trenches* they were used to create *fire bays*. Also; purpose-built changes in angle of direction in any trench to achieve the same effect.

VAD: Voluntary Aid Detachment, women volunteers providing auxiliary nursing assistance to the Red Cross and registered nurses.

Very Light: A white or coloured flare fired from a Very Pistol. Used for signalling or illumination at night.

Vickers Machine gun: Water-cooled, belt-fed machine gun. Heavy and bulky, but more accurate than the Lewis.

Whizz-Bang: A German 77mm high velocity shell.

Windy: Or *to have the wind-up;* apprehensive or anxious about a situation.

Wipers: Tommies' name for the town of Ypres, in Belgium.

Woolly Bear: The distinctive smoke burst of a German high explosive shrapnel shell.

Pat Kelleher is a freelance writer. He has written for magazines, animation and radio. He served his time writing for a wide variety of TV licensed characters, translating them into audio books, novels and comics. Yes, he's written for that. And that. And even, you know, them. He has several non-fiction books to his credit and his educational strips and stories for the RSPB currently form the mainstays of their Youth publications. Somehow he has steadfastly managed to avoid all those careers and part-time jobs that look so good on a dust jacket.

UK ISBN: 978 1 906735 35 7 • US ISBN: 978 1 906735 84 5 • £7.99/$9.99

On November 1st, 1916, nine-hundred men of the 13th Battalion of The Pennine Fusiliers vanished without trace from the battlefield, only to find themselves stranded on an alien planet. There they must learn to survive in a frightening and hostile environment, forced to rely on dwindling supplies of ammo and rations as the natives of this strange new world begin to take an interest. However, the aliens amongst them are only the first of their worries, as a sinister and arcane threat begins to take hold from within their own ranks!

UK ISBN: 978 1 907992 15 5 • US ISBN: 978 1 907992 16 2 • £7.99/$9.99

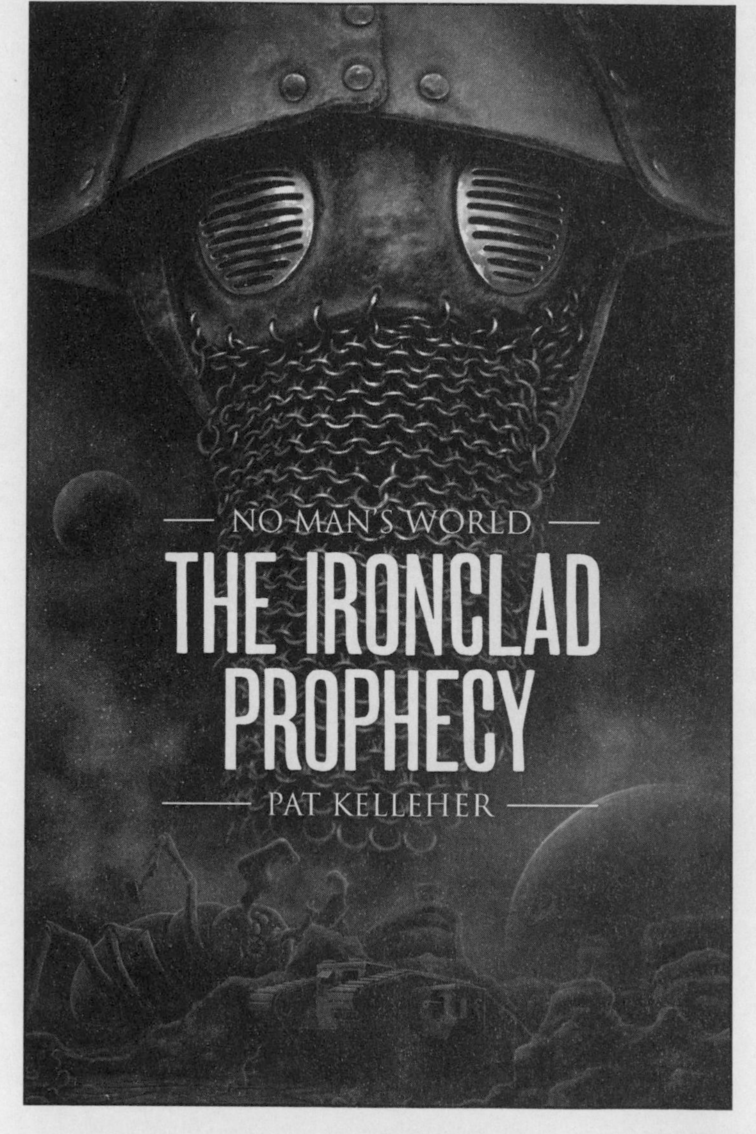